Copyright Matthew
Edited by
All rights reserved. N
reproduced in any form or
inclusion of brief quotatic
permission in writing from the publisher.
This book is a work of fiction. The characters and situations in this book are imaginary. No resemblance is intended between these characters and any persons, living or dead.
This book is sold subject to the condition that it shall not, by way of trade or otherwise, be lent, resold, hired out or otherwise circulated without the publisher's prior consent in any form or binding or cover other than that in which it is published and without similar condition including this condition being imposed on the subsequent purchaser.
Published in Great Britain in 2024 by Matthew Cash Burdizzo Books Walsall, UK

FÜHRER: PART ONE

Matthew Cash

FÜHRER:

PART ONE

MATTHEW CASH

BURDIZZO BOOKS
2024

FÜHRER: PART ONE

Matthew Cash

Prologue

FÜHRER: PART ONE

1.

Suffolk

1983

Andy studied the house martins' nest beneath the eaves, fascinated by the tiny, intricate balls of compacted dirt. For the past two weeks, the little birds had been building their home above the window of his bedroom.

They built their nests on the terraced houses every year; he looked forward to hearing the chirps of the chicks at dawn.

He stared over his back garden and beyond, over a valley of sunlit fields. The skeleton of a new housing estate, an eyesore, jutted up beyond the back garden fence and obscured some of the picturesque view.

Even though the scene would be forever tainted, he was excited about the building site. New houses meant new people. He thought that was good, even though his parents insisted the families who were to occupy them would be toffs. It wasn't a council housing estate like theirs. Andy didn't care, as long as there were new children to play with, and that no more countryside would be ruined.

The doorbell rang.

Andy checked his watch and ran down to answer the door.

It would be Ben: he was always on time.

FÜHRER: PART ONE

A boy a month younger than him stood on the doorstep, with messy hair, grazed knees, and a t-shirt that was miles too big.

"Hey, Ben." Andy jumped over the threshold, shouted goodbye to his mum, and slammed the door.

"So, what are we gonna do?" Ben said, swatting him with a sprig he'd pulled from the garden hedge. He was forever fiddling with something.

Andy kicked the garden gate open and let it swing back on the latch. "Did your mum give you any money?"

"Nah, but I've still got fifty pee Uncle Reggie gave me when we went to see him on Sunday," Ben said, checking his shorts for the coin.

"Oh, God, did you have to walk it all the way to Stutton?" Andy groaned; just the thought of having to walk four miles to the next village tired him out.

They left the row of terraced houses and headed towards a footpath which would take them into the wilds of the village.

"Yeah," Ben sighed, "we always have to see Dad's looney lot on Sunday afternoons. We did get a lift back, though."

They cut between the houses and immediately descended into the valley. High-panelled fences lined the sides of the footpath, casting it in shadow.

"Fancy checking out the building site?" Andy said, as they were already headed in that direction. "We can go to the shops after."

They slipped through a gap in the fences where a newly laid footpath led into the new estate.

A flat dirt road ran down what had been a field only the year before. It was strange to think people would be living there soon.

The foundations of the new houses were in various stages of completion, the interiors unfinished and the plumbing and inner workings protruding from the ground.

"Reckon anyone cool will move here?" asked Ben.

Andy walked towards a house which had all of the brickwork done. "Probably," he said, peering into the confines at the muddy floor. "Mum reckons they'll all be snobs, though."

"Yeah, that's what Dad says."

Andy stepped through the empty doorway and into semi-darkness. He spun around. "Hey, look, I'm standing where someone's living room will be."

Ben laughed, joined in. "They'll probably be so posh they'll eat their dinner at the table every day."

"Yeah," Andy agreed, and then added in a posh voice, "this will be our dining room."

"Bit muddy!" Ben laughed.

Andy peered through the empty window frames. "'ere, keep a lookout, why don't you?"

Ben frowned and moved back to the doorway. "Whatcha gonna do?"

"Add something special to the foundations." Andy grinned, dropped his shorts, and squatted in the middle of the room.

"Andy!" Ben gasped as violent laughter took control of him.

Andy grunted loudly whilst he tried not to succumb to his own mirth. He turned around, waggled his bare arse at his friend and shouted, "Look, I've got a tail."

Ben half-collapsed, his hands clamped on his knees and let out belly-rippling laughs.

FÜHRER: PART ONE

"Stop laughing," Andy said, "you keep making it go back up."

This sent both boys into a whole new level of hysteria.

Andy wiggled his hips, dancing around like a headless chicken as he tried to detach the clinging turd.

"What the bloody hell are you two playing at?"

Ben jumped a foot into the air as a shadow fell over him.

A man blocked the doorway.

One of the builders from the site.

He growled in disgust when he saw Andy yanking his shorts up and the brown thing lying on the ground. "You dirty bugger. I'll be having a word with your dad about this."

Ben ran to Andy and pointed at a double doorway, where patio doors would eventually go.

Without hesitation, the boys fled, but soon found their way blocked by another man, this one had a huge black beard. Another builder. He locked eyes with his colleague. "What's this pair up to, Nige?"

Nige pointed to the shit on the floor. "Hold them, Baz, they ain't going anywhere until they tell me their names and where they live."

Big, black-bearded Baz clamped his hands over the lads' shoulders.

Ben's cheeks reddened and tears began to well. "We were only mucking ab—"

"I don't care what you were doing," Nige interrupted, "you ain't supposed to be on the site, there's enough bloody signs telling you to clear off. It ain't safe."

Shame and embarrassment stung Andy's face, then he became overwhelmed with fear at the thought of what his parents might do. "Please," he whined, trying to think of a way to convince the builders not to tell on them. He looked at the man called Nige—he seemed to be in charge of the situation—and was about to give him one hell of an apology when a searing pain ripped through him.

At first, he thought he needed to crap again, but the pain intensified.

He fell to his knees.

"What the fuck have you done to him?" Nige cried out at his workmate.

Baz stepped back, hands in the air. "I didn't do anything!"

"Andy?" Ben shouted, crouching next to his friend and placing a hand on his back. For a second, he thought it was an elaborate ruse, something to throw the men off, but Andy landed on the mess he had made just moments before.

"What's wrong with him?" Nige asked Ben, worry etching his face. He stepped forward and reached to help Andy back up onto his feet, but the boy suddenly growled and snapped his jaws at Nige's hand.

"Calm down," Baz said, gesturing for Nige to back off.

Andy crouched in the mud and shit, his lips drawn back, baring his teeth like a wild animal.

Baz circled around and stood next to Nige and was surprised when Ben also backed away. "Is your mate mental, or something?" Baz whispered.

Ben shook his head, but the way Andy was acting made him think twice. "Andy—" his words were cut off when his best friend from school came across the dirt on all fours.

FÜHRER: PART ONE

"What the fu—?" Baz yelped and backed out of the house as the wild-boy launched himself at Nige.

Andy knocked the builder onto his back and tore at his clothes, scratching and gnashing his teeth.

"Help me, he's fucking possessed or something," Nige yelled, and thrust his forearm beneath Andy's neck, keeping the twelve-year-old at bay with great difficulty.

Baz rushed back into the house and reached to pull Andy off his workmate, but his head snapped around lightning-quick and his teeth clamped down.

Baz held his hand up, horrified: a chunk of the webbing between his thumb and forefinger was missing.

Vomit rose when Ben saw Andy with blood around his mouth and his jaw moving from side to side as he chewed on the scrap of flesh.

He puked.

He had known Andy for eight years; he had never done anything like this before. He didn't even get into squabbles at school.

The prone builder shouted something about possession.

Ben knew what that was, they had watched The Exorcist, even though they weren't allowed—

A flashback: Goswell's wood, the summer before, when they had made a five-pointed star out of branches.

What if they had conjured something by accident?

"Andy, stop!" Ben screamed as his friend drooled strings of bloody saliva onto the builder's face.

"Fuck this," Baz shouted, seizing Andy around the waist and hauling him off his workmate.

Andy roared. He bucked in the builder's embrace, arms and legs paddling in the air, and tried to twist around to bite Baz's throat. Baz shoved him away but he was too slow. Andy darted forwards and latched onto his face. Baz beat at him with his fists, harder than Ben had seen anyone being hit, but still Andy wouldn't let go.

As Nige went to Baz's aid, there was an audible rip and a spurt of red.

Andy had torn off the man's ear.

Baz threw him to the ground, clutched his head and mewled.

Andy raked Nige's legs and Ben ran, leaving the building site amidst a cacophony of what sounded like a ferocious animal attack.

FÜHRER: PART ONE

2

Budapest

1955

Gwen Krauss stared blankly at the cellar wall, lost in time. A time long ago, but a place not far from where she was sitting now.

The cellar was a dreary affair, with no electricity, and bare walls that wept damp tears for eight months of the year.

They could afford more luxury accommodation— Victor had laundered enough money during his time working for Liebermann to set them up for several lifetimes— however, there weren't many places that were willing to accept payments from a person who didn't want to leave a paper trail.

Victor circled the decrepit, white-haired woman strapped to the metal hospital bed, and despite the weathered exterior, he still pined for the woman she had been.

He picked up a saucer that was holding a lighted candle, one of a dozen or so dotted around the cellar and checked the thick leather restraints around her wrists and ankles.

"Why don't you fight?" Victor addressed the monster inside of her as if it were a thing that could be reasoned with. "I *could* harm you." The buckles were

FÜHRER: PART ONE

secure. "You let her deteriorate for weeks on end, and then just get her ready for your takeover."

Every month, a week or so before the full moon, Gwen would suddenly become radiant, her skin softer, her hair lush. It angered him that she was being used this way, when his own wolf kept him in prime condition.

If he wanted, he could torture her, leave her in her own filth, and the beast wouldn't do a thing to help her. It only showed itself if there was a major life threat.

He picked up a cane he'd had custom-made, long and black with a decorative wolf's head. He twisted the handle and drew out a long, thin blade, which he slowly brought to Gwen's cheek.

Her far-off expression changed at once; something ignited in her glazed eyes, and the rumble of a distant thunder reverberated in her chest and throat.

Her beast was reacting to the silver in the sword.

Gwen's face rippled, the skin tightened across her sunken cheeks, and her lips drew back, widening beyond their normal boundaries. Long white canines sprang out through empty gums, filling the air with a fine red mist. She was a perversion of a woman, grey fur sprouting across her realigning jaw as her nose began the process of its recreation.

It took mere seconds.

Victor held the blade millimetres away from her, knowing that just resting the blade against her would singe and blister the skin.

He sighed, lowered the blade, and slunk away.

As soon as the threat was gone, Gwen's change stopped and she reverted back to her perpetually trapped senile state.

"I hate you," Victor roared, and hurled the sword and its casing across the cellar. He tore himself away from her and slumped over his workbench, tears running free. "Why can't you heal her? Why?"

"It's a lovely day," Gwen said, happily staring through the cellar walls at the sunshine over the Danube.

Victor howled his frustrations at the damp walls.

Without even knowing what he was doing, he clawed deep furrows into the crumbling stonework; his fingernails tore away and fell to the floor like flaked almonds.

He watched his fingertips, bare to the bone, repair themselves almost instantly.

It only added to his rage.

Victor stared at the sunlight on the water. Yet another reenactment of one of the few memories Gwen was still trapped in.

She sat with him on the boat deck, a glass of champagne in her hand, reliving the river cruise of their honeymoon. Every few minutes, he would encourage her to raise the glass to her lips.

Gwen's deterioration had come to a standstill at the time he had infected her with the Schäfers' blood. To begin with, he had been foolish, allowing it to give him hope.

If lycanthropy can halt the process, then surely it can reverse it?

It was always this slight chance that had stayed his hand since they'd left Germany.

Maybe I haven't given it enough time.

FÜHRER: PART ONE

Maybe there is a way of manipulating it.

If there was a chance it would save her, there was no way he could end her life.

Budapest was a great place for Victor to learn more about the areas of science and medicine he was unfamiliar with.

Psychology and psychiatry.

Potential immortality meant he had time to expand his knowledge, heighten his intelligence, so perhaps one day he could begin to understand what it was that was inside them.

Using the money from his squirrelled stash, he had secured rooms in a building by the Danube. In the cellar, he had perfected his hold over his own wolf, tested the limits and variations of transformation, and restrained Gwen whenever she was due to turn.

The dementia was a match for the wilderness inside her, and Victor theorised that one of the many reasons it left her in such withered state between transformations was because it was focusing all its energy on this ailment of the mind. When her wolf did come, it was a ravenous but clumsy thing, and had none of the cunning that he felt coiled within his own.

Victor's wolf was a constant, unseen presence, a schizophrenic shadow, always there, always aware, waiting to pounce and take over at any given opportunity.

So why wasn't Gwen's?

The Schäfers had hinted that the key to controlling your wolf was resisting the initial takeover, the first transformation.

Victor thought back to his own horrifying process in the Black Forest and how he had pinned himself beneath the log pile whilst Gwen tore apart everything she came across.

The realisation that her wolf couldn't take over completely gave him a certain level of reassurance, but also told him that it was just as trapped as she was, being allowed freedom only with the full moon.

Unlike Gwen, who would revisit this place day after day, this would be the last time Victor journeyed beneath these bridges.

Hungary was too close to Germany.

Liebermann would pick up his trail soon enough.

The boat slowed as it approached the dock and Victor tipped his hat to the city. "Farewell, old girl."

FÜHRER: PART ONE

3.

Boxford

2016

His eyeballs were bubbling, red-hot, molten pools that dripped over his cheeks. The pain, now the fire had burnt through the nerve-endings, was finally over.

Inside Herbert, the lycanthropy raged, battling against the flames and the never-ending trauma.

He welcomed the smothering oblivion and looked forward to being in his dead wife's embrace.

That should have been the end.
But it wasn't.
The pain returned as the parasite in his brain repaired him from the inside out.

Awareness returned, too, both physical and psychological.

There was nothing else at first, apart from the effects the inferno wrought on his skin, and then his olfactory senses returned sluggishly, strengthening all the time, allowing him to experience the aroma of his own burnt flesh.

Movement wasn't possible, but when his vision returned and the fog began to clear, he saw strip-lighting above.

FÜHRER: PART ONE

4.

Cyril had played in Bluebell Woods since he was a child. Back then, he had known all its secrets. He had been an expert at spying, finding the best places to hide away from the beaten path. He'd watched people shagging, set fire to stuff, and buried dead pets.

The only building in the entire green expanse was a ramshackle warehouse, a throwback from an era Cyril didn't remember. Its last purpose, before it had fallen into dereliction, was as a music studio.

In the seventies, he had hung around with the bands and the patrons, ferrying them back and forth, as he was the only one who could drive.

When the studio closed, the woodland had become even quieter.
Times had moved on, and the attitudes and behaviours of courting teenagers had changed. What were once hotspots for drinking and listening to music had become picnic areas for hiking groups.
When Cyril's mum had died, he was free.
He'd sold his parents' house, moved into a council flat, and bought the studio for next to nothing. At the time, he didn't know why he'd bought it, other than it held good memories and would be a useful place for storage, but as he cleared out the derelict building and noticed the studio's soundproofing, ideas had begun to form.

FÜHRER: PART ONE

Matthew Cash

PART ONE

drain every last drop of blood from the pair of you. You think I'm worried about infection?" He pressed a fingertip to his half-drooping face. "I'm not, I'm—"

"Tepes!" Cyril shouted.

"Shut up," Tepes bellowed, not taking his eyes off Tony for a moment. "And my eager friend here is going to rape you in as many ways he can think of."

Tony looked at Cyril behind him and laughed.

Tepes turned to see the source of the bound boy's hilarity and was almost knocked over by Cyril running towards the stairs.

"Where the fuck do you think you are going?" he shrieked at the lanky freak, grabbing hold of his arm and nearly losing his balance.

Then he turned and saw Danny.

Chapter 2

Gustav studied the men's injuries. "I can't believe they're still alive."

The doctor beside him was a man of average build, with a grey beard and a matching tuft of hair. "Lycanthropy is one of the most resilient things I've come across."

"Aren't you the one who first had access to the brain?" Gustav asked. "Where are you from, Doctor Blair?"

The doctor basked in the glory of his reputation. "To answer your first question, yes, I dissected a specimen's brain back in Germany. And although my accent has dwindled over the years, I am from Scotland."

Gustav nodded. He couldn't take his eyes off the thing in the glass tank, nothing more than a head attached to a spinal column. "Is it a parasite?"

Doctor Blair chuckled. "I'm afraid we had to sign a non-disclosure agreement about that very thing. Let's just say the repercussions, if any of us were to break that agreement, are the most severe imaginable. Only those who are permitted to know, know." He patted the man on one of his broad shoulders. "Don't worry, I don't even think your boss knows."

"Speak of the devil and he shall appear," Gustav grumbled.

Sir Jonathan Butcher came into the room, a living cadaver amidst a wheeled junkyard of technology. He tapped out words for his automated voice. "How are our survivors, Doctor Blair?"

FÜHRER: PART ONE

Blair rapped a knuckle against the glass tank. "As you can see," he smirked, "my fellow Scotsman here is a little worse for wear. However, I know from my studies that lycanthropy can recreate almost the entire body. The source of lycanthropy is remarkable, a complex network that spreads like a many-limbed octopus in the pituitary gland. First, it invades the hypothalamus—"

Butcher rolled his eyes. "Please, spare me."

Blair nodded and pointed to the remains inside the tank. "Currently I think it's processing what it needs to do, what it needs to rebuild, trawling the patient's memory banks for the original body's blueprints, as it were. I can't estimate how long this process will take."

Gustav tutted. "It is like the Windows Update, yes?"

Blair roared with laughter and slapped the deadpan Ukrainian on the back. "Exactly, my friend, exactly."

"And the others?" said Butcher, his failing voice a mere croak.

"This way, please." Blair gestured across the room to a hi-tech grey glass sarcophagus, linked to various monitors and equipment. "Your recent escapee suffered the least amount of damage, mostly exterior burning. I've subdued him until his regeneration is complete. We cannot take any risks with those who have already changed until we know just how much control they have. Even those in full control of their abilities can find themselves slaves to the lycanthropy after such tremendous damage."

"How long?"

"Judging by his recovery so far, and the fire damage, I'd hazard a guess at forty-eight hours, maximum."

Gustav peered into the cryochamber at Herbert and recalled the experiments Mortimer had performed on him. He pitied the old man. The tests, the torture, had all been for nothing once the Germans and their teams were informed.

Herbert was a big, sunburnt baby submerged in translucent gel as the lycanthropy focused on repairing the fire damage.

Blair moved to another cryochamber and once again, his cheerful countenance radiated. "A funny thing with the Jamaican," he said, laughing at the memory, "when I'd finished extracting all traces of the silver from his system, I shaved all the hair off his body, just going on a theory I had." Blair rapped on the glass. "As you can see, the lycanthropy has returned him back to how he was. It's as if, in some aspects, it retains the image of its host when they were infected, and recreates that facsimile, albeit with a few modifications."

"Any more survivors?" Butcher asked.

"Unfortunately not; as you know, Krauss was shot in the head, the silver obliterated the lycanthropy instantly, and the female suffered incredible damage before she was shot. These things are hard to kill, but not impossible."

Butcher tapped his touchscreen; using the keypad exhausted him. He was yellow, on the brink of collapse. "Is that it?"

Blair nodded. "There is nothing else aside from the two adolescents who are awaiting collection."

"What about the other woman?" Gustav asked.

FÜHRER: PART ONE

Blair frowned and consulted his notes. "Ah, yes. Elizabeth Holder. We found remnants of her dog, which we believe was also infected and suspect somehow stole her corpse from the hospital, but as yet we haven't found her body. There's a team going over every millimetre of that park, so don't worry."

"Search quicker, and report to me," Butcher's speaker boomed.

Blair raised a finger and an awkward smile. "Of course, Sir Jonathan, but you must remember that you aren't in charge here anymore. You will be kept informed, but after my superior."

Butcher glared at the doctor and moved from the room.

"He's a barrel of laughs, isn't he?" Blair said once the drone of Butcher's motor faded.

"He has his good days," Gustav replied, peering in at the comatose Jamaican.

"Really?"

Gustav turned back to the doctor, his moustache twitching — the closest he ever got to smiling. "No." He returned to the man in the futuristic tomb. The scars from Trevor's gutshot and the subsequent operations were visible, but looked months-old, rather than hours.

Herbert was in even better condition. Aside from the discolouration of his skin, he looked normal.

The rational part of Gustav, the part that had grown up with loving, humble parents in Antratsyt, the part that had gone into medicine to help people, wished those in charge would consider the good they could do with this discovery.

They had enough information to cure so many of mankind's ailments, perhaps even stall or prevent death itself. But despite the Germans having studied it since the second world war, he knew full well how it would all pan out.

Butcher would infect himself and join forces with whatever was lying in wait in Germany.

He returned to the remains of the Scotsman.

A few days earlier, he'd resembled a macabre Christmas tree. He had been little more than a disembodied head attached to a spinal column, with a spindly nervous system reaching outwards to the tank sides like jellyfish tentacles, but now that he was practically whole again, it was just a matter of time before the lycanthropy repaired the remaining layers of skin and muscle.

FÜHRER: PART ONE

Chapter 3

"Please, Gustav," Mortimer whined, the tendons in his neck straining as he lifted his head from the gurney. "Let me try to do this on my own."

Gustav harrumphed. "You are not so high and Mister Mighty now the shoe is on the opposite foot, are you?" He jabbed a cannula into a vein on Mortimer's arm.

"I know, I know, but that was before. This was all new to us, a medical miracle with the potential to save millions of lives. It still is. I was just following orders."

"That is all I am doing. You think I can stop now? You think I want the bullet in my brain, maybe?" Gustav shook his head and sighed. He inserted another cannula in Mortimer's other arm. "This is just a backup line."

Mortimer rolled his eyes. "I know what you're doing, I *am* a doctor. But please, there must be another way."

"Oh-ho, last minute nerves, eh, Doctor?" came a jovial, Scottish voice.

"Who the fuck is that?" Mortimer asked Gustav as the newcomer, a man with grey hair and a beard, slipped into view.

"Haven't we met, Doctor?"

"No."

"Pardon me. Allow me to introduce myself. I am Doctor Matthew Blair, would you like to see my qualifications?"

"Who are you?"

FÜHRER: PART ONE

"Oh, no one important in the grand scheme of things, just here to oversee my right-hand man Gustav and make sure he follows the procedure to the letter."

"The procedure?"

Gustav smirked behind his epic moustache whilst he attached intravenous lines to the cannulas. "Doctor Blair is modest. This man invented this procedure."

Blair laughed. "You give me too much credit, my friend."

"Please." Mortimer addressed the doctor as he moved back out of eye line. "Let me do this unaided."

"Don't worry, this is a standard procedure which has been performed many, many times."

Oh, Jesus. Mortimer realised the implications. *Many, many times. But how many? Dozens? Hundreds? Thousands?*

Gustav finished readying the intravenous lines and began running saline through them to check they were good to go.

A large part of Mortimer hoped the procedure would go wrong. Although his previous thoughts were of earning a place amongst the Powers That Be, he thought that maybe death would be preferable to whatever plans they had in place.

Everything took on a clarity like never before, the euphoria he had experienced since becoming infected was reaching a high point. Noises too loud, colours too bright.

Gustav and Blair sounded like a couple of warthogs; he could smell them: sweat, expensive cologne and something spicy.

He could hear their heartbeats.

His vision was beyond his normal capacity, too: he could make out the tiny print on the little vials metres away.

Pentobarbital.

Pancuronium bromide.

Potassium chloride.

"Please," he begged one last time.

Gustav didn't meet his stare, but injected him with a high dose of pentobarbital, which on its own would be enough to slow his breathing and kill him.

Mortimer felt the darkness close in and wondered briefly, before it became all-consuming, if there really was a god.

FÜHRER: PART ONE

Chapter 4

For the first time ever, Bartholomew Tepes was speechless.

Where the youngest Scarborough brother sat was a scene from a horror film; half-man, half-dog, an adolescent boy rapidly morphing into something canine.

It turned towards him, its human mouth splitting at the corners, and Danny's scream shifted from human to animal as his cheeks tore and spewed forth a wolf's muzzle.

The boy's melting limbs were still lashed to the bondage chair, but the foot Tepes had freed stamped against the concrete floor.

Tony carried on laughing.

Cyril was gone.

The door to the cellar was wide open.

Tepes raised his good arm and pointed at Danny. When he spoke, his slur had worsened. "What is that?"

Tony scooted away until he felt the cellar steps against his back and pushed himself to his feet. "It's what you're going to turn into on the next full moon," he said, malice glinting in his eyes. "You are so fucked."

Tepes knew it was true, he just couldn't believe it. He braced himself on his hospital crutch and hobbled closer to Danny.

Although this form wasn't much bigger than his original one, this new body was taut with bunched muscle and the lesion on his throat wasn't visible, proof of the mythicised regenerative abilities.

FÜHRER: PART ONE

Tepes studied its teeth and claws, the strength in those jaws, listened to the straining of the leather straps, and now it was his turn to laugh. "You don't know what you've done."

He could feel it inside him like a stimulant, filling him, assessing the new body in which it grew. Even his stroke-weakened, lop-sided grin felt better.

Tepes moved to the stairs as quickly as he could. Tony said something as he passed but Danny's creature's snarls drowned him out. He carried on up the stairs, slammed the heavy door on Tony's screams and fastened the bolts.

The sound of a car engine took his focus and he went through the kitchen.

Anger at Cyril made him quicken his pace.

If that freak has deserted me, more fool him.

He came out of the house and into the road just in time for Cyril's blob of pus to rocket up the street towards him. He brought the handle of the crutch down across the car bonnet.

Cyril slammed on the brakes, his jack o'lantern face unhinged.

Tepes all but fell into the passenger side and grinned. "Drive."

Tony scurried up the stairs, not daring to take his eyes off his brother.

The leather restraints tore with a loud *rip* and Danny rose steadily to his newly formed feet, inspected himself, gazing down as he opened and closed the wide hand-paws, lifted his snout, and roared with approval. He swiped the chair away and set his yellow eyes on Tony.

"Danny."

Tony sounded like the younger brother now.

Danny leapt at the sound of his voice, scaling the cellar floor in one coiled spring, and pinned his brother to the stone steps.

Tony felt piss soak his trousers.

Danny lowered his face towards him, his nostrils flared at the stench of urine.

Tony knew what these things were capable of.

Danny's wolf jaws opened and Tony waited for his throat to be torn out. He closed his eyes, ready for the end, but all that came was a brief rush of air as Danny leapt over him and ploughed through the cellar door.

Cyril stared in the rearview mirror and saw the shape stagger into the light of the moon. He jammed his foot on the accelerator. "What... what was that thing?"

Tepes sat in the passenger seat clenching and unclenching his hands, beaming with delirious wonder. "In the films, they call them werewolves or lycanthropes."

"But—"

"You saw what I saw."

"Yeah, but it can't be that. It must have been a costume, or—"—Cyril's garbled words flew out of his mouth—"there are people who dress up in that kind of stuff."

Tepes roared with laughter and slapped his thigh. "I don't think the boys are furries, Cyril."

"Cosplay or something."

"Balderdash." Tepes reached up and switched on the interior light. "You watched him change before your very eyes. Look at me, Cyril."

Cyril slowed and turned to his friend.

FÜHRER: PART ONE

Tepes flashed his shark-like grin. "Look at my face. It's already healing me."

The lop-sided half of Tepes' face, a side-effect of the stroke, had rectified itself.

"Fucking hell."

"There are more things going on in this world than what we're told about, Cyril, you know that. Look at how much is hidden on the dark web."

Cyril's mouth flapped open and closed, open and closed, but no words came.

"We are indoctrinated to believe what those in charge of us want us to believe. I'm not a conspiracy nut but I'm sure there are a lot of things which are covered up." Tepes paused and focused once again on his weaker side. As impossible as it was, he really could feel something working inside him. "Do you honestly think they would let something of this magnitude out? *This* is why the boys are in hiding, the younger one is obviously the cause of the hoo-ha in Boxford."

"They said it was street gangs—"

"No one's going to admit to bloody werewolves, are they?"

"No. Well, what do we do?"

"Did you check my place?"

"No, I took the two boys on, remember?"

Tepes smiled and nodded. "Yes, but not in the way you were hoping, I'm sure."

Cyril turned away and checked the side mirror. "Do you think I like being like this?"

"Like what? Explain yourself."

Cyril flicked the indicator and turned onto a busy road. "All my life I've been an outcast, a flaming weirdo. Even if I wasn't socially inept I'd still be trapped in this out-of-proportion freakshow of a body. I never wanted to kill people, I really didn't."

Tepes rested his forehead against the window. "I remember it was Jeffrey Dahmer, or Dennis Nilsen, who said something along the lines of, 'If I had been able to hold down a relationship I would never have turned into a serial killer.'"

" Nilsen," Cyril confirmed which murderer had

uttered those words.

"There you go, then," Tepes said, as though that solved the issue. "Does that sound like you?"

"I understand where he was coming from."

"But *you* are not like them," Tepes snapped. "You were a swaddled little mummy's boy right up until the moment she popped her clogs, and the reason you never had a relationship with anyone is because you're a closet homosexual and you didn't want dear old Mummy to find out." He took a breath. "And you've repressed yourself so much you are permanently trapped in the era of your own sexual awakening and now you just take what you want, regardless."

Tepes' words hit a nerve.

Cyril felt his anger boiling, but when it rose, it morphed into self-pity. Tepes was right, in a way: it was as if he could see right into his soul.

Tepes rested his hand on Cyril's forearm.

Cyril stared at it confused. It was an uncommon act of affection from somebody who rarely showed any to somebody who rarely received any.

"I understand you," Tepes said. "Just because we are taught right from wrong doesn't mean we have to

FÜHRER: PART ONE

abide by those rules. *We* are different. *We* take what *we* want and *we* mask behind the facades that society expects and endorses. With this stuff flowing through me I can finally be who I truly am."

"But it's going to turn you into a monster."

"I already am one."

Chapter 5

"What's going on, fatso?" Trevor asked Gustav when the sounds from outside reached their room. Over the course of the day, the three old men had been awakened from their drug-induced slumbers.

Gustav's eyes widened at the iPad in front of him and swore in Ukrainian.

"It's all gone tits-up, hasn't it?" Norman said, bemused.

Gustav scowled at the two men. Neither one had shut up since coming out of the cryochambers.

The Jamaican was fully healed, but the Scot remained a weeping sore whilst the lycanthropy fixed the last few layers of skin.

The Brit was physically well but had reverted to the same depressive state he had been in before his near-death experience.

They are nice men.

That's what troubled Gustav the most: they reminded him of his father, his uncles.

None of them asked for this.

The Jamaican, the first that Blair roused, still reeled with the guilt of murdering his grandchildren. Until he was reunited with his friends he was a compliant zombie, but once the other two were awoken, he became more animated.

Gustav thought about how none of this would be used for good. How preparations were already in place to move everything at the facility and merge it with the empire General Liebermann had built beneath the Black Forest.

FÜHRER: PART ONE

The Jamaican hung his head in defeat.

Gustav slammed his fist on the computer desk. "Enough." He picked up the iPad and approached the men.

"What are you going to show us? A bluey to test our sexual reactions? You fat pervert," Norman snapped.

Gustav ignored the Scot, addressed the Jamaican, and stopped differentiating them in his mind by their nationality. "Trevor, isn't it?"

"Eartha Kitt," Trevor mumbled.

Norman huffed out what Gustav assumed was laughter.

"You want to get out of here? Escape?" Gustav made no attempt at trying to understand their sense of humour.

"No," Trevor said, "I want to die, but you bastards won't let me."

"Hear, hear," Herbert whispered, the first words he had spoken all day.

Gustav couldn't believe what he was about to do.

He tapped the iPad and the red lights on the CCTV went off. He brought up footage of the terrified twins being taken into the facility and strapped to beds.

He turned the screen for Trevor to see.

At first, Trevor refused to look at whatever it was Gustav wanted to show him, but once he did, he couldn't look away.

"You did not kill your grandchildren," Gustav said. "I'm afraid what you did was much, much worse."

"Oh, Mother Mary, no," Trevor murmured.

"Yes," Gustav continued, "they are alive."

"Oh, Jesus Christ, I've turned my babies into monsters."

"No," Gustav shouted, startling both himself and the men. "You've given them life. Long-lasting, enduring life. This thing that's inside you, inside them, can be controlled. I've seen it. The doctor, he showed me videos of a place in Germany. Despite what your friend believed, there are people who have known about this for decades. Krauss left a trail and it was picked up by the very people he took it from." Now he had their attention. "This thing is a psychological monster, a battle of wills. It can be controlled if you are strong enough. Determined enough." He tapped his temples. "Mentally."

"It's true." Herbert raised his head. "It's like that little voice inside you that tells you to have another cake," he looked at Norman, then at Trevor. "Or, in your case, another drink. You have to show it who's boss."

Gustav agreed. "There are people in Germany who have been studying this since the end of the Second World War. God only knows what they have planned, but it can't be good. They need to be stopped." He allowed a moment for this information to sink in. "But there are two children who need your help now." Gustav's hands were shaking as he unfastened their bonds.

For once in his life he was doing the right thing. Years of keeping secrets was at an end, and he didn't care if they tore him apart; it was no better than he deserved.

The three men stood before him in hospital smocks.

FÜHRER: PART ONE

The bald man, Herbert, seemed to be animated with a new zest of life. It was as if he had been suffocating but could now finally breathe. "We can do this."

"Aye," Norman agreed, puffing out his chest. "Or at least die trying."

Gustav locked eyes with Trevor. "Just believe you can control it and you will. Go and save your grandchildren."

Trevor stepped towards Gustav, could smell his fear, his alien senses had gone into overdrive now he was free. The creature inside him made itself known, ready to go, to start the transformation, but a new level of determination stopped it from rising.

Do as you are told.

A low animal grumble rose in Trevor's throat but he swallowed it back like bile.

Not yet.

The three old men pushed past Gustav, left the room, and headed towards the sounds of thumping boots and shouting.

Chapter 6

Doctor Charlotte Smith stood behind the line of soldiers, her hands held behind her back by Agent Davis.

She watched the black van rock violently as Kiran and Kayleigh tore their mother apart. At least that's what she presumed was happening.

She couldn't believe what she was seeing: the change, the frightened faces of the children as their bodies went through spasms of what looked like an agonising process.

"Why aren't they helping her?" she asked Davis as the soldiers formed a ring around the van, the pilot lights of their flamethrowers flickering.

The darkened windows of the van gave nothing away.

Davis whispered, breath hot against her neck, "They don't want to kill them. These things are valuable."

"What about their mother?" Charlotte cried, although she already knew the answer to that. Juliet was expendable, so no doubt she was, too.

The rocking reached a crescendo.

The soldiers raised their weapons and, in an explosion of glass and metal, the twins burst from the van.

Sparse black fur covered their lithe bodies as they ran with an unnatural volume of muscle.

The twins hadn't grown much but they crouched like wildcats, ready to pounce. Their hands sported talons almost as long as their hooked fingers. As they bared their teeth at the soldiers, their teeth looked too big for their mouths.

"Oh my God," Charlotte said. "They're frightened." She craned her neck, looking at Davis. "They're frightened. Don't let them hurt them."

Whistles came from the soldiers' guns.

Charlotte thought they were using some kind of silencer, but then she saw the little darts protruding from the children's necks.

One of them, it was hard to distinguish who was who, as they were even more identical in their new form, moved forward groggily before both collapsed against one another and crumpled to the asphalt.

"Don't!"

Charlotte ignored Davis; she wasn't running to the fallen children, their modified bodies could withstand more than that; she was running to the van. She needed to see what they had done to Juliet, to see if there was anything she could do to help, but when she reached for the door, Juliet heaved herself out of the vehicle.

Charlotte recoiled, half-expecting Juliet to be undergoing her own metamorphosis, but instead, she staggered into the light shaken, clothes torn, with no visible injuries.

She smiled at Charlotte. "They didn't hurt me."

There was no chance for Charlotte to respond.

Juliet spotted Kiran and Kayleigh on the tarmac and fell over their naked bodies. "Don't hurt my babies."

"Get them confined," Butcher boomed from unseen speakers. "We evacuate in two minutes."

Davis rushed towards the two women and trained his gun on Juliet. "Let them take them. If you don't, they'll be hunted down and killed."

Charlotte choked.

Soldiers swarmed the children and threw Juliet aside whilst more stood guard.

"Where are they taking them?" Juliet asked, but Davis' answer was drowned out by gunfire and shouting.

They turned in the direction of a new commotion.

Three large shapes, two bipedal, one quadruped, exploded through the front of the facility.

FÜHRER: PART ONE

Chapter 7

Hunger was God.

The host's stomach contained nothing of value. It was on the brink of malnutrition and it burned through the meagre number of calories within seconds of its first transformation.

There was something primal in the host itself preventing it from devouring the mewling prey strewn on the stairs.

It tore through the house, following the scent of the fleeing men.

Once outside, beneath the night sky, it froze in the silvery luminescence of the heavenly glowing orb.

Something roiled within its new body; increased vigour, heightened awareness.

It tipped its head back, beheld the moon with new eyes, and cried out a mixture of violent ecstasy and incurable pain.

This distraction allowed its prey to get away.

Even though it gained some kind of sustenance from the moon, it was incredibly weak, starving. It needed easy prey, this was no time for challenges.

The wolf turned back to the place where it had been caged and sprayed the entry with scent. There was prey there, albeit unattainable, so it would return if it wasn't strong enough to find better.

It moved across the road rifling the air for smells of other living things.

Something small and furry scuttled along the gutter.

FÜHRER: PART ONE

The wolf gave a few lazy steps in pursuit before realising a cat was too meagre a morsel to make a difference.

The cat hissed when it made eye contact with its potential hunter, arching its spine and its fur bristling.

The wolf scared it rigid with a hiss of its own.

Then the cat vanished with a flash and the wolf followed it farther along the road until its ears pricked with nearby sounds.

More prey.

What strange bleats and mewls this prey made. Their scents and calls were plentiful and their lair glowed like nothing it had ever seen; it was full, ripe for the picking.

The wolf stuck to the shadows, instinct telling it that such an abundance of food must be protected.

Bright lights attracted it but also made it cautious.

Nevertheless, it stalked closer to the building.

"There's something out there," Suki said, pressing her face up against the glass.

"Of course there is, dur-brain. The whole world is out there," Matt said, trying his utmost not to sound freaked out.

Although he was a sceptic, he didn't disbelieve enough to rule anything out and knew perfectly well how kids were rumoured to be tapped into stuff adults couldn't see. It both excited and scared the horror fanatic in him.

He remembered when he'd been on his own with his eldest having a late dinner in the flat.

Ebbie had sat, all small, cute and chunky, in her highchair command centre overlooking a battleground of turkey dinosaurs and potato letters.

He'd frozen, ramrod-straight, in his besmirched surroundings and raised a chubby, saucy finger and pointed over Matt's left shoulder. "Daddy, I do not like that little boy and girl standing there."

Matt felt his insides curdle into half-defrosted cauliflower. Gooseflesh rippled across the nape of his neck and for a moment, before he turned around, there really was a pair of spectral children behind him pulling obscene faces at his son. He could feel them, hear their excited whispers.

There was nothing there when he spun around, of course.

"You're not funny, Matt," Suki said, pouting. She used a chocolate bar as a baton and thwacked it against his big, silly head. She loved her uncle; she thought he was funny and liked his crazy green hair and colourful tattoos, but his sense of humour made her groan.

About as funny as a fart in a two-man tent, her dad would say.

She pulled at a strand of her brown hair and twisted it between her fingers.

"Come on Suke, eatey-eat choccy-choc and make the hypo go away," Matt said in a baby voice.

Suki huffed and pressed her face back against the window.

Matt slumped on the cushioned bench beside her and returned to his normal demeanour. "What's up? You pissed off 'cause you couldn't go swimming?"

FÜHRER: PART ONE

Suki turned towards the families coming out of the changing area with excited faces, wet hair, the smell of chlorine.

Matt saw her face go pale, a sign that she either needed to eat that bloody chocolate bar or she was going to cry.

"A bit, I suppose," she grumped.

"Come on," he said, and playfully punched her in the bicep.

He loved her as if she were his own, but it was difficult being a bloke: he had to be careful showing affection to other people's children, relatives or otherwise.

He wanted to give her a great big bear hug that lasted several minutes, just as he'd done with his own kids when they were younger, but he was always conscious about making them uncomfortable, which is why he resorted to lovingly playful violence.

Suki returned his punch and he was equally surprised and proud that it actually hurt. "Jeez, Suke," he said, rubbing his arm, "don't actually hit me and mean it!"

"I do mean it," she said sulking. "Every *single* time."

"Look, we'll come again next week, I promise, and we'll make sure to keep an eye on your blood sugar beforehand. And I'll get Manjo to pack extra OJ in her poolside bag just in case."

Suki nodded, slumped against him, and picked at the wrapper of her chocolate bar.

Her aunt, Manjo, her mum's sister, was a pro at diabetes. She had lived with it herself for thirty of her thirty-seven years.

Suki thought she was going to die when she became diabetic, she had been really ill and had had to stay in hospital.

Matt and Manjo had bought her a toy wolf, her favourite animal, and all she could remember of that time was hugging Aurora, Matt's name for the wolf, and sleeping lots. The doctors gave her medicine, and after a while she started feeling normal...ish. When she'd got an insulin pump, just like Manjo's, they'd had a special party because they were pump-twins. It made the condition a lot easier for she and her parents knowing they had someone at their beck and call who was a walking encyclopaedia on diabetes.

Suki pressed herself against Matt's arm, ignoring his fake yelps of pain and protest. "At least I still get to have Maccies."

"There you go, there's always a silver lining," Matt said. "I mean, I didn't get an hour and a half of quiet reading done like I hoped, and had to endure sitting next to you moaning about your school week, but hey ho."

"You mean pretending to stare at the same page of your book whilst you perv at the receptionist with the red hair?"

Matt gasped and hoped the girl with the letterbox red hair, who sat at the reception desk across the foyer, hadn't heard.

Suki looked at the clock above them and sighed heavily. She took a miniscule bite of her chocolate bar and twisted around to stare back out at the darkness.

Something definitely moved out there. It was hard to see with the glare of the leisure centre, but something definitely shifted in the shadows.

FÜHRER: PART ONE

"Shit the bed," Matt exclaimed, kneeling on the seat beside her. "I think I actually saw something out there in the bushes. Maybe it's a homeless guy getting shelter for the night. Must be the heat coming from the pool vents."

They recoiled as an inhuman shape broke from the cloak of darkness and sprang like a tiger towards the giant glass panels.

Twenty. Twenty fucking lengths without barely stopping to breathe. I'm fucking Aqua Man.

Rich thrust his head and chest out of the water, expecting the entire pool full of people to go crazy with applause at such an impressive athletic achievement.

But the only reaction was from an elderly man, doggy-paddling so slowly it seemed he was going backwards, who tutted at him for standing in his way.

Balls bounced above the surface as kids carried on playing with their parents.

Across the large expanse, his wife Caz stood opposite her sister, Manjo's kids forming a circle around them as they pushed baby Martha backwards and forwards in an inflatable ring doughnut.

Ebbie, Matt and Manjo's teenage dirtbag, glared hatefully at the happy family units around him, probably picturing them all being eaten by a shoal of ravenous piranha.

Rich covertly scanned the pool for the young blonde in the bikini with the amazing boobs. He'd clocked her earlier and had made a mental note to swim by her and get a closer look at those beauties when wet.

A few athletic teens, nothing at all like his nephew Ebbie, cut through the water like dolphins, making his twenty lengths look like nothing.

He spotted the blonde, and as he readied himself to dive and scope out her attributes, something smashed through the glass wall above them.

People shrieked as a black mass barrelled into the centre of the pool, causing a mini tsunami.

As it rose from the pool, the first thing Rich noticed was a mass of dark, wet fur. The second was that it was a monster, something that should not exist this side of a movie. Just as he decided it must be exactly that, a really life-like cosplay, it swiped a long spindly arm through the air like a scythe and raked its wide paws across the nearest swimmers.

The water turned scarlet, and people rushed towards the sides with ragged red zigzags across their chests and faces.

Rich thawed from his frozen-solid state and swam immediately towards the side. He slapped his palms on the tiles and tried to hoist himself out of the water but he was closer to Whale Boy than Aqua Man. He twisted, and finally set eyes on the blonde who he'd instantly, moronically, nicknamed *Tits.*

Her cry drowned out all other noise as the beast snatched something from her hands.

A flailing little body, complete with orange armbands, dangled above its open jaws.

Rich saw the baby's head resting on the monster's wide red tongue for a second, as if it were savouring the anticipation, and then it clamped its teeth together, destroying the head of the child and the heart of its mother.

"It's a fucking werewolf," Rich said as finally, after the fourth attempt, he managed to haul his arse out of the pool, colliding with a doddery old couple. A man, who only moments before had tutted at Rich for obstructing his path, and an equally sour-faced old battle-axe, a network of wrinkled sagging skin in a bathing suit cut way too high, revealing an overgrown shrubbery sprouting from the crotch. "Bloody terrorists," the man said, rushing his spouse towards the exit at a speed that surprised Rich.

Everyone made for the sides but either their injuries were too severe or the sides were too high.

Rich grimaced as a rope of intestines floated past in the red water, still attached to a frantic swimmer, trailing behind them like goldfish shit; the monster grabbed it and reeled them in.

Rich's only concern was his family.

Manjo's dayglo pink hair was a beacon in the panicking crowd and he saw her standing at the poolside, Martha's squealing red face tucked under one arm. Ebbie actually showed emotion for once and batted at the water with a blue pool noodle.

All of them screamed at his wife, who rushed towards them as fast as her bad knees would allow.

The beast in the water set eyes on her and decided she was a more bountiful meal than the baby and the skinny teenagers it had just tried to eat.

It splashed towards her, ribbons of flesh hanging from its black claws.

"Oi!" Rich shrieked. "No one's eating my wife but me." He jumped up and down, clapping his hands trying to get the thing's attention and scanned the walls for anything he could use as a weapon. He pulled the long-handled net from the lifeguard's seat, briefly wondering where the staff were, and slapped its looped end at the water's surface.

The creature paid it no heed, raking its spindly body through the water after its tasty, curvaceous prey.

Caz ploughed through the water at a pace far faster than normal while Manjo and Ebbie threw anything they could find at the wolf-thing. Pool noodles and did nothing but bounce off the flouncing beast. It wasn't until Ebbie had the initiative to hurl one of the spectator chairs at it that it even flinched.

Rich reached over the surface and hooked the net over the creature's large head. It looked ridiculous but it stopped and turned its attention on him.

He looked into its burning animal eyes, and for a moment, seriously considered letting it eat his family, before it jerked its head and dragged him back into the pool.

Matt's reaction, when the shadows exploded and the thing collided with the leisure centre, was to grab his niece and throw himself to the floor on top of her.

"What the fucking hell was that?" shouted the red-haired receptionist as she ran towards the entry.

"Something's come through the glass and into the pool," Suki cried, thrusting her chocolate bar with each word.

"I don't know what the fuck it was, but it was big," Matt added, moving gingerly towards the entrance.

FÜHRER: PART ONE

Whatever it was had to have some propulsion behind it as the glass walls were at least ten feet up, and so thick they were virtually soundproof.

Being the only male in the vicinity, he figured it was up to him to play the hero and venture out into the night to investigate.

Sometimes he hated being a man.

"Suki, stay here with the nice reception la—"

"—the lady you perv on?"

"There's a time and a place, Suke," Matt said, avoiding the receptionist's disgusted glare.

Well, he thought, *now's as good an opportunity as any to get the fuck out of here. Anything is better than staying with a smug twelve-year-old and a twenty-something woman who is looking at me like I'm the embodiment of all male wrongdoing.*

He came out of the well-lit leisure centre and scouted the area by the pool wall.

Nothing to see, aside from a huge hole in the glass, and nothing to give a clue about what had gone through it.

He went to go back inside when the first bloodied swimmers began their stampede from the pool area; covered in deep scratches and cuts, they fell over each other to get away.

"Fuck," Matt shouted into the ruckus and raced back inside to get his niece.

That's what this is, a fucking knife attack, the more accessible choice of attack for your average terrorist now that guns are pretty much obsolete.

He had a fleeting image of running into the throng and bringing the attacker down and getting his picture in the papers, but then he remembered he wasn't brave or knowledgeable enough in combat matters to even bring one of his own kids down, let alone an armed terrorist.

Rich floundered beneath the surface, his vision limited due to the clouds of diluted blood. Two thick black things came towards him, the monster's legs.

He kicked out and drove himself upwards, gasping for air as soon as he could. The thing still had the pool net over its head, lacking the dexterity to get it off.

He saw Caz finally drag her arse out of the pool, helped by Manjo and the kids.

The beast roared in frustration and made towards them.

Even with assistance, Caz's tired, arthritic knees prevented her from moving too quickly.

Rich knew he had to buy them time. He slapped his palms against the water and shouted at the retreating animal. "Oi, you great big cunt, ain't there enough for you to eat here?" His hand brushed a floating, severed arm,, and he grabbed it with a grimace.

He flung it at the creature, striking it in the centre of its back.

It gave a nonchalant grumble but continued towards Caz, its ultimate prize.

Of course it wants to eat them, Rich considered, *who wouldn't?* They were both tasty looking women, his wife and her sister, and he had to admire the monster's taste although it had left Tits floating face-down, uneaten.

He dove across the pool and yanked hard on the net handle.

FÜHRER: PART ONE

Surprisingly, the beast lost its balance and fell over backwards, the net now looped below its jaws.

Rich grabbed the handle and dragged it towards the deep end, wondering if he could drown it. He left it clawing at the pool bottom and clambered up the closest edge.

"Drown, you wanker!" he shouted and ran towards the exit and his wife.

"Oh my God." Matt ran to his family as they rushed into the foyer. They didn't seem to have any injuries but the attacker was still at large.

Caz was slowing them down so he rugby-tackled her and attempted to get her up on his shoulder in a fireman's lift.

"You can't pick me up," she hollered, slapping at his broad back.

"Chill out," Matt said, face pressed against her hip. "I lift heavy at the gym."

His back gave out immediately and Caz landed on top of him.

The doors to the pool area slammed open and Rich collided with them. "Stop fucking about," he said, yanking Caz to her feet one-handed, "that fucking thing's coming for us."

"Go," Matt moaned heroically, belly-down on the carpet.

"No," Manjo wailed. "I'm not leaving you. I don't want to look after these bloody children without you."

"Yeah, dickhead," Ebbie added, almost affectionately, and grabbed hold of his dad's right ankle. Manjo and Suki held on to the other and together they dragged him across the sodden carpet.

Behind them the doors exploded and Suki stopped. "It's a werewolf," she said with a bit too much delight, frozen to the spot in starstruck wonder at coming face to face with her favourite monster.

It bared its teeth but she ignored its carrion breath and the strands of flesh dangling from its jaws.

"Aww, he's only looking for something to eat," she shrieked as Rich threw her over his shoulder. She threw her half-eaten chocolate bar at it and smiled when it caught it in its mouth and instantly swallowed it.

"Good boy, good boy," she called as they burst through the leisure centre doors and out into the night.

Outside, blue flashing lights swathed the building; the night was alive with screaming and sirens.

"Good boy," Suki whispered sadly towards the thing in the foyer as half a dozen armed police ran inside.

She saw the werewolf retreat into the pool area. Her dad plonked her beside Martha, Ebbie, and a group of other survivors.

"What the hell was that?" Matt said, bracing his back and getting to his feet.

One of the survivors, an old man, muttered, "Bloody terrorist."

"That was not a terrorist," Matt snapped.

Gunshots echoed from the centre and the top half of a police officer flew through a broken window, followed by the creature itself.

It landed, flattening the bushes, and glared at them malevolently.

FÜHRER: PART ONE

"Does that look like a fucking terrorist?" Matt asked the old man, who shrugged, took hold of his wife's arm, and frantically shuffled off as the so-called terrorist pounced, bringing them both to the ground with its terrorist paws.

"Bad dog!" Suki scolded and slipped free of Rich.

The werewolf appraised her with a somewhat alien expression of confusion and then chomped down on the old man's head.

"Ew," Suki squealed, "no more chocolate for you."

"For fuck's sake, Suke!" Caz shouted at such a volume even the wolf flinched. It turned back and focused on tearing the old woman's throat out. The sound of its teeth grating against her spinal column told them it was time for them to go.

The adults fled, carrying and dragging the children.

It was only Ebbie and Suki who looked back with a mixture of admiration and sorrow.

There was too much prey, and that had been a problem.

It had chosen its hunting ground poorly and only succeeded in brief mouthfuls of rushing prey when it needed to glut itself.

It turned away and retraced its way back to where it had marked its scent.

Chapter 8

What Tepes had said was wrong.

Cyril was a mummy's boy, but she knew about his sexual orientation.

She knew alright and had done ever since the trip to Tenerife back in 1984, but, like a lot of stuff back then, it had been covered up, brushed under the carpet, bound and tied and hidden in the closet with all her other skeletons.

It was the last holiday Cyril ever went on. Right before his dad's aneurysm popped whilst he came down the stairs with half a tin of white gloss. They never did get that out of the carpet.

Cyril had been obsessed with his image back then, he knew he wasn't typically good-looking so he tried hard with fashion and hairstyles.

Back when he'd had hair, he'd worn it long to mask his disproportionate features.

Tenerife was a hotspot for his parents and they'd visited almost every year since he was born. When he was officially old enough to be left on his own, Cyril would split away from them and lounge around the hotel, a familiar place he knew as well as his own home. There was no need to go sightseeing; he'd already seen everything a dozen times or more. He hung around the bar and the swimming pool, watching the other holidaymakers.

From a young age, Cyril knew he liked boys. At primary school, he was besotted with one boy in particular, Michael Harper.

FÜHRER: PART ONE

Michael Harper, who would beat him up on an almost daily basis for not being able to control his freakish, roving eyes. Michael Harper, who was a blue-eyed, yellow-haired cherub, whose expressions of amusement and vicious delight were things of beauty, worth every punch, slap and kick.

At the time, Cyril had known how wrong his feelings were, he had heard all about it from jokes on the television, and conversations between his mother and father about what was right and what was wrong. They would go on endless tirades, using vile words and terms to describe people's creed, culture, race, and sexuality.

Hypocritical arseholes.

If his father wasn't lambasting 'queers' and 'bloody foreigners,' he was shouting about fighting evil Nazis in the Second World War; ironic, really, given that his own outlook wasn't that far removed from theirs.

Since their previous visit to Tenerife, the hoteliers Alfonzo and Marie had hired new staff, and one in particular caught Cyril's eye.

Philippe was French, with dark, Celtic looks and blue eyes.

Cyril's past experiences told him there was no point in trying to achieve anything other than passing platitudes, but nothing, no matter how much he hated this, could stop the hope inside him. Hope that maybe this time, if he did let his guard down and make a move, he wouldn't be greeted with looks of disgust, laughter, or a kick in the teeth.

Although he was only in his mid-twenties, he'd learned there was no point in bothering; he was destined to be alone.

However, Philippe was different.

They discovered mutual interests in music, became friends, and over the two-week vacation, things escalated. Much to Cyril's amazement, it was Philippe who made the first move.

Cyril confided in him, told him it was the first time he had been kissed by a boy, by anyone, like that.

Cyril lost his virginity to the barman; he was twenty-five, Philippe nineteen. Love, undying, was declared over a bed wet with Ouzo sweat and spunk beneath loitering clouds of cigarette smoke.

It was the only truly happy night of Cyril's life.

The following morning they overslept. Cyril's dad came in to rouse his son and found them tangled, half-naked.

He flew into an apoplectic rage, dragged the young bartender from the bed by his hair, and hurled him towards the open balcony door.

Cyril froze.

The horror on Philippe's face as he smashed through the balcony's poorly built railing would haunt him forever.

His parents convinced everyone it was an accident, that his father had found the bartender ransacking his son's room whilst he lay comatose, and that Philippe had run to the balcony to escape and had fallen.

Cyril had known from then on just how wrong he was for wanting such things, but as time went by it became harder and harder to deny his compulsions.

FÜHRER: PART ONE

Chapter 9

The soldiers with the children rushed away, ignoring their comrades' distress, using their deaths to distract from the more important part of the mission. Blair wanted those twins.

One of the creatures came below the spotlight. It had the appearance of a skinned bear, completely bald and wet with blood. It swatted at the soldiers almost lazily, their bullets peppering its body but doing little to slow it down.

Another one pounced past it, bigger in both girth and height and covered in grey-black fur. It ploughed into half a dozen soldiers, a fury of tooth and claw sending ribbons of flesh and viscera into the air. With a single swipe of a paw, it took one soldier's head clean off.

The other, red-furred beast, larger than a traditional wolf, was less calculated, but wilder. Without any kind of strategic planning it slashed at everything in its path, taking bites from whatever it could before moving on to its next fresh victim.

A klaxon rang out and more soldiers came with tranquiliser guns.

Juliet sprang from Davis and ran in the direction Kiran and Kayleigh had been taken but managed only a few metres before she received a gun-butt to the face.

Charlotte ran to Juliet, hands in the air. "Please don't shoot," she begged the soldier who dropped the children's mother. His evident fear betrayed his age;

he was barely an adolescent. He shouted something in another language and ran to help his friends.

The screaming and gunfire as the troop fought the trio of beasts was suddenly swamped by a deafening noise.

Charlotte remembered the Chinook they'd passed when they'd arrived at the facility.

The gurneys with Kiran and Kayleigh vanished around the side of the building, towards the sound of twin rotors.

Charlotte checked Juliet, who was beginning to stir, with a huge lump on her forehead.

"The twins," she slurred.

"They've taken them," Davis said, panic-stricken, not knowing his next move. He looked at the two women on the tarmac briefly before shrugging and running toward the helicopter.

The sound of gunfire died out as the remaining soldiers left the attacking beasts and headed for the safety of their escape route.

The faster quadruped pulled its wet maw from the open stomach of a soldier it had felled and sprinted in the direction of Charlotte and Juliet, the black-furred biped joining in the hunt. Charlotte scooted back across the tarmac away from Juliet; she knew they would both be defenceless against the things.

As the red wolf left the ground to pounce on the groggy Juliet, the black beast drove a fist into its side, sending it crashing to the ground in a heap. It roared at the fallen animal and crouched over its potential prey.

They're fighting over her, Charlotte thought as it towered over Juliet and dripped bloody drool onto her screaming face.

Though Charlotte was several feet away, she could smell offal on its breath.

The quadruped red wolf righted itself, shook its gigantic head, and crept slowly towards them, a low rumble in its throat.

Charlotte waited to be torn asunder.

Juliet straightened up in the shadow of the massive black beast, spat at its feet, and ludicrously prodded its wide chest.

"Always late to the show, aren't you, Dad?"

Rather than being obliterated, Juliet's voice had a different effect on the creature. It began to shrink, fur retracting back into the body and revealing blood-slicked skin.

Trevor panted with exertion and hacked up a torrent of red gore.

The red wolf beside him went through a similar transformation.

Charlotte was dumbfounded.

Before anyone had a chance to speak, the Chinook took to the air and hovered above the facility. Something pink and muscular clung to one of its wheels.

"Oh, Jesus fucking Christ," Norman said, pointing up at the sky and crouching to hide his nudity. "It's like that scene from *Jaws: The Revenge*. What the hell does Herbert think he's doing?"

The Chinook listed as the pilot tried to shake off the monster clinging to its side.

Unlike what usually happened in the movies, Herbert's claws, as strong as they were, could not penetrate the chopper's armour, but he clung on regardless, hoping his weight would force them to land.

Tendons strained in his forearms as gravity took its toll. He dug his modified feet against one of the wheels and climbed farther up the side of the aircraft. A door slid open, and a soldier aimed his gun at him and fired.

Herbert swung a paw, but the bullets ripped through the appendage quicker than he could strike.

The soldier fired point-blank at his chest, so Herbert pressed closer to the metal, thinking the soldier wouldn't risk damage to the helicopter.

He clung on, but with one hand destroyed by gunfire he could feel himself slipping.

The massacred stump stopped pumping blood and began to clot, but the miraculous regenerative properties of the lycanthropy failed to restore the damage in time.

The soldier vanished inside the chopper and leant back out with one of the tranquiliser rifles.

Darts zipped from the barrel and spiked Herbert's chest and neck, numbness coursing through instantaneously.

With one last roar of frustration, Herbert scrambled up the side of the Chinook, wrapped his bloodied stump around the soldier's waist, and let the loss of sensation consume him.

Something tore and he fell from the helicopter.

The last thing he saw as he plummeted towards the roof of the facility was the horror on the dying soldier's face.

Chapter 10

The cold of the cellar steps made Tony feel like he had frozen solid. The skin around the zip-ties was purple, his hands numb. He had seen numerous YouTube tutorials on how to free yourself from sticky situations like this (zip-ties, not werewolf siblings), but refrained from doing anything about it. The freezing numbness was more than just physical.

It's over, Danny's gone.

As he sat with the cold concrete pressing into his back, he decided he was going to go to the police; there wasn't any other choice. If they didn't believe him they soon would, there was only so much stuff they could blame on teenage hoodlums, especially with the Green Man Crew being virtually extinct.

The floorboards creaked as something passed over the house above.

Tepes or Cyril had come back, he knew it. God only knew what evil would be unleashed now that man had become infected.

Tony had no doubt the manipulative psychopath was now going to go through the same experiences as Danny, although how the thing inside him would react to something whose bloodlust probably matched its own wasn't worth thinking about.

He sat up, let sensation crawl back into his legs, and climbed the stairs, ready for anything but fully prepared to die; he had no more fight left.

The first thing he noticed was the wide-open door, then the bloody footprints leading across the kitchen.

FÜHRER: PART ONE

Tony followed them into the lounge.

Danny lay on the settee naked and red, his stomach abnormally distended, with horrible stretch-marks zigzagging over the shining skin like someone made heavily pregnant overnight. He had obviously eaten — Tony didn't want to guess what, or whom — and briefly wondered why he hadn't stayed in wolf-form to digest his meal. He looked like he would literally split.

"Danny?" Tony said, inching closer, noticing ruddy pockmarks where something had penetrated his skin but was healing rapidly.

Danny snored heavily like a satisfied bear after gorging itself post-hibernation.

Tony relived his close proximity to Danny's beast only hours before, as it had drooled over him before fleeing the cellar.

Why didn't it kill me?

Did it think I was already captured?

Did it want to leave me bound in the cellar and keep me in its larder for another time?

"Why didn't you kill me?" Tony's voice faltered as he succumbed to the tears. "I wish you had."

Chapter 11

Tepes' prominent limp wasn't as pronounced as it had been before the car journey. Cyril followed him, awestruck by the rapid state of his recovery when just hours before he'd been a weakened version of himself.

Tepes climbed the stairs confidently but this renewed vigour didn't last; he began to struggle by the time he reached the top.

"Are you okay?" Cyril said, pawing at his back.

Tepes nodded. "Look at how quickly this thing is working. I don't even need the crutches anymore. It's miraculous." Nevertheless, he leant on a doorpost and pointed through the open doorway. "Under that bed are three cases. Get them out."

Cyril moved into the room, crouched down and pulled the cases from beneath the bed.

Tepes fumbled in his coat pockets and swore. "Those little shits still have my keys."

Cyril pulled a bunch of spare keys from his pocket.

"No, there aren't any copies."

"Can't you force them?"

"You're right. Bring them down to my shed."

Cyril stacked the cases on top of one another and followed Tepes back down through the house and out into the old builder's yard.

Of the various Victorian outbuildings, only one was in usable condition.

Cyril had been there numerous times; he liked Tepes' home, it reminded him of his youth.

FÜHRER: PART ONE

An archaic concrete coal bunker, its metal cover rusted into ruin, was now a home for spiders and other creatures that liked the dark and the damp.

A half-collapsed outdoor toilet showed a devastated porcelain basin and a graveyard of ancient garden implements.

The largest building other than the house was a more modern affair; a big, secure shed made from red corrugated iron filled half the yard.

Tepes opened a chunky, heavy padlock and led Cyril into the large space. He flicked switches and strip lighting flickered on, showing walls covered in sparkling tools of every variety.

Cyril clocked a row of lethal meat hooks, which glinted on the high rafters above a tin trough.

Looks like something you'd find in an abattoir.

Cyril wondered why Tepes had bothered murdering his last victim in the house when he had all the necessary utensils and space here.

"I don't need to tell you what all this stuff is for, do I?" Tepes said, noticing Cyril's inquisitive looks.

"You've got everything here," Cyril said, putting the cases down on a workbench.

"First things first," Tepes said, moving towards a large chest freezer. He lifted the lid and revealed the frozen body of a skinny black-haired boy. "Have you ever tried human flesh, Cyril?"

"What?" Cyril said transfixed by the naked youth.

"Cannibalism, dear boy."

Tepes slammed the lid, opened one of the others, pulled out a neatly-wrapped package and showed the label to Cyril.

Belly draught.

"I don't know about you, but I'm starving."

"What about the cases?"

"Why don't you see if you can crack them open whilst I go and put the oven on?" Tepes waved at the tools. "I'm sure you're capable. Come and find me when you've got them open."

Cyril stared dumbfounded as Tepes left him to it. He eyed the tools; most of them looked as if they had never been used.

Several rows of knives and bone-cutting saws added to the slaughterhouse ambience.

He knew that Tepes' kink was drinking blood, but he'd never taken him for an actual killer. For the first time ever, he was in the company of someone quite possibly worse than him.

Tepes hadn't bought his sob story back in the car, and it was no surprise. They were cut from the same cloth: they both killed for some type of pleasure or need.

Is there anything sexual in it for him?

How does he feel when he consumes their flesh?

Does he think that a part of them lives on? Inside him?

Cyril raised the lid of the chest freezer and stared at the dead boy's perfect alabaster skin. He cupped the feminine face, the flesh hard as bone, ran his thumb over the blue lips, and let the tip of his little finger slip inside his cold, dark mouth. He groaned and pushed his finger in deeper.

"I knew you'd not be able to resist," Tepes whispered, his hot breath against his neck.

Cyril cried out and fell across the open freezer, his finger stuck in the cadaver's mouth up to the second knuckle.

"Relax!" Tepes laughed. "What say I leave you to it for a while? The cases can wait."

Cyril's nerves overrode his speech and whatever did come out was indecipherable bilge.

"Don't be ashamed of what you are, Cyril." Tepes' stare was penetrating, like all the best vampires. "Embrace it. Be proud."

"Why?" Cyril stammered, "why are you doing this? Sharing this?"

Tepes gazed around, seeking inspiration from the hammers and chisels. "We are kindred spirits, you and I, and now we're privy to a power beyond our imaginations. Well, I am," he corrected. "And besides," he said, smiling warmly, "every vampire needs his Renfield."

Chapter 12

"Sweet Jesus," Charlotte said to the two naked old men.

The Scot was a mass of weeping red flesh, virtually skinless from the neck down.

Juliet shrieked up at the sky, beating her fists against her father's wide chest as he held onto her and howled out his own sorrow.

"So, I take it he's Juliet's father, but who are you?" Charlotte asked, trying to process the slaughter of the soldiers.

"We're the good guys. At least I hope so," Norman said sheepishly.

"Can you control the thing inside you?"

"Kind of." Norman grinned awkwardly. "But to be honest, that just then was a bit of a blur."

Juliet pushed away from her father and scowled at Norman. "What the hell have you two been dabbling in?"

"Hey, this is not our fault," Trevor protested.

"It was all Victor and Ethel," Norman said.

"You're like a couple of guilty schoolboys," Juliet scolded.

A silhouette appeared in the entrance to the building and lurched towards them with the awkward gait of someone carrying a few stones too many.

"Who the hell is that? Victor?" Juliet stepped towards the newcomer.

"That's not Victor, you daft woman," Trevor said, reaching for her arm. "Victor was about seven foot tall, this bloke's got the physique of an Oompa Loompa."

Charlotte watched the thick-set man waddle towards them. As he came below the floodlights, she saw he had thinning brown hair and a moustache so long and full that it almost covered his chin. He was carrying something draped over his arm.

"That's Gustav," Norman said.

Juliet pushed him aside and strode towards him. "Who are you? Why didn't you leave with the others?"

"Relax," the man said, raising a palm. "I am nobody, just a dogsbody."

"What's going to happen? Where have they gone? Are we in danger?" Charlotte fired the questions at him.

"Relax. Your children should be safe, on their way to Germany, and there is probably no danger." He paused and took in their deserted surroundings. "Well, for now, anyway."

"Germa—"

Charlotte cut Juliet off. "You know quite a lot for a dogsbody."

"Everything of importance was permanently stationed on the Chinook in case of an emergency evacuation. As a failsafe, everything on the computers will have automatically been wiped. I tried to stop the process, to gather more information, but I was unsuccessful."

"He told us about you, that Kiran and Kayleigh are alive," Trevor said. "He gave me a reason to control my wolf."

His daughter spun around and spat in his face. "Wasn't attacking your grandchildren reason enough?"

Trevor hung his head.

Charlotte looked at the dozens of dead soldiers littering the tarmac; amongst them were Davis and the other agents who had abducted her and the twins. "But all this? What for? They have taken those kids anyway."

Gustav handed Trevor and Norman hospital smocks. "Please. I know there are lots of things to talk about, but can we do it inside and see to your other friend? I believe he got hit several times with the tranquiliser but he is a big man and it may not be as effective as it was on the children. And we need to leave this place. We may not have a lot of time. They will send someone."

"I don't care," Juliet growled.

"Don't you want to know where they have taken your children?" Gustav shouted.

Juliet kept her mouth shut and her anger bled into heartbreak.

Gustav pointed at the facility. "Inside."

They wove through the carpet of dismembered dead.

The foyer was wrecked, with smashed ceiling tiles, shattered strip lights, and Herbert sitting like a newborn baby covered in blood from its mother. He smiled groggily. "That was great fun."

"And this," Norman said to Charlotte, "is Herbert."

Herbert waved the massacred stump of his hand.

"How many of you are there? Where are the others?" Juliet asked Trevor.

Norman and Trevor helped Herbert to his feet and handed him a smock.

"Just us three," Trevor said sadly.

"Ethel and Elizabeth didn't make it," Norman added.

"I understand how awful this all is, and pointing fingers won't do anyone any good," Herbert said, getting dressed, "but—"

"It was Victor's fault!" Norman blurted.

"Yes, we understand that Victor and his wife were like us, they brought this here."

"But it was Ethel who infected us," Trevor said, slumping into a chair. "She used samples of their blood to infect us. She thought we would live forever."

Norman nodded. "It wasn't our choice."

"I believe Krauss and his wife had been lycanthropes since the nineteen-forties," Gustav said. "They discovered it, and he studied it. Once he realised how dangerous it was, he tried to keep it from the Nazis, despite being foolish enough to infect himself and his wife."

"Jesus!" Norman sighed. "He kept it quiet for so long only for that nosey old cowbag to screw it all up."

Gustav shrugged. "It was all for nothing, his subterfuge; the Nazis had access to it all along."

"What? Why haven't they done anything with it?" Charlotte asked. "Surely something like this would be used."

"They have been finding out all they can about it before—" Gustav stopped and turned to a nearby computer monitor.

"Before *what*?"

"Before they pick up where they left off eighty years ago."

"God." Charlotte was horrified by those implications, but knowing the evil ways of humankind, it didn't come as much of a surprise.

"Why do they want my children?" Juliet asked quietly.

Gustav rubbed a hand over his moustache and shrugged again. "I don't know, probably their youth, the fact the young are more malleable, and of course they want every lycan on their side for whatever it is they have in mind."

"However," Herbert said, dumping an armful of bandages on the floor, "we are apparently expendable."

"You were a threat. They will send people to get you," Gustav said, eyeing the contents of the first-aid kit.

Charlotte studied Norman's ruined skin. "What happened to you?"

Gustav answered for him. "He is still regenerating after the Boxford incident. There wasn't much left of him when he was brought in but the source of the lycanthropy was unharmed and able to rebuild him."

"Aye," Norman said, "it's the second time it's made my legs grow back."

"Jesus Christ!" Charlotte gasped. "This thing is impossible."

"If I remember rightly," Norman continued, turning to Herbert, "you pulled me apart."

A red flush rose on Herbert's cheeks. "Oops. Yes, I'm sorry about that. If I knew then what I know now, maybe things would have gone differently."

"Why? What do you know now?" Juliet asked.

Herbert's unnaturally cheery manner evaporated. "We,"—he pointed to his friends—"died. I welcomed it. I couldn't wait to be reunited with my wife. I climbed on top of a pile of bodies and embraced the flames like a lover." Herbert's face fell further. "We died. I honestly thought I would be taken into my wife's loving arms. All my life I've believed devoutly in God and an afterlife." Herbert saw Trevor and Norman lower their eyes. "But there was nothing. Nothing at all."

"Aye," Norman whispered.

Charlotte understood the importance of faith. "That doesn't mean there isn't—"

"There is *nothing*," Herbert stated, "nothing at all." He turned to Juliet. "I know you might not see it now, but what Victor had, what your dad has passed on to your children, it's a gift." He raised his hand before anyone could protest. "If, *if* it can be controlled. Oh, I still feel the same way as I did before I found out Ethel had infected us. That hasn't changed but seeing that this is really all there is has made me want to try my hardest to rectify things. Our friend Gustav has given us a mission, I'll do it alone if I have to, to stop those who want to use this against humankind."

"I never thought I'd see the day you turned vigilante," Trevor groaned.

"Herbie goes bananas!" Norman smirked.

"We can do this." Herbert thrust his bloody stump at them. "We can get those children back."

Lights twinkled in Trevor's eyes and he nodded at his friend affectionately. "Yeah, Herbie, man, or die trying."

"And that," said Herbert, "takes some doing."

"You're all completely crazy," Charlotte said. *It doesn't matter how resilient you three think you are, how the hell can you expect to take on an army?*

"What choice do we have?" Norman said. "The bloody Nazis are preparing to take over the world with a nigh-on indestructible infantry."

Charlotte snorted. "And you're going to go *Dad's Army* on them? Just the three of you?"

"Well, what would you suggest, Doctor?" Trevor asked, angry and exhausted.

Gustav cut in before an argument could start. "This is bigger than anything. Governments will be overridden, nations will fall, and people's fingers will be hovering over the big red buttons."

"Exactly," Charlotte agreed. "So, how are three old men from Boxford going to prevent World War Three?"

Gustav moved awkwardly to a computer monitor and avoided the question.

It was Trevor who answered. "I don't know, but can we at least try and get my grandchildren back? Then we'll all vanish to the Outer Hebrides or somewhere and the world can go fuck itself."

Silence befell them, aside from the sounds of Gustav tapping at the computer.

"Do we know where in Germany they have been taken?" Charlotte asked him.

He held a finger up. "I am already searching what remains of their database. I halted the information purge. I suspect they're located near the place where all this began: Offenburg, and the Black Forest. It will obviously be a top-secret facility, big, possibly masking as something else or entirely hidden. There is only one way to find out."

"You're suggesting we go there?" Charlotte laughed. "If these people are as big as you say, won't there be people watching us?"

"Of course," Gustav said coolly. "There will no doubt be a team headed here as we speak. Each one of our heads will have a bounty on it. We are loose ends."

"They already sent someone to kill me," Juliet said to Trevor. She thought of killing the courier back at the Green Man Estate.

"I'm not going to let that happen," Trevor said, his chest puffed up with bravado.

"They know how to put you down for good," Gustav said. "We are nothing, they can destroy us in the blink of an eye."

"Hark at Mister fucking positive, here," Trevor said to his friends, before switching back to the Ukrainian. "So, what do we do?"

"Well," Charlotte said, focusing on Herbert and Norman's wounds, the things she could do something about. "I guess I'd better start by playing doctor. Come on, you two, let's get you fixed up. Just promise you'll not try and eat me."

There was a palpable tension between Juliet and her father. Charlotte left Gustav to handle them, gathered up the meagre offering of plasters and bandages Herbert had found, and led her two patients away.

They needed to be gone. Nobody knew what Butcher's next plan of action would be, but Gustav's guess was probably right, they would send a clean-up party.

The men's regenerative abilities weren't doing much for their current conditions.

Herbert's arm was a tattered ruin below the elbow from where the soldier's bullets had ripped through it, but the minor cuts and grazes from the fall had already healed.

The flesh around his severed arm hung in grey wet strips like doner meat around the splintered bones of his forearm.

"I have no idea what I'm doing," Charlotte said, trying to gather up the dangling mess.

Herbert grinned despite the pain. "You and me both. But I can tell you it's already hurting less, which means it's at least doing something."

Charlotte lifted a scrap of skin with a gloved fingertip and saw the end was already necrotic. "But your hand isn't going to ping back any time soon. I presume these bits will fall off or shrivel away?"

Herbert remembered his time under Mortimer's care and the brutal tests he'd put him through. "Yes. Once the flesh is separated from me, it seems to decompose unnaturally quickly. Just wrap it up the best you can and let this thing do the work."

Charlotte nodded and set about cutting squares of gauze to pad and wrap the wound.

Norman pulled up his hospital gown and moaned as a thick layer of semi-healed skin came off with it.

Herbert and Charlotte grimaced.

"Yah bastard," Norman winced when the partially healed skin across his chest split open and wept. He was a mess of wet suppuration; not one area, aside from his face, was free from gunky, yellow-green pus. "I guess you'd better get me wrapped up like the Invisible Man."

They came back to the others.

Herbert stamped his foot to get everyone's attention. "This is what's going to happen. First, we need to find somewhere to hide. If there are people

FÜHRER: PART ONE

coming to deal with us, we need to be gone. Then we will worry about how we're going to get to Germany."

"There are facilities here to make passports and identification," Gustav offered. "It will take minutes."

"Good man," Herbert said.

"The power has gone to his head," Norman said, nudging Trevor.

"Oh, I don't know," Trevor ruminated. "He does have a look of Winston Churchill about him."

Herbert scowled at them and mimed the removal of a cigar. "We shall fight them on the beaches, fight them in army barracks, we shall fight them in the streets and in the Black Forest. We shall never, ever surrender."

Charlotte failed to stifle a smile. "Okay, that was pretty good." She admired his vibrancy. "You really think we stand a chance?"

"We?" Juliet shook her head. "You don't have to do this."

"I'm already involved, Juliet, and I would rather see this through to the end doing something other than waiting for someone to put a bullet in my head."

"She's a bobby-dazzler, isn't she?" Norman whispered to Trevor.

"Not half, man, not half. If I was twenty years younger," Trevor said through the side of his mouth.

"Twenty?" Charlotte spun at the two men and gave a wry grin. "Sorry, guys, you're too old, and too male."

"No way," Trevor said, exasperated.

Herbert chuckled. "Come on, let's get ready to leave this place."

"Blow this joint," Trevor said. "*Blow this joint* sounds a lot better. If you're going to wear the leader pants, at least learn the lingo."

"Gotcha!" Herbert winked. "Okay, let's get ready to blow this joint."

"That's better, Herbie, man."

Herbert beamed. "Then we'll go to Germany and bust a nut in their arse."

Trevor grimaced. "As you were, Herbie, man. Just be yourself."

FÜHRER: PART ONE

Chapter 13

They were walking for at least two hours, occasionally hiding from the odd passing vehicle. Three elderly men in hospital smocks wandering country lanes late at night would draw more than a little attention, but there were plenty of hedgerows and ditches on their journey.

The scenery barely changed; Butcher's Facility, a functioning army barracks, was in the middle of nowhere.

Gustav led this worn and filthy bunch tirelessly whilst mumbling a combination of English and Ukrainian, mostly to himself.

He finally stopped at the entrance to a field. A wooden stile filled a gap in the hedges and the sun began to set alight a dark pasture. He climbed the fence and sat atop the gate. In the field, the silhouettes of squat farmyard buildings began to manifest in the morning light.

A dirt track cut across a meadow of overgrown grass leading to a static caravan site.

Charlotte caught up with him and stopped by his side. "What is this place, Gustav?"

"It is like my holiday home."

Even from this distance, Charlotte could see that a couple of the caravans had collapsed in on themselves. "Are you sure?"

"Yes, it's where I stayed when I was working at the facility." His moustache rose in the hint of a smile. "I keep the money for the hotel they pay for."

"And they don't know anything about it?" Charlotte asked, surprised by his wiliness.

"Oh, they don't know about this place. It is mostly derelict. Has been for a decade or so. When you are working for corrupt people, it is wise to be a little corrupt yourself."

Charlotte had to agree. She leant on the gatepost whilst they waited for the others.

Herbert was the first.

He was animate with newfound enthusiasm, as if he was enjoying every minute and mile of this impromptu country hike.

"Are you a part of the travelling community, Gustav?" he asked cheerfully before turning back to his friends. "We can't say 'gypsies' now, lads."

"No, but the caravans were."

They took off across the field.

Most of the caravans were abandoned, most not much more than burnt-out shells, but the largest one, centre circle, looked sturdy and maintained, and perfectly hidden from the small road they had come from.

"Is there anyone else here?" Trevor asked.

"No one but me." Gustav headed towards the central home.

"How can we all stay here?" Juliet said.

"Relax," Gustav said, unlocking the door. "Looks are deceiving, there are plenty of beds."

Norman eyed a small caravan which was semi-submerged, as if it had fallen into a sinkhole. "I call dibs on one with a roof."

"It is just somewhere to lie low for a while."

Gustav led them inside to a gigantic lounge which was adequately furnished.

"But what about my children?" Juliet asked.

"We need to rest and plan, hen," Norman said, his eyes lighting up at a huge, plush four-seater settee, which he collapsed on.

Trevor joined him.

Herbert took Juliet's hands and smiled somewhat serenely at her. "We will get your children back, Juliet. I promise."

Trevor twirled a finger around his temple. "Do you think he's gone…"

Norman sighed and plucked at his sodden bandages. "I wouldn't blame him, after all this."

"Yeah, man, you're right, but with how he was before..."

Across the lounge, Juliet burst into tears and fell into Herbert's arms.

"What did you believe?" Norman said softly to Trevor.

"You mean about God and whatnot?"

"Aye."

Trevor rubbed a hand over his face and leant back into the sofa cushions. "I don't know, man. I mean, I liked the idea of there being at least something afterwards, otherwise what's the bloody point?"

"But that's not belief."

"No, you're right, it's wishful thinking. I don't think I believed in anything, just hoped, like you said. Dolores did, though." Trevor felt his heart ache at the sight of his daughter's distress. "She does, n'all. Well, she did."

"And when we were, *you know*, dead, did you experience anything? Anything at all, consciousness even?"

Trevor shook his head slightly. "Not a dicky-bird."

"How does that make you feel now?"

"Like I want to make this life last as long as possible."

"Aye," Norman ruminated, "me too."

Trevor clapped his hands on his knees. "But I know I'd give it all up to keep my family safe." He turned his red-rimmed eyes to Norman. "I don't want the babies going into that nothingness."

"Aye, I agree, and you know I'll be there as long as I can," Norman said, patting his old friend on his shoulder. "I just don't know if I can control this beast in my head and I know I definitely can't control the flashbacks I've been getting of ripping people to shreds."

"It's grim, man; mega grim, but we have to make it all worthwhile, use this thing we've got, and rectify the damage."

"You really think we have a hope in Hell?"

Trevor laughed, but sad tears rolled down his cheeks. "Not in a month of Sundays, man. We'll be lucky to make it out of the country with our heads still attached."

"Aye, that's what I thought. Glad we're on the same page."

"I remember something your Bridget told me after we were banned from *The Flagship* in the eighties," Trevor began.

"Oh, Jesus," Norman said. "I've not thought about that place in years. They whacked a McDonald's on the spot where that place stood. I bet Malky still haunts the place begging for a fag and a drop of whiskey."

"Ha!" Trevor remembered the old drunk, who used to be part of the pub furniture. "He was like Beaker from *The Muppets* after he'd seen a ghost."

"Aye."

"But ghosts and Big Macs aside, man, if you remember correctly, we were kicked out for fighting."

Norman burst into laughter so loud everyone stopped their separate conversations and stared. He waved them away and let them go back to whatever it was they were talking about before continuing. "You twatted that City fan around the head with one of those big churchy candles for calling you a dirty ni—"

"Yeah," Trevor cut in, "I know full well what he called me. Anyway, your Bridget told me to persevere through all that racist shite, that one day there would be this golden age where nobody would give two shits about creed or colour, to keep my head held high and my fists to myself and that you don't fail until you stop trying."

"Aye," Norman said wistfully, "she was always coming out with pish like that, probably got it from bloody Reader's Digest."

"We've killed people," Trevor stated, drying up all remaining humour in the room. "Or rather, this thing inside us has, but we've proven we can control it. You with your legs in the disabled toilets, for example." His smile returned at the memory of Norman thrashing around in the tiny bathroom, his red, furry legs sticking out below him like something out of Narnia. "We've proven we can control it. Back then, you must have had some form of influence, or you wouldn't have stopped when you did."

"Maybe," Norman considered. "I don't know if I could do it again, to order."

FÜHRER: PART ONE

"But we have our man Herbie there to show us how to master it. We have to get those kids back."

"I heard my name," Herbert said, joining them. "What are you two old codgers twittering about?"

"About controlling these things inside us."

"Norman," Herbert said, eyeing him sternly, "we have to make sure we're all on the same side. There was a moment at the park where I honestly thought you were going to elope with Victor."

"Aye," Norman said shamefully, "I don't remember that, but I do remember you tearing me apart for some reason. I guess it was survival instinct."

"Are you scared of dying?"

Norman thought about it. "I was, but not now. How can you be scared of nothing?"

"It sounds like the most terrifying thing imaginable."

"Aye, but when your existence is fighting for control over a monster who wants to eat everyone, nothing sounds like a day in the park."

"But isn't that, *this*, if we can learn how to control it, better than absolutely nothing?"

Norman was silent.

"And so we go on," Herbert said. "*We* have sent people into that nothing. We *have* to see this thing through. We *have* to do this so even more people aren't sent into that nothing before their time. From what Gustav says, there has been stuff in the works since the Second World War. None of us wants this burden, but we *have* to use what we've got and at least try to make a difference." Herbert looked away from Norman and Trevor and saw he had everyone's attention. "We *have* to try and save those kids. We *have* to try and save ourselves. We *have* to try and save the world."

Gustav moved to the centre of the room and cleared his throat through the palpable tension.

Everyone waited in anticipation for what he was about to say.

"I am making some coffee."

After Gustav brewed a pot of tar-like coffee, the three old men fell asleep on each other like overexcited schoolboys at a sleepover.

"I can't imagine what they've been through," Charlotte said, staring into her mug.

Gustav filled her and Juliet in about their deaths and resurrections.

"Are they aware of what they are doing when they turn into those things?" Juliet wanted to know. She still couldn't forgive her father for what he had done.

"Some are, some aren't, and I understand that it can change at any time," Gustav said. "Most are aware of all sensation, even if they are not in control of their new bodies. It is like a possession of sorts."

"My God! How the hell does someone live with that?"

Gustav shrugged and sipped his drink. "Forgive me, I have only worked with these three and one other but I believe it was the guilt of your father's act which made him become an easy target at the park. He gave in, wanted to die, and that overpowered his wolf. I also believe it was the knowledge that the children were actually alive and held captive nearby which gave him the willpower to control his monster at the facility."

"You know we don't stand a chance against an army of werewolves, don't you?" said Charlotte.

"It is like Herbert said," Juliet said, staring at nothing. "We're already in this up to our necks, we're loose ends."

"There must be someone we can go to," Charlotte insisted.

"Not at this stage." Gustav drained his cup and refilled it.

Charlotte held her own out to be topped up. "So when?"

Gustav lowered his eyes and sighed heavily. "When they make their first move. When the existence of werewolves becomes public. When they declare war."

Chapter 14

Herbert came out of the caravan and sat on the doorstep. He had only managed to grab a few hours' sleep but was grateful for even that.

His wrist and forearm throbbed. The speed of the regeneration made his flesh sing, the bandages were too tight, and his skin was alive with an insectile crawling.

He tore the wrapping off, studied the freshly healed pink stump, and wondered how long it would be until his hand regrew.

If it regrew.

This thing inside him couldn't be relied on completely.

Just because Norman had regrown limbs more than once didn't mean he would.

The cool air on his skin felt good. Dawn still hadn't purged the night sky of all its stars and it was a long time since he had been anywhere remote enough to see through the light pollution.

1995, in fact. The Lake District His and Emily's last holiday.

They had rekindled some aspects of their courting days by sitting out in the dark and peering up at the heavens. When they were younger, they would lay stargazing for hours in the summer, holding hands, talking, just existing, both happier outside than in.

Herbert left the caravan and lay flat out on the grass.

Emily was adamant there was a creator scrutinising all above and below. Up until his time on the pyre and his subsequent death, he'd had faith in something similar, but it was hard to distinguish whether it was faith in a god or faith in his wife's belief. She was so certain it made him believe, but now, without her, he didn't know what he believed in.

What if I'm wrong?

What if the experiences we shared were due to lack of faith?

What if the reason we didn't see an afterlife was because we don't believe in one?

"Are you up there?" Herbert asked the cosmos. He didn't need his glasses anymore and the clarity of his vision was something he was still coming to terms with.

He sat up, removed the clothes borrowed from Gustav, and spoke to the wolf inside him. Without uttering a single word, he changed.

One fluid motion.

No pain at all.

He lowered his good paw to the ground and willed himself to change further. The joints of his elbows snapped backwards into knees as he went from biped to quadruped.

He loped across the fields as fast as he could, testing this new form to the maximum, surprised at how well it did on just three legs. Over ploughed land he went, through neighbouring pastures and deep into the surrounding woodland. He bounced off tree trunks and leapt over dead logs, determined to test his limits of endurance.

Within no time, he found himself back at the barracks, Butcher's facility.

He skirted the perimeter and was surprised to see it still lay deserted.

Surely there should be some kind of clean-up party by now?

He couldn't believe they were that expendable.

During his return to the site, he sensed another large creature's strong musky odour on the breeze.

He followed it back into the dense woodland and relaxed his hold on his wolf and allowed it to hunt, a treat for being subservient.

Herbert allowed it temporary control, letting it press its snout into the ground and nearby bushes to pick up the prey's scent. Once it found the trail, it stalked with slow deliberation.

With a thrash, the deer sprang from behind a bush but against the supernatural sensitivity of the wolf, it was no competition.

Herbert was disgusted but exhilarated at the thrill of the kill, at how good the fresh meat tasted.

He remained an animal and allowed his wolf to feed and clean its hairless skin.

When he returned to the campsite, he slipped back into human form, the transition so smooth now his monster was sated and grateful.

Perhaps this is the way.

To master lycanthropy you must respect the inner beast, treat it like a loyal pet.

Love thy wolf.

A small caravan next to the main building rocked with the combined snoring of Trevor and Norman.

Herbert finally knew how he would teach them to tame their wild sides.

Love thy wolf.
Love thy wolf.

FÜHRER: PART ONE

Chapter 15

Her head was a jumble of stills: scenes and memories. Whether they were real or not, she had no way of knowing.

Altercations with blurry faces in a supermarket café which smelled of wet coats, baked beans, and coffee.

Lying beneath a relentless sun, her skin blistering in Armageddon's death glow.

She rolled onto the wet grass, her broken fingertips sinking into the dirt like roots, her mouth open in a silent scream at the very earth itself.

Her skin was grimy, slick with the rich black soil from her grave, and beneath this filthy layer, her veins throbbed.

A child's face popped up out of nowhere, familiar, the café worker's little brother. He had a syringe in his hand; not for her, but for Victor.

He was going to poison her friend. She intervened, threw herself at the lad, her new vibrancy making her motions liquid. The needle pierced her neck and she became filled with an unholy silver fire. Victor's long, haggard but handsome face stared mournfully at her before even her eyes succumbed to the acid in her veins.

Then nothing.

Nothing until the moon and stars above told her to rise.

Elizabeth was alive, albeit with a throat packed tight with wet soil and a body recovering from some torturous realignment.

She turned back to the sky and held her ruined hands above her face, unable to comprehend how she was able to see in the dark. Her flensed fingertips swelled with the coming of new flesh, regrowing from the cuticles up, a time-lapse animation.

The inferno beneath her skin changed in the moments she lay beneath the moon's radiance, flowing through her with the intensity of a class-A drug.

Euphoria guided her movements and she sprang to her feet without any effort.

Grey lightning zigzagged along the arteries in her arms. She expected her fingers to spark.

Turning to observe the hole she had clawed her way out of, she wondered why they had buried her in such an isolated location.

Everything was drenched in shades of green. The moon suggested it was night, but she could see as clearly as if it were daytime.

Far away through the closely grouped trees, Elizabeth could see lights.

She headed towards them and whatever answers they held.

More memories returned as Elizabeth pushed through the trees towards civilization.

She knew the place like the back of her hand, but hadn't frequented it at night for some years, since the town had held their version of Blackpool's illuminations, stringing lights up amongst the trees, colourful displays of the latest kid crazes.

The town had been better then, and she had been a lot younger. Back then, there was more to the nightlife than street-cruising and vandalism. Back then, she would take her friend's son, Jez, to the fair. She would take him to see the lights, and they would overdose on chips, fizzy pop, and chocolate-covered honeycomb. He would call her 'aunty', that was before she had Frankie, when she'd had Dolly the Yorkshire terrier.

Frankie.

Where is the love of my life?

Elizabeth clutched her hands to her chest, noticed her nakedness, and gasped.

Where is he?

Is someone looking after him?

Who?

Ethel or Herbert?

She quickened her pace through the foliage towards the path nearby, worried about her dachshund but concentrating on her next move. She floated across the playground like a ghost, her feet barely registering the soft paving as she wove through the swings, slides and roundabouts.

There were two squat circular buildings in the area, one housing the public toilets, the other a staff shack where the Play Park supervisor sat during the day.

She headed across the new splash park, an addition paid for with a lottery grant. A network of fountains and sprinklers occupied children on sunny days.

The door of the staff hut was locked but she tugged at the iron handle and was amazed at how, after the second attempt, the door jamb splintered.

The interior was basic, nothing much apart from a few folding chairs, the controls for the water park, and a couple of large plastic storage boxes.

FÜHRER: PART ONE

She rifled through the lost property boxes: hats, socks and towels left behind after a day's play, all children's stuff. She found a pink swimming costume made for a teenager and thought it might fit her petite frame.

It stank of mould and chlorine but fit reasonably well.

She wrapped the largest towel she could find around her waist and left the building.

Something had happened in the park; numerous areas were sealed with blue-and-white police tape. She passed beneath the solar-powered lamps and headed towards the entrance.

Thankfully, the roads were quiet, it was that dead time of the morning, Ray Bradbury's 3am, where everything everywhere seemed to just stop, the silence surreal.

The closer she got to Boxford town centre, the more likely it was she would be seen.

Commuters, street-cleaners, and postmen might be surfacing from whatever cracks they hid in. There was no way she would be able to make it across the town without being spotted.

Remembering her outings with Jez, she realised there were people closer she could go to.

Elizabeth headed towards the Green Man Estate.

She pressed the buzzer three times before someone answered the intercom. Answered, but cancelled the call straight away. They were always being woken in the small hours by drunken residents who had misplaced their keys, and the homeless seeking shelter in the hallways and stairwells. It was instinct, unless expecting a visitor, to reject such intrusions at certain times of the day.

Herbert told her he had switched his own to private from the moment he went to bed until when he rose in the morning.

Emergency personnel had their own way of entering, or they could buzz whichever caretaker was on the grounds.

Sometimes residents would hang their sleepy faces from bedroom windows to see if they recognised their callers.

Elizabeth pressed the buzzer again and again until an angry male voice shouted, "Look, I'm not letting you in, they've been up our arses about this sort of thing."

"Jeremy, let me in," she said softly. She heard the clatter of the handset bashing against the hallway wall.

Seconds later, a window opened five floors up and someone peered down at her.

She looked up and smiled.

The person stared at her for a moment before retreating inside.

Soon, heavy-breathing came from the intercom. "What the fuck? If you're a vampire, this doesn't count as an invite. This is a council building so I'm not technically the owner, and I ate half a halloumi and garlic pizza a few hours ago. My breath could strip the flesh from your bones at six paces."

She smiled at Jez's outlandish response. "Do you still have the other half of the pizza?"

"Yeah," he said, his nervousness finally detectable, "and I'm not afraid to use it."

FÜHRER: PART ONE

"Be a love and zap it in the microwave. Oh, and put the kettle on."

"Okay," Jez said, zombified, and buzzed her in.

"This can't be happening," Jez said to himself as he went to answer his front door.

It was a long time since he had taken LSD, or any other hallucinogens, but he heard that sometimes, especially with LSD, it was possible to have flashbacks, or instances of psychedelic delusions, decades after taking it.

This had to be one of them.

The phone call from the snooty old cow Ethel was still fresh in his mind, telling him how some teenage yob had attacked Elizabeth in the supermarket café.

An explosion of horrific trash on the news added another level of insanity to the events. It was all about werewolves, street gangs and somehow the bunch of OAPs his aunt was part of.

And now this.

What the hell is going on?

He opened the door without looking through the spyhole; if he had, he might never have opened it.

He fought the urge to scream.

Elizabeth shuffled from bare foot to bare foot, her long grey hair matted, filthy with dirt and dried blood. She smelled of wet soil and was dressed in a swimming costume. She looked like an extra in a zombie movie. But unlike the undead in those films there was an unholy silver light in her eyes, and her veins stood out, prominent beneath her pale, translucent skin.

"Jeremy," she purred mournfully.

He remembered Louis Creed's wife at the end of the Pet Sematary film. Elizabeth sounded exactly the same as the living dead spouse.

He slid toward the floor, the archaic Artex shredding the skin on his back like a cheese grater and let his dead aunt inside.

FÜHRER: PART ONE

Chapter 16

Roasted human flesh.

The smell was both nauseating and appetising.

Appetising, because Cyril liked food. It smelled great. Nauseating, because he knew without a doubt what the mouthwatering aroma was.

Roasted human flesh.

Cyril pushed the door, lugged Tepes' three briefcases in, and dropped them onto an empty worktop.

Tepes looked up from what he was doing, running the edge of a carving knife across a sharpener. Eyeing the busted locks, he smiled. "You were successful, then? Good, good. Did you open them?"

Cyril shook his head. He felt his eyes flit briefly to the knife in Tepes' hand.

Tepes could sense his discomfort. "You don't trust me, do you?"

"Yeah, yeah," Cyril began, several octaves higher than his usual tone, his eyeballs spinning behind his increasingly fluttering eyelids. "Of course I do."

Cyril had spent all his time in Tepes' shed using numerous tools to break open the cases.

There was no chance of being himself around the dead kid without Tepes knowing about it.

Plus, Cyril was no necrophiliac. He preferred his boys living.

"Come here." Tepes beckoned him with the knife.

Cyril took a reluctant step forward but couldn't raise his twitching eyes from Tepes' hand.

FÜHRER: PART ONE

Tepes' amusement switched to anger. He slammed the knife into the tabletop, the tip sinking into the wood at least an inch. "You're a liar. You don't trust me one bit."

Cyril couldn't help but notice that he had used his previously weak side.

Whatever was happening to him was happening fast.

"Don't you realise I could squash you in an instant, if I really wanted?"

Cyril didn't answer; he knew he was no match.

"I could have put you down just after I'd had the stroke," Tepes boasted. "Now. Come. Here."

Cyril stepped across the kitchen and stopped a foot away from him.

"Take the knife."

Cyril wiped his sweaty palm on his slacks and curled his fingers around the handle.

Something inside him told him to plant the knife into Tepes' chest. Stake the vampire, steal his hoard, and vanish.

Cyril passed the knife back to Tepes, handle-first, and made sure the tip pointed back towards his own stomach. "I trust you."

He closed his eyes and felt the knife-tip press a little harder against a spot above his navel. A large part of him wanted Tepes to stick it in, or for him to muster up the courage to throw himself onto the blade.

Tepes grabbed Cyril's shoulder, watched him tense for a second before relaxing and accepting whatever card fate dealt. He dropped the knife onto the table and patted him on the cheek. "We're in this together, Cyril. Now, let's see to the cases."

Tepes opened the top briefcase.

Inside it were stacks of identity cards, bank cards, student IDs and driving licences.

"Bloody hell," Cyril started, "are these all your—"

"Victims?" Tepes butt in. "Yes. One likes to keep a little memento. I understand how foolish that is, so they will be eradicated forthwith."

Tepes rooted through the cards until he found a student ID with a photograph of a chubby, brown-haired youth. "Ah, Nicholas," he said, flipping the card towards Cyril. "He is the one we'll be tasting tonight."

Cyril looked at the oven.

"He was such a gentle giant," Tepes said fondly. "Squealed like a fat little pig when I slit his throat, though, ha-ha." He flicked the card back into the case and slammed it shut. "Let's see if they took any of the good stuff."

The second case contained a handgun, ammunition, and bags of assorted pills.

The third, stacks of bound twenty-pound notes.

"Everything seems present and correct. Stupid boys should have taken the stuff when they had the chance."

"What are we going to do?"

Tepes moved away from the cases and gestured to the dining room chairs. "There is something bloody miraculous growing inside me, Cyril. I can feel it flowing through me like a drug, and I fully intend to use it. There's enough money here and in my bank for us to do whatever our hearts desire. We know one another's perversions and, rest assured, there will be no secrets between us." His black eyes bore into Cyril.

"What would you like more than anything else in the world?"

To be someone different.

That was his initial thought.

To not have such compulsions.

Regardless of what Tepes believed, Cyril hated the way he was. But he remembered his words about embracing the monster inside him and not being ashamed.

But he was ashamed. He hated the things he had done and the things he knew he couldn't help but do again.

Both men jumped when the buzzer on the oven went off.

Tepes leapt up, donned oven gloves, yanked open the door, and stood back up with what looked like a slab of pork, a thick layer of crackling glistening with juices.

He sat the steaming tray in front of Cyril. "Ah," Tepes said, lowering his face into the steam, "doesn't Nicholas smell divine?"

Cyril turned away and retched.

"Oh, come, now. You can do this. What's one more taboo?"

Cyril forced himself to look at the meat. It did smell amazing and looked more than a little appetising. It was knowing what it was that put him off. "I can't."

Tepes put a pair of plates on the table, lowered the carving utensils to the sizzling meat, and thrust the fork into the crackling, eyes half-closed with an almost sexual gratification. "Be like me, Cyril. Become something more than human."

Cyril thought about the monster growing inside him and wondered if he meant that, or just the cannibal part.

Tepes cut into the tender belly draft.

FÜHRER: PART ONE

Chapter 17

"Do it."

Tepes studied Cyril closely as he raised the fork to his quivering lips.

This was an initiation, something of importance to Tepes, and Cyril doubted he had ever shared this experience with anyone else.

He closed his teeth on the meat and pulled it slowly from the fork, his stomach threatening to betray him, knowing what it was about to consume.

He fought the urge to gag and forced himself to chew.

The immediate explosion of flavour roused his taste buds to such an extent it overrode his queasiness.

The meat was ambrosial, food of the gods, the most sublime thing he had ever tasted.

His knife and fork were forgotten in an instant. He picked up the slice of meat and tore at it with his teeth.

"Haha!" Tepes clapped and carved himself a thick slice.

Cyril looked at him with a childish grin, an expression both alien and unfamiliar, his lips and chin slick with grease.

There was no conversation whilst they ate, just the smacking of lips and the appreciative grunts of two predators devouring their prey.

Afterwards, they half-dozed like glutted lions, sleepy with content.

FÜHRER: PART ONE

Cyril leant back in his chair and sighed. He felt like a different man; he felt stronger somehow, like the old belief was true: consumption of one's enemy increased strength and knowledge.

Although it hadn't been an enemy.

It was an innocent kid.

"How do you feel?" Tepes said, patting his full belly.

"Different," Cyril told him, and tried to ignore the queasy guilt.

"It's like that every time, and this," he said, sliding a fingertip over the grease on the plate, "is just one part of the body. Every piece of every person tastes different. I have so much to teach you, if you're a willing pupil."

I have no choice. Cyril smiled lazily. "Does everyone taste the same?"

"Yes and no," Tepes started, a connoisseur describing his art. "Every victim has the same general flavour but, just like the differences between caged birds and free-range, it can depend on what they are fed and their lifestyle prior to slaughter. They all have subtle differences that make them unique."

Like any new thing, Cyril wanted to submerge himself in it, glut himself until he was sick, but the voice inside him (which was sometimes his mother's and sometimes his father's) had plenty to say on the matter.

You are a cannibal.
You've eaten human.
Somebody's son.

He thought about Tepes' question: what did he want most in life? And he considered his own answer: to be someone else. Was this the start of it?

"I need to go."

"Where? Be more specific," Tepes said warmly.

"I have commitments."

"*You* have commitments? Don't tell me you're one of these nutters who has to go and run around in your dead mother's skin every day."

"We've been up all night." Cyril pushed himself away from the table. "I just have stuff I've got to do."

"Off you pop, then." Tepes waved towards the door. "Busy, busy."

Cyril turned back. "If you need me to come back later, message me."

"Need you?" Tepes laughed. "Why would I need you?"

"You know, in case something happens."

"You think those kids will go to the police?"

"I don't know. I meant with you, *you know*, your health."

"Oh, I'm sure if I turn into a bloody great werewolf, the first thing I'll do is text you."

FÜHRER: PART ONE

Chapter 18

Trevor leapt from the caravan and landed on all fours.

"Look at you. You think you're one of those bloody X-Men," Norman said behind him, his head poking through the neck of a jumper.

"Ah, as shit as this thing is," Trevor said, brushing dirt from his hands, "I don't miss waking up feeling like I'd gone to rust like the Tin Man." He stretched his hands skyward, as though he could grab fistfuls of cloud.

"Aye," Norman agreed, "it's good not being legless all the time, too."

Trevor chuckled. "You think once we've learnt to control these things, we'll be able to have the odd snifter now and then?"

Norman shrugged. "I'm kind of getting used to the whole teetotal thing now."

"What?" Trevor turned and stared at him in disgust. "You're a letdown to your nation, man."

"Pfft, just 'cause I'm a Scot doesn't mean I have to be a pisshead all my life."

Trevor shook his head. "Man, I'm so gasping I could drink a pint of Pernod."

"You hate the stuff."

"That's right, but I'd still happily drown myself in it."

Norman clapped him on the shoulder. They started to walk across the field towards Gustav's holiday home. "Remember that time we went to that flaming kids bar back in Sudbury? You know, the one with the beer steins hanging up all over the place? I forget what it was called, now—"

"The Stein Bar."

"D'oh!" Norman laughed. "That's right. You went ape when they told you they didn't sell pints and ranted for over an hour about all the bloody steins hanging around everywhere."

"Bloody stupid name for a bar that doesn't sell proper beer. Should've sold it by the litre." Trevor smiled at the memory of one of their many drunken exploits. "Then I asked for a Pernod on the rocks, the first bloody bottle I saw, and had a fucking tizzy because the bloody stuff changed colour when it hit the ice."

They roared with laughter.

"We were a proper pair of eejits," Norman mused.

"But now look at us, stuck in our seventies for Christ knows how long." Trevor sighed.

The door to Gustav's caravan was wide open and the aroma of toast and coffee wafted toward them.

As they neared the entrance, they heard raised voices and slowed to investigate. They were familiar voices, however, Herbert and Gustav's, so they carried on inside.

The two men sat in the lounge breakfasting, Herbert poking the air in front of Gustav with a triangle of toast.

Charlotte and Juliet looked on with bemused expressions.

On a central coffee table amidst half-emptied cups were the passports Gustav had quickly made before leaving the facility.

"Do you know how to spell the Ukrainian word for *nicotinamide adenine dinucleotide phosphate*?" Gustav shouted at him red-faced.

Herbert rolled his eyes. "Don't be so ridiculous. Of course I don't—"

"It is one of the longest Ukrainian words. But I bet you don't know how to spell any word in another language—"

Norman, no stranger to breaking up feuds despite it being several decades since he had hung up his uniform, interrupted the two men. "What's all this about?"

"It'll be fine, Herbert," Charlotte insisted, "we'll think of something."

Juliet hid her face in her hands.

"What's all the hoo-ha?" Trevor asked, inching towards the coffee pot.

Herbert sank back into the sofa cushions and threw his hands in the air. "That's bloody what," he said, pointing at the passports.

Trevor filled his cup, sat between Herbert and Gustav, and cast a worried eye over his daughter. Resigned to yet another catastrophe, he reached for one of the passports, sipped coffee, and promptly spat it back out.

"Ah, come on," Norman started, "none of us looked our best last night."

"It's not the *bloody* photographs," Herbert said, exasperated, his Yorkshire accent suddenly broadening. "It's the ruddy names."

Trevor flipped a passport to Norman. "There you go, man. See for yourself."

Norman snatched it from the air and opened it.

FÜHRER: PART ONE

Herbert's unflattering portrait was the run-of-the-mill convict-chic that seemed to be a necessity for all acceptable passport photos. Beside his slightly startled, tired face were the details Gustav had forged on the spur of the moment. They'd discussed changes to birth dates with him but had left their new names to his discretion.

"Oh!" Norman nodded, chewing the insides of his cheeks to stop himself from smirking. He handed the fake passport to Herbert. "Here you go." He tried hard not to say, but couldn't contain it, "Mister *Smimpson*."

Trevor's laughter rattled the cups on the table. "*Smimpson*," he cried. "*Brain Smimpson*."

"You can all rot in Hell," Gustav said, slamming down his empty cup and storming out of the caravan.

"For pity's sake," Juliet said, following him outside.

"It's not his fault, guys," Charlotte said, getting up to join them. "We need to keep him on our side."

"Aye," Norman said with fake sincerity. "That's right, you pair."

"You won't be saying that when you see what your name is." Herbert quickly rooted through the passports until he found Norman's. He cleared his throat and introduced him by his new moniker. "Nail Flips."

"*Nail —* " Norman took it from Herbert and lowered his face. "Oh, sweet Jesus."

Trevor slapped his thigh and wheezed with laughter.

"Jeez, someone get the lad here some Ventolin," Herbert said to the crying Jamaican.

"Yours is the worst," Charlotte said as she left the caravan.

Herbert chuckled. "Oh, yes. Yours is a thing of actual beauty. I think what he meant to spell, as in Eastwood, was *Clint*."

Trevor's fit ceased mid-laugh and he stared at his friends in abstract horror.

Both he and Norman lunged for the passports.

Norman was the quickest.

He took the passports and fled to the other side of the room.

"Ah," he said, tapping a finger against Juliet's new name, "this one isn't too bad. He was no doubt going for Carole but actually put *Creole*, Creole Brown. That's plausible." He opened Charlotte's and grimaced. "Debra Hooker. Okay, worse written down." Finally, he opened Trevor's. "Oh, Jesus, Mary, and the gullible one," he muttered through quivering lips. "I cannae say it."

"Told you," Herbert said smugly.

"Oh, Christ," Trevor said, peeping between his fingers. "I can't take any more."

Norman attempted to say the name but couldn't get past the first syllable before hysteria stole his voice. "He meant... but he put—" Norman choked. "Oh, I cannae do it captain, I havenae got the power. Tell him, Herbert, I've died. I'm dead."

Herbert thought this was such a special announcement that he stood and bowed as if curtseying before royalty. "May I present to you,"—he paused and added a throat-clearing for effect—"Mister Cunt Packer."

Trevor choked. "Oh, man, we are so, so screwed."

Chapter 19

"Gustav," Charlotte and Juliet called in unison as they raced after the Ukrainian.

"No," he said, waving a hand over his shoulder. "I will not be mocked."

Charlotte sprinted, overtook him, and tried to block his path.

"Gustav, stop. Please," Juliet said, lightly grabbing his arm. "Don't you realise that with my father and his friends, mockery is considered a term of endearment? Surely you are like that with your other male friends. It means you're part of their crew now." She paused to take a breath now she saw she had his attention. "Jesus, you should hear the things they say to each other when they think us younger generations aren't listening. Racist, sexist, outdated slurs, it's no holds barred with them lot."

Charlotte backed her up. "She's right, my dad's their age, he never normally swears at all, but I heard him answer the phone to one of his lifelong friends when he didn't realise I was behind him and he greeted him with 'alright, you senile old bastard.'"

"Pah." Gustav swatted at the long grass like a child having a tantrum.

"Please!" Juliet grasped his hand. "We need your help. Help me save my children."

He said something in Ukrainian, which sounded like a curse, and sighed. "What are we to do about the misspelt names?"

"I do actually have an idea about that," Juliet said.

"Look," she continued, gathering everyone around the laptop. On the screen was an advertisement for a coach trip to the Rhine Valley.

"A coach trip?" Herbert asked, incredulously.

Juliet looked at her dad. "Last-minute booking. It leaves next week. Do you remember when we went on the coach trip to Calais, organised by the Green Man Estate?"

Trevor shrugged. "Only vaguely. That was before the twins were born. What's that got to do wi—"

"Do you remember when we were at Dover and how the customs officer checked everyone's passports?"

He frowned. "Didn't we just stick them against the window as he walked around the bus?"

"Yes!" Juliet smiled. "And there's no way they could have spotted any spelling errors. I'm surprised they could even see the photos properly."

Herbert laughed. "Oh, that's good thinking. Plus, everyone knows that only old biddies go on these trips, so we should fit right in."

Norman typed something into the search engine and clicked on the top link before reading something off the official government website.

"'All passengers must get off the coach with their passports at border control so that a Border Force officer can check them face to face. You can make sure you are prepared for crossing the border by:

- Asking passengers to put on shoes and coats.
- Checking each passenger is holding their passport or travel document.

- Letting passport control know that you are the leader of the group.
- Checking that passengers leave any food and drinks on the coach.
- Leaving all luggage on the coach; if Border Force needs to search the luggage this will be organised separately.

"That's the correct procedure, especially since 9/11, however, I know officials, and I know how bloody slack-arse they get when greeted by a bunch of people who they think aren't a threat. It could work. Could. We'd have to split up, no holding hands or even pretending we know each other."

"And if we get through Border Control we wait until we reach the hotel in Germany and then abscond?" Gustav summarised. "When do we get to the German hotel?"

Juliet scanned the itinerary. "There's a sleepover in France on the first night and then to the hotel in Goldscheuer the day after."

Gustav tapped his phone. "Good, Goldscheuer is not far from the Black Forest and Offenburg."

"You had no trouble spelling Goldscheuer?" Herbert commented.

"Boil your head," Gustav grumbled.

Norman and Trevor laughed.

"Do you think that's where they are?" Juliet asked.

"It's likely. Or at least somewhere in that vicinity. A lot of wilderness to hide things in, or beneath, and it was where Liebermann and Krauss were in the forties. That's all we have to go on."

Matthew Cash

"It's decided," Trevor said, putting his arms around Gustav and Juliet. "We're all going on a summer holiday."

FÜHRER: PART ONE

Chapter 20

Cyril drove like the devil was on his back. He had been gone so long; overnight, too, shirked his duties. It was stupid and irresponsible.

On his way to Bluebell Woods, he pulled into a drive-thru McDonald's and bought some Happy Meals. His stomach was still fighting with breakfast at Tepes', caught somewhere between delight and disgust. The tastes and textures repeated on him to the backing soundtrack of Tepes telling him over and over again that they were the same now.

"No," Cyril snapped, and pressed a button on the car stereo in an attempt to use music to drown out his intrusive thoughts.

It's not like I killed him myself.

The voice in his head was his own and it whined like he had done as a child.

What's one more taboo?

No, he wasn't like Tepes, he didn't like killing, it just seemed like the only thing to do.

He slowed as one of the lesser-known roads to the woods appeared in front of him, Freddie Mercury on his mind.

Freddie Mercury had been on the stereo that day, almost a year and a half ago.

Music was Cyril's life, and every event had its own soundtrack, just as certain songs were windows to memories both rich and forgotten.

He was driving back from Sudbury General, music blasting in the car after an afternoon spent listening to the sounds of his mother's heart monitor

FÜHRER: PART ONE

and the geriatrics groaning in pain. They, however, were the backing orchestra to his mother's laboured breathing as she fought for life through tar-blackened lungs. When she was conscious, all she did was scream for him to fetch her cigarettes. The same line over and over again, ever since he was old enough to go out alone.

Get my fags, boy, or I'll toss you out on your ear.

It was smoking that had put her in the hospital but he always did as he was told. He'd learned a long time ago never to say no to her. He would get her her cancer-sticks until she died, but the last time, she couldn't even leave the bed to go outside and light up.

So she'd taken her rage out on him.

She had been a horrible crone most of his adult life, but even more so on what would be her last day on Earth.

She sat propped up on pillows, hacking blood into her oxygen mask, and stared at him with poison and accusation in her eyes. "This is all your fault," she wheezed through the fogged-up mask.

The ward was fairly busy with relatives visiting their loved ones and talking low-level but if his mother wanted attention she would get it.

"He got locked up, once," she started, pulling the oxygen mask aside and looking around at the people in the room.

Cyril stood, ready to leave, but she snatched his wrist in one withered, taloned hand.

"Used to sell dirty magazines on Felixstowe market."

"Muuum," he pleaded, feeling himself shrivel.

"Got banged up, he did, for selling illegal ones, ones with— "

"Mum!"

"—kids in." There it was. She'd got her reaction.

A man and a woman sat by the bedside of an old man, a teenage boy and girl with them. The old man shook his head in disgust and the woman rushed out of the ward.

Cyril tried to pull away but she started another coughing fit, her fingernails digging into his wrist as she spasmed.

She spat blood onto his jacket sleeve and glared wickedly at her captive audience. "Look at him, will you? Got child-molester written all over him."

The woman of the group came back into the room with a nurse.

"Better take them kids or he'll get 'em."

Cyril yanked his arm away, leaving several layers of skin underneath his mother's fingernails, and hot-footed it out of there.

"Poof!" his mother shrieked.

Cyril pushed through the door, her words still coming in rapid-fire.

"Imbecile. Idiot. Pervert!"

Everyone in the reception area turned to the noise and scrutinised the freak who fled past them.

"Paedophile!"

That would be the last thing he ever heard his mother say.

That afternoon, he was just as foul as his mother and the weather.

There was torrential rain. Storm Harry had been working its way across the country, obliterating coastlines with terrific gales and photogenic waves.

FÜHRER: PART ONE

Luckily, as he had come from the Atlantic, Harry had lost most of his bite by the time he hit Suffolk, and all they were faced with was heavy rain.

Cyril had driven from the town centre, his tears making his visibility even worse. He felt like deep-fried shit. He was just contemplating a trip to McDonald's to eat away his sorrows when he pulled up at a set of traffic lights and saw an angel standing by the roadside.

Initially, he thought it was a girl, a teenage runaway,, holding a sodden cardboard sign, begging to the drivers of the idling cars.

Queen was playing from his stereo: Under Pressure.

The teen approached him as he was waiting for the lights to change, one pale hand outstretched holding the limp placard telling everyone she was homeless and hungry.

He tried his best to ignore her but she tapped against the glass and motioned for him to wind down the window.

He wouldn't have done it if he hadn't noticed the light dusting of blond hairs on her — no, *his* — jaw.

The boy — sixteen at best — leaned into the car. "Hey mate," he said in a Liverpudlian accent, quite out of place in Sudbury, and pointed at the stereo. "I was named after Freddie Mercury."

Cyril was so flummoxed by the latent gender reveal he spun the volume of his stereo up as David Bowie sang a portentous *this is our last dance, this is our last dance.*

The homeless kid's smile wiped all recollection of his nightmarish afternoon at the hospital.

Cyril quivered with excitement and stammered out an invitation to McDonald's.

The kid wolfed down his food as though Cyril was suddenly going to stretch out one of his Mr Tickle arms and snatch the meal away at the last minute.

He didn't.

He was so nervous, his appetite had vanished. The boy was beautiful. His long blond hair, which obscured his face and had made Cyril assume he was a girl, dried in the warm restaurant and fuzzed into thick metal curls. He wouldn't have looked out of place at a Led Zeppelin gig.

"You have nice hair."

That was the moment the kid realised Cyril wanted something in return for his act of generosity.

A darkness passed over the kid's eyes as he focused on the French fries poised near his lips. "Why are you doing this?"

Cyril sat back and scoped the place out. Nowhere was safe nowadays, well, not for people like him.

People were obsessed with child molesters and paedophiles and there was always some wannabe vigilante who probably harboured their own hidden perversions, on the constant lookout for confrontation, a hero moment to make them feel better for their own sordid ways.

Cyril fake-laughed, sounding like an escaped mental patient, and forced himself to sit back and relax. After all, body language is everything. "I'm just being nice."

Freddie pushed the fries into his mouth, chewing thoughtfully. "What do you really want?"

FÜHRER: PART ONE

Cyril shook his head and out came another loony hoot. "Nothing. My mum always taught me to care for those in need." That was his biggest lie. His mother was a heartless bastard.

Freddie nodded.

"I mean," Cyril continued, and saw something ignite behind the kid's eyes, the eureka moment. "If you want to come back to mine, I'd let you have a bath and stuff. Stay as long as you want, my mum's in hospital. I'll get you some dry clothes."

"You still live with your mum?" A sinister glint sparkled in the kid's eyes and Cyril knew exactly what he was thinking: that he was a vulnerable adult, autistic or something. This was confirmed when the kid spoke again; his whole demeanour had changed, a condescending smugness overriding his previous fear. "Did you say your mum was in hospital? Oh no, that's a shame. I hope she's okay."

It was time for Cyril to turn his acting skills up a notch.

His face sagged and he stared at the devastation of fast-food wrappers on the table. "She's very ill. She smokes too much."

The kid made a sympathetic face that wasn't even close to the high standards of Cyril's acting. "I'm sorry to hear that. I guess with your mum in hospital, you get really lonely?"

Cyril nodded. "I don't even like going shopping, and I"—he lowered his eyes in shame— "hate the dark. I don't know what to do. Her pension has just stacked up the last few weeks; she says, "You need to make sure you eat properly,' but I miss her so much."

"Come on, then," the kid said.

"Did your mum choose this car?"

"She chooses everything for me," Cyril lied, adding another layer to this painted persona.

The kid stifled a laugh and Cyril hit the stereo on.

"Jesus, this is the stuff my dad listens to."

Cyril concentrated on the wet road.

Office blocks and eateries turned into dilapidated shuttered stores and bedsits and soon enough he took the turn towards Bluebell Woods.

The way through the woods was narrow but Cyril knew it like the back of his hand. The trees crowded the road as if they were trying to get a glimpse inside his car.

The kid scrutinised everything about his parents' house with an air of amusement but stopped short of saying anything derogatory.

Even though Cyril wanted the boy, he was already starting to hate him.

How could someone so desolate act so privileged?

How dare he?

How dare he look down his nose at his surroundings, like it was no better than the gutter or the doorway where he usually slept?

"Do you want me to run you that bath?" Cyril asked after he had led the kid into the living room and sat him on the sofa.

"That your mum?" The kid pointed to a photo of Cyril, back when he'd had hair, wearing double denim, standing next to a short woman with curly black hair and a constant look of disgust.

FÜHRER: PART ONE

"Yeah," Cyril said, "we were on holiday in Clacton."

"Jesus," he heard the boy whisper under his breath before offering another fake smile. "Go and run that bath, then. I'll make us a cup of tea, if that's alright?"

"Coffee," Cyril said, pointing through to the kitchen. "Everything's in there."

"Good place to keep it."

Cyril ignored the kid's joke and left the room. On his way upstairs he double-checked the front door was locked.

He turned on the taps and squirted a generous amount of bubble bath into the swirling water, Lily of the Valley, his mother's favourite.

When he went back downstairs, he saw that the envelope, which held his mother's pension book, had been moved slightly. The kid had wasted no time.

Cyril spotted him in the kitchen, opening and closing cupboards. He took in a deep breath, moved stealthily behind him and revelled in the way he flinched when he realised he was right up close, practically breathing down his neck. "The mugs are in here," Cyril said, pressing himself against the boy's back and opening a door.

There was an element of doubt in the kid's eyes, as if maybe he realised he had underestimated the situation, that maybe Cyril wasn't as vulnerable as he'd originally thought.

Cyril pulled one of his biggest grins, the one which made him, in his mother's words, *look like a fucking spastic*. The kid's smugness returned, and he slid out from in front of him. "I'll have tea, white, with four sugars."

Cyril nodded towards the stairs. "I'll bring it up to you when I find you some dry clothes."

"Just stick these in the washer and dryer," the kid ordered, like the entitled prick of a teenager he was, and yanked off his hoody and t-shirt in one go.

Cyril averted his gaze from the boy's naked torso— there would be time for that—and focused on making the drinks. He heard the kid's shoes drop to the floor; the rustle of material as the rest of his clothes followed.

"I'll hang this in the bathroom." The kid walked past him, his dripping coat draped over one shoulder.

Cyril eyed his slender calves and trembled with excitement.

He finished in the kitchen and took a scorching hot mug upstairs.

When he got to the half-open bathroom door, he rapped on it with a knuckle and, once again tried to sound more dopey than he really was. "I've got your white tea with four sugars. Shall I leave it out here?"

"Bring it in," the kid said, with the confidence of a con man. "I've got nothing you haven't got."

The expression on the kid's face when he came into the bathroom was priceless.

He had been luxuriating beneath a deep layer of Lily of the Valley bubbles but when he saw Cyril enter completely naked he sat up and yelped.

Cyril threw the contents of the coffee mug, scalding hot water, over his face then drove the empty mug into his left temple.

FÜHRER: PART ONE

The kid thrashed and sent water everywhere, his skin reddened with the hot liquid.

Cyril climbed into the bath,, his massive feet finding space between the boy's legs, and he dropped his full weight on top of him.

He landed knee-first on the boy's abdomen; the breath whooshed out of him and Cyril wrapped his big pink spider hands around his feeble neck and squeezed.

Cyril's dick grew hard as Freddie screamed beneath the creamy surface and he wondered if it was possible to drown at the same time as being strangled.

The science didn't really matter, the kid was malnourished, and it only took a few minutes of struggling, puny little slaps before the life left his eyes.

He stood by the side of the bath and pulled the plug.

Freddie stared lifelessly at the ceiling as the water drained around him.

Whilst the fluids from both bath and boy were emptying down the plughole, Cyril switched the shower on, pushed him into a seated position, sat behind him, and lathered the boy's hair.

Lily of the Valley again.

He kept him as long as possible, using him for both sexual activity and companionship.

Unfortunately, after four days of persistent pestering from Sudbury General, his mother chose to interrupt Cyril's special time by dying in a similar way to his latest love, except the fluids she drowned in were all her own.

It was a special moment, Freddie and his mother dying in the same week, and it was the only time in his prolific history when he left any evidence.

Before wrapping Freddie tightly in polythene, he doused him in Lily of the Valley perfume and dressed him in one of his mother's best frocks. He rode to the hospital with the corpse in the boot of the car, Queen's Greatest Hits playing full blast in honour, crying for the loss of his lover rather than the loss of his mother, and wished to God he could get one of his future suitors to stay.

A long-term lasting relationship was on Cyril's mind from that moment on, and with his mother out of the way he finally had the funds to do this.

The building that once housed Bluebell Studios was virtually invisible to see from the road cutting through the wood, and that was exactly how Cyril liked it. Ivy smothered it like camouflage netting and the path toward it was long overgrown.

He parked up in the lay-by of a picnic area and waded through the foliage the last few hundred metres, a brown paper sack of McDonald's food in hand.

Good memories are made here, he thought as skirted the outside of the building checking everything was in place.

It was.

He rested against a pair of giant barn doors and scanned the trees opposite until he spotted a tiny red light high up. He took out his phone, opened up an app called SecLock, and checked there were no notifications on the eight surveillance cameras: four in the trees, four inside, looking down at the place.

There was nothing on the outside cams and only a generic shuffling from inside.

He unlocked the heavy padlock securing the doors and went inside.

The interior of the studio was in better condition than the outside, most of the original furniture remained, and vandalism and graffiti had been minimal when Cyril purchased it. He squeezed around the large reception desk and unlocked a door behind it.

He turned his phone torch on. The recording studio had no windows and was pitch-black, so he'd left the boys with the little plastic battery lantern.

In a corner, under a mountain of beanbags and blankets, Adam and Taylor clung together like frightened refugees, their tears clearing channels through the dirt on their cheeks.

"Hey, kids," Cyril said, searching for the plastic lantern and finding it overturned on the floor amidst a graveyard of batteries. He switched it on and a weak orange glow filled the room. "Did I wake you? Were you sleeping?"

Adam, the older of the two boys, gave his head a barely perceptible shake.

"Got you something to eat," Cyril said, shaking the McDonald's bag at them. "I got double the amount as I didn't come last night." He walked over to the boys' grabbing hands, their hunger outweighing their fear, but he held the bag out of reach. "What do you say?"

"Thank you," Adam said straight away.

Cyril looked at Taylor, Adam's classmate. "Don't you have something to say?"

Taylor turned his head away with a snap and buried his face in the mound of blankets.

Cyril crouched down to their level, his knees audibly clicking.

Around them, empty packets of crisps and biscuits were strewn, along with half a dozen bottles of mineral water. Cyril passed one to Adam and gave him the McDonald's bag. The boy tore open the paper sack with ferocity, spilling French fries over the concrete floor.

"Slow down!" Cyril laughed. "You'll make yourself sick. And save some for Taylor." Cyril saw the other boy's shoulders tremble and a puddle of vomit at his feet. "For when he's feeling better."

Adam went at the food with ravenous abandon; his filthy face was covered with sauce in seconds.

"Gonna have to clean you pair up," Cyril said, and ruffled the fuzz of hair on Adam's little head. "I'd better bring the razor next time, your hair's getting long. You don't want to get nits, do you?"

Adam shook his head without making eye contact. His chin ground into the clunky metal collar fastened around his throat, where a raw-looking red mark glistened with fresh irritation.

"Have you been worrying at that again?" Cyril asked.

Adam stopped chewing.

Cyril sighed. "I'll put some antiseptic cream on it. You don't want to get an infection, do you?"

Adam stayed still and silent.

FÜHRER: PART ONE

"It's a good job you've got me to look after you, isn't it?" Cyril said, clutching the boy's bony shoulder. "Isn't it?"

Adam nodded.

Cyril stood and absent-mindedly tugged on the two heavy duty chains that linked his pets' collars to strong fixtures in the wall.

"Better eat something, Taylor," he said, turning from the boys and setting the plastic lantern down on a metal shelving unit. "You don't want to get poorly like Nathan did."

The beanbags muffled Taylor's scream.

Adam reached over, grabbed a fistful of his jogging bottoms and yanked on them, pleading, "Come on, Tay, eat something, please. Don't leave me alone with" — he locked eyes with Cyril — "him."

Those words were like a knife to the chest. Cyril stooped and picked up a metal bucket which was full to the brim with the boys' combined waste. "I'll leave you two to it whilst I empty your slop bucket." He met Taylor's eyes; with how the child was acting, Cyril knew he'd likely be the next to leave. "I'm sorry it has to be this way."

As he tidied up their mess, he noticed Adam encouraging tiny Taylor to eat; the small boy took pitiful bites between body-wracking sobs. Both of the boys had looked after Taylor like he was their little brother. He wasn't, though, he knew that much.

He also knew they were in Year 8 at Sudbury Comprehensive, that Nathan had an older brother who looked just like him, a mum who catered for them, and a dad who had a well-paid job in London. He knew Adam was from a council estate, had four half-siblings, all younger, and lived with his mum.

Taylor was a gamer nerd, had two younger sisters, and divorced parents.

It was amazing how much information he had discovered about them on the local news.

"Right," Cyril said with a yawn, clearing up was done, now he could finally settle down for a few hours.

He walked towards the stack of beanbags and blankets, Taylor immediately throwing himself as far as his chain would allow and sat between them. "Ah, that's better," he said, kicking off his loafers and slipping an arm around Adam. "If you bite me again I'll take it out on Taylor," he whispered, his thin lips pressed against the boy's ear.

Adam stiffened but made no attempt to struggle as Cyril hugged him close and got comfortable.

Taylor trembled amidst the McDonald's cartons.

"Try to calm down," Cyril said, "you can't really afford to throw that up as well. Remember Nathan."

"You killed him!"

Both Adam and Cyril turned towards the hunched kid in the corner.

"I…" Cyril spluttered, offended, "…I did not!"

Taylor staggered to his feet, an emaciated waif, ghoulish in the soft light from the plastic lantern. "Yes you did!"

Cyril smirked, and all of a sudden he realised who the kid reminded him of: Fiver, the weakened little runt in Watership Down. "Don't say such nasty things. Any more stuff like that from you and I won't come back tonight."

"I don't care," Taylor seethed, and kicked the McDonald's empties at him. "One less meal is a step further away from you."

FÜHRER: PART ONE

"Wow." Cyril pushed Adam aside and stood up. "After all I've done for you boys."

"Fuck you," Adam said, and got up next to his friend.

Cyril felt a lump swell in his throat. "Look at you pair, my boys, my little rabbits. What's happened to you?"

"You," Taylor spat. "You've happened to us."

Cyril smiled sadly; things had escalated a lot quicker than he'd hoped. The boys had lost their fear; he'd known that would happen. "You bloody kids grow up too quickly these days," he said through tears, then added, "oh well."

Sudden grief threatening to overwhelm him, he felt the sting of tears. Without a word, he fled the studio. When he got outside his phone was ringing.

Tepes.

Chapter 21

Bartholomew Tepes studied himself in the mirror. There were no signs of the stroke. His slackened face had rectified itself overnight and there was no weakness in the side of his body affected.

He felt alive, stronger than ever, even the fatigue he should have been experiencing after being up all night wasn't present.

This was going to be the start of a new, interesting chapter in his life.

Now someone knew about his crimes, he had to destroy evidence of his wrongdoings.

He gathered up his briefcase full of souvenirs and carried it into the yard, where a rusty oil barrel sat. It was a rookie move keeping trophies.

The theory was that most serial killers longed to be caught, for the whole world to know.

Maybe that was one of the reasons a lot of them kept such trinkets. But not for Tepes, he had never wanted to be caught, his lifestyle was far too pleasurable to give up.

He did save their ID cards to catalogue them, but even that was stupid.

His victims were something to consume.

They were food.

Cyril's face, when he opened the briefcase, had been a picture, *the goggle-eyed freak.*

Tepes found it hard to believe that someone like Cyril didn't keep something of the boys he abducted, sexual predators like him usually did.

FÜHRER: PART ONE

He emptied half the contents of the briefcase into the oil drum and poured petrol over the lot.

As the cards melted and burned he thought about the inventory of his chest freezers and sighed. There was enough evidence there to get him convicted for several lifetimes. "Shit," he said, leaving the smoking barrel and heading to the shed.

"Cutting up bodies, especially when frozen, isn't easy work," Tepes mused to himself as he hooked his fingers beneath Lestat2000's armpits and hauled him from the freezer. Even with this new lease of life it exerted him to the point where black stars twinkled in his vision.

After he had lifted the teenager onto one of the workbenches, he needed another breather.

"It's always best," Tepes said to his imaginary audience, revelling in the sound of his own voice, "to dismember your corpses when they're still warm, after draining them of any unwanted fluids, of course." Tepes laughed to himself and moved to the racks where he kept his saws and other cutting equipment.

If he had been the one to dispose of Lestat2000, this would have been a lot easier, but fate had chosen to intervene. His little apprentice, Tony, had thrown him in the freezer intact, fully clothed.

"The first thing to do," he continued, "when securing one's victim, is to find a suitable container to catch the immediate evacuations. If there's time, and you have sufficient funds, might I suggest investing in some heavy-duty incontinence pants. There are certain excretions that you don't want contaminating your crucial supply." He pressed a hacksaw blade against the boy's frozen throat. "Again, these things shouldn't be rushed. I recommend using a strong tape to cover the mouth and nose, too. Once you've bled them dry and stored their life fluid safely, remove all clothing and burn them."

Tepes grunted as he began to saw through the neck bones.

"Once you've stripped your chap, unfasten all previous safety measures, tapes and nappies, and just let everything drip out. Leave them for a few hours if possible. Usually, once this process is over, I hose them down. It's helpful if you have a drain beneath them. Then…" He swore as the hacksaw blade got stuck halfway through Lestat2000's spinal column. "Then you can dismember them."

Lestat2000's head broke free of the neck and Tepes grabbed it by the long hair. "Such a fucking waste," he said, staring into the boy's dead eyes. "The brain's one of the best parts."

He carried the head over to a large furnace, pulled open the iron door, and threw it inside.

"Enough of this mindless patter," he said to himself and switched on a small radio that sat on one of the tool cabinets.

Stevie Wonder was in the middle of telling everyone about his cherie amour.

"I'm sorry," Tepes said, running a hand across Lestat2000's headless corpse. "This music is probably not to your particular taste, but" — he looked at the furnace door with a smirk — "I doubt you can hear it where you are."

As Tepes began the task of sawing off an arm, Stevie Wonder finished and the midday news came on. Tepes paid little attention at first; cutting through a frozen body was hard, even with the advantages of lycanthropy.

He hoped once the thing inside him matured, he'd be able to tear the limbs from people's bodies.

He stopped sawing when he heard the words *massacre* and *Sudbury*.

"...*has confirmed fourteen dead...*"

Tepes concentrated on the remainder of the news bulletin as the reporter repeated the details of the event for new listeners, telling them about the attack at the swimming pool. A dark smile crept across his face and he chuckled. "Oh, boys, what have you been up to?"

He fished his mobile phone out and hit Cyril's number.

"Yeah?"

There was a subtle waver in his tone that Tepes detected immediately. "That's no way to answer the phone to your best mate."

"Umm, yeah," Cyril said with a wet sniff. "What do you want?"

Tepes could hear birds singing in the background. "Where are you?"

"Umm, nowhere, really."

Tepes straightened up and strode across his workshop. "You're hiding something."

"No, I'm not. I just fancied a walk."

"I would have thought you'd be asleep after last night."

"You're not."

"I have things I need to get done asap."

"Me too."

"Okay, be like that. But you need to come here. There have been developments."

Tepes heard Cyril swear and drop his phone. He waited for him to pick it up before continuing. "Don't go getting your knickers in a twist, it's got nothing to do with you or me. Yet."

"Tony and Danny?"

"Yes. I just heard a news report about an incident in Sudbury last night. An incident involving the attack of a pool full of swimmers."

"Oh."

"Yes. Oh."

"That means they definitely won't go to the police."

"That's what I was thinking," Tepes said. "I need your assistance in disposing of anything incriminating here, just in case."

"Oh, I, well, I-I was b-busy," Cyril stammered.

"Doing what?"

"It's okay, it can wait," Cyril said, evading the question. "I'll be there as soon as."

Tepes hung up and picked up the hacksaw. "What are you hiding now, Cyril?"

FÜHRER: PART ONE

Chapter 22

"So you know who I am but I'm not allowed to know about you?" Tepes said, trying his best to sound wounded. "How long have we known each other, Cyril?"

"Thirty-three years."

"And it seems you know a lot more about me than I do you," Tepes said, hurt.

"You know enough," Cyril said quietly, but realised how rude he sounded and added, "I don't like talking about it."

"If they catch you, you'll have to tell them."

Cyril turned towards him, wide-eyed.

"I want to know everything you've done, not just suspect it."

Cyril brightened somewhat and Tepes realised his error, he had just admitted to not knowing anything concrete about Cyril's crimes.

"You know about me being banged up for dealing in them dodgy magazines."

Tepes grabbed Cyril's wrist. "What about Bluebell Woods? How many are there?"

Cyril shrugged and tried to pull away but Tepes' new-found strength held him in place and he forced Cyril's hand over the incinerator. "How many?"

"Fifteen!" Cyril cried.

Tepes let him go. Cyril recoiled and stared at his reddened hand. "What the hell is wrong with you?"

Tepes laughed. "I don't like secrets, Cyril. Things are different now you know about me."

"Look, I'm not going to dob you in or anything." Cyril offered an awkward smile. "I get it, though: you're worried the boys will be found and squawk, but—"

"If I get caught I get caught, but I meant what I said at the hospital: if I go down, you go down," Tepes spat, marching towards the house. "I'll tell them we were a double-act."

"But why?" Cyril pleaded. "All I've ever done is support you."

"But I was foolish, I let you know too much." Tepes growled, punched his fist through the back door, and stared in fascination at his hand.

He held his bleeding knuckles up to show Cyril and they both watched the skin heal itself, in mutual awe.

"We're in this together now, Cyril. At least until we know those brothers are in the fucking ground."

Cyril stayed for the rest of the day, painstakingly helping Tepes to rid his home and surroundings of the evidence. All the while, Tepes forced him to divulge all his own secrets.

"I still don't believe you don't keep anything of them," Tepes said, as they sat down to afternoon tea like a pair of old fogies.

Cyril sighed. "I've always been able to remember everything about them, not *just* them, about everything. I think nowadays, they'd probably say I was on some sort of spectrum, label me with something."

"Having a photographic memory doesn't mean you're autistic, Cyril."

"No, but all this other stuff," he shuffled in his seat, "the bumbling awkwardness, the nervous fucking twitches. I honestly don't know how I've gotten away with it so long, it's different for you."

"Different for me? How?"

"You're cold, meticulous. I worry, all the time, apart from when I'm doing these things, and the boys,"—Cyril touched a trembling finger to his chest— "they never, ever leave me."

Tepes pitied him. "You love them, don't you?"

Cyril nodded.

"I guess that's something I'll never truly be able to comprehend. Emotions. You're right, I have always been an emotionless freak."

They sat in silence over cups of tea like loved ones who had just shared a heart-to-heart.

"Jesus!" Tepes laughed. "Enough of this sentimental shit. We are what we are. What are we going to do about the Scarboroughs?"

"If they'd been talking about us, they'd already be locked up."

"They're the cause of all this werewolf claptrap, at least we know that now. Our only hope is that they keep running. But we can't risk that."

"No, we can't. So what are you suggesting?"

Tepes looked at his healed hand. "I think we need to find out how to kill a werewolf."

"Silver?" Cyril said, looking over his mug.

"That's the most common one." Tepes yawned and gazed around his living room. "I wonder if any of Mother's junk is silver."

FÜHRER: PART ONE

Aside from modern appliances, not much had changed since he'd inherited the place from his parents.

The ghastly brass ornaments his mother had collected gathered dust in the same places they had sat for decades.

"Jesus," he said, "why the hell have I kept all this crap?"

Cyril crossed one long leg over the other. "What you on about?"

Tepes waved at the things adorning every nook and cranny. "All this shit?" He jumped up, grabbed a brass bedpan, from beside the electric fire, and held it by its long black handle.

"Isn't that what people used to shit in in the olden days?" asked Cyril.

Tepes roared with laughter. "Not quite, not quite. They used to fill it with hot coals or water and shove it in their beds. An old-fashioned hot water bottle, if you will."

Cyril's face reddened.

"My point is, why have I kept all these things? I'm not sentimental at all," Tepes whined in exacerbation. "Even you sold all your folks' shit and got yourself a bachelor pad."

"Are you thinking about moving or something?"

"I don't know, it's like I'm seeing it all with new eyes. This thing inside me is making everything clearer." He bent down to replace the brass bed pan and keeled forwards into the mantelpiece.

"Whoa!" Cyril leapt from the settee and began to dither at Tepes' side, hands hovering millimetres away, as if he were afraid of contact. "Are you alright?"

Tepes braced his palms against the stone fireplace, his long hair obscuring his face.

"It's not another stroke, is it?" Cyril pined.

"Help me into the chair," Tepes said weakly.

Cyril did as he was told.

Tepes rubbed his hands over his face and puffed out air. "I thought I was going to black out."

Cyril moved towards a land-line telephone. "Should I call someone?"

Tepes shook his words away. "No, I think I'm just tired."

"We've been up all night." Cyril drew back his coat sleeve to check the time. "I've been up for nearly thirty-five hours."

"Christ," Tepes said, his eyelids drooping. "We're too old for this shit. Help me upstairs and come back tomorrow morning."

Cyril nodded and pulled Tepes from the armchair. He led him up the stairs like an invalid, someone frail and old.

"Keep your phone on, please, Cyril," Tepes said, and for the first time in their friendship there was fear in his eyes.

Cyril offered him a comforting smile. "If you want, I could stay?"

Tepes' stare was glacial. "Get some matching pyjamas like Morecambe and Wise, Bert and Ernie?" he slurred with exhaustion. "You'd love that, wouldn't you?"

Cyril didn't know how to respond until a dark but tired grin crept across Tepes' face. "I'm joking, Cyril. You're a good friend. Thank you."

Cyril's heart fluttered at the unaccustomed sentiment and he cursed his stunted libido at automatically assuming it must have been the start of something sexual.

Not daring to do anything other than nod, Cyril helped Tepes into his bed and watched him fall asleep.

He waited like a faithful friend outside the bedroom until he heard heavy snoring.

He needed sleep too, and, although his bachelor pad, as Tepes referred to it, had almost everything he desired, it lacked the one thing he wanted most. Company.

He lay back on a black leather recliner, in which he slept far more often than his bed. He found comfort in the chair's restriction.

At times like these, his mind would wander beyond his sordid cravings, his basic animal urges, and he would fantasise about what could have been.

He wasn't stupid: he knew physical appearance wasn't important for finding love, and that there really were people who saw past such trivial things.

Like Philippe.

Echoes from another life haunted him when he was alone.

In another dimension he was with Philippe. The French bartender would have aged well, his dark, smouldering looks would have gotten better with age. They'd have their own bar, Cyril would supply the music. Maybe they would adopt.

He saw it all, what could've been; it lulled the excruciating guilt of his reality, and in a way, gave him a reason for why he was the way he was.

His parents.
His dad.

If they had been different, *he* would have been different.

Maybe this life he dreamt of would have been the actuality if his father hadn't killed Philippe in his fit of homophobic apoplexy.

When they returned to England, the accident, as his parents had put it, forcibly forgotten, he'd given up all hope of ever finding another Philippe, and his urges had taken a darker route.

No, he thought, and tried to close that shadowy room in his mind, the attic where the horrors danced, and focused on the fantasy, what could have been, but as he drifted into slumber, the physical similarities between Bartholomew and his imaginary middle-aged Philippe made themselves known.

He thought about Tepes asleep on the other side of town and the thing growing inside him.

Sleep did not come easy.

FÜHRER: PART ONE

Chapter 23

Suffolk

1990

Andy checked himself in the taxi's rearview mirror.

He liked what he saw.

His mum was right, he really had grown a lot in the last few years.

For his eighteenth, his dad had taken him for his first pint at The Gardeners Arms, a proper, old-man pub riddled with retired farmers and gamekeepers. Picturesque and quaint, not for young people at all, and the beer tasted like rainwater from a stinking Welly boot.

His dad assured him everyone's first beer tasted like shit, but despite the foul-tasting liquid, it made Andy feel grown-up.

He watched Cilla Black welcome in the start of a new decade with his parents and knew the next New Year's Eve would be different.

He felt older, wiser.

Andy's time at Suffolk college was due to end in the summer, and university beckoned.

During his early-teen years he rediscovered his passion for reading fiction, poetry, and his love for the English language, the way a good author could stir a palette of everyday words and proceed to paint illustrious worlds.

FÜHRER: PART ONE

He aspired to do the same.

The beginning of his teens had been somewhat troubled, and this new-found love helped him tell the careers advisor what he wanted to do with his life.

He wanted to write.

Andy dabbled, in secret, for years, starting with fan-fiction, sequels to his favourite films, before learning to create his own universes from scratch.

He always struggled to fit in anywhere so he tried his best to build up his tolerance for alcohol in time for university.

Hollywood's opened just before he turned eighteen, and even though his friends got into the nightclub underage, he hadn't been bothered.

However, all that was before he plucked up the courage to ask Ginger Morgan out on a date.

Ginger Morgan, real name Tracy, was the girl of his dreams. He knew it the moment he first saw her step aboard the ninety-six to Ipswich.

She took his breath away.

A petite, red-headed vision of Celtic beauty, with skin like bone china, she had eyes so green they made everyone freeze.

His friends took the piss over his infatuation.

Ginger was boyish, flat-chested, with no well-defined curves, and apparently her pixie cut made the statement that she didn't even like boys.

But Andy was in love, and she was a fairy in human form. He wrote sickly-sweet love sonnets where she cavorted barefoot in forests wearing dragonfly wings.

It took him six months just to say hello but once he did, he discovered her great personality, too.

Ginger was an art student. She rambled on about artists and paintings like Andy did writers and books. They shared common ground with music, both being fans of the Madchester scene.

After eighteen months of talking to her, Andy found the courage to tell her exactly how he felt, albeit with a majorly diluted version.

He gave her a poem inspired by her erratic dancing in the student bar.

"Storm-Girl," she said, wrinkling her nose and mouthing the words again.

"Yeah." Andy felt himself flush with embarrassment and lowered his eyes. "It's something I wrote spontaneously, you know, without thinking."

"I know what spontaneously means, knobhead," she grinned. "Can I read it out?"

"Oh, God," Andy grimaced, "if you must."

"'Storm-Girl' by Andy Cooper. My best mate."

His heart skipped a beat when she added that, afraid that if he told her how he really felt, it would end their friendship.

Ginger stood, brushed imaginary crumbs from her baggy Joy Division t-shirt. "Storm Girl.

"She twists with the unpredictability of a tornado.
Her lightning fingers strike at their power-line glances.
Her feet cough up dust but it's their hearts that provide the thunder.
She whips and she wails the song of her sorrow.
They stare, breath taken, at her relentless devastation.
This storm-girl ravishes and takes without knowing, without asking.

Leaving them swept and destroyed in fear of her encore."

Andy wanted the earth to swallow him whole.

"So," Ginger said, her radioactive eyes scanning the verse one more time. "Is this really something you wrote without thinking?"

"Yeah, you know me, always putting stuff down in that notebook of mine."

"It's...er...not about anyone in particular?" She bit her lower lip nervously.

Andy went a deeper shade of crimson and knew it was time to tell her. He took a deep breath and closed his eyes. "It's about you dancing to Waterfall in the student bar."

Ginger clutched the scrap of paper to her chest and her eyes moistened.

Before she had a chance to respond he continued, heart slamming, "I really like you, Ginge. Yes, in that way, from the moment I first set bloody eyes on you. I'm sorry if this fucks our friendship up but I can't keep it in anymore." He sighed, stared at his fingers, and welcomed any repercussions. The weight had been lifted.

When he finally looked up, her smile almost reached her eyes and he knew the risk had been worth it, for that grin alone.

"Well," she said, "there's a new indie club night at Hollywood's, if you fancy it?"

It wasn't until he saw her walking towards him in the queue outside the nightclub that he actually believed it would happen.

It was the first time he had seen her in a dress since the summer before, when she had simultaneously stepped on the bus and his heart. Her white summer dress had been swapped for a sleek black number, and she looked divine.

"You look amazing," he said as she slinked towards him like a cat.

"Fuck off," Ginger said with an embarrassed laugh and plucked at the dress. "This was my mum's."

Andy smiled and waved his hands up and down his white shirt. "Dad's, circa 1979."

Ginger laughed again. "It looks good," she said, and leant close. "Although, judging by the amount of band t-shirts and jeans about, I do feel a bit overdressed."

"Yeah, I thought these places had a dress code? I didn't know what to expect from indie night."

"I wonder if the DJ takes requests," she said dreamily.

"We should just ask him to play the entire Stone Roses Album."

"Why, so you can write another poem about my bad dancing?" Ginger teased.

Andy covered his face with his hands. "I'm never going to live that down, am I?"

Ginger shook her head. "Nope. Hey, maybe I can write one about your dancing?"

"Oh, God, no! It'd be more like a bloody limerick."

"I could use the experience to paint a portrait," she said, winding him up.

"It'd be a Picasso, I can't dance."

"Mate, we've come to a nightclub. You're dancing."

FÜHRER: PART ONE

"I don't even know how."

"Me neither. There aren't any rules, you just close your eyes, move to the music, and don't give a shit about anything else around you."

"You make it sound so easy."

"It is if you don't care about what anyone else thinks."

"Promise you won't laugh?"

"I'm not making any promises, Buster."

They followed the queue towards the redbrick building.

When Andy's dad was younger, the place had been a maltings, and Andy was intrigued to see what the inside was like. Historical buildings had more character than new ones. He turned to look at the queue behind them and when he saw how many people had joined, he was glad they had arrived early.

Then he spotted someone he recognised and his face fell. Ginger prodded him in the ribs. "What's wrong? You look like you've seen a ghost."

Andy spun away, turning his back to the queue. "I've just seen a dickhead who used to go to my high school."

Ginger turned as if she had a dickhead-detector and shrugged. "Ah, it's been years since high school. We're all grown-up now."

"Yeah, I hope so." Andy risked another glance and saw the boy and three friends pushing one another, mock-fighting, and wondered if that was the case.

"Shit," Andy groaned when his fellow ex-pupil spotted him.

"Cooper!"

"Fuck's sake," Andy swore as the boy broke away from his friends and came their way.

"Hey, Howard," Andy said, calling the lad by his surname.

He hated that fad from high school.

It was callous, impersonal.

Howard hadn't changed much, his athletic scrawniness had morphed into something bulkier. He was one of those kids who magically grew into an adult overnight, bigger than the teachers. He was stereotypically handsome, dark-haired, dark-eyed, and all the girls at school fancied him. Andy doubted he had much trouble attracting them now.

He was one of the biggest wankers Andy knew, and if it wasn't for Ginger, he would disappear.

"How are you?" Andy mumbled.

"Great, man, great," Howard mumbled, his eyes roaming the queue like he was already bored of the conversation.

"Howard, this is Ginger."

Howard's eyes roamed over her before being distracted by other people in the queue, in particular a couple of buxom blondes. "Alright?" He never waited for Ginger to reply, he just came out with what he really wanted. "Here, do you mind if me and my mates barge in with you?"

The whole inadequacy Andy had felt at school returned. He knew he wouldn't be able to say no, like it was ever an option in the first place.

Howard didn't wait for him to answer in any case, he just jogged off to round up his trio of clones.

"I'm sorry, Ginger," Andy whispered.

"It's cool. You're right, though, he is a dickhead. Did you see the way he just looked right through us?"

"Yeah. I doubt he's changed much, his sort don't."

FÜHRER: PART ONE

Ginger threaded her arm around his and he felt the tingle of electricity as she interlocked her fingers with his. Her touch empowered him.

"We'll lose them once we're inside, I promise."

"That'll be hard, they're like fucking lighthouses," Ginger said, as the four six-foot-plus lads made their way forward. "With really shit wigs on top," she added.

Andy exploded at such imagery, one of those sudden laughs that gets everyone's attention.

Howard sneered at Andy's outburst and said something which brought years of schoolyard ribbing fresh to the surface. "Alright, Cooper? You ain't going to wolf-out on us, are you?"

Unsurprisingly, after the attack at the building site, the police were involved. Luckily for Andy, even though one of the men lost part of an earlobe, their injuries were only superficial and neither pressed charges.

Andy had hardly any memory of the event other than the intense anxiety, the fear, and the feeling he was being torn apart.

Something had changed inside him and everything had vanished behind a red rage-blur. He had come round in the foundations a few minutes after one of the men knocked him out.

And so followed months upon months of appointments with doctors and psychologists.

They had concluded that it was a one-off explosive act of madness; rare, but not unheard of during adolescence.

The damage, though, was done.

His best friend Ben told everyone about the encounter, in particular the animalistic noises he'd made while attacking the builders. So from then on, Andy was known as Wolf-Boy and the term wolf-out was coined.

Don't piss Cooper off or he'll wolf-out on ya.

It was unfair that an incident in his past, which had lasted only a few minutes, had followed him for so long. But kids will be kids.

Ginger frowned.

Andy cursed Howard's flapping gob. "It's something we used to say at school," he said half-heartedly, hoping Howard wouldn't elaborate.

He tried to forget about the appointments, particularly the ones with the eccentric psychologist who wanted to recreate his ordeal to see if he would react the same way.

There was already a mass of bodies around the bar but Andy joined the queue regardless. Eventually, after waiting for what seemed like half the night, he bought a couple of drinks and considering how much they cost, he wouldn't be getting drunk.

"Uh-oh, what's up?" Ginger said, accepting her Bacardi and Coke.

"I think I understand the concept of pre-drinking," Andy said, repeating a term he'd overheard in the student bar.

"You don't have to buy me all my drinks."

"No, I want to, I just—"

"Look, we're both poor students. We'll go Dutch."

"Why do they call it that?"

"Ah." Ginger raised her palm. "I know this, it's an old Americanism and has nothing to do with people from the Netherlands, but with Germans, and the Swiss, who settled in Pennsylvania in the 17th and 18th century."

"You are a crying, walking, sleeping, talking encyclopaedia."

"It's embarrassing, isn't it?"

"No, I like people that read. I just wish I could remember stuff like that."

"Oh, God," Ginger said, "here comes your mate."

Howard and his friends were heading over from the bar, laden with bottles of lager.

"Let's go check out the dance floor." Ginger took his hand and led him away.

For someone who had never been farther than the student bar, the loud music was a shock. His eardrums pulsed with the vibrations and he wondered how the hell people could hear themselves think.

Andy shrugged and cupped his hand to his ear as Ginger was saying something he couldn't hear.

She stood on her tiptoes, pressed her cheek against his, and repeated herself.

He still couldn't hear, but he loved her being so close, her skin against his, her perfume.

She laughed, pointed to the DJ stand, and held her palm out for him to stay put. Andy watched her weave towards a platform haemorrhaging different-coloured lights.

He lost sight of Ginger amongst the throng and panicked. *How the hell do people find one another in these places?*

He gulped half his drink to try and quell his anxiety and Ginger reappeared beneath violet lights as she slid back down from the DJ platform.

As she stepped back onto the dancefloor he saw Howard swoop beside her and do something which made her slap his face.

Andy elbowed his way through the crowd and headed towards her.

She was livid until she saw him, and then all that vanished.

"What did he do?" Andy shouted, but Ginger either misheard him or chose not to answer. She put her arms around him and he lip-read *Waterfall* before the current song ended and a familiar melody began and then everything else in the world was forgotten; there was only him, Ginger, and the music.

Chimes on Sunday morn.

She smiled at him.

The surrounding lights glittered in her eyes and turned them into emeralds, her face curved upwards in rapturous bliss, as though she had been waiting all her life for a moment like this.

Andy flowed with something other than panic but just as electrifying. His hands rested on her lower back and she crushed herself into him. They swayed in time to the music, and he followed her lead.

Ginger closed her eyes and sang along, and as Andy plucked up the courage to lean in and kiss her, she planted her lips against his and he was in Heaven.

The tip of her tongue poked gently at his lips and then they were closer than he had ever dreamed possible, as though they were trying to push their way through each other, two ghosts on the dancefloor.

FÜHRER: PART ONE

Then there was something else between them.

A pair of hands grabbed Ginger's breasts and Howard leered down behind her.

A bomb exploded in Andy's chest; he felt his skeleton shatter.

Ginger recoiled, staggering away.

He shrieked, louder than the music, as, once again, after seven years, Andy Cooper wolfed-out.

Howard laughed as Andy squatted, ready to attack.

Fur burst from his pores, the sudden growth of tooth and claw filled the air with a blood-mist, but still Howard laughed.

People nearby began to notice and joined in Howard's mocking.

Andy bent over, the lava inside him desperate to erupt. He wanted to rip Howard into the smallest of pieces, pull the skin from his skull.

Everything intensified: his senses enhanced, the lights became too bright, the music too loud.

A hand reached out to him and he lashed out, rending the soft skin with his fingernails.

Blood.

There was blood.

There was blood, there were screams, and then there were heavy punches pummelling him to the sticky dancefloor where feet stomped and kicked, back and forth, back and forth into his abdomen and ribs.

Clarity soon returned, with the beating delivered by Howard and his friends.

Andy saw someone else lying on the dancefloor, someone being dragged away from the assault, their face covered in blood, their eyes wide with fright.

Once Andy saw the deep scratches across Ginger's face the kicks stopped hurting.

This was more painful by far.

Andy's scream was monstrous: unholy, but human.

FÜHRER: PART ONE

Chapter 24

Norfolk, England.

1955

Money could buy you anything if you knew the right people.

Victor had altered his and Gwen's histories and identities with each one of their moves. Names on paper didn't mean anything, he knew who they were.

He was almost always called Victor, despite changing his surname numerous times.

The Victor Krauss who had been the only child of a loving mother and father had officially died at the end of the Second World War.

Medicine and healing were in his blood, and as he and Gwen settled into a quiet life in a coastal Norfolk town, he began to focus on aspects of the brain in a bid to further understand Gwen's condition and how their joint mutation could affect it. It wasn't easy; as far as he was concerned, they were the only two lycanthropes in existence.

He acquired the latest psychiatric drugs to see if any of them could subdue, tame or invigorate Gwen's wolf.

A newly-tested drug was chlorpromazine and although it calmed the aggressive aspects of her

Alzheimer's, it did little for the thing she would turn into once the moon was full.

Although risky, as he was already in total control of his own wolf, he too took the drug so he could monitor the effects firsthand. The only thing he noticed was that the inner voice, or constant presence of his beast, quietened with the bombardment of antipsychotics.

It was this he was thinking of, and the increased dosage they were on, as he rode through the latest place they called home.

Great Yarmouth was a busy seaside resort and the ideal place for an old couple to spend their twilight years.

A modest three-storey house with an impenetrable cellar in a quiet cul-de-sac was enough to keep them hidden and safe. Gwen's changes came like clockwork; it was easy to prepare for them as he was in sync with her and felt the urges growing stronger with the fattening of the moon.

Whilst they were in Budapest, whenever he sensed their monsters readying to rise, he would lock up the house, send the carers and cleaners away, and barricade himself in the cellar with Gwen until it had passed.

There was no reason to suspect their routine couldn't be transferred to another country.

Before coming to England, he had made sure everything was to hand, including a secret, fortified room leading from the original cellar.

A strong but comfortable place to hold his wife captive.

He knew something was wrong as he clamped the handrail of the bus.

The wolf was rattling its shackles ahead of schedule.

He had everything prepared, down to the last meticulous detail.

The house had everything they needed, the housekeeper and carers were instructed to leave upon his return and not come back for three days.

He told them they were going away to visit relatives.

He had calculated the phases of the moon a month in advance.

But one mid-afternoon, on a blusterous October day, he felt the surge inside him and realised he had made a grave error.

It was the drugs, it must be. They had somehow altered the time between cycles.

Victor gripped the handrail and doubled over as his insides roiled.

"You alright, guv?" said a dirty-faced worker, jumping up and taking him by the elbow.

A snarl escaped. Victor struggled to contain it and fought his usual politeness to the surface. "Sorry, my friend, just a touch of travel sickness."

"Ginger biscuits are good for that," an old white-haired woman suggested from her seat.

"Humbugs, too," came another remedy from her friend beside her.

Victor closed his eyes, thanked the young worker for giving up his seat, and mentally whipped the beast inside him. "I shall certainly try your methods. Thank you, ladies." Starting to feel more in control, he rang the bell for the next stop.

FÜHRER: PART ONE

The harsh sea air hit him when he stepped off the bus.

He hurried homeward as quickly as he could at his age.

When he rounded the corner to their quiet cul-de-sac, he heard the screams.

Victor cursed himself for thinking he could have contained this, that they could hide in such plain sight.

Crowds lined the pavements near their home. Two men, still in their work overalls, stood poised by his front door as if planning to break it down.

"Don't panic," Victor shouted, shouldering past them. "My wife is ill and prone to violent outbursts. If you go in, it will only scare her more."

The oldest of the two men crossed his chunky forearms across a paint-speckled belly. "This used to be a quiet street before you foreigners turned up."

"And it will be again," Victor said, ignoring the slur and ushering the men away from his door. He entered the house quickly, slamming the door behind him before either man could nose his way in.

He expected a repeat of the train catastrophe, blood splattered up the freshly decorated walls, offal on the plush new carpets, but there was no immediate sign of anything untoward.

Mrs Baylock was at the top of the stairs, her usual leaden features morphed into those of a frightened little girl.

"She's..."—the housekeeper stumbled over her words—"she's..."

Victor simply nodded and squeezed past her.

Gwen's transformation wasn't yet complete but the beast had her, and her carer, Miss Thorn, in its clutches.

The young nurse was pressed against the wall, her feet a foot off the floor, bloody rivulets dripping down over her kicking, stockinged legs.

Gwen's arm was buried up to the elbow in the nurse's abdomen, the ribcage preventing her from sliding lower. Blood bubbles popped over the nurse's still-quivering lips as she stared pitifully at Victor.

Gwen's head snapped around, her grin bestial, eyes the feral yellow of the wolf, a woman possessed — quite literally.

The wolf was taunting him, proving that it couldn't be contained through drugs or binds.

Her body slowly undulated beneath her nightdress; the cracking, twisting bones sounded like burning twigs.

She pulled her fist out of Miss Thorn and flung a handful of warm viscera into his face.

A growl escaped, and his incisors burst through his lower lips, the taste of the young carer's blood rousing his demon.

Knowing there was nothing he could do for the nurse, Victor allowed himself to undergo full transformation.

He turned to Mrs Baylock, standing in the doorway, mouth agape.

Victor pounced and tore out her throat before she could release the scream building inside her.

Victor looked through the net curtains at the empty street below.

FÜHRER: PART ONE

The neighbours had lost interest when the screaming had stopped.

Behind him, Gwen lay decrepit, spent, asleep, covered in the drying gore of her latest victim.

Once her wolf had satisfied its needs, it reversed the transformation whilst it retreated to wherever it was they went.

Outside, darkness brought the new moon and cast the street in its glow.

There was so much about the lycanthropy he didn't understand.

Movement distracted him.

The disembowelled Miss Thorn twitched, her fingers spasmed.

Once again, the job was incomplete.

He fetched his silver blade and thrust it through Mrs Baylock's head, just to make sure, and then approached Miss Thorn.

A small part of him hesitated and he stayed his hand.

Maybe I can keep her alive and study her brain to see what this thing really is?

He froze, standing over her as he wondered how he could keep two monsters prisoner. The new one could be even more of a guinea pig than Gwen.

Yes, he felt the animal inside him say, *yes.*

Victor shook his head, leant against the handle, and pressed the sword's silver tip against Miss Thorn's temple.

Matthew Cash

PART TWO

FÜHRER: PART ONE

Chapter 25

The colour drained from the blonde woman's face, the water around her clouded yellow as her bladder emptied into the swimming pool. She grabbed the baby in the b floating ring, lifting the float as well as the curly haired tot.

Danny's wiry, dark-furred arm reached out and snatched at the infant, puncturing both the inflatable and the child with its black talons.

Its shrieking hurt his sensitive ears, it wailed louder and more high-pitched than anything else in the pool.

As he lifted the child to his mouth, the mother fell forwards into the chest-high water, her fingers reaching out for one of her baby's feet.

The little thing squealed and squealed, and a waft of hot shit engulfed him as its screaming head rested on his tongue for a moment.

The flavours excited his taste buds. Chemicals from the water, a faint taste of soap, and salt from the baby's tears.

He closed his wolf-jaws and modified teeth pierced the baby's skin.

The bones beneath offered no resistance as he bit down...

Tony's shrieking roused him from the horrific flashback.

Danny roiled on the sofa, clutching at his abnormally extended abdomen.

FÜHRER: PART ONE

Tony rushed to his aid as he rolled onto his side in time for a clumpy red geyser of partially digested raw meat and blood to splatter on the floor.

Tony recoiled: the torrent missed him by inches.

Danny continued to eject the grisly vomit for at least a minute before falling back, exhausted.

Tony looked at the mound of gruel and felt his own gorge rise when he saw scraps of flesh and fragments of bone. He fell onto the sofa and waited for Danny to finish retching and panting, his eyes streaming with the pressure of it all. When—finally—it ceased, he slumped with an air of utter desolation. "Oh, God," he moaned, "what the fuck have I done?"

It was obvious what he had done; neither boy needed to answer.

"You need to find a way to kill me," Danny said with a sincerity beyond his years. "Please, T."

"No," Tony began but honed in on the tiny finger that floated amongst the human stew.

"I can remember it all," Danny wailed. "I was aware as it tore people apart. I couldn't stop it, T. I murdered people. I *ate* people. I can't do this!"

"Stop!" Tony shouted, stepping over the pile of sick. "We can do this. This was a one-off. We need to go back to the flat. I have enough money hidden to get us away."

"No, Tony, I can't forget the things I've done."

"It wasn't you, and you can forget it. I won't let it happen again, I promise." Tony meant what he said, although he had no idea what they were going to do.

"I ate a fucking baby!"

Tony hid his face in his hands. "It wasn't you, it was that thing inside you."

"It needs to die."

"Okay." Tony had known it would come to this eventually, either his or his brother's death. "But please just let us get away from here first, I beg you."

Danny nodded weakly. "What choice do I have?" Unless they had access to another gun and more silver-doctored bullets, he doubted suicide was even possible.

Danny thought of Herbert crawling over a heap of burning bodies and sitting on the top like Satan himself. He would never have that courage. As much as he wanted this to be over, he knew he couldn't do it without his brother, no matter how much the ghosts from the swimming pool haunted him.

They left as soon as Danny was fit enough.

Both knew the risks of staying put when Tepes and Cyril were aware of their location.

The town of Sudbury was big, but a whole section of the centre was cordoned off due to the previous night's slaughter.

They were fugitives, still sought by the police, but the pressure of everything made Tony want to give himself up. He thought it would only be a matter of time before that was their only choice left.

Going back to the Green Man Estate to see if his stash of cash was still there was their last chance. If there was any sign of a police presence, however, he didn't know whether he could trust himself not to just quit there and then.

Flowers and other tributes were left at the entrances to the five tower blocks, by the play park and the old houses in the middle of the estate. Memorials to the victims of the recent attacks.

Danny spotted a photograph of Germ's little brother and froze. "I wish to God I'd just left things alone."

"Which one of them took the kid?"

"Krauss, or whoever he had locked up in his cellar."

Tony thought back to the old man's café visits and snippets of overheard conversation.

"He supposedly cared for his wife, who had dementia."

"Yeah, I think she probably had a bit more than that. It was obvious that it was them who caused all this shit. I saw his journals, remember? He'd been studying this for years."

"I just want to know how the others got involved, they were really nice people," Tony said sadly. "I mean, I'd known them for a few years. You might not remember but Mum used to speak to Trevor and Norman all the time. Dad used to drink in the same pub."

"You reckon his wife is still out there?"

Tony shrugged. "I don't know. When you went back to his house, didn't you say all the werewolf stuff had been removed?"

"Yeah." Danny paled at the memory of unearthing the freshly buried remains of Germ's little brother. "We didn't do anything, T, we just left the kid in his garden. And now their mum has lost both of them."

"The cops will have combed the place; don't worry, they'll have found him."

The Green Man Estate was a strange mismatch of social housing.

Aside from five tower blocks which were laid out at all five points of a pentagram, there were six archaic semi-detached houses slap-bang in the middle, like some sacrificial offering.

The houses were tiny remnants from a long-lost era.

Before the flats were built, a street of old turn-of-the-century workhouses ran across the grounds and for some reason, six of the houses were kept and incorporated into the estate.

Despite the homes being actual houses everyone still referred to them as flats, Tony and Danny especially. Since their mother's death, their dad lived downstairs, the boys had their own bedrooms, and they all lived so independently from each other that it was as if they were living in separate flats.

Once they passed between the first two tower blocks, they could see their own miniature apartment block. Metal shutters covered the windows and the doors were padlocked.

Three of the other houses were in the same state, one having been unoccupied for the best part of a decade.

"I don't know why they don't just knock them down," Tony said as they passed the graffiti-covered buildings.

The sole remaining occupied house was in a state of disrepair, with hanging gutters and drainpipes, and two of the bedroom windows boarded up. Their own wasn't much better.

FÜHRER: PART ONE

They stepped over the remnants of a concrete fence and inspected the boarding.

Tony slid the first paperclip into the padlock and probed with another to feel for the individual lock pins.

Danny thought it ironic that he had been the one involved with street crime, and yet it was his clean-cut brother who was the lock-picker. Tony had been obsessed with puzzles when he was younger and when someone bought him a lock-picker's kit. "It's a pity you never learnt about car locks."

"What's the point," Tony said, "if neither of us could get the bloody thing started, let alone drive it."

They went into the cold, dark house.

Someone had gone through everything, and Tony prayed they hadn't been too meticulous. "Just pack what you need and we'll get out."

Tony headed straight to his bedroom and flipped his mattress up.

There was a moment where he felt the bottom drop out of his world but then he spotted the jiffy bag full of notes. He snatched it and checked the money was still in there.

Last time he'd counted it, there was almost two grand, nowhere near enough. He thought about Tepes' stash. His own meagre savings were a pittance compared to that treasure trove.

Danny slumped in the doorway, bag over his shoulder. "We can't do this anymore. Let's just give ourselves up."

Even though Tony had been thinking the same thing, he disagreed. "They won't understand. They'll make things worse."

"We need to tell them about Cyril and Tepes."

Tony rested his head against the doorjamb. "Isn't there anyone else you know?"

Danny shook his head.

The remnants of the GMC would have been taken in for questioning, and their families, too.

He thought about the town's abandoned places but what was the point in hiding when all it was doing was delaying the inevitable?

"We just need somewhere to hole up where Tepes can't find us. I need time to think."

"What about number seven in Jack flats?" Danny suggested. Number seven of the Jack-in-the-Green block had been unoccupied so long that it had become an urban legend around the estate, a local myth and ghost story.

From outside, the first-floor flat's windows were obscured by ancient, dust-filled net curtains and the desiccated tendrils of a houseplant that somehow hadn't completely disintegrated over time.

The kids used to dare one another to knock on number seven's door, and they would imagine they could hear something shuffling up the hallway towards them.

Once, Tony had plucked up the courage to spy through the letterbox, only to find it was glued shut, adding another element to the mystery.

To the kids of the estate it was a whole lot more than an empty flat. It was a time capsule, the secret hiding place for an immortal monster.

As it was only one floor up, Danny had been one of the kids to brave climbing up to peek at its balcony, and he had never forgotten the deep layers of bird shit and the number of dead pigeons in various states of decay, from freshly rotting corpses to fossilised bones.

FÜHRER: PART ONE

Everyone who lived there fantasised about breaking into number seven, but no one ever thought it would be worth the trouble.

It would be the last place anyone would look for them.

The door of number seven was old compared to the rest of the flats in the block; the other apartments had had refits every decade or so.

A mixture of childish fear and excitement filled Tony, with the prospect of uncovering the answers to the estate's mysteries.

In a horror novel, or on screen, this lost-in-time flat would play an integral part in the story's narrative, it could be anything: the prison of an abducted deity, the portal to another dimension. Although he doubted the answer to number seven's conundrum was anything half as interesting as that, his skin still prickled with gooseflesh when the lock clicked open.

He turned to Danny in genuine fright. "What if we're about to unleash Hell?"

Danny gave a wry grin, thought about the devastation he'd brought on the swimmers at the pool, and everything that had happened with Cyril and Tepes. "Don't you think it's a bit too late to worry about that?"

Chapter 26

It must have been a nightmare.

For a fleeting second, Jez thought and even hoped that it had been, but when he saw the lump beneath the blankets on his sofa, he knew it was real.

Not much was said the night before.

Automatically, he had acted as normal as possible around the woman he had called Aunty Liz all his life.

It didn't matter that she was supposed to be dead.

She had turned up in such a state in the middle of the night. He gave her food, drink, clean clothes, and somewhere to rest.

Some colour had returned to her face but it did little to vanquish the deathly pallor.

It must be some kind of mix-up.
Things like this happen all the time.

He'd read stories about people waking up in the morgue after being declared dead.

There were peculiar conditions where people were mistakenly classified as dead, such as catalepsy and locked-in syndrome, which often made the person rigid, unresponsive, and to the untrained eye, appear to be in the beginning stages of rigor mortis. And then there was Lazarus syndrome, where a flatlined heart could suddenly restart itself minutes after stopping.

People really could come back from the dead.

No one could forget the attacks on the town, how something or someone had attacked people at the hospital and how an unnamed corpse had gone missing.

What if that 'corpse' had found themselves alive in a mortuary freezer?

He was pretty sure that that alone could account for a spontaneous violent outburst of insanity.

Is Aunty Liz the monster terrorising the town?

As he stood watching her sleeping form, she stirred and peered around the room in confusion before setting eyes on him.

"Oh," was all she said, and she looked down at the baggy Pink Floyd T-Shirt she was wearing. "Oh, how ironic."

Jez had no idea what she was on about as she traced her fingertips over the design, a beam of light passing through a triangular prism.

"The Dark Side of the Moon," she said with an ounce of her usual sense of humour. "Quite apt, considering."

Jez found himself speechless again, his mouth and throat as dry as sandpaper. He forced himself to sit in the closest chair and say something, anything. "What are you on about?"

"I really don't know, Jeremy. I think I need to find my friends."

"The folks you used to hang around with at the café?"

"Yes, Victor and that lot. That boy tried to stick Victor with something—"

"They're dead."

Elizabeth gasped. "They're what? How? What happened?"

"There were attacks around town after you..." He couldn't say it, he didn't know the end of the sentence. "The police station, hospital, a nursery, for fuck's sake, and the park. They put it down to some barney between the Green Man Crew and a gang from Sudbury. People were torn apart. Apparently, your friends were somehow involved."

"Oh, God," Elizabeth said to herself, "he couldn't control them after all."

Jez stared in horror. "He couldn't control them? Who? Who couldn't control who? Do you know something about this?"

Elizabeth nodded. "There's no rational way of saying any of this, Jeremy so I'll just come out with it. Victor and his wife are werewolves."

Once again, Jez was lost for words.

"He showed himself to Ethel, it was him that killed those poor boys along the canal, they tried to mug him and once he retaliated he had to make sure the deed was done properly so this thing couldn't spread."

"This is insane."

"Quite definitely," Elizabeth agreed. "Victor kept his wife locked up in his cellar and tried to work on a cure, or at least some way to harness the good parts, the regenerative properties and longevity, and get rid of, or at least control the monster. There were samples of his and his wife's blood for him to test. Ethel stole them and infected us all."

"So you're a—"

"Jeremy, I don't know what I am. I know there was something inside me that I had no control over, and that Victor created some kind of poison to kill someone like himself. That's what the boy who tried to attack him had. I got in the way. Somehow the stuff didn't work. What happened at the park?"

FÜHRER: PART ONE

"There was a fight between several groups of people which started here at the flats. The newspaper put it down to gang warfare, and your friends were collateral damage, they got in the way. Most of the Green Man Crew were killed, and so did whoever they were fighting. Someone tried to clear it all up by burning everything. Authorities have tried to hush everything up but there are families who want to bury their children but they have no remains."

Elizabeth was stunned into silence.

"The police are still looking for the boy who sticked you and another called Anthony Scarborough."

"Tony?"

"What are we going to do, Aunty Liz?"

Elizabeth reached out and gripped his hand. "You've not called me that since your mum died. I promised her I'd look after you and I will."

Jez laughed.

"I suspect we'll have to go to the authorities. Somebody will have some idea of what to do."

Jez shook his head and sighed. "They'll dissect you and you'll just become something else to be hushed up."

Elizabeth smiled sadly. "There's nothing else we can do. This has to end. What if I change and hurt someone?"

"I think it's too late to worry about hurting people, Aunty Liz," Jez said, exasperated. He showed her his phone.

A news article showed a grainy image of something big and bulky standing in the swimming baths foyer, a little girl fleeing, and the headline: ANOTHER WEREWOLF MASSACRE.

"Oh my God."

Jez nodded. "I hate to say this but, do you think this was your doing?"

Elizabeth's face sagged with the possibility. "All I can remember about last night was waking up freezing cold and naked in the back of the arboretum."

"Yeah, that's what worries me."

"Oh Jeremy, what if it was me? You could be in danger."

A hollow, humourless laugh escaped him when he thought about her makeshift wardrobe when she'd arrived at his place in the early hours. "Well, it would explain the child's swimsuit you had on."

Elizabeth gasped. "But I remember getting that from lost property. I told you that, at least I think I did."

"You were covered in dried blood and dirt when you got here," Jez said. "You looked like you'd clawed your way up from Hell."

Elizabeth shuddered. "I remember waking up beneath the stars, not able to breathe, my throat was clogged with soil and worms."

Jez paled. "Do you think it was your friends who buried you in the park?"

Elizabeth shook her head. "Victor knew what he was doing. You said about the funeral pyre, the remnants of all those people. Only the Scarborough brothers were accounted for, you said."

Jez studied the news article once more. "Well, if this wasn't you, it means there's another one of these things out there."

"But everyone was accounted for."

"Apart from the brothers."

Elizabeth sat silently ruminating before slapping a palm against the coffee table and forcing a smile.

FÜHRER: PART ONE

"Let's have a nice cup of tea and then I'll go to the police station."

"So that's it, then?" Jez asked. "You're going to hand yourself in?"

"What else can I do?" Elizabeth said. "Once they run their tests, they'll see that the danger is real and be more vigilant in finding out who's out there killing people."

Jez sighed. "When?"

"No time like the present, Jeremy. You've already done enough. God knows what danger I could have put you in coming here in the first place.

"Well, I'm not letting you do this alone. You can't. If you're adamant it's the right thing to do, then we'll do it."

Chapter 27

They left the caravan site in the early hours of the morning. Three separate groups travelling to three separate destinations, none of them really knowing if they would see each other again.

The money, Gustav's savings, had virtually dried up after they'd spent it on their ludicrous method of travelling to Germany.

None of them knew what would happen once they got the kids, *if* they got them.

They would still be fugitives, still be privy to something that would change the world and be sought after at all costs.

Travelling was costly and Gustav doubted they would even make it past Dover.

The group went their separate ways that morning to nearby towns, to the various pickups the coach was due to make on its way to Dover.

They said their goodbyes at a tiny country train station, two unmanned platforms in the middle of nowhere, six desperate-looking people, three young, three old.

The three old men got together away from the others.

Norman and Trevor listened intently to Herbert. Somewhere along the line, he had taken charge.

They nodded doubtfully at Herbert's words but he offered encouragement, reinforcement, and clapped them on the shoulders. Herbert had enough faith for all of them.

FÜHRER: PART ONE

Their pairs were as mismatched as they thought possible, Herbert partnered with Charlotte. For the sake of the trip, they would be father and daughter. They had the farthest to travel, and in the early light of dawn, they found themselves at Colchester railway station, an old redbrick affair that hadn't changed since Herbert's childhood.

For him, just approaching the station brought back memories both good and bad, but unfortunately, the bad overrode the good.

There he was as a young boy, screaming blue murder at his panic-stricken mother as she dragged him towards another term at St Botolph's boarding school, another term under the reign of Simon and his cohorts.

It had been a long time since he had travelled, willingly, outside of Boxford. Overall, aside from its surroundings, the train station was a nostalgia-drenched timepiece which made him long for some of the better parts of his past.

There's still so much bloody hurt in her eyes.

It was all he could think about as he hugged his daughter goodbye. She would never forgive him, could never forgive him, and Trevor knew he deserved Juliet's hatred.

The knowledge of what he had done to his grandchildren made him all the more determined to get them back, no matter what the cost.

Since the battle at the facility, he hadn't felt hide nor hair of his wolf. He hoped the control he had over it wasn't a fluke. Perhaps the way he'd gorged on the soldiers had lulled it into a temporary hibernation, a fattened, sleeping dog, its bloodlust sated, but now he was separate from his friends he worried how short-lived that would be. His anxiety returned and threatened to overwhelm him.

What if I turn and Gustav can't handle it?
How can we deal with that situation on our own?

Neither of them said much on their way to Cambridge.

Once away from Herbert and Trevor, Norman felt his confidence dwindle. His seeping skin felt constantly moist and uncomfortable, refusing to heal, as though his supernatural healing abilities were being held back for some unknown ransom.

At the facility, he had killed soldiers, more lives taken because of this monster inside him, a monster put there against his will.

He had ripped those men apart but hadn't feasted on their flesh.

Maybe that's the problem.

Did the sustenance the beast received during its killing frenzies fuel its regeneration?

Who knew what fuelled these things other than their hunger?

It made a modicum of sense and for a second Norman mused over the idea of werewolves living off high-calorie protein shakes.

His monster was carnivorous and he had hardly consumed his daily quota of protein since fleeing the barracks. God only knew what stuff they had been pumping into him there. Whenever he closed his eyes, glistening internal organs filled his head and made his stomach growl.

FÜHRER: PART ONE

Before she patched him up, Charlotte asked him and Herbert not to eat her, a joke laced with more than a little genuine fear. Now, as he waited with Juliet, he wondered whether his beast would swipe a claw through his and Trevor's friendship by killing her before they reunited.

A black coach with DEHANEY'S on its sides drove towards a group of people standing outside a boarded-up building which had once held the town's job centre.

"This isn't going to work," Trevor said, feeling exposed to the elements.

"Just remember to keep a low profile," Gustav said, and rubbed at his bare top lip.

They'd had to pin him down, ignoring his protests, to shave off his epic moustache, and discovered it had been covering a scar from cleft-lip surgery.

Afterwards, the group felt guilty as sin.

"Pretend we're going on holiday," Gustav whispered, and nodded to an elderly couple. "Good morning."

The coach door opened.

A rotund man with short brown hair jumped from the deck. "Morning, all, I'm Barry."

"This is where it all goes pear-shaped," Trevor said, stepping forward with his coach ticket and passport.

"Ah, don't worry about that now, son," Barry said with a wink. "Just tell us your name, leave your bags by the side there, and get in the warm and

Cheryl will be round with some hot drinks as soon as we're off."

"Clint Parker," Trevor mumbled, and climbed aboard.

Gustav said something to the driver and followed quite swiftly.

"What name did you give him?" Trevor asked as he sat in his allocated seat.

"Gustav," Gustav said.

"No." Trevor looked to see if anyone was within listening distance. "Your fake name."

Gustav lowered his eyes, wary of the old man's teasing.

"Gustav Gustavson."

Trevor bumped his forehead against the cold glass in despair. "Oh, Jesus."

"I have the accent. I'm being Icelandic."

"Oh, Jesus."

"All us foreigners sound the same to you Brits anyway. Who's going to tell the difference between Ukraine and Iceland?"

"I'm Jamaican," Trevor corrected him. "And I hope to God you're right."

Gustav tapped the passport in Trevor's hand, stifling a grin. "I think you'll find you were born in Surrey."

"It's a grey day," Trevor sighed, studying the fake identification, and shook his head. "Surrey. Jesus Christ, not only do I have a stupid bloody name which will get me arrested as soon as someone looks too closely, but I'm also from Surrey. Couldn't you have picked somewhere a bit more exotic?"

"Milton Keynes?"

FÜHRER: PART ONE

Trevor's groan startled the old couple Gustav had greeted moments before as they came down the aisle.

"He has the—" Gustav said, trying to explain his sudden outburst but momentarily forgetting the English for травлення, *indigestion*, and going with the first ailment he could think of. "Haemorrhoids."

Trevor stiffened in his chair at the old couple's shocked reaction. The lady, with long silver hair and red glasses, smiled sympathetically and told him it was the cold mornings that set hers off.

"Marvellous, Gustav," Trevor said, once they passed, "now I have images of that old mare's arsehole in me head. Thanks for that."

When the coach pulled into Cambridge, Trevor spotted Norman and Juliet with the waiting passengers even though Norman was doing a pretty good job at being incognito.

He found a pair of walking sticks from somewhere and hobbled up to the coach with Juliet clutching at his arm.

Trevor didn't know what their story was.

They all agreed it was best to leave them as a surprise and introduce each other in front of other people like they were strangers.

He hoped and prayed Norman wouldn't go as far as telling everyone Juliet was his girlfriend, and God help them all if the old Scot attempted an accent.

Luckily for all involved, Norman didn't alter his voice at all other than to make the accent broader and more indecipherable.

"It's pronounced *Niles*," he barked with the aggressive tone that some people seemed to have naturally. "It's Gaelic."

"Weren't they those pepperpot things in Doctor Who?" Barry jested, something Norman would usually have laughed at, but this new persona was obviously a cantankerous old bastard.

"Away, and don't talk pish, you flaming idiot!"

"I'm so sorry," Juliet said, scolding Norman with her eyes, and apologising to Barry. "He's just excited to be going on holiday." She reached out and took Barry's hand. "My name is Creole, I'm his carer."

Trevor cringed as Barry bent to kiss Juliet's hand, heard him say something about *Kid Creole and the Coconuts*. Together they helped the decrepit Norman onto the bus in a flurry of nonsensical swear words and blasphemies.

As Juliet and Norman passed them, Trevor mouthed the words "Low profile."

Oh my God.

Gustav felt guilty as soon as he had thought it.

The folk waiting at the coach stop at Colchester bus station were a mixture of ages but mostly over fifty, aside from one guy who stood out over the rest of them.

Gustav hated himself for staring.

He forced his face away from the window but still couldn't tear his eyes from the man.

The horror and revulsion he felt, at himself, at the man, soon diluted into pity.

The guy stood around seven feet tall and probably weighed at least thirty stone.

FÜHRER: PART ONE

He wore black. Black everything. Dark snatches of mottled purple skin bunched up around his ankles. His beard and hair, grown long, spilled over his broad chest.

Gustav had struggled with weight issues all his life, but he had never reached these proportions this man.

Gustav guessed the man was in his late twenties to early thirties and, once again, tried to avert his gaze.

The woman with him was quite literally half his size. She was bleached blonde and dripping in gold jewellery.

The big man picked up their two suitcases, which seemed tiny in his grasp.

"Jesus fucking Christ, he's huge," Trevor blurted out.

Gustav wanted the ground to swallow him up. He feigned ignorance. "I do not understand."

Trevor thrust a hand under his nose and pointed out the window. "Bloody Weight Watchers over there," he said, and roared with laughter almost loud enough to shake the coach.

Gustav turned to the Jamaican, trying his best to keep the anger from his voice. They didn't want to attract unnecessary attention. "How dare you?"

Trevor's face was a picture of shocked innocence.

"Morbid obesity is an illness."

Trevor lowered his eyes. "Ah, come on, man, it's not like I said anything to his face."

"It is not good enough," Gustav continued. "Your generation knows no tact. These people have feelings, they are just like you and me."

"I know, man, I'm sorry."

"It is illness," Gustav said. "Tell me, you and your Scottish friend, you used to enjoy a drink, yes?"

"That's the understatement of the century," Trevor said with a dry laugh.

"Food is the only vice that you need," Gustav stated.

"What do you mean?"

"Alcohol. Drugs. Sex. Cigarettes." Gustav turned in his seat. "Food is the only thing that is there from the word go. We eat from when we are a baby. Our bad habits start at such a young age, defensive-eating because of an older sibling, maybe. Overeating. It all starts as a child. It is the hardest vice to give up. We need to eat."

Although Trevor had his own opinions on the matter, he chose to let Gustav have his moment—and he was making rather a good point.

The big guy got on the bus and Trevor tried his best not to grimace as he squeezed up the aisle.

Among the other holidaymakers were Herbert and Charlotte.

Trevor seized the opportunity to change the subject. "How about that one over there in the hat?"

Herbert donned a trilby he had picked up somewhere.

Trevor chuckled. "He looks like he belongs in an afternoon detective program."

"Kojak?" Gustav suggested, and honestly thought Trevor was going to die.

"What's funny?"

The two men turned towards the blonde woman, who in turn stared at them maliciously.

"Just an in-joke," Trevor said.

FÜHRER: PART ONE

The woman was sceptical. She waited until her big companion reached the back seat. "Let's just get one thing straight, guys, I'm extremely protective of my son, Vince, there," she said, flicking her eyes to the rear of the coach. "And I'm not blind to how people start when they first lay eyes on him. I get it, he's likely the biggest man you've probably seen, but he's my baby, has a heart even bigger than the rest of him, and I will rip anyone to pieces who even so much as points a finger at him." Her son looked her way and she flashed him a toothy smile.

Trevor stood. "You can rest assured we were not making fun of you or your son." He offered her his hand. "My name is Clint, and this is my good friend from Iceland,"—he winked—"not the supermarket, Gus."

The woman's whole demeanour changed when she lay eyes on Gustav, and Trevor could have sworn he heard the twang of Cupid's bow.

"Wow!" Her voice rose several octaves. "Icelandic. A real-life Viking, eh?"

Ignoring Trevor's hand, she plucked Gustav's from its resting place on his belly and mimicked Trevor's wink. "And do you have a long or a broadsword?"

Trevor collapsed backwards into his seat and panted with laughter at Gustav's shock and the flush of embarrassment on his cheeks.

"I'm Valerie," she said to Gustav, "and I'll be your Valkyrie any day."

Gustav's mouth opened and closed but no sound came out.

"We'll catch up with you later, Valerie," Trevor said between laughs. "I promise you my friend here will be more talkative."

Valerie looked hungrily at him. "It's okay, darling, you don't need to say much, but you'll be screaming by the time I take you to Valhalla."

Trevor roared again and heard an angry Scottish voice bark, "Jesus wept. Keep it down back there." Norman's way of reminding his loudmouthed friend to remember their low profile.

Herbert looked quite fetching in his trilby. He had also acquired a tweed suit, which added to his new persona. He waved towards the bus and allowed Charlotte to get on board first, as though she were royalty. "Yes," he said to Barry, "she's my daughter, my pride and joy."

Aside from smiling at all the passengers already seated, Herbert and Charlotte paid them no attention.

Trevor read the itinerary and saw there were two more pickups before they were headed to Dover.

"Right, ladies and gents," Barry the coach driver boomed through the speakers. "There are tailbacks all the way to Dover so we're going to stop here for a pitstop for thirty minutes." Here was a service station on the outskirts of Canterbury.

Charlotte put her hand on Herbert's shoulder and shook him gently to rouse him from sleep.

"You know you could get away here," Herbert whispered from the corner of his mouth as the passengers began to leave the coach.

Everything still felt surreal and dreamlike, her senses numbed and subdued. A lucid dream from working too many hours. How could any of this be real? She wondered if their faces were on news

FÜHRER: PART ONE

bulletins already, whether they were wanted fugitives or whether the powers that be were still trying to cover it up.

When she and Herbert had left for Colchester in the early hours, he'd continued to reassure her it wasn't too late for her to back out, to do a runner, that despite his own persistence to see this thing through to the end, it really wasn't her fight, and the chances of it ending well for any of them were slim.

She had been tempted, but how could she go back to her normal life now, after all this? Her whole belief system had changed. She knew she had seen too much for whoever was in charge to let her go free. She was a loose end, and loose ends were the start of everything unravelling. The most she could hope for, even if she did go her own way, would be a lifetime of hiding and constant paranoia. And every time she closed her eyes, she saw the twins writhing in agony as their little bodies buckled and changed in the back seat of that van.

Her life had been over the minute the hospital administrator had made her escort them to Butcher's facility.

There was no going back.

"I've already told you. If I run, I'll always be running. I'd like to have a destination in mind. Now, quit it before someone overhears us. Dad."

Herbert sighed and pointed to the front of the coach. "After you, daughter of mine."

Norman let Juliet help him down the steps to the tarmac. They followed the line of passengers towards the service station toilets. He had already clocked the majority of the others on board, his ex-copper observation skills never quit making assumptions about new people. On the journey so far, he'd unwittingly eavesdropped on the two men sitting behind them, listening to them discuss both ailments and alcohol with equal enthusiasm. He couldn't wait to get five minutes away from their constant yatter.

Norman nodded at the men who shuffled ahead of them. "Couple of old pissheads," he said to Juliet with an eye roll.

"Pot, kettle," Juliet replied.

"Pfft." Since discussing it with Trevor, he'd been grieving for his last pint. "Do you reckon once Herbert has taught us how to control this, we'll be able to partake again?"

Juliet's expression was enough.

"Aye, I guess it's for the best."

Norman continued the pretense of struggling with his mobility in front of the coach party.

They went in the disabled toilets together, for appearance's sake, and when they came back out, saw a group had gathered around Barry, the coach driver, and they caught the end of whatever he was telling them.

Juliet smiled at a regal-looking elderly man and a woman close by. "What was that all about?"

"A spot of bother back home," the man said, with a posh upper-class accent. He stood to sharp attention. Everything about him was pristine, his three-piece herringbone suit looked expensive, but Juliet noticed immediately that his pencil-thin moustache was a few millimetres lopsided on the left.

The woman who had been mid-conversation with the man clutched at the front of her blouse, ashen-faced. "It's bloody typical, is what it is."

FÜHRER: PART ONE

"What's happened, hen? Problem with the bus?" Norman interjected.

The woman softened at Norman's approach, a hand flitted upwards to check her blue-grey hair was in place. "Trouble in Suffolk."

"Oh, Jesus. What kind of trouble? Terrorists?" Norman asked, hating that it was the default assumption nowadays.

"They've not said." The man seemed only capable of one volume: loud. "Barry there says he's going to fill us in when we're on the coach."

"It better not fuck our holiday up," came a crass northern voice from behind.

Norman immediately recognised it as belonging to one of the two pissheads sitting behind him. He turned to get a better look at them.

The swearer wore a flat cap over a scraggly yellow-grey mop of hair which fell onto the dandruff-freckled shoulders of his anorak.

Norman would bet money on there being an archaic band t-shirt beneath his navy coat: Rainbow, Pink Floyd or The Who, he could almost guarantee it.

The man had a permanently pissed-off expression, even when he gave what was presumably a smile, it looked like a painful grimace. He flashed crooked, plaque-yellow teeth at Juliet. "Alright, love. I'm Ted, and this here is Oliver."

"Ollie!" Ted's acquaintance barked. Ollie was a foot taller than Ted and had crazy grey hair like a mad scientist's.

"Creole," Juliet said, and tried her best not to squirm as Ted took her hand and pressed his thin lips against it.

"Leopold Alcocks," the toff shouted, and thrust his hand out to Ted, who took it with a lingering side-eye to his friend.

"I'm Ivy," said the woman with the blue rinse, before Norman could offer up his introduction.

"Are you travelling alone?" he enquired.

"Ey-up!" Ted cackled and drove an elbow into Ollie's ribs. "Matey here's on the pull before we've even left the country."

"I am doing no such thing," Norman snapped at the northerner.

"Alright, keep your hair on, Grandpa, it was only a joke."

"I'm a widower," Norman added, and got a sympathetic look from Ivy.

"Don't mean you're dead, though, does it?"

Norman's stare was venomous.

Juliet grabbed him by the arm, and before he could respond, Ivy took the other.

"It's okay, love," Ivy said, giving it a squeeze. "They don't mean no harm. I'm the same. My Ernie has been in his grave for fifteen years now. When you get wed, it's for life, there aren't any plan B's for whatever happens next, are there?"

Norman smiled, she had hit the nail on the head and simultaneously diffused what could have been an ugly situation. "Aye, hen, there aren't." He winked at her and addressed the two men. "How about you two? What's your story? How long have you been together?"

Ted lunged at him like a rabid Pit Bull, but Ollie held him back. His yellow-nailed finger stabbed the air. "I'll have you know," he seethed, white froth at the corners of his lips, "I'll have you know..."

FÜHRER: PART ONE

"Pack it in, you ruddy scallion," Leopold steamed in, albeit only verbally.

"Ten years," Ollie said, making them all stare at him in shock.

Ted goggled at his friend. "I didn't think we were going to tell anyone on this trip? You know what these old 'uns are like."

"Fuck 'em." Ollie shrugged indifferently.

"Language, boy," Leopold barked, "ladies present."

Juliet burst into laughter. "You'll get no prejudice from us. It's hardly groundbreaking news, being gay."

"Plenty of poofs in the army," Leopold mused to himself.

Ivy appeared to be more startled than the rest of them but then came to her senses. "Well," she said, appraising Ted and Ollie, "good for you. Ummm... well done."

Ted flushed with embarrassment. "Okay, so, now that we've all aired our skiddy skivvies, maybe we should get back on the coach and find out what all this bollocks is about in Suffolk and how it affects us."

"Aye," Norman said, flipping one of his walking sticks in the direction of the coach. "Lead on, MacDuff."

Once everyone was back on board, Barry stood at the front and got everyone's attention. "I'm afraid there's some rather disturbing news coming from—"

"Oh, here we fucking go," Ted boomed from the back of the bus, drowning out Barry's words.

"Quiet," Norman hissed over his shoulder, "let the man talk."

"Hear, hear," said Leopold.

"Last night," Barry continued, "there was a massacre at a swimming pool in Sudbury, Suffolk. I know a few of you are from that area, so I thought I'd make sure you had the opportunity to check up with relatives.."

A chorus of cusses, blasphemies and blessings erupted throughout the coach.

"Oh, Jesus Christ, what now?" Norman shouted out before he'd had a chance to control it and was promptly shushed by Ted.

Barry smiled with embarrassed confusion, as if he was about to divulge something ludicrous. "That's the thing I can't get my head around; the news said it was someone dressed up as a werewolf."

"Oh, don't be so ridiculous," Ivy shouted.

The bus thrummed with a dozen simultaneous conversations.

Barry held his hands up to silence them. "I know how it sounds, trust me I do, but I saw it on the news back in there." He cocked a thumb back towards the service station.

"What about our holiday?" Ted yelled.

"Why should it affect that?" Barry asked. "You ain't got any relatives there, have you? Picked you pair up in York. That's a long way from Sudbury."

"Never heard of the place," Ted said quietly.

"Well, then, this doesn't affect you, does it?"

"I suppose not."

Barry shook his head in disbelief and raised his palms. "Look, I'm just keeping you lot in the loop, okay? If there's no further questions, it's wagons roll."

FÜHRER: PART ONE

A few rows from the front, Trevor whined quietly to Gustav, "Oh, Jesus Christ, what the hell is this?"

Gustav seemed on the verge of vomiting. "We need to find out what happened at Boxford."

"No shit, Sherlock."

"Something, someone must have survived the park attack."

"Oh Jesus," Trevor said, and bumped his forehead against the coach window.

It took just over two hours to get from the services at Canterbury to the Dover Port Control.

As predicted, they didn't have to leave the coach, just press their passports against the windows, and by the time the coach had boarded the ferry and parked in its designated area, the three men from Boxford were desperate to get reacquainted and talk about the recent events.

The passengers readied themselves to explore the P&O *Spirit of Britain* during its ninety-minute channel crossing.

Norman caught his friends' attention and pointed upwards.

Whilst other passengers chatted about finding something to eat and raiding the duty-free shops, they prepared to convene up on deck.

Trevor and Gustav were the last to arrive at this particular meeting, the latter taking several minutes stilling the advances of his new admirer, who tried everything she could to coerce him into having a drink with her. After promising to give her his time once they got to the hotel in France, he escaped with Trevor and his constant teasing over what Valerie would likely do to him in an amorous situation.

"So much for being incognito and not mingling," Trevor said as they strode across the wet deck.

"Let's face it," Norman sighed and scratched at his red beard, "they're not looking for us, are they?"

"We don't know that for sure—" Herbert began, but Gustav cut him off.

"I think he is right. I don't think they are caring about what we are getting up to."

Juliet scowled; she didn't believe they were so expendable. "But we could go to the press, or anything."

"That is what concerns me even more," Gustav said gravely. He rested his arms on the deck railing and stared at the water.

"How so?" Charlotte asked.

"If they do not care whether this gets to the paparazzi, it could mean they do not worry about it becoming public knowledge."

Charlotte squinted at Dover's cliffs, bright white in the sunlight.

"Do you think they're planning something?"

Gustav nodded glumly. "I predict so."

"Like what?"

"As I said, after the facility, picking up where they left off in the forties."

"You think they're gearing up to invade somewhere with this new army they're building?" Herbert said, horrified.

Gustav nodded again. "I predict they will recreate Hitler's strategies and occupy surrounding countries, unless the old dogs have learned new tricks."

FÜHRER: PART ONE

"How the hell are we supposed to compete with something on this scale?" Trevor whined, hawked up a mouthful of phlegm and spat it over the side.

Herbert put his arm around his shoulders. "Come on, old friend, we know how slim our chances are, but what choices do we really have?"

They all stared at the water as it frothed with the ferry's movement.

"We have to remain positive." Herbert sounded like he was beginning another pep-talk. "Let's focus on what we can do. As soon as we get to the Novotel, we'll find somewhere to have our first training session."

"Training session?" Gustav said, confused.

"Not for you, Gustav. You and the ladies can relax at the hotel. This will be our first group session on how to train our bodies to cope with—"

"Herbert!" Juliet shouted, stopping him mid-sentence and nodding to Ted and Ollie who appeared beside them, bags full of clinking bottles.

"Alright," Ted greeted Norman and winked at Juliet. "What are you all up to then, making friends? Saying au revoir to Angleterre?"

"Och, nothing much," Norman said, "just introducing ourselves to some of the other holidaymakers." Norman offered an uncomfortable grin.

"That's nice," said Ted expectantly.

"Hello," Herbert chirped with his usual joviality. "I'm Brian."

"No, he's not," Ted squeaked in a high-pitched voice, "he's a very naughty boy."

Everyone, including Ollie, looked at him in confusion.

"Don't you remember? Monty Python? The Life of Brian?" Sudden disgust clouded Ted's face. "You ain't all Bible-bashers, are you? Because if you are I'm jumping overboard."

Herbert smiled awkwardly.

"Quote's wrong," Ollie told him in as few words as possible.

"How the bloody hell should I know?" Ted said, scalding his boyfriend. "We've not watched that one in years. You always insist on the bloody Holy Grail, which, in my own personal opinion, is an inferior film."

Norman cleared his throat.

"Sorry about that," Ted said, and thrust his hand at Herbert. "Pleased to meet yo—" He clocked Herbert's wrapped wrist. "Oh, what the hell have you done?"

Herbert waggled his bandaged stump. "Oh, this? 'Tis nothing but a flesh wound."

Ollie's laugh, like most of his conversation, was monosyllabic. "Grail," he barked.

Ted remained stoic; he rarely laughed at anything but his own jokes.

Herbert lowered his arm. "I got it shot off by a soldier whilst I was trying to single-handedly hijack an army Chinook."

Ted rolled his eyes at Norman and cocked his thumb. "Proper fucking comedian, this one, innee?"

"Brian," Norman said, "this is Ted and Ollie."

The pair of newcomers nodded.

Ted's eyes lit upon Charlotte. He offered her a flash of his disgusting teeth. "And who is this angelic vision of loveliness?"

FÜHRER: PART ONE

For a horrifying moment, Charlotte forgot her fake name but Juliet jumped in to rescue her.

"This is Deborah."

"Never Debbie, Debs, or any other abbreviation," Charlotte added, just to prove she hadn't lost her voice.

"How about you pair?" Ted quizzed Trevor and Gustav.

"I'm Clinton," Trevor said proudly.

"Gustav," said Gustav with mild embarrassment.

"So, what's this I hear about training sessions?" Ted asked, seeing their faces fall.

Juliet broke the silence. "That's none of your bus—"

"It's okay," Herbert intervened, "they're only interested, and they might care to join us." He smiled at Ted and Ollie. "As you may have heard me telling these two, I will be partaking in some training sessions at my earliest convenience once we get to the hotel in France, and Niles and Clinton here are interested in what I do. You may have noticed that we three here are the most senior amongst our small collective, and I'm an instructor of yoga for the over-sixties."

Trevor exploded into a bout of raucous laughter before managing to disguise it, badly, as a cough.

"A one-handed yoga instructor? Pull the other one!" Ted paused. "Well, I guess you can't."

"One doesn't let one's disabilities hinder them."

"Besides," Norman chipped in, "it's for OAPs, so I doubt it's handstands and cartwheels."

"Namaste," grunted Ollie.

"Too fucking right," Ted said. "Namaste in the fucking pub whilst them lot do that shit." Ted wheezed at his own joke.

"Well," Herbert continued warmly, "although you certainly don't meet the age criteria, you are both most welcome to join our little soirée. After all, yoga is for all ages."

"Nah, mate, you're alright." Ted shook his duty-free bag. "Me and Oliver will be doing some heavy-lifting in the hotel room."

Trevor eyed the bag of booze solemnly. "It'll keep you young, man."

"What, drinking, or pratting around sticking your feet behind your ears?"

"The yoga, man, the yoga. Us three don't touch that stuff."

"Aye, he's right," Norman agreed. "You'd be sooner off chucking that into the Channel."

Ted and Ollie clutched their precious purchases to their hearts.

"You can keep your yoga and we'll keep our Jägermeister." Ted pronounced the word with a hard J.

"Each to their own," Charlotte said, "but us two and Gustav have no qualms about drinking and will be around in the hotel bar if you lads fancy sharing some stories with us."

Juliet and Gustav were gobsmacked.

Ted softened at Charlotte's words. "We might just hold you to that one. In the meantime," he said, fishing out a dark-green bottle from his carrier bag, "Anyone fancy a snifter as we wave bye-bye to Blighty?"

Norman caught Trevor's mournful expression and shared his pain when Ted offered the bottle to the others. He turned to the receding cliffs and everything they had left behind.

FÜHRER: PART ONE

Chapter 28

Boxford Police Station had been on its last legs before the attack that had set Danny Scarborough free.

Most of the seven-storey building had now been stripped of anything of value, ahead of its planned demolition.

The attack that had killed numerous police constables, among them DCI Craig Saunders, saw the place close two weeks ahead of schedule and the reins of law enforcement pass to the bigger, newer station at Sudbury.

DS Grace Brown had been on annual leave but had heard all about the attacks from messaging colleagues whilst she and her girlfriend Lorna were sunning themselves in Ibiza.

Werewolves.

Although it sounded complete and utter bollocks, as if her workmates were all in on some elaborate joke, it wasn't until she saw the grainy images that showed up on the news that she believed there might be something in it.

She didn't believe it was actual werewolves; she wasn't that stupid, and it wasn't long before each and every piece of visual evidence online was meticulously debunked and proven fake.

Zoomed-in photos of a monster in a lift at the local housing estate showed highlighted areas where stitching was apparently evident, and someone had conveniently wiped Boxford Police Station's CCTV.

By the time she arrived back in England, it had all been pinned on a group of OAPs and local thugs.

FÜHRER: PART ONE

It wasn't the first time kids and pensioners had become got mixed up together.

Back in the late noughties, when she'd joined the force, there had been a massive bust-up between a group of old fogies and a couple of drug dealers when the old 'uns decided to up their costs on the prescription drugs they were flogging.

By the sounds of it, this fiasco was a similar thing but on a more serious and deadly scale. She had to admit, though, the werewolf aspect was a cool new twist.

The local degenerates and other vultures had cheered as the Boxford cop shop was demolished, and the town sank into further destitution as the numerous crime scenes closed for refurbishment — or for good.

Even the local hospital was closed for two days when one of the old folk's corpses was stolen.

And then everything was regurgitated when another attack was reported at Boxford's swimming baths, this time with dozens of witnesses and CCTV images being released to the press. But Grace was more ready to believe in a psychopathic cosplayer than an actual living, breathing werewolf.

Grace had never liked the shitty little town anyway, although the coppers who died were pretty good guys. Boxford just seemed like somewhere they stuck all the shit, it was practically one great big council estate with a few shops, at least half of which were boarded up.

Little else was heard about the werewolves and riots aside from the odd family member who didn't have a body to bury and wanted to know why. And bodies were the reason she'd rushed to the Sudbury station.

Someone, claiming to be the corpse that was stolen from the hospital morgue weeks earlier walked into the reception and declared herself alive.

Obviously another hoaxer. But Grace wanted to at least interview her before they wasted resources trying to determine if she was or she wasn't who she said she was.

DS Brown rapped a knuckle on the interview room door and went in.

A slim older lady with long silver hair smiled at her as she moved across the room and took a seat opposite her.

Grace noticed the woman's oversized clothes: a Pink Floyd t-shirt and rolled-up tracksuit bottoms. An outfit far from befitting a lady of her age.

"Hello, I'm DS Grace Brown," she said, offering the woman her best grin.

The woman said her full name and Grace asked if it would be okay to call her Elizabeth.

She said that it was fine.

Before she'd come in, Grace had noticed a man in reception, wearing hippy clothes.

"Is that your son outside?"

"Oh no," Elizabeth said, "that's Jeremy, he's the son of a friend of mine long gone now."

"And did he bring you in?"

"He came with me for support but I'm here under my own steam." Elizabeth sat bolt upright, palms on the table. "I'm not an invalid in body or mind. Just for the record."

DS Brown smiled again. "Okay, Elizabeth. Well, go ahead and tell me why you are here."

Elizabeth nodded. "A few weeks ago, I'm not one hundred percent certain of the date, the younger brother of the supermarket café worker Tony Scarborough, who I must add is a very nice boy, tried to inject my friend Victor Krauss with something, I don't know what. I got in the line of fire, as it were."

Grace consulted her notes and told Elizabeth the exact date.

"Oh lord, was it really that long ago?"

"Yes. And you were held in the mortuary at Boxford hospital, awaiting autopsy, for eight hours before someone stole your body. If you're really who you say you are I'd be more than a little bit interested in hearing how you went from being declared dead, spending hours in a mortuary freezer, to sitting here with me several weeks later."

"It does sound very far-fetched, doesn't it?" Elizabeth said with mild embarrassment.

"Just a wee bit, Elizabeth. Why don't you tell me what you know."

"Victor Krauss was a werewolf, and my friend infected me, herself, and three others with his blood."

"Okay," Grace said, trying not to laugh at the absurdity of her statement. "So, does that mean you're one too? A werewolf?"

"I believe so."

"Tell me about life being a werewolf." Grace couldn't help but patronise her.

Elizabeth ignored her tone and smiled ruefully. "Oh, we noticed the changes immediately. The thing that spread from Victor to us coursed through our decrepit old bodies like a steam train, righting all the wrongs, making us feel fantastic, like we were in our twenties again." She paused and considered her words.

"Victor barricaded us in the village hall, you'll know it was he that paid for its refurbishment, of course, that was so he had somewhere local in case he or his wife needed to change unexpectedly."

"Into werewolves?"

"That's right."

"Sorry to interrupt, but I just need to confirm we're talking half-man, half-wolf horror movie monsters here?"

Elizabeth said, "I never really saw any of us change completely. Victor was able to change the tiniest parts of himself: he changed his arms right in front of us."

"How do you mean, changed his arms?"

Elizabeth recalled them all sitting in Ethel's kitchen, Frankie growling under the table. "They thickened, grew fur, and his hands changed into paws, complete with claws. You could hear the bones and muscles adjusting."

"Okay," Grace said, "going back a bit, you mentioned Victor Krauss's wife. Where was she in all this?"

"Oh, he killed her after she broke out of his cellar and killed a little boy. After all that time, he was somehow careless."

"After all that time?"

"Victor and his wife Gwen got infected at the end of the Second World War. He thought it would repair her mind—she had dementia, you see—but it didn't, just turned her into a monster once a month."

"And she escaped and killed a little boy? Do you know who this little boy was?"

Elizabeth shook her head. "No, I'm afraid I don't."

"Okay, then what?"

"We barricaded ourselves in the village hall to try and resist our first transformations at the full moon."

"Resist your transformations, you say?"

"Yes."

"Why would you want to do that?"

"Oh, I'm sure you've seen enough films to know the tropes, DS Brown. Everybody knows them, they're second only to the vampire in the murky world of horror, aren't they? Well, one thing that comes part and parcel with lycanthropy is an almost miraculous healing ability."

"Apart from dementia?"

"Yes, Victor was frustrated that no matter what he did, it couldn't heal ailments of the mind and the brain."

"So you all wanted this to avoid getting older?"

Elizabeth tutted. "Oh, we didn't want it at all, remember? My friend, Ethel, found out about Victor and his wife, stole samples of his blood and spiked some—" Elizabeth stopped mid-sentence. "I know how this will sound, but it's true. She put the blood in some brownies and gave them to me and my friends, and…" Elizabeth gasped, "…even Frankie ate some."

"Who's Frankie?"

"My dachshund."

Grace snort-laughed. "Oh, come on."

Elizabeth's stare told her she was being deadly serious. "He ran away, I remember now, so it doesn't matter anyway."

"So you wanted this gift for the good bits, not the bad. What happened next, did you change into a werewolf?"

"No, we managed to resist our transformations."

"Of course you did," Grace muttered under her breath. "So tell me what happened at the hospital."

"That is all a blank, I'm afraid. The last thing I remember was being in the café and the young Scarborough boy trying to attack Victor. Then I woke up covered in dirt at the back of the Arboretum and found my way to Jeremy's."

"This was last night?"

"Yes."

"So you were possibly buried for—" Grace added up and told her the number of days between her body going missing and her waking up.

"I understand this is all very hard to believe," Elizabeth snapped. She could tell the DS was humouring her, and no doubt thought considered her doolally. "So run whatever tests you have to, and it'll prove I'm right."

Grace sighed; everything about this whole situation smelt like the rankest of bullshit to her, but then she remembered the recent attack at the swimming pool, which, according to Elizabeth's story coincided with her resurfacing. Plus it was also situated between the park and the Green Man Estate.

She dropped her pen on top of some hastily scribbled notes and wished she was back in Ibiza.

"Okay, Elizabeth, let me have a chat with..."—she checked her notepad—"...Jeremy, and then we'll get someone to sort out some tests to prove you are who you say you are."

FÜHRER: PART ONE

Matthew Cash

PART THREE

FÜHRER: PART ONE

Chapter 29

As someone who often suffered with bouts of insomnia, Bartholomew Tepes found waking up refreshed and vibrant a rarity.

If this is another side effect of Danny's gift, then I'm all up for whatever else it can throw at me.

Gone was the stiffness in the joints, which had endured over half a century of indulgences and excesses. He stretched his palms to the ceiling and felt twenty years younger. "Oh, what a beautiful morning," he half-sang, and thought about arranging another meetup with some twenty-something sad act. It felt like a long time since he'd indulged in the claret, even though it was only but a matter of a day or so.

Surely those boys would have gone to the police by now?

He wondered if he and Cyril had in fact reached a kind of stalemate with the Scarborough brothers, both sides had shit they could slather one another with.

He wouldn't truly rest until the boys' silence was guaranteed.

"Still, we must seize the day," he said to himself and walked through to the bathroom, where he noticed there was less grey in his hair.

From the handle of his bathroom cabinet dangled a plethora of chains and necklaces with a number of different trinkets attached, and it wasn't until he snatched up the crucifix a past conquest had bought him and it stung his palm like a red-hot branding iron that he remembered his and Cyril's discussion the previous day.

Silver.
How to kill a werewolf.

He scrutinised the skin on his hand and watched as it reddened and blistered in the perfect shape of a cross.

"Ha," he said, running cold water over his hand, "and there I was thinking she had been a cheapskate. Jesus, that hurts."

So, silver works.

He picked up the necklace with a wad of toilet paper and flushed it. There was no way he could hope to kill the kid with a piece of jewellery.

Silver, though.

Silver was the age-old weapon of choice when it came to killing or maiming a lot of cryptozoological species, but only when fashioned into something that could penetrate.

If made into swords and knives on its own, it would be expensive and far from hard enough to retain sharpness. And Tepes was hardly in the place to fashion swords and bullets.

The question is, how does the modern werewolf hunter dispatch his victims?

"I'm sure if I could get him into my shed I could figure something out."

He remembered who'd got him the archaic handgun in his briefcase, back in the early nineties.

Cyril.

It hadn't just been illegal pornography that he dealt in.

Tepes went back into the bedroom and saw Cyril's twee note, *Call me when you wake up, C,* like a lover's message. He shuddered at the thought and picked up his phone.

After six rings, Tepes quit waiting for him to answer and hung up.

What the hell is he up to that makes him so busy?

FÜHRER: PART ONE

Chapter 30

"Morning," the old man said cheerfully as he strode into the picnic area.

Cyril was about to leave Bluebell Woods' busier spot and head onto an overgrown, less-used pathway.

Smiling was unnatural for Cyril. It heightened his unconventional looks and made him even more ghastly, so he simply nodded his head, took in the man's black Labrador, and shielded his face beneath the peak of his baseball cap.

"Nice day for it," the man continued, added a chuckle, and did what all socially awkward people dread: he stopped.

Fuck off, Cyril thought, and tried to skirt around him, but the stupid dog blocked his path and panted up at him with its shit-eating grin.

"Oh, don't mind Daisy. She's a good girl, more loyal than any of my wives."

The elderly were always desperate for conversation.

Well, why don't you go back home and fuck the fucking thing? Cyril thought whilst offering the smallest of smiles.

The dog paddled its front paws against Cyril's thighs and left muddy prints on his beige slacks.

"She just wants to say hello," the man said with another laugh, and laughed even harder when he saw the mess Daisy had made of Cyril's trousers. "Oops, sorry about that. Bit of a daft colour to be wearing out here, though, ain't it?"

"It's okay," Cyril grumbled, and lowered one shaky palm to pet the animal's head.

FÜHRER: PART ONE

Bloody thing should be on a lead.

It wasn't that the dog's interested that pissed him off, or that it had dirtied his trousers, it was the expectation of most dog-owners that everyone would love their animal. He wasn't an animal lover, although he didn't hate them either. People were worse than any animal.

Once, out of morbid curiosity, he had researched fatal dog attacks in the UK on Wikipedia after considering getting one to guard the studio, but knowing his luck, the thing would turn on him.

Right, I've said hello to your fucking hound, now let me past.

Cyril tried to skirt around the bouncing dog.

"So, where are you off to?"

"What are you, the police?" Cyril grimaced and offered a nervous laugh.

"Just passing the time of day," the man said, unsure now how to take him. "Seen you a fair bit around these parts."

Cyril felt his blood cool. "Oh?"

"Yeah." He crouched to fasten the dog's lead. "We're always coming down here for a wander."

Shit.

The man eyed the rucksack Cyril had over his shoulder. "I know what you're up to," he said with ominous suspicion. "Don't think I don't. I've seen you at that old place, the old music studio."

Cyril gripped his bag strap in one shaking hand and jammed the other between the small of his back and the rucksack. "Y'wav?" His words wouldn't come properly. His eyelids flickered like mad beneath the peak of his cap. He wet his lips and repeated himself more clearly. "You have?"

"Yeah," the man said, and tapped a finger against the side of his nose. "I can spot *our kind* a mile off."

"Our...k...kind?"

"Don't try and deny it, I've seen the cameras you *tried* to hide, too."

Cyril's heart began to race; there was nothing in his bag to use as a weapon, just food and drink for the boys. The man was a lot older than him, shorter (well, everyone was shorter than him), but his dog was big and would no doubt try to defend its master.

He tried to regulate his breathing and felt the beginning of a panic attack bloom in his chest.

"It's okay," the man said, "your secret's safe with me. I won't tell anyone."

"Y-you won't?" Cyril managed to stammer. He had to get the guy in the studio, try and leave the dog outside. *Although then it might alert someone.*

"We're a dying breed," the man chuckled.

There has to be something in the studio.

Cyril tried to think of something heavy enough to bludgeon him with.

A broom? No, there's a spade.

"Us twitchers are a dying breed," the man continued, "it was my old man who—"

"Twitchers?" Cyril blurted out.

"Mate," the man tapped him playfully on the shoulder, "it's what we're called, innit? I ain't one for them fancy words and I can't even say 'em anyway." He laughed. "What's it called then, *horny theologist* or something?"

"Ornithologist!" Cyril's laughter was genuine, one of both relief and humour. "You think I'm a bird-watcher?"

FÜHRER: PART ONE

"Either that or a serial killer," the man whispered from behind his hand.

Cyril went quiet.

The man attempted to speak, maybe apologise for his crass joke, but Cyril held up a hand to silence him. "Sparrow, blackbird and songthrush," he said, "and, I believe, a green woodpecker."

"Blimey, Charlie, you've even learnt their tunes," the man said, amazed, "I am impressed."

Yeah, I bet you are, seeing as I made all that up. I couldn't tell the difference between an owl's hoot and a pigeon's coo.

Cyril's smile slowly evaporated. "Would you like to see my lookout?" *Either way, he has to go.*

"Of course," the man said, and turned towards the hidden building. "So did you buy the studio for that reason?"

An unusual serenity came over him. "Well, I'll admit it has some sentimental memories, too."

"Oh, were you in the music business?"

"You could say that."

"Were you in a band?"

Cyril found this equally as funny, the prospect that someone as nervous and uncool as he was could have ever been in a band. "No, but I ferried enough of them to and from this place, haha." *What the hell? Haha. I've been hanging around Bartholomew so much I'm starting to talk like him.*

The man's smile took on a sudden sombre shade. "Yeah, I used to come up this way a fair bit. God, must be at least knocking on for fifty years."

Cyril picked his way through the overgrowth. "To the studio?"

"Yeah, my son was in a band. Called themselves *The Buttons*, daft bloody na— "

Cyril didn't hear the rest of his words; he stumbled, his left trouser leg caught on a bramble and he nearly pitched face-first into the bushes.

Samuel Ellington was always fresh in his memory whenever he came here. Everyone remembered their first victim.

Samuel had been bass player in a band that recorded at Bluebell Studios, a band called The Buttons. At the time of the band's conception, they were stumped for a name, and gazed around for inspiration. Samuel had been munching on a bag of Cadbury's Milk Chocolate Buttons, a favourite since he was little, and the band's name was coined.

How the hell can you be one of their dads?

Cyril's maths was never good, but the guy would have to be at least eighty. If he was that old, he was in remarkably good condition.

"Think I remember them," Cyril said as they approached the studio. "The singer had a 'tash like him from Motorhead."

The man cleared something from his throat and mumbled something to his dog.

"Sorry?" Cyril said, unlocking the studio door.

"Ah, nothing, I just remember that bloke being nothing but bad news." He gave an exasperated sigh. "'Twas probably him that made Sammy run off. Bugger died in a motorcycle accident after holding up a post office in 1984. Good bloody riddance, I say."

Cyril was struck dumb and it must have shown on his face as the old man suddenly froze. "What's up with you? Don't tell me you were related to the thieving scallywag."

Cyril shook his head and tried to speak. The old man was his first victim's father.

FÜHRER: PART ONE

"Even if you were, I wouldn't apologise." The man raised his chin in defiance. "He was scum of the earth, that man, and it weren't long after my lad met him that he scarpered."

"Your lad," Cyril managed to get out, "ran away?"

The man's eyes lit up at the interior of the studio. "You've got it nice in here, ain't you? I best leave Daisy outside guarding the place." He ducked back out into the sun and tied Daisy's leash around a tree trunk before he came back inside. "Sorry, what were we on about?"

"Your boy, Sammy," Cyril said, feeling the word on his lips. "Samuel."

"Yeah, he ran away for some reason. 1975, don't know where to, don't know why, but the last he was seen was driving off with some fella in a red car. Broke his mum's heart, made her hit the bottle something hard, I can tell you. It's what killed her in the end."

Shock and revulsion were two alien feelings Cyril had come to acclimatise himself with over the past few days what with Tepes' revelations, monsters and cannibalism, but they still threw themselves at him like newcomers at a bar brawl.

He felt his cold hand rest on his lower jaw as it slackened over this new information. Fate had been dealing some interesting cards recently, and this was one of its best.

Forty-two years peeled away the half-rotten façade around him and he was momentarily back in 1975. The Buttons had finished another rehearsal where they had to waste almost half their allocated time waiting for Gerry Forsyth to finish throwing up so he could lead them in song.

The old man was right.

The frontman was bad news, constantly drunk or high, always hanging around drug dealers and rough, dodgy-looking people, but he did sing well, better than any of the others.

That night, after Cyril had pulled a trailer full of equipment to and from the drummer's garage, he had given Samuel a lift home.

Things had got out of hand once he'd parked up by the woods. After buying them alcohol, the others went out to score more and more potent stuff, but Samuel was the youngest and already suffered the effects of the booze.

He was semi-conscious when Cyril stopped in the lay-by, malleable and compliant but completely out of it.

"You alright, son? Look like you've seen a ghost."

Cyril blinked away the memories and leant against the old reception desk. "Yeah, sorry, I lost my train of thought just then." He reached a long arm behind him and felt for the handle of the spade propped there.

"Comes to us all, son," the old man said, tapping a finger to his temple. "Once you hit fifty, it's all downhill."

"I remember your son, Sammy," Cyril said fondly, "he was the most beautiful boy I had ever seen."

The old man's initial look of surprise soured at the prospect of being in the company of a homosexual.

Cyril watched as he forced the politeness back onto his face.

FÜHRER: PART ONE

The old man knew things were different now, gone were those halcyon days where top-notch comedians could mock disability, race and sexuality on prime-time television and get away with it. You had to answer for that kind of stuff nowadays. "As far as I know, my Sammy wasn't like that. I mean, he had a girlfriend at one point—"

Cyril remembered the sobering look of disgust on Samuel's face when he had woken from his drunken stupor to find Cyril grasping his semi-erect penis.

They have the same eyes.

"No, Samuel wasn't queer," Cyril said quietly, "at least not willingly."

The old man looked confused.

Cyril used that confusion to bring the spade up and around and swung it hard against his face.

A spray of blood and shattered dentures arced through the air as the man dropped to his hands and knees.

Cyril planted a foot on his shoulder and pushed him onto his back.

The old man mewled like a baby. He spat blood.

A red fissure opened above his ear.

His hands hovered feebly, seeking protection.

Cyril kicked them aside and rested the cutting edge of the shovel against the old man's windpipe and pressed hard until he made no more noise.

"I'd bury you with him," Cyril said sadly, "but they put the kids' playground right where he lies in the late-nineties."

Samuel Ellington's was the only grave he remembered the location of.

The old man's hand snapped around the spade handle, his strength surprising Cyril, one last chance for vengeance spurring him on. He tried to speak through his mushed mouth, but Cyril had no desire to hear his final curses. He pushed down on the spade handle and watched as the skin on the old man's throat separated, felt the muscle's resistance and then the sudden erotic ease as the blade sliced through his oesophagus and crunched against bone.

Something shifted in the secured room behind him.

"It's okay, boys," Cyril called over his shoulder, remembering the reason why he had come to the studio. "I'll be in there with you in a mo."

He rested a foot on the spade and finished the job.

FÜHRER: PART ONE

Chapter 31

Suffolk

1990

Andy sat in the cafeteria of St Clements.

After the fateful night at the club, he was admitted to the psychiatric hospital whilst doctors and psychiatrists alike tried to fathom out what to do with him.

The café was busy for a weekday afternoon.

A couple sat saying nothing as they stared into polystyrene foam cups.

A young girl, probably a year or two older than Andy, stood holding the hand of a silent, rocking boy with a wad of newspaper cuttings clutched so close to his face that the dye had left a black smear.

A plump, middle-aged couple sat with a little boy with Down's Syndrome, who pored over a glossy book with the word 'Magic' on the front.

Andy saw a few kids like that come for their appointments, the majority had parents who were old enough to be grandparents, or perhaps some were. He wondered whether late motherhood played a part in their child's condition.

The kid was an outpatient for sure; the inpatients, those who could dress themselves, rarely bothered to don anything other than pyjamas and slippers.

FÜHRER: PART ONE

There wasn't much point unless you were planning on venturing onto the grounds outside.

This kid wore sensible clothing, a mini replica of his father.

Some kids would come for respite visits, some came for temporary stays whilst new medication was trialled or if they became more difficult as they grew up, and some remained when their parents died. Andy felt sorry for those ones the most, he saw the way some of the staff treated them, especially the ones who couldn't respond or speak for themselves.

Most of the innies, as Andy liked to call them, were subdued with either drugs or whatever abuse or mental issue had left them in a near-catatonic state. They were more lively on his ward, though; he was stuck with the schizophrenics and labelled a potential threat but was allowed to wander the public areas and grounds, as long as he was being supervised.

The only things Andy looked forward to were his mum's Saturday afternoon visits. She would bring him sweets, writing materials, and books.

It was a miserable existence and he cried himself to sleep almost every night, but he never once asked to be let out.

Every night he saw her lying on the dancefloor, her beautiful face ruined, the purple lights painting patterns on her soft skin, three slits across her pretty mouth deep and black, The Stone Roses playing slow and distorted like a funeral march.

Ginger.

Despite what he had done to her she still begged his mother to let her visit, but Andy wouldn't allow it, couldn't face her.

As yet he was unmedicated, and they were waiting to see what happened if he had any more attacks.

Multiple personality disorder and schizophrenia were the phrases on the professionals' lips, but no formal diagnosis had been made.

Once again, as he did after an attack he'd had when he was thirteen, he came under the eye of a psychiatrist called Friedrich, an eccentric Austrian. He was the main reason for Andy not being medicated. Friedrich wanted to wait for another attack.

Andy finished the dregs of his lukewarm coffee, letting the sugary mulch at the bottom ooze onto his tongue, and left the table. He smiled at the little magic enthusiast and stopped in front of a pedal bin. He balanced the empty polystyrene cup on his shaved head and put his heel on the bin lever.

"Now you see it," he said, flicking his head back and hearing the cup drop into the bin, "now you don't."

The little boy beamed with what could almost have been religious ecstasy.

Andy flashed an awkward smile at the kid's uneasy looking parents and headed for his appointment.

Doctor Friedrich hadn't changed in seven years. He was still dressed head-to-toe in beige.

He was still tall, old and gaunt and reminded Andy of the old priest in The Exorcist.

"It's good to see you again, Andrew."

Andy slumped into the chair opposite his desk and said nothing.

"I'm sure you don't feel the same," the doctor said lightly. "Now, I've read about the alleged events in the nightclub, but it would be nice to hear your version of events. Would that be okay, do you think?"

Andy shrugged, then nodded.

"Was it the same thing you experienced as a child?"

Andy shook his head. "No. This time around, I was aware it was happening. I felt myself changing into something else."

"Can you tell me what you felt and saw?"

Andy had been forced to relive the scene over and over again through nightmares, flashbacks, and the insistence of numerous doctors. It never became any easier.

"It was like that film," he started, but was pretty sure the old man wasn't a fan of trashy horror films. He continued regardless. "An American Werewolf in London."

"I see," Friedrich said, scribbling in his notes. "Do you remember the first time you saw this film?"

Andy thought he knew where this was going.

"About three years ago. I rented it from the video shop."

"Okay, please carry on."

It had been the most blissful moment in his life, so close to Ginger he could feel the heat from her body and smell her perfume.

"We were dancing, me and Ginger, and this pillock I knew from school came up behind her and grabbed her tits."

"How did that make you feel?"

Andy laughed bitterly. "How the hell do you think it made me feel? I thought I was going to explode, and I guess in a way, I did. I wanted to tear him apart and I turned into a monster." He paused, lowering his wet eyes. "Or at least I thought I did."

"And you say you were aware of your transformation, no blackouts or gaps?"

Andy nodded. "I remember it all."

"And you acted out on your anger knowingly?"

Andy lowered his eyes and gave a barely perceptible nod.

Friedrich began to ask another question but Andy cut him off.

"I lashed out. I-I thought I'd grown claws. I *did* have claws, and Ginger got in the way."

"Ah, Miss Morgan," Friedrich said, scanning his notes. "I understand she has been in contact with your mother several times in order to see you. Her own description of events collaborates with yours, apart from one thing."

"No one else saw me turn into a monster, I know." That was how Andy knew he was nuts.

As a kid, he'd been spared the memory of the attack on the two men. All he remembered was the building tension before.

Spontaneous act of madness, that was what they called it back then.

Friedrich put down his pen and smiled emphatically. "A most unusual development. Tell me Andy, have you heard of clinical lycanthropy?"

Andy laughed. "I've heard of lycanthropy. Are you telling me there's an actual condition?"

"Oh, yes, it's very rare, but there is. There are a few documented cases of people who believed they are—or that they frequently change into—wolves. There are others who think the same about other species: bears, buffalo, even reptiles and birds."

"Why?"

"It's the same as a lot of other psychological disorders and delusions, there doesn't have to be a reason, and of course everything feels very real to the patient. Many of the case studies showed the patients were abused, or suffered a terrible childhood trauma, but I have seen in your notes you say you can't remember any such occurrences."

Andy nodded. "My foster parents have always been there for me. I wasn't even bullied until after the first time."

"As I said, there doesn't have to be a cause," Friedrich said. "There are cases where patients suffering from clinical lycanthropy showed signs of abnormal strength, agility and speed, sometimes needing several people to subdue them. Again, that is nothing that can't be explained."

Andy was sure the doctor was holding something back.

"What concerns me is this. When you were arrested, your general practitioner contacted me, your medical records will have an account about the talks we had when you were thirteen, so I took the liberty of examining Miss Morgan as her wounds were being treated."

"You did what? You saw what I did?"

Friedrich nodded. "Yes, and I saw the marks on her face—"

"What about them?" Andy cut in. He didn't know if he could handle any more. "Oh, Christ, they didn't get infected, did they?"

"They healed fine, with minimum scarring," Friedrich insisted. "However, what I found the most alarming were the injuries themselves; they resembled claw-marks. No weapons were found on the night, and it would be difficult to imagine what could cause such injuries. They appeared to be exactly what you said they were. Claw-marks. But how? That's the conundrum. Your hands were examined after the attack and if you had done such a thing with your own fingernails, there's no way such deep lacerations wouldn't damage them. They were made by three claws with a similar spacing to your fingertips."

"I was searched. I didn't have a weapon. Why would I—"

Friedrich waved his words away. "No, you possibly misunderstand my implications: I believe you really grew wolf claws."

FÜHRER: PART ONE

Chapter 32

Suffolk

1990

Three weeks had passed since Friedrich had ended Andy's appointment with that insane cliffhanger.

I believe you really grew wolf claws.

The idea was absurd and made Andy instantly doubt the old doctor's integrity.

Friedrich added that he had a theory but wanted to witness one of Andy's attacks firsthand before sharing his thoughts on the matter.

Andy continued to refuse the doctor's attempts to instigate an attack, and as far as Andy was concerned, he would just have to carry on waiting and theorising.

Friedrich didn't have to wait too long.

Yet another appointment arose where Andy would talk about his childhood, whether there were any hidden aspects of life with his foster parents that he kept under lock and key, any possible events that may have led to a fracturing of the mind.

The corridor outside Friedrich's office was suspiciously quiet. It was usually the main thoroughfare for patients and relatives to venture to the secluded garden at the rear. When Andy was halfway to Friedrich's office, he heard someone quickly approaching from behind.

He turned: there was no mistaking Ian Bragg. Andy recognised him straight away.

Bragg was an ape of a man who looked like someone had bred a white-van driver with a bulldog. Thick-set, bald, and covered in crude tattoos of big-breasted mermaids, England flags, and weaponry.

Bragg was a schizophrenic who had put four men in hospital after a football match, one paralysed from the neck down.

Andy only ever saw him sleepily pacing back and forth in the company of two equally heavy-set male nurses. Just the sight of Bragg wandering around alone worried him and there was no sign of his usual sedated state, the usual dragging feet and slurred words. Bragg was alert, possibly even ready for something to happen. When he locked eyes on Andy there was a spark, a recognition, despite Andy never having spoken to the man before.

He charged at him like an angry rhino.

Andy ran the last few steps to Friedrich's door and snatched at the door handle, crying out when he found it to be locked. He hammered his fists against the wood and shrieked for the doctor to open it.

There was no answer.

The shrink had set this up.

Andy turned, raising his palms in a placatory manner, but all twenty stones of Ian Bragg slammed into him and knocked him to the floor.

As they landed, one of Bragg's knees went into Andy's stomach and the air whooshed from his lungs.

Bragg grabbed a fistful of Andy's t-shirt, lifted him up and bashed him back down onto the floor, his head striking the tiles.

Black dots and stars danced in his vision as Bragg huffed stale breath into his face. "Where is it?" Bragg hissed, spraying Andy with spit. "Where the fuck is it? What have you done with it?"

Andy tried to push against the man's chest but moving him was impossible. "I don't know what you're on about."

Bragg grit his teeth in rage. "You've got it. They told me you've got it. If you've been playing with yourself and looking at it, I'll rip it off and make you fucking eat it."

"I haven't—" Andy managed to get out before Bragg clamped a hand around his throat and squeezed the life out of any further opportunities to speak.

"They told me." Bragg released his other hand and tapped his temple. "Special ops. Friedrich, they speak to him too, that's how I know I ain't mad."

Friedrich.

Andy knew that old bastard was behind this.

Bragg hauled him to his feet and thrust him into the nearest wall. "Friedrich said you'd deny it. That you're a filthy little pervert who likes wanking over pictures of old ladies."

Andy fought to speak against the hand choking him but nothing would come out.

Bragg drove his fist into Andy's solar plexus, and he fell heavily to the floor, where Bragg drove his foot into his ribs.

Andy coiled into the foetal position in time for Bragg to kick him in the kidneys and straighten him back up.

One of his filthy size twelves pressed on Andy's windpipe and the spots and stars in front of his eyes melded together to form the creeping dark ivy of unconsciousness.

As the black cloud threatened to blot out the world, Friedrich's door opened and Andy felt the weight of Bragg being torn off him and saw him sliding across the floor on his backside.

Friedrich crouched between them. "Ian, stop. I'm wrong. I was wrong. Special ops lied. Your mum's photo fell down beside your bed. Quickly go and check."

Bragg stared at the doctor in wild fear and scrabbled away quickly on his hands and knees.

"I could've been killed," Andy shrieked. "Just because you wanted to witness one of my attacks." He got up and scowled at the doctor. "I can't believe what you've done. I'm going to...I'm going to—"

Andy felt something tear across his stomach, fire pulsing through his body. He doubled over.

"It's happening, isn't it?" Friedrich said as Andy roared with apparent agony.

Andy had no control over his body but was still aware of the ease in which the old doctor had scooped him up and half-thrown him into his office.

Once inside, Friedrich pinned him against the door. "Are you still aware? Can you control it at all?"

There was no way Andy could talk through the pain. His shrieks reached a new crescendo, the sockets of his shoulders dislodged, and his thin arms ran with transforming muscle.

Friedrich stared at the wonder of it all.

Andy's eyeballs peeled apart and reformed and the fracturing and realignment of his skull swamped everything else out. Temporarily blinded, he lashed out with changing limbs and threw Friedrich across the room.

Andy could see again, the doctor hunched feebly on the floor behind his swept-clean desk. He appeared more excited, rather than frightened.

Andy remembered the damage this thing had to Ginger and miraculously felt some control over this new condition. His mouth was overcrowded with his new sharp teeth and his transformed vocal cords weren't capable of speech. He growled a warning at Friedrich and held up a paw, claws splayed, to keep the doctor at bay.

They stayed that way for three minutes, silent apart from the sound of Andy's ragged breathing, then Andy began the equally painful process of changing back.

"Remarkable," Friedrich stated once Andy had reverted back to his usual self.

"Happy now?" Andy sneered, barely able to contain his anger.

Friedrich straightened behind his desk and scribbled in a notebook.

"That's right, you go on making your fucking notes."

"You seemed to be in a lot of pain. As if you could actually feel your body transitioning from one form to the other."

Andy spun around and yanked the door handle.

"Oh, it's on automatic lock, I'm afraid."

"You can't keep me in here. Let me out, now!"

"Andy," Friedrich said, finally looking up from his notes, "please sit down. I have a proposal."

FÜHRER: PART ONE

Andy pressed his head against the wood and dug his fingernails into his palms. "I have no interest in anything you have to propose."

"Sit down!" Friedrich shouted, his accent pronounced, heightening the authority in his voice.

Like a sulking teenager, Andy reluctantly sat at the desk.

After a moment, he spoke. "The pain was excruciating. I could see and feel myself change."

"And yet none of your clothing appears to have been destroyed," Friedrich said, casting his eye over Andy's tracksuit. "Although I believe your temperature went up several degrees."

"Look," Andy spat, "I know it's all in my fucking head, don't I? But it doesn't stop it feeling real to me, does it?"

"Oh, it's real, alright. Not only real to you but there was a considerable amount of change from my perspective too."

Andy showed interest.

"As I said, your temperature rose, your skin grew clammy, your pulse quickened, and your pupils dilated." Friedrich dropped his pen to the desk. "And, most importantly, your strength increased at an almost supernatural rate."

"How the hell do you know all these things?"

Friedrich smiled. "I'm a doctor. I observe. Plus, you literally threw me across the room."

"But how can I have actually gained strength?"

"Oh, come on," Friedrich said, "every human is capable of seemingly superhuman feats of strength and heightened ability when in danger, it's called adrenaline." He paused and stared once more at his notes. "Tell me, did you ever watch, or read *The Incredible Hulk*?"

"You don't have to patronise me. I read, I know exactly what adrenaline is."

"I've studied a few cases of clinical lycanthropy and I'm amazed at what one's body is capable of at times. I merely mentioned The Hulk—*Bruce Banner* as a similarity. I don't believe you're going to change into a green giant." Friedrich laughed at his own joke.

Andy didn't.

He continued. "I don't want to drug you. I don't want to stop it. I want to know how we can control it."

Andy laughed. "How? How the hell can I control this without the same sort of sedatives you give Ian Bragg?" He paused, then added scornfully, "*Usually.*"

"Mentally. I want you to be able to tap into this at will, control it, harness it, and use it. See it as a self-defence mechanism."

"What the hell?" Andy said, incredulous. "It sounds like you want to turn me into a fucking superhero."

To his surprise, Friedrich nodded. "That's precisely what I want to do."

"You're joking? What? Why?"

Friedrich stared off into space as if he were about to divulge top-secret information.

"In case you have to defend yourself..." his voice petered out as if he was suddenly unsure, "...against a *real* lycanthrope."

Andy's jaw dropped.

The doctor was being serious.

"What I'm about to tell you is between the two of us. It doesn't really matter if you tell anyone as I'll deny it and, once you've heard what I've got to say, I'm sure you'll understand how believable people will

FÜHRER: PART ONE

think it is, especially coming from a psychiatric patient." The doctor's cold eyes burned into Andy's. "There are people who can change themselves into wolves. Real lycans exist."

Chapter 33

Suffolk

1990

It took several appointments for Andy to realise Friedrich was serious and therefore completely insane.

He believed in werewolves, had a theory that a lot of mental health conditions originated from the same source, that the insane were the results of millions of years of lycanthropic breeding with humans.

It was ridiculous, but the mental exercises Friedrich had given him helped him to relax, and it was a novel approach to embrace this thing than batter it into submission with medication.

On the fourth appointment after Friedrich had told him werewolves existed, he told Andy he had a special visitor.

Andy's heart somersaulted when the old doctor called to whoever it was outside his office door.

He hadn't seen her since that night at Hollywood's.

Ginger's hair had grown since he'd last seen her; an auburn fringe hid her face for a second but he recognised her slender physique.

He recoiled, out of shock rather than horror, and felt the beast inside him lurch in his stomach.

FÜHRER: PART ONE

Since Friedrich had taught him how to tap into his other side, it seemed a lot closer to the surface.

"Hello, Andy," Ginger said, brushing the hair from her face. Three pale pink slashes ran from her left cheek to the corner of her mouth, a disfigurement he had caused.

Guilt overwhelmed him.

Nothing would come out other than loud wet sobs at what he had done to her beautiful face.

She wrapped her arms around him.

"It's okay," she said through her own tears. "I kind of like the scars, they make me look a lot tougher than I actually am." She pressed his hand against her mouth, making him touch the raised scar tissue.

He tried to pull away, but she held fast.

"We have something special. I don't want to lose you."

Her words were everything he'd ever wanted to hear, but now, after everything he had done, he didn't know what to think. "I'm fucked up. I hurt you. I'm dangerous."

"You're not fucked up, there's just something different about you. Something he says can be controlled."

Andy glared at Friedrich. "How dare you get her involved."

"I'm already involved," Ginger said softly.

"Tell him about the nightclub," Friedrich said, glancing down at his notes.

Ginger made Andy sit down. She held his hands.

"Before Howard and the others beat the crap out of you, you were amazing, like Spider-Man or something. At one point, you threw Howard across the dancefloor like he weighed nothing. You cracked three of his ribs. That was why his friends, and several others, got involved and even they took a beating trying to bring you down. It wasn't until you saw me and what you'd done,"—she saw Andy's hurt resurface—"*accidentally*, that you seemed to give up and let them batter you."

Andy covered his face.

"Don't you see, if you were to control this, it needn't be a bad thing. It could be an advantage."

"Like I'm some kind of bloody superhero? You're starting to sound like him."

"Why the hell not? Wouldn't it be better to be able to help people than hurt them?"

"Yeah," he said. "But surely you don't believe in all this werewolf claptrap?"

Ginger grinned sheepishly. "Yeah, that part is a lot to swallow, a bit far-fetched for my liking."

"Told you," Andy said.

"Fine," Friedrich said, throwing down his pen. "You want proof?"

Both Andy and Ginger nodded.

"Tomorrow."

"Tomorrow?" Andy asked.

"Tomorrow, we're going on a day trip."

Andy and Ginger exchanged a worried look.

"Where to?" Andy queried.

"Not that far." Friedrich slammed his notebook shut.

FÜHRER: PART ONE

Chapter 34

Suffolk

1990

Friedrich drove his little red Fiat like a typical old-aged pensioner: slowly, but for Andy it felt good to be outside of *St Clement's*, especially with Ginger by his side. She had spent a few hours in his company the previous day, filling him in on the things he had missed out on and what she had been doing since the incident at the nightclub. Ginger was off college for several weeks after her attack whilst the stitches in her face healed.

Andy couldn't believe Ginger's devotion after what he had done, how Friedrich had managed to get her involved in whatever this was, and how she appeared to buy into all this werewolf nonsense.

The Fiat protested as Friedrich drove it up a ludicrously steep hill towards five tall apartment blocks which looked ominous, giants waiting to trample everything. A few battered bangers were parked in the car parks. Strangely, in the centre of the estate grounds, sat four semi-detached Victorian houses, leftovers from a bygone era.

"Where are we?" Andy asked but received no answer.

FÜHRER: PART ONE

Friedrich stopped in front of the tower blocks. Andy squinted through the windshield at the name plaque and frowned. "Jack-in-the-Green?"

Ginger smirked. "That's so cool. Don't tell me you haven't heard of *Jack-in-the-Green*?"

Andy saw Friedrich smile at Ginger in the rearview mirror. "Is he a relative of *The Incredible Hulk* or *The Jolly Green Giant*?"

Ginger elbowed him in the ribs and sniggered. "Actually, you're not far off with *The Jolly Green Giant*, as he has to be a modernization of the Green Man. Jack is an embodiment of a pre-Christian fertility ritual."

"This whole area is steeped in rich folklore, Andy," Friedrich said. "Boxford is built between two hills, one on the eastern side and one on the west. If you look out of the back window, you will be able to see the spires of St Matthew's church on the western hill."

They turned and located the impressive grey building half a mile away. Andy thought he was giving away a lot of information about the place, especially if he wanted to keep its identity secret, but aside from the signage on the tower blocks they hadn't seen anything else to name the place and the other things Friedrich said could all be made up to mislead.

"It is said that when the foundations for the first church were laid here, the original placement was going to be on this hill, but every time they staked the markers out for the digging to begin, they were moved overnight, as if by magic." Friedrich grinned at them with the enthusiasm of all good storytellers. "Superstitious folk believed there to be a fairy ring here, something hallowed by pagan rituals long preceding the God whose church was to be built, and they were scared of building on what may have been cursed land." Friedrich laughed. "So they built the church over there."

"And they thought it was okay to build flats here?" Andy said with mock shock.

Friedrich nodded. "Before the flats were here, this area was the poorest part of the town, the cheapest houses available, old workhouses and slums, factories for leather and brass."

Andy surveyed the surrounding area, the dilapidated car ruins, litter blowing across grass speckled with dogshit. "Maybe the land is cursed, then," Andy offered, thinking the tower blocks had taken on a more foreboding aspect.

Ginger giggled. "Imagine if the flats were built on integral parts of the fairy ring and that the fairies lived on the energy of the people inside, like some kind of psychological prayer wheel."

Andy appeared horrified.

Friedrich laughed. "I can see why you like young Tracey, Andy."

"Ginger," she corrected.

Friedrich nodded as he turned the ignition off and got out of the car. "Well, let's hope you don't change your hair colour."

"So why have you brought us here?" Andy said, following Ginger out of the vehicle.

She pressed herself against him, gave a maliciously cheeky smile, and whispered, "He reckons he's caught a werewolf."

The close proximity to her sent Andy's heart racing but seeing that constant reminder of what he had done to her on her face stopped him from getting too hot under the collar.

FÜHRER: PART ONE

Friedrich walked up a slope and used a key fob to open the main entrance of the Jack-in-the-Green flats.

"Do you live here?" Andy was surprised. "I thought doctors had massive houses."

Friedrich held the door open for them. "Let's just say it's a holiday home."

Andy hesitated and Ginger slipped past him. He reached out and took hold of her arm, preventing her from entering.

"I'll wait inside," Friedrich sighed, and left them.

"How do we know he's not a serial killer?" Andy asked. "Luring innocent kids in, and..." he mimed slitting his own throat.

Ginger smiled crookedly. "Yeah, that's why I brought this with me." She took something from her pocket, a small, black-handled switchblade.

Andy's eyes widened. "Where the hell did you get that?"

"One of my mates gave it to me after hearing about me being attacked," she said, grimacing at his reaction and quickly adding, "not by you, by the twat who groped me."

Andy nodded grimly.

"Trust me?" Ginger's Arctic eyes, equally capable of freezing and melting, bore into him.

"Of course, it's whether you trust me, and him that bothers me."

She gripped his hand tightly. "Come on."

Inside, Friedrich waited at the foot of the stairwell.

"Is the lift not working?" Andy asked.

"We only have to go up one flight."

They followed the old doctor up the steps and came to a small landing, big enough for the entrances to two apartments. One door was painted sky-blue and the other red. Friedrich took out a bunch of keys, unlocked the red door, and went inside, making no attempt to force them in or lock the door behind them. They entered a narrow, dimly-lit hallway, which was empty aside from a telephone cabinet with a black ring dial telephone. Friedrich walked straight towards a door at the end of the hallway and opened it.

As the contents of the room came into view, Andy felt the bottom drop out of his world.

An emaciated woman in a hospital smock hung by her arms from a fixture in the ceiling.

Andy instinctively turned to run but heard Ginger let out a frightened yelp.

Friedrich's forearm was wrapped around her shoulders, confirming everything Andy had suspected.

"Please don't be alarmed," Friedrich said, quickly holding Ginger in place. "No one is going to get hurt."

"You're crazier than I am." Andy growled at him.

Behind Friedrich, the woman, who didn't have any visible signs of trauma, raised her head. "Help me, help me please."

Friedrich backed into the room with Ginger in tow. "Just give me a chance to explain. This woman is infected with lycanthropy. She's a werewolf."

"You're delusional," he spat, livid this man had spent months teaching him to train himself when he obviously couldn't contain his own lunacy. Ginger's hand slowly inched towards her pocket but Friedrich's reaction was quicker. He snatched the switchblade from her grasp. "Ah, just the thing," he said, flicked the button, and plunged the knife into the woman's stomach.

All Andy's instincts screamed *run!* but there was no way he was letting Ginger down again. His guts exploded and he fought the beast inside him, concentrating on his awareness like the psychopath in front of him had taught him.

Friedrich's methods weren't always successful. He'd endured one or two outbursts which were out of his control, and he wasn't surprised to hear the room reverberate with a hideous animal growl, but soon realised it wasn't coming from him.

The woman was changing. She gyrated against the bonds and her skin discoloured as waves of dark grey fur covered it.

Ginger slipped free of Friedrich and ran into Andy's arms. When she faced the woman, she screamed.

The crackling and reshaping of the woman's bones lessened as she reached her fully changed form.

Friedrich pulled the knife from her abdomen, retracted the blade after wiping it clean on her coarse fur, and handed it back to Ginger. "As I said: Lycans are real."

They stared at the captured beast as it thrashed against the restraints, a thing both hideous and beautiful.

Andy saw fear in its eyes as well as intense hatred. "What..." he started but had no idea what he was going to say.

"What are you going to do to her?" Ginger finished.

"I want to learn from her," Friedrich said. "I have been doing so. I want to cure her. Don't worry, she's heavily drugged, her transformation won't last long."

The psychiatrist studied the creature. "Ah, you see, it's already beginning to reverse."

The creature's body rippled and twisted and made the same sickening sounds as before, as it turned back into an exhausted woman.

"What are you going to do with her?" Andy said, repeating the question Ginger had asked.

The woman flopped lifelessly against her ties.

"Learn."

"And what does this have to do with me? With us?"

"I want to help you use this ability of yours."

"Why?"

"As a fail-safe."

"A fail-safe for what?"

"In case she ever gets free and makes more like her."

FÜHRER: PART ONE

Chapter 35

When they cracked open the door to the flat, they were blasted by an array of odours. Danny was more receptive than Tony, it made his eyes instantly water. "T, stop. This place smells wrong, man."

"It's coz it hasn't been opened for years, that's all."

Beneath the musty smell of age and mould there was animal filth, and something meaty and sweet.

Danny's stomach flipped as he followed Tony into the darkness.

The flats on the Green Man Estate were all laid out the same way, an L-shaped hallway with two bedrooms to the left, or right, depending on whether the flat was front or rear-facing.

Most of the apartments had skylights above the doors, but a few people had painted over them or they'd been broken and replaced with plywood, a cheaper alternative.

The darkness in number seven's hallway was like a grave, the skylights had been painted over with thick black gloss.

Tony swung his bag around and felt for his keys, where there was a Maglite keyring attached. "I take it you can't see in the dark?"

Danny huffed against his neck. "I could when I turned into that thing, but I can't now."

"Good job I have this, then." Tony switched on the torch on and lit up a mountain of junk mail heaped against the opposite wall. He crouched and picked a takeaway flyer from the top of the pile.

FÜHRER: PART ONE

"Whoa," Tony said, showing Danny the leaflet. "This place has been sealed up for yonks, mate. Look." He pointed at the telephone number of the takeaway.

"What's the matter wi— They've got no ones."

"Exactly." Tony dropped the menu and proceeded to educate his brother on his brief knowledge of British telephone numbers. "When I was little, Mum had an address book with everyone's phone numbers in it and I remembered she'd added ones in red ink after the zeros in the area codes. Apparently they changed in 1995."

"You are such a fucking nerd," Danny winced.

Tony pressed a light switch to see if there was power. He'd read a story about a lady in London who was found in her flat with her television and heating still on and undelivered Christmas presents at her side. She had been dead for three years. His initial reaction, after how tragic the story was, had been confusion over the cost of the running amenities. How come the bills were still being paid?

Unsurprisingly, there was no electricity running to number seven.

Tony turned, moved Danny aside, and shone the torch at the door. Two heavy bolts sat at the top and the bottom. "That'll save us trying to relock the door," he said, sliding them across.

"Please, T, there's something dead in here."

"Well, we're in now," Tony said, "it's probably a fridge freezer full of rotten food."

"Or body parts."

"Yeah, cheers for that, Jeffrey Dahmer." Tony punched Danny in the shoulder. "Come on Scoob, let's investigate."

Danny scoffed. "Yeah, I'm definitely the mutt, aren't I? Who are you, Daphne or Velma?"

"I'm Fred. Good-looking blonde."

"Not anymore."

Tony remembered dyeing his hair back to its natural colour. "I'm still blonde on the inside."

"I wish it was just Scooby Doo on my insides."

"Come on."

The hallway was empty aside from the shattered remnants of a wooden telephone stand. The flooring was bare, black vinyl tiles that had been installed by the council, and a drift of dust, dirt and detritus, through which feet had worn a track up the hallway to each of the doors.

"Someone's been here," Danny said.

"Not for a while, though."

Tony timidly touched the door handle of what he knew to be the larger of the two bedrooms, the metal icy against his palm.

He took a deep breath and pushed it open.

Daylight seeped into the room through net curtains that were black with filth and mould.

A wooden double-bed frame, most of the slats broken, took up a lot of the space, along with a stack of bin bags, grey with dust, which sat in the body of a half-collapsed white wardrobe. Clothing littered an off-pink carpet which was black with rot, no doubt from the mildew that speckled the ceiling and the walls.

"Nothing much in here," Tony said, not stepping into the room.

They moved up the hallway, past the dilapidated telephone stand, to the last bedroom.

FÜHRER: PART ONE

"Holy shit," Tony exclaimed when he opened the door and saw an old hospital bed, a metal table and enough knives, saws, syringes and other apparatus to create a makeshift operating theatre. "Fuck."

Tony considered how he'd felt about the place when he was growing up, how his imagination had deemed it mysterious and sinister, but he'd never believed it would be something like this.

Danny clutched at his arm. "T, let's go. We shouldn't be here."

Danny's words went unnoticed; Tony was transfixed on the dried blood that stained the rubber mattress and which had soaked into the carpet.

Several medical posters covered the walls: detailed diagrams of the human anatomy, the nervous system, and blown-up pictures of the brain and eyeball.

"This is some fucking serial killer shit, T, we need to go."

"Not yet."

Tony pointed at a stack of notebooks on the metal table. "Have a look through them. Stay here. I've got to check the rest of the place."

Tony knew Danny was right, there really was something dead in the place, and it was in the living room. Again, curiosity got the better of him.

How could someone get away with this kind of stuff in a tower block?

Wouldn't the neighbours notice?

He thought back to that lonely woman in London and how the neighbouring tenants had put the smell of her decomposition down to the bins.

Yeah, cheers for that, Jeffrey Dahmer.

Didn't that guy run his reign of terror in a similar place?

Tony rested against the living room door and covered his mouth and nose with his sleeve. In films and real-life alike, crime scene investigators carried tubs of vapour rub for this very thing.

He wondered how many bodies he would find and had visions of dismembered parts pickling in barrels.

Danny knew the handwriting: a spidery scrawl with the odd German word in capitals, indecipherable to everyone but the author.

Anatomical drawings of various parts of the body were depicted in pencil and ink, copied with precise artistic detail.

He knew who these belonged to, he had seen something similar before.

Tony's sudden shriek made him drop the notebooks to the floor.

Tony rushed from the room, hands over his mouth, amidst a swarm of fat flies. Danny saw something black through the cloud suspended above the living room floor.

Tony burst into a closet-sized room housing the toilet and puked up everything he had in him.

"Kitchen," he spluttered, "open a fucking window."

The kitchen was dirty, but tidy.

Ancient appliances sat alongside outdated units and furniture.

A forest of brown desiccation blocked the window, houseplants left to fend for themselves with nothing but sunlight and condensation. Danny remembered looking at their skeletal fingers when he played down below.

He pushed through the jungle, coughing as it all disintegrated at his touch, and pried open the window. In his peripheral vision, through a greasy serving hatch, he saw the shape in the living room.

He slid the glass aside to allow air into the stinking room and caught a fleeting glimpse of a blackened foot resting against a threadbare sofa cushion.

Chapter 36

With an empty stomach, Tony faced the thing in the living room.

Human.

He could tell it was a woman by the breasts and the straggly strands of long hair which clung to a virtually bald scalp.

She hung by wires attached to her wrists and ankles and fastened to countersunk screws in the corners of the room.

Her skin was the darkest of greens, almost black with decay, flies crawling over every inch of her, feeding and tending to the millions that wriggled in every orifice.

Her head hung, facing a massive, writhing patch of collected body evacuations, maggots dripped from her open mouth.

"Oh my God," Tony cried, suddenly overwhelmed with sadness rather than disgust at how much this woman must have suffered. "Who did this to you?"

"Krauss."

Tony spun; he hadn't heard Danny enter the room. "What? How do you know?"

Danny pointed into the hallway. "I found more notebooks like I did in his cellar. More werewolf shit."

Tony moved from the putrid seething thing, swatting flies from his face. "Show me."

Danny's jaw dropped.

Tony saw the shadow of the corpse on the wall, gently swaying.

FÜHRER: PART ONE

The woman convulsed as if a live current ran through her.

She turned her face in their direction, and maggots scattered the floor.

Her eyes were putrid, fly-blown messes of yellow rot, her mouth a black cave of necrotic flesh where tiny white things wriggled like stalactites. Her breath, ice-cold, came out in liquid, chest-heaving expulsions.

Pus the colour and texture of stewed apples seeped from a split in her stomach.

"How the fuck is that still alive?" Danny said, cowering behind Tony.

Tony had read about how sometimes corpses moved; the process of decomposition was never the same and depended on a lot of things.

It was impossible to believe the person was still alive, despite the signs, with the creatures infesting her, but her mouth snapped open.

"Is she trying to speak?" Danny asked, expecting his big brother to have all the answers as usual.

"Can you hear me?" Tony asked.

"Mate, she's a fucking zombie," Danny croaked. "First werewolves and now zombies. Fuck me."

"If this has something to do with Victor, then nothing would surprise me."

"What the fuck do we do?" Danny whined, staggering back. "Don't you dare cut her down."

Her head snapped around so fast the taut, swollen skin on her neck split and exposed the bones of her neck.

"We just need to go. Now that we've opened the windows, the smell will alert someone. It's not our problem." Tony walked away. "Bring those notebooks."

"Where are we going to go?"

"Fuck knows, but we can't stay here."

They made to leave the stinking, buzzing room but a low moan came from the corpse.

It sounded like every zombie from every film, combined with the heartache of a thousand grieving mothers.

"We can't leave her like this," said Tony.

"What do we do?"

"I don't know, Danny. I guess we have to put her out of her misery."

"I can't do it."

"No, you just kill people in wolf-form!" Tony pushed past him angrily.

The guilt from what Tony had said derailed him; his brother had done so many horrible things, all because of him.

When will this end?

Danny stared at the animated corpse, noticing more and more gross little details about her.

An expanse of pale-green skin across her left hip pulsated with a squirming, spaghetti-like mass.

She was rotting, being eaten alive, and the pain in her death-rattle moan suggested she could feel every single thing, too.

"Please," Danny said, thinking about the people he'd killed at the swimming pool. "We're going to end this. Put you out of your pain. I don't know if you can understand me, but I promise you we'll stop this."

Her perpetual groan coalesced into something resembling coherence, as though she was trying to force words over her maggot-infested tongue stump.

FÜHRER: PART ONE

Danny leant in, ignoring the flies, the stench and the putrefaction, telling himself over and over again that this was a person, a woman, and she deserved to be heard.

Her pus-slickened, split lips pursed and her voice was like that of something which had spent its entire life in a sewer. "Aaaa—"

Thinking if these were her last words they could be vital, Danny pressed closer.

A thick, gushing torrent of liquid black rot exploded from her gullet and sprayed into Danny's mouth.

He recoiled, retching, and let out a geyser of his own rancid filth, which crawled with corpse-flies and maggots.

Tony ran into the room and brought something down on the woman's head with a loud, wet crunch.

Danny, hunched over, saw Tony wielding a steak mallet, the end dripping with congealed blood and brain matter.

Something wriggled across his tongue and he vomited again.

"What the hell did you do, Danny?" Tony said, gagging, "kiss her?"

Danny heaved again, his throat raw, when he looked inside her caved-in skull.

"At least she's at peace now," Tony said, turning from yet another corpse.

"Oh my God." Danny pointed.

Something moved inside the cavity, something attached to her brain.

Black tentacles, fine threads like fibre optic cables, moved and blossomed from the skull opening, sensing the air around them.

Tony screamed and out came the rage of all the past weeks' traumas.

He swung the hammer again and again and again, pummelling the cadaver's head and the alien thing inside until there was nothing left.

FÜHRER: PART ONE

Chapter 37

Cyril leant across the old reception desk with a painful sigh, unscrewed the lids on two small bottles of mineral water, and took a strip of triazolam from his trouser pocket. As he crushed half a dozen of the tablets he said a mental prayer to Jeffery Dahmer; triazolam was the Milwaukee Cannibal's sedative of choice to incapacitate his victims..

One good thing about not visiting his boys since the fiasco the day before was that they would be starving and thirsty. He pulled a couple of half-melted Mars bars from his coat.

The reek of their evacuations hit him as soon as he opened the door.

Both boys lay huddled together, eyes swollen red from endless crying.

Forgot to bring the cleaning stuff.

Cyril cursed himself for not having thought that far ahead, but it was nothing a trip to the nearest supermarket wouldn't solve.

The batteries in the little plastic lantern were weakening; the orange light flickered on and off.

"Wakey wakey, hands off Snakey," Cyril called with a nervous giggle.

Adam opened his eyes and sat up slowly. "Taylor's not well."

Cyril stepped closer; the smaller of the boys, his Fiver, was groggy and pale.

Cyril kicked through the detritus on the floor, every scrap of food gone, regardless of their earlier protests.

FÜHRER: PART ONE

"Probably dehydrated," he said to himself, moving empty water bottles with his toe. "Good job I've got you some water."

Cyril stooped, picked up one of the beanbags to sit on, and let go of it instantly, disgusted. It was sodden and stank of piss. Without thinking, he wiped his hands on his trousers, then swore at how stupid an idea that had been. He caught Adam's quiet snigger. "Oh, you think that's funny?"

Adam nodded, his face screwing up with the same bravado he'd found the day before. He hawked up a mouthful of phlegm and spat it on Cyril's loafers.

"Disrespectful little—" Cyril started, before forcing his anger back down. "Oh, what's the point?" He threw the water bottles and Mars bars at Adam's feet. "Here."

Adam snatched up one of the bottles, went to unscrew the cap but stopped, suspicious. "You've opened it."

"I ain't buying any more water for you pair of ungrateful little urchins," Cyril said, revelling in the boy's sudden horror.

"W-why?" Adam stammered.

Cyril did his best to fake sad sincerity, staring at the saliva on his shoes like a scalded schoolboy. "Letting you go, aren't I?"

The boy's suspicion doubled and Cyril dropped his face into his hands and turned his acting skills up to eleven. "I just can't do this anymore. I'm so sorry for keeping you here."

Adam's eyes glowed with hope but there was still an underlying amount of doubt there. He unfastened the water bottle and took the tiniest of sips. Deciding it tasted alright, he drank the rest greedily and reached for the Mars bars.

Taylor slowly propped himself up on his elbows.

"He says he's letting us go," Adam said, unable to keep the excitement from his voice.

Taylor shivered and glared. "And you believe him?"

Cyril stood and walked away.

"Wait!" Adam called, a palpable fear in his voice. "You said you were going to let us go."

"I am," Cyril said over his shoulder. "I'm just going to bring my car closer so you don't have to walk so far. I'll take you to the police station in town." With that, he carried on, leaving them to the rustle of chocolate bar wrappers and conspiratorial whispers, and, as if the man had psychic powers alongside his regenerative abilities, his phone bleated. *Tepes.*

Cyril pulled out his phone out and smirked at the picture of Christopher Lee's Dracula, which stared up at him whilst the theme tune by James Bernard echoed throughout the studio.

Since their friendship had escalated, he thought it would be an amusing touch.

He hit answer and pressed the phone to his ear but before he had a chance to speak, Taylor screamed out for help.

Cyril recoiled, smothered the phone against his chest, scowled at the boy and closed the soundproofed studio door.

"What was that?" Tepes demanded.

"Just the telly," Cyril lied. "What's up?"

"I know where they are."

"What? How? Where?" He whined with anxiety. *Why now, for fuck's sake?*

Tepes laughed at Cyril's reaction. "As that old annoying singer once sang, the night has a thousand eyes."

"Bobby Vee," Cyril mumbled. "Where are they?"

"They were spotted on the Green Man Estate, going into one of the blocks."

"They went back there?" Cyril found it hard to believe that the boys would have gone home.

"The younger one was part of the local gang, they obviously still have connections there who are willing to hide them."

"So what are we going to do?"

"I've got people keeping an eye on the place; they'll let me know if they leave and will follow them. We're going to go catch ourselves a werewolf, Cyril."

"What? How?"

"Don't you have anything in your arsenal that would enable us?"

"My arsenal?" Cyril asked with innocent confusion.

"Oh come on now, no secrets," Tepes purred. "I know about your other little hobbies."

Cyril seethed. *Is there anything this bastard doesn't know?* "I've got some stuff I never managed to shift in a lockup, yeah."

"Got something that might be able to trap us a werewolf?"

Cyril thought about the boxes of weapons he hadn't looked at for several years: covert stuff from Russia, ex-military spy gadgets, lipstick knives, James Bond stuff, firearms, ammo, swords, machetes. "I'll have to go and see, I don't know offhand."

"Okay," Tepes said, "get to it now. Drop whatever it is you're doing, or about to do, this is our priority. Get whatever it is you think will do the job and restrain them and come on over."

"We can't do this in broad daylight," Cyril said, thinking about his other priorities, the boys in the room behind him.

"We'll do it as soon as possible, Cyril," Tepes growled. "My people are tailing them and have even gone to the trouble of loaning us a van, which is sat outside my fucking house right now."

"We'll be seen!"

"You'd better stop at the fucking fancy dress shop on the way and get us some bloody masks, then, hadn't you?"

Cyril growled with his own frustration.

"I know you bought the old music studios, Cyril."

Cyril felt his spine freeze.

"Just help me with this and I promise not to pry any further. You have my word."

Cyril thought about Adam and Taylor and, if they had both drunk the spiked water, wondered how long it would take for the sedatives to kick in, and how long they would be unconscious for. "Fuck's sake," he groaned.

If it comes to it, I'll just have to drug the bastards again.

"Okay." He saw the headless corpse of Samuel Ellington's aged father and remembered the dog was still chained up outside.

It's just one thing after another.

He cursed his bad luck silently and said his farewell to his vampiric friend. "I'll go to the lockup and get there as soon as I can."

FÜHRER: PART ONE

There was no time to bury Old Man Ellington so he left him where he lay and dealt with his dog.

Daisy went apeshit when he walked towards her, barking, growling and pulling at the dead branch the old man had tied her lead around. Cyril stood over her with the blood-spattered spade and looked into her ferocious face. He lowered the shovel towards her snout and let her inspect it. Once she had caught her owner's scent on the blade, she suddenly quit barking and whined.

"Yeah," Cyril whispered, "your master's dead. That's his blood you're sniffing. I cut his head off."

The dog backed away towards its branch anchor.

"Maybe I should cut yours off, too, and swap your heads around." Cyril giggled with the comic absurdity of the idea. "Would you like that?" He quickly scanned his surroundings and raised the spade.

The dog leapt up at him, front paws on his chest, jaws snapping at his throat, and there was a loud crack as the dead wood she was tied to broke in two. Rather than carry on her attack, now she realised she was free, Daisy bolted away from Cyril and vanished into the brush.

"Shit."

Chapter 38

Suffolk

1995

Andy hit the button for the steel shutter, watched it rise slowly and waited for Friedrich to back the armoured van into the warehouse.

Ginger handed him a katana, its handle bound with black leather, and unsheathed its twin.

The guilt of what they were being paid to do never went away, but Friedrich had convinced them it was for the greater good.

Friedrich.

That wasn't his real name, as they'd found out shortly after visiting his so-called holiday home in Boxford. Friedrich had come clean, told them who he really was, and had even showed them, eventually.

Victor Krauss, a doctor who had worked with the Nazis fifty years before but had stayed the same age almost indefinitely.

A lycan; a werewolf.

The woman in his flat was a guinea pig, something for him to work on, test his little theories in an attempt to understand the condition he had inflicted on himself and his wife. "When you are both ready I'll put her out of her misery," the old man promised.

FÜHRER: PART ONE

Andy closed the shutter and watched as the van rocked on its axis.

Krauss climbed down from the driving seat and nodded a greeting to them.

"How many more times do we have to do this?" Ginger asked coldly. She fully understood what the point was, Krauss was more than a little paranoid of a secret organisation somewhere in the world breeding these things to be used in warfare, but it didn't make it any easier.

"You know, we only do this with a live specimen once a year now," Krauss said sadly. "We must be prepared."

"Have your researchers found any hard evidence of these things anywhere else?" Andy asked the same question every time.

"No," Krauss said, "but there are still regular whispers, sights and sounds amongst the Black Forest."

"Okay," Andy sighed.

"Have you been practising regularly, still?"

"In between the things we actually want to do with our lives, yeah."

"That's all I ask of you," Krauss said sadly and took a bunch of keys to the van's rear doors. "This specimen," he said, "as requested, is a serial rapist who, despite being convicted twice, still hasn't learnt his lesson."

Since Andy and Ginger had honed their skills enough to take on live opponents, they insisted that each infected victim be a repeat offender rather than innocent.

"I will warn you," Krauss said to Ginger, "he is a vile man, even more so now the darkness inside him has taken hold. As usual, I only want you to be a bystander, let Andy do his thing, and only get involved if you have to."

"Where the hell do you find these people?" Ginger asked, staring at the rear door of the van.

"I have my ways."

"Let him out, then," Andy said, gripping his katana. "You know, I still think you should make me some silver-plated Freddy Krueger gloves."

Krauss unlocked the rocking van and pounced on its roof.

Seeing the old man's true strength and capabilities was something Andy could never get used to.

The van still shook from side to side, the sound of snarling coming from within.

Andy waited but knew from experience lycans weren't renowned for their dexterity, opening doors wasn't usually an issue if you could plough through them as though they were made of paper.

The thing in the van hadn't even dented it.

Steeling himself, he gripped the handle, yanked the door open, and was instantly thrown out of the way when something barrelled into him.

He rolled across the concrete and was up straight away, the fire in his belly gearing up to enable his own transformation. This was usually almost instantaneous, but the shock of the werewolf's appearance slowed the process.

It was jet-black, darker than anything he'd ever seen.

It hunkered in the corner, bipedal, drinking in its surroundings. Great yellow eyes locked onto Andy's and it roared.

FÜHRER: PART ONE

Andy felt a sudden rush of energy and strength, his muscles bunched and grew, his fingernails toughened and lengthened a few millimetres.

The wolf growled at the two men and licked its teeth with a wide pink tongue when it saw Ginger.

"Jesus," she said, "it even looks like a pervert in wolf-form."

"Nesbitt," Krauss shouted at the creature. "If you can get past us, you're free. We're in the middle of nowhere, plenty of places for you to hide."

The lycan grumbled deeply, stepped forwards, and started circling Andy.

Andy's senses were in overdrive, the werewolf's scent filled the room, a musky concoction of animal, sweat and piss.

Changing, for some people, was like dying, and when you had no authority over your bodily functions anyway, dignity wasn't paramount.

He held the katana over his shoulder, ready to strike.

It didn't matter how bad the victim was as a person, the last thing he wanted to do was prolong the fight.

It stomped towards him and he swung the sword, missing its face by a foot.

It crouched, the thick muscles in its thighs tightening, and jumped.

Andy swung the sword again but misinterpreted the lycan's actions. Its jump hadn't been aimed at Andy but at the van; it hit the metalwork with its feet and rebound into Andy, knocking him to the ground.

Andy clawed his way across the concrete, knowing just one bite or scratch from one of these things would turn him into a monster.

It ploughed into him and landed on his back whilst he sliced the air above and behind his head with the sword.

The blade caught on something and the lycan yelped in pain; as the sword ended its arc, blood splattered the grey walls.

Andy flipped over and saw a red slash in the monster's left shoulder. With the silver in the blade, that cut would be enough to kill it, but not quickly enough.

In one movement, Andy went from lying flat on his back to being back on his feet, ready to attack again.

The wolf roared, grabbed at the van, and swung a paw up at Krauss, who fell back across the van roof and out of sight.

Andy yelled and brought the sword down towards the thing's broad back.

It spun, lightning-quick, and clamped a paw around the blade and howled when the silver sliced the leathery paw pads.

Andy tried to pull the sword free but the thing held on tight, lifted Andy in the air, and slammed him against the wall.

"Andy!" Ginger cried when she saw his head collide with the wall. She raised her own katana ready for attack, but unlike him, her defences and reactions weren't abnormally fast, and the wolf grabbed her around the throat.

Krauss swore in German; he had underestimated Nesbitt. Krauss changed mid-air, his clothes exploding around him, but Nesbitt ducked out of his path and leapt across the room, Ginger still in his grasp.

Andy rolled onto his back groggily.

Nesbitt raised Ginger high in the air above his head, holding her away as she tried to reach him with her sword.

Krauss coiled, ready to pounce, but Nesbitt swung his arm around and used Ginger as a shield.

"No," Andy screamed, all his advances blocked by the hanging form of his girlfriend.

Nesbitt was in control of his wolf, something rare amongst the opponents Krauss brought in; his own wiliness exacerbated the wolf's.

There was no way of getting past Ginger to attack so he did something he had never done before during one of these fights: he relaxed and dropped his weapon.

Surely, if Nesbitt was aware of his predicament, he would realise just how valuable Ginger was.

If he killed her, he and Krauss would attack him.

Nesbitt knew, alright, and he used it to taunt them. With his free paw he grabbed Ginger's flailing wrist, the one with the sword in it, let go of her throat, swiped a claw across her, tearing her clothing apart, and held her up half-naked to show them.

"No, please," Andy begged. "Just go. Leave. Leave her alone."

Ginger looked at him, defeated.

Krauss roared.

"No, change back," Andy shouted, "let him go."

Krauss glared at him through his feral yellow eyes and his fur began to retreat until he was just an old man again.

"Please," Andy said, stepping towards Nesbitt, "just let her go."

If werewolves could grin, that was exactly what Nesbitt did.

He stripped away the remaining clothes from her skinny body, dripping great strands of saliva to the floor, and pressed his muzzle against her naked flesh.

"No," Andy cried. All he could see was Nesbitt, a vile rapist in every form, and his wide wet tongue as it slid up Ginger's body from foot to face.

Andy didn't see what Ginger was doing with her free hand until her red hair suddenly cascaded down her back and he remembered the silver kanzashi he had made for her.

She held the two long needle-like hair ornaments in her fist and smashed them down through Nesbitt's left eyeball and into his brain.

Nesbitt let go of Ginger, a look of confusion crossing his animal face, the two kanzashi sticking out of his eye.

Ginger landed on her feet and shrieked with cold-blooded fury as she went about the gigantic beast's legs with her sword.

Nesbitt crumpled to the floor, his body rapidly undergoing the reverse metamorphosis, his hands realigning and fluttering towards his injuries.

Ginger roared, swung the katana and sliced off the top of his skull and brain, before staring straight into Andy's soul and screaming.

It was three whole days before Ginger spoke to Andy again. Although the one-bedroom flat they lived in was tiny, she managed to ignore him as long as she could.

It wasn't Andy she was angry with, but Krauss.
She rued the day she'd met him.

FÜHRER: PART ONE

Even though he had rescued Andy from a long stay in a psychiatric hospital, their lives had been barely normal.

The rigorous training for something that might not ever happen, and the guinea pigs Krauss had created to test their mettle.

They'd had some close calls at the start of their trials against live opponents, both experienced enough that the recently infected people were quickly dispatched, usually by Andy, with his souped-up strength and reactions.

But Nesbitt was different.

He had known exactly what he was, had embraced it, and he had violated her.

Ginger wasn't stupid, she knew if Krauss's fears were realised and werewolves were unleashed upon humanity, there would be wilier ones than those who were pure beast, ones who reached some kind of symbiosis with their wolf, but that this would even happen was pure speculation. As far as they and Krauss knew, he and his wife were the only two lycans in existence.

It was with this thinking that she broke her three-day silence.

"We should kill him," she said, startling Andy after such a long silence.

He put down his notebook and pen and gave her his attention.

"I know he helped you," she said, "he helped us to be together, but we don't need him. If he's out of the picture, then it lessens the chances of this shit ever getting out. He doesn't know it's out there still. Currently, it's only out there because of him."

Andy smiled bitterly. "I never wanted to do any of this. I just wanted to be rid of that thing inside me, to be with you."

She sat down beside him. "Me too, which was why I even listened to him in the first place. I don't know what he really wants from us, maybe this is it? Maybe he doesn't have the bottle to end himself and his wife so he trained us up to do the job."

"But what if he's right and one day the werewolf apocalypse arrives?"

Ginger laughed. "And do you honestly think two lycan hunters are going to be able to go up against an army of these things? We've only ever done one at a time and most of them have only been rabid for a few weeks. What happens if they really have been breeding these things in secret for decades? What the fuck is the point anymore? I say we keep what's ours, get rid of him, and try to lead normal lives."

"And if World War Wolf happens, we've at least got the training to defend ourselves?"

"Exactly."

Andy took her hand and nodded. "Okay, I'll do anything for you."

Ginger rolled her eyes. "No, we do it for us. To free ourselves from this bullshit."

FÜHRER: PART ONE

Chapter 39

1965

From the moment Victor had put an end to the Schäfers, he had a feeling they wouldn't be the last of their kind.

The trouble with creatures which were classified as mythical was that there was no science to fall back on.

In a way, although he doubted it was the case, he was the first person to document the existence of lycanthropy from a scientific perspective.

Gwen's wolf became subservient, recognised Victor for what he was: the alpha male, the alpha wolf.

Life became a tedious drag of routine.

Gwen's dementia never worsened, but it never improved, either, and she spent most of her days sitting opposite a radio; then, with the advent of television, she would zone out in front of the box. Victor knew he should end her suffering; he had spent years putting all werewolf superstitions to the test, but there were some methods too painful, too barbaric to put her through.

That was where Jennifer Thorn entered into the equation.

Gwen's infected nurse presented quite the opportunity; despite his initial misgivings, he kept her alive. The cellar of their townhouse became quite crowded around the time of the full moon and he was lucky to have total control over his wolf.

FÜHRER: PART ONE

Every month, he secured Gwen in the secret room with Miss Thorn, who stayed in there permanently. At first she had been vocal about her capture, scared of the things happening to her body and the ordeals Victor was putting her through, but her wolf kept her in prime physical condition.

It wasn't long after the twelfth month of her captivity that she slipped into a seemingly permanent catatonic state, Victor's experiments having destroyed her mentally.

He examined the effects of silver on her flesh and her blood. Pressed directly onto her skin, silver left burns that took months to heal.

Wolfsbane was combined with liquid silver and samples of her blood so he could watch the reactions beneath the microscope, a sudden destruction of the cells.

It was difficult to test these methods on blood or skin samples from the body as the lycanthropic flesh deteriorated rapidly once removed.

Lycan blood went bad twice as quickly as that of humans, but he discovered that it remarkably resurrected when it came back into contact with something living.

It would be possible to infect someone with lycan blood long after it had coagulated.

The thing inside them had methods of defence and attack on a molecular scale, which meant the only way one could successfully test their weaknesses was to experiment on a live specimen.

Eventually his studies came to a standstill.

Over the years, he had examined every inch of Jennifer Thorn's body, inside and out, for the source of the lycanthropy. But the secret was in the brain.

Somehow, something invaded the mind and took over, like a personality with the ability to physically change its host, just like Jekyll and Hyde.

After two decades of going over the same research and undertaking new experiments, he went back to the beginning again: the Schäfers.

There were more answers there, he knew it.

The answer, which opened more doors into this world, had been staring him in the face all along.

The Schäfers were a family of werewolves.

They hadn't all been bitten by an infected creature, but their lycanthropy was hereditary. That meant this thing could be passed on through genetics.

Is it necessary for both parents to be lycan for this to happen?

What if one is uninfected?

What if the child was produced with less lycanthropic genes, would half-breeds be possible?

He pulled apart everything he knew and studied it again.

The word *lunatic* had been about for at least two thousand years, derived from the Latin *lunaticus*: moonstruck.

For centuries, people had believed diseases of the mind to be brought on by the moon's influence, and for nearly as long, there had been legends of shapeshifters and lycanthropy.

FÜHRER: PART ONE

It was a fact that werewolves were affected by the moon at its fullest and he devoured texts about mental health conditions that came and went in irregular cycles.

What if they are connected?

He researched a number of different conditions and tried to find their origins, and the more he delved, the more he was sure that whatever had caused a lot of these defects must have come from the same source.

Somewhere down the line, lycanthropy had mixed with human DNA and brought about diluted, purely psychological versions of itself.

Was lycanthropy the original mental health condition?

If he couldn't cure this thing, or make it fix his wife, he was going to find out everything he could about it.

Chapter 40

Danny caught sight of the putrid puddle of maggot-speckled vomit and retched again. "Aw, man," he whined, "we need to get out of here."

Tony was transfixed by the blackened mess of the devastated body.

Both boys startled when the hammer slid from his gore-caked hand and clunked to the floor. "What the fuck was that thing in her head?"

"You saw it too, then?"

Tony slumped to the floor and held his hand up in front of his face, the fingers beginning to shake. "I can't do this anymore, Dan. This is too much."

Danny spat once more onto the floor and dropped beside his brother.

"We'll give ourselves up. That's got to be better than this. At least we can tell them about Cyril and that bloke."

Tony nodded. "I don't see any other way."

Danny reached for Krauss's notebooks. "Maybe someone will be able to decipher these, too."

"I'm sorry I couldn't look after you," Tony said tearfully.

There was nothing left to do, hopelessness overwhelmed them.

They stole one last look at the rotten, headless corpse and made to leave.

Danny fumbled with the bolts on the door, without checking through the spy hole to make sure no residents or grounds staff were in sight of the unoccupied flat.

"Come on, T," Danny said, just as his brother was about to warn him to be more inconspicuous.

As Danny opened the door, he saw the two black-clad figures, yelped, and tried to push the door closed, but one of them kicked a heavy boot against the wood, knocking him back into his brother and into the flat... whilst the other shot them both with a handgun.

Chapter 41

Suffolk

1996

Ginger drove them to the airfield in a navy-blue Volkswagen Beetle she called Blueberry.

Krauss paid them enough that they didn't need to work, but neither of them liked the control that came as part and parcel of the deal.

To begin with, Krauss had rented a small house with a built-in garage in Brantham, the village Andy had grown up in. This was where he showed Andy how to control his own dark side and make his Mr Hyde work for him.

Once Andy had mastered this unusual power, Ginger had joined them and they began to learn about different types of combat via various tutors Krauss sent in.

When both were ready, Krauss brought them their first opponent, a homeless man he had infected with his captive's blood.

It never seemed to end: victim after victim, month after month, until Andy refused to carry on the slaughter.

Krauss begged and pleaded, and that was when they insisted that future werewolves would be convicts or criminals. They knew Krauss had the money to investigate such things. But throughout their years-long training, all either of them could think of was the poor woman imprisoned in Krauss's flat.

Ginger parked outside the small hangar for light aircraft, Andy took a bag from the VW's boot, and they entered the building through a door next to the heavy-duty hydraulic shutter.

It was what Andy referred to as their Dojo, where they honed their fighting skills and dispatched all of the lycans Krauss brought to them.

Andy dropped the black holdall onto the concrete floor, unzipped it, and took out a black-and-brown rifle.

"Where the hell did you get that thing?" Ginger said, running a finger along the barrel.

"Farmer's auction," Andy said, looking down the barrel. "They used to use this for putting cows and horses down," he said, then clocked the look of horror on her face. "Mostly if they needed an op, or to be inspected by a vet."

"You sure it'll work?"

"Nope."

"Great," Ginger said and opened a metal cabinet which housed their arsenal. "Katana for back-up, then."

Andy nodded, and as Ginger retrieved their swords, he checked to see if she still had the silver pins in her hair.

A flashback of Nesbitt the year before replayed in his mind; it had haunted him ever since, horrific visions of Ginger being set upon by the serial rapist.

It would take a lot for Krauss to top that piece of shit, but Andy had to remember they weren't just trying to take out a newbie Lycan this time. This time, they planned on taking out someone who had taken fifty years to get used to his condition.

Raydon airfield never saw a lot of traffic, so they knew it was Krauss when they heard an engine approaching.

"Fuck," Andy said, panicking; he was earlier than scheduled. He fished a small case from the holdall containing the darts for the gun and inserted one into the weapon. "We only have one chance at this. I doubt we'll have time to reload."

Ginger paled.

The vehicle stopped by the hangar and there were three toots of the horn to signal his arrival.

"Let him in," Andy said, hiding behind the weapons cabinet. "He'll reverse as always. As soon as he gets out of the van, I'll do it."

Ginger hit the controls and the shutter rolled up.

Krauss backed the armoured truck into the hangar.

Once inside, Ginger lowered the shutters.

He switched off the engine and got down from the van.

Krauss nodded, his face then darkened when he saw only Ginger. "Where's Andr—"

Andy stepped out from behind the cabinet, aimed the tranq gun, and fired before he had a chance to hesitate and Victor had a chance to move.

The dart zipped towards Victor's throat, dead on target, but in the last millisecond, he dropped to the floor.

"What the hell are you doing?" he shouted, his face inches from the concrete.

Andy fumbled with the other tranquiliser darts.

"This has to end," Ginger said, readying her sword. "If you're gone, it will."

FÜHRER: PART ONE

"But you know I'm not the last one," Victor said in disbelief.

"We'll see to whatever's in your van, and we'll sort what's in your flat." Andy paused before adding the lines that he knew would get them both killed: "And we won't stop until you and your wife are dead. You were right in the forties, Victor; this should not have spread, but you've let it." Andy raised the reloaded gun.

"Stop!"

Andy tried to aim the gun at Victor again, but he was too quick, jumping from beam to beam.

One of his arms thickened into a clawed, muscular limb, and he smashed a hole in the hangar roof.

Before he vanished, he looked back at them once, his face somewhere between human and animal, and snarled, "Very well."

It would be twenty years before they saw him again.

Chapter 42

Boxford

2016

Over the years, the subject of making their knowledge public came up several times, but without hard evidence they would be fobbed off as insane.

They kept a close watch on Boxford and were satisfied when the caretakers at the Green Man Estate said the flat he owned had been unoccupied for over a decade.

All signs of Victor Krauss had vanished, and eventually, Andy and Ginger let themselves be absorbed by their lives and tried to forget the horrors they had been subjected to. They hypothesised that eventually the old man had done the right thing and either ended his own and his wife's lives or vanished far away where they could hurt no one else. Either way, there was no mention of unusual animal attacks or werewolves.

They both turned into teachers of their chosen crafts: Ginger, high school art, and Andy, storytelling. He ran creative writing groups and taught English part-time.

Andy had almost forgotten about the stuff that had happened when he was younger.

His fits and compulsions, which he'd had control over ever since Krauss had taught him how, were a rarity now, usually brought only on by intense emotion. Both kept up with their physical training, but Andy rarely used that strange power inside him, so it lay dormant.

However, when Ginger came home from school one evening and dropped a regional newspaper in front of him, he felt its hackles rise.

DOG MASSACRES TEENS

"Oh, Jesus," Andy said, thinking of the panic over Alsatians and Rottweilers in the eighties. "Please tell me it isn't any of your kids," he said, referring to her students.

Ginger was silent as he scanned the write-up to see what breed it was this time around. He remembered his mother's tirade about bringing back dog licencing, but then he spotted the location. "Boxford?"

Ginger nodded, slumped beside him on the sofa, unfastened her greying ginger hair, and sighed. "Read it, there's more on page five."

Andy read the brief summary on the front page beneath the large bold headline; not very much detail was given other than the location and how a group of friends were attacked by a canal, but on the other pages were photographs of the boys themselves and they were not what he was expecting. These boys, virtually adults, were tough-looking fuckers with facial and neck tattoos. The report said they were literally torn apart, all five dead before any kind of help arrived, and the only witness was a man in his nineties, who it seemed they attempted to mug.

"It's him."

Andy finished reading and nodded. "It has to be."

"I can't believe he's still nearby," Ginger said, "after all this fucking time."

"Fuck," Andy said, rescanning the article, "but it says they tried to mug him? That rather than let the hooligans have his belongings, he threw them into the canal. That definitely sounds like something he would do. And then—"

"And then," Ginger finished, "some dogs came along and ripped them all apart."

Andy grimaced. "It sounds complete bollocks, doesn't it, but what's more far-fetched, a pair of passing Cujos, or a bloody werewolf attack?"

"And when your victim's a frail old man…"

"Shit," Andy said, "shit. I honestly thought he would have fucked off by now."

"What do we do?"

"I mean, they attacked him, and if this shit is as infectious as he let on, then maybe he had to…you know, finish the job?"

Ginger shot him a scornful look, and Andy knew she was keeping something from him. He wondered whether her sudden change of mood was due to his seeming to defend the old man's actions. Then he spotted the date at the top. "This was over a week ago." The crushing realisation sank him into the sofa cushions. "Oh shit, you've got more, haven't you?"

Ginger eyes were wet with tears as she fumbled in the brown leather satchel she used for school.

"That's been sitting in the staffroom all week." She handed him a fresh, folded edition. "This is tonight's."

Boxford again, but this time, a child's face filled the front page: small, cute, with a huge tumble of light brown curls, with the simple headline: WHERE'S MILLER?

FÜHRER: PART ONE

Andy read about a little boy, a resident of the Green Man Estate who had been snatched from his ground-floor bedroom. One broken window, several traces of his blood found on the pavement nearby. "Oh, shit."

Ginger nodded, her hand shaking as she wiped her eyes. Andy took the other hand in his. "We're going to Boxford."

The only thing they could remember of their trip to Boxford twenty years earlier were the five tower blocks at the top of a steep hill, looming ominously over a row of shops and facing a cathedrallike church on an even higher mount opposite.

That view hadn't changed.

Andy also remembered Krauss's folk tale about the fairy ring and imps moving the plans for the church to the other hill, and the whole paganism theme.

No visible improvements seemed to have been made to the tower blocks, their cladding patchy and weather-beaten, a few balconies in various states of disrepair.

Mothers so young they were still children themselves pushed prams across dog-shit speckled grass whilst the males of their species dawdled behind in their oversized sportswear, puffing out swirling blue vape clouds.

"Jesus," Andy said as he hunched over the steering wheel and looked for a space in the parking lot. "This place is the pits."

"It wasn't exactly Knightsbridge twenty years ago," Ginger replied.

"Yeah, but it wasn't this bad when I came and tried to find out about his flat."

"Do you think we should check on that?"

"I don't know, I have no idea what to do now we're here." Andy switched the ignition off and they sat gazing up at the tower block. Across the small car park, they saw that one of the ground-floor flats of the adjacent block had its window boarded up.

"That'll be where the kid got snatched," Ginger said sadly.

"What do we do, Gin? How the hell do we find him?"

"Can't be many six-foot old Germans wandering around here," she suggested, "but I'm willing to bet he keeps himself to himself."

Two teenagers, a boy and a girl, burst out of the block in front of them with school bags over their shoulders.

"I guess we'd better start asking some questions," Andy said, and climbed out of the car. "Excuse me," he called over to the group. They looked trustworthy enough, too young to be involved in any gangs, and judging from the boy's long dark hair, too alternative, as well..

The boy glared his way and put his arm around the girl's shoulders protectively. Andy smiled and waved; it made him think of his own younger years. "Hi," he said, stepping away from the car.

The boy stared at him suspiciously but seemed to relax a bit when Ginger showed herself. "Yeah?" he said, in a voice half-gruff with the changes of puberty.

Andy pointed at the boarded-up window across the car park. "Do you know anything about that?"

The kid frowned. "You a cop, or something?"

FÜHRER: PART ONE

"No."

"Reporter?"

Andy smirked. "I'm just a nosy bastard, to be honest." He nodded to Ginger. "Me and my wife have applied for a flat here, just wondering what the area was like."

The boy grinned, but it was the girl, a small blonde with a nose piercing, who answered. "It's not that bad, really, if you keep yourself to yourself."

"So that's just modifications?" Andy said, pointing to the window again.

The girl smiled sadly. "'fraid not. A lad was snatched from his bed."

"What?" Ginger said.

The girl nodded. "The other night, someone smashed the glass and took him."

"Oh my God. Was he left on his own or something?"

"Dunno," the girl told Ginger. "Some reckon the mum was out of it when it happened." She mimed smoking a spliff.

"Jesus."

"I reckon it was something to do with the gang the kid's older brother was in."

"Oh?"

The girl pointed to a spray-painted white tag on a nearby lamppost. "The GMC. The Green Man Crew."

"So is there trouble with these gangs?" Andy asked.

"Not anymore," the boy sniggered, and received a thump in the arm from his girlfriend.

"A lot of the main members were killed recently," she said, with casual indifference. "People around here reckon they had a run-in with a bigger bunch from Sudbury, ones that'd brought their dogs with them."

"Dogs?" Andy said. "I think I read something in the local paper about a dog attack."

"Yeah." The boy's face lit up with malicious glee. "Killed five of the cunts by the canal."

"Tay!" The girl flushed red and began to storm off.

The boy turned to them sheepishly. "Sorry, but she don't know what they were like. They were bastards."

"Hey, we're not here to judge," Ginger said. "Do you both live here?"

The boy cocked a thumb over his shoulder at the Jack-in-the-Green block. "I live on the twelfth floor, and Zara's in one of the blocks at the back."

The girl came bac to tell him off. "Don't tell them where we live!"

"I didn't tell them what number."

"I don't care. Come on," she said, tugging at his arm, "we'll be late for school."

"Wait," Ginger called, "please."

The girl spun around, her face like thunder.

"Do you know anything about the old man they tried to mug?" Andy blurted out and stopped them in their tracks.

"Everyone knows that prick," the boy scoffed, "local bloody celebrity, they all flock to him, the old 'uns, cuz he's minted as. He refurbished the old village hall so they could all play bingo or whatever."

"He's alright, Victor," the girl butt in, "my nan talks to him loads."

"Do you know where he lives?" Ginger asked.

The kids shared a look, the boy shrugged.

FÜHRER: PART ONE

"No," the girl said, "but my nan sees him and his lot in the café at the supermarket most days."

"Okay, thanks for your help; no doubt we'll see you around if we become neighbours," Ginger said, mustering a warm smile. The kids left them to ponder over their next move.

Andy took out his car keys. "Let's go and check this supermarket out."

Andy and Ginger scouted the town for the supermarket, it wasn't hard.

A great grey edifice which contained a gym and a multi-storey car park stood over a row of older, independent shops that had either been closed for decades and were boarded up or had given up the ghost when the new supermarket had stolen their customers.

Above the gigantic red lettering of the supermarket's logo, a glass frontage spanning a fifth of the building showed an eating area.

"There's our café," Ginger said, stating the obvious.

They walked past a pub which had two mobility scooters parked outside and tried not to stare too much at the mournful-looking old men nursing half-empty pint glasses. "Jesus, I'm getting depressed just walking around here."

"Yeah, it's grim, isn't it?" Ginger said.

Two homeless people sat swaddled in blankets in the supermarket entrance and rattled paper cups for change. Andy apologised as they walked past them and into a corridor that ran parallel to the carpark. A lift, stairs, and travelator all led the way to the supermarket up above.

They stepped onto the travelator and as it brought them higher, they saw the café directly opposite. A generic supermarket café full of shoppers and shopping.

Breakfast was still being served, and the aroma of fried food stirred hunger pangs in Andy's stomach.

"Let's get something to eat and just have a look." He joined a shuffling queue and grabbed a tray. "See anything?"

Ginger casually turned around to survey the customers: parents having breathers after the school run; a couple of uniformed workers on their own; one Royal Mail, the other, McDonald's. A graceful, silver-haired older lady sitting scalding a man who Ginger presumed was her wheelchair-bound husband, whilst an overweight man in a Rastafarian cap sat watching them, trying not to laugh and tapping his fingers against a Tupperware tub that sat between them amidst their dishes. She noticed, with vague surprise, a fat brown dachshund curled by the woman's feet. He wore a little jumper which said, 'Service Dog', and which made her stifle a laugh. *Wily old coot,* she thought, as Andy loaded their tray with teapots and cups. *There's no way that thing is a service dog.*

The dog side-eyed her, as if it could hear her thoughts, licked its chops, and then melted back into the floppy-skinned puddle it had formed beneath the table.

"No sign of Krauss," Ginger said, squishing into Andy's side.

A blonde woman in her forties handed them mugs to go with their teapots and pointed to the hot water dispenser. Andy waited for her to retreat until he spoke. "Do you think we should ask these guys?"

FÜHRER: PART ONE

He nodded to the blonde woman and a skinny lad in his early twenties.

Ginger shook her head. "They might alert him."

"Let's just get something to eat and wait a bit, then. What else can we do?"

"I suppose so. I'm going to sit down, get me a bacon sandwich," she gave him a quick hug and made her way to the nearest space. When she passed the table with the three old people, she heard the man in the wheelchair ask, "You gonna divvy up them cakes or what?" She was surprised to hear he had a Scottish accent, and he noticed he had caught her eye. He smiled politely as his lady friend lowered her teacup and opened the tub to reveal some delicious-looking brownies.

"Hands off," he said jovially, "or it's a pound each."

She returned his smile and patted her flat stomach. "I've only got space in here for my bacon sarnie this morning."

"A woman after my own heart," the other man said with a beautiful Jamaican accent.

The Scotsman sucked air through his teeth. "Big question is this, though, hen: red or brown sauce?"

His friend laughed like this was the funniest thing in the world.

"Mustard all the way," Ginger said defiantly.

"Now you're talking, man," the Jamaican said with a slap of his thigh and a gaze at Andy. "Hope you got your woman her mustard."

Andy looked at them all with amused confusion.

"Oh, ignore this pair of buffoons and enjoy your breakfast," the lady said.

"Thank you," Ginger replied, and led Andy to a table. Even though they were a few spaces away from the elderly group, their voices carried, especially those of the two men, who occasionally cracked what they thought were jokes and looked around at everyone in the vicinity to see if they had heard their attempts at humour.

Andy and Ginger attacked their breakfast but Ginger couldn't help but continue to eavesdrop on the trio, especially when the atmosphere at their table took on a sombre tone when a note was discovered at the bottom of the brownie box.

From then on, the three spoke in hushed voices until she saw the woman give her dog some of the cake (which she thought was irresponsible and stupid), then one of the men cracked another joke and the lady blurted out, "Ethel? And Victor? You're joking."

She locked eyes with Andy. "Bingo."

Luck was on their side.

They knew he was in town somewhere, and by chance alone, he passed them whilst they sat in the car in the parking space outside the bakery.

It was the first time in twenty years they had seen him, and although their own skin had taken on the blemishes of natural ageing and their hair had begun to turn grey, Victor Krauss hadn't aged a day.

He was still a stick-thin yet formidable figure, tall and stooped. With his long black coat, Roman nose, and thinning white hair he resembled a vulture, a cadaverous old bird, the angel of death, Death in human form.

"He's still got that cane," Andy pointed out as they stared through the car windscreen at the man on the opposite side of the street. He remembered Krauss showing him firsthand the effects of silver on lycanthropic flesh.

He had held the stiletto-thin blade against the skin on his forearm for a few seconds, before removing it and subsequently a layer of skin. "If it were pure silver, I expect there would be smoke and fire," he had said with a dry laugh. "The tip of the blade has to be made from metals that can be sharpened repeatedly, the rest a high percentage of silver to cause enough lasting damage to get the job done."

"Just adds to the old man image, doesn't it?" Ginger said as they watched Victor pass by a row of boarded-up shop fronts. The street was busy for one with so few retailers. The hustle and bustle of a usual weekday, pedestrians going to the supermarket, the chain bakeries and betting shops. Victor dropped a handful of change into a paper cup held aloft by a waif sitting on a flattened cardboard box.

"What's the plan of action?" Ginger asked.

"All we can do at the moment is try not to be seen and follow him. He's a clever old crow and we can't underestimate him."

Victor continued until he came to a bus stop, where, three minutes later, he got on a bus marked 'Hospital'.

Andy started the car and followed.

Krauss got off the bus outside the hospital and entered the giant building.

Andy parked in the nearest available spot and they jogged to keep him in sight as he slipped through the automatic doors.

By the time they were inside, they could see him on the escalator across from the busy reception area.

Beside the row of three escalators, two up, one down, there was a row of three lifts. Andy hit the call button and they waited.

"Wouldn't it be quicker to use the escalator?" Ginger asked, peeking around the exterior wall of the lift shaft to see Krauss slip from view on the first floor.

"He's only going up one floor," Andy said. They followed him in the lift, but almost missed him as he turned at the end of a corridor.

Andy cussed and ran after him. Unlike the reception area, the first-floor corridors were virtually empty.

"What the hell is he even doing at a hospital?" Andy complained.

"He's old, has old friends," Ginger said, stopping and risking a glimpse around. She smiled smugly and nodded towards the new direction Krauss had taken.

Far up the next corridor, they saw him towering over a little old lady with short white hair and glasses, who took one look at him, jumped, and ran as quickly as her old body could carry her.

"What the fuck?" Ginger said as Krauss casually gave chase. "There's no way that's his wife, is it?"

Neither of them had seen the elusive Gwen, but they were aware of her mental condition, and apart from being terrified, the lady Krauss was after seemed completely level-headed.

She slammed into the bar of a fire exit door, and a split second later, Krauss quickly vanished into the stairwell with her.

"He's gonna kill her," Ginger said. She ran a lot faster than Andy and caught the fire door as it swung back to the doorpost.

Andy followed suit but stopped when he collided with Ginger, who clamped a hand over his mouth and pointed down the stairs.

They heard Krauss shout from a floor or so below. "Will you stop and let me talk?"

"Please don't hurt me," the woman answered, and they heard one of them slump to the floor.

The rest of the conversation was hushed, as though they were frightened someone would hear, although they did hear the old German swear at something she said.

There came the ruffling of clothing and heavy sighs and then the sound of the couple heading back up the stairs.

Andy opened the fire door as quietly as possible and they moved back into the corridor.

He turned and hugged Ginger, a ploy so he could spy on Krauss and his lady friend as they left the stairwell and headed back down to the reception.

=

After a minute or so, Krauss left the hospital with the lady and got into a small car with her.

"Well, I presume that's the Ethel the folk at the café were talking about. Reckon they're an item?"

Andy shrugged. "I have no idea what to do now. All we have to go on is a bunch of old cronies in a supermarket café."

"I don't think he's planning on going anywhere soon," Ginger surmised. "We need to find out where he lives so we can get him on his own."

"Fuck."

"Oh, come on, you didn't think this was going to be easy, did you?"

Andy shook his head. "So what? We just keep eavesdropping on the oldies until one of them lets slip where he lives?"

Ginger watched the little car pull out of the hospital car park. "We know he's here in Boxford and whatever has happened so far has been covered up. We go home, go back to work, and plan our next move."

They managed a week of normality before Boxford hit the headlines once more.

As soon as Andy heard the place mentioned he assumed it would be another gruesome slaying, but from what little the radio report described, live from the scene, it sounded like a vendetta of sorts. A woman had been attacked with a syringe full of some as yet unknown substance, which had killed her instantly.

Nothing else was mentioned apart from the suspect being a youth rumoured to be part of a much-feared local gang who called themselves the GMC, the Green Man Crew.

Andy continued the drive home without giving the bulletin a second thought, other than to briefly consider whether Victor's initial attack on some hoodlums on Boxford canals had been justified.

Once again, it was Ginger who found the glaringly obvious.

Another newspaper was thrown at him when she burst through the door a few days later, her face like thunder.

FÜHRER: PART ONE

The front page of the regional rag ran a photograph of a graceful-looking elderly lady with long silver hair.

He recognised her immediately, she was hard to miss. She was one of the trio from the café.

A quick scan of the fine print told him it had been she who'd been killed the day before, although the headlines told a more elaborate story.

BOXFORD HOSPITAL HORROR AS THUGS STEAL BODY.

"Says a local hoodlum stuck her with a needle in the café, and later that night, they stormed the hospital, killed numerous people with the aid of some type of dog, and stole the body," Ginger ranted. "And, on page seven, there's an article about a park warden being attacked by a large dog later on in the evening."

Andy scanned the front page as quickly as possible before turning to page seven.

"It's him, isn't it? There's no way local thugs would attempt bodysnatching from a bloody hospital. We went there, for fuck's sake, the place was massive, riddled with CCTV. Surely they'd know exactly what went down."

"We need to go back to Boxford," Ginger raged. "Now."

Chapter 43

For the second time in a matter of days, Danny was restrained. Tight metal wiring cut into the flesh of his wrists and ankles, his hands and feet sticky with what he presumed was blood.

His head swam, and when he opened his eyes, the shadows in the room told him it was either late afternoon or early morning.

He moved his head and saw a wrapped black parcel bound with duct tape, clearly a body.

"Tony," he cried, trying to wriggle free.

He remembered the two figures, the guns.

"It's alright," Tony said from somewhere behind him. "I think it's the body of that woman."

Footsteps came from the hallway and a tall, thin man entered the room, dressed head to toe in black tactical gear. He had greying dark hair, messed up from when he'd removed the balaclava. Krauss's notebooks were in his hands, and he said nothing as he moved out of Danny's vision.

More surprising was the appearance of a woman following him.

She wore similar clothing, and sixteen-hole black leather boots that covered most of her shins. She had big green eyes and long curly ginger hair that was scraped behind her head. When she made eye contact, she smiled sympathetically and Danny noticed pale scarring across her lips, as if she'd had corrective surgery as a kid.

"Who are you?" Tony shouted at the man, who took a seat on the ancient dusty sofa in front of him.

FÜHRER: PART ONE

They had been unconscious for a while. While they were out of it, these people had wrapped the body of the captured woman and opened all the windows in the place.

He was rope-tied to one of the kitchen chairs, and Danny's bare wrists and ankles had been bound with wire. He was dripping with blood.

After the recent turn of events, it was unusual to see his brother bleeding so copiously.

The man ignored his question, flicked through one of the notebooks and swore, tears wetting his cheeks. "I can't fucking believe it."

The woman sat next to him and held him. "It doesn't matter, it doesn't change anything, doesn't change what we have to do."

"But," the man whimpered in the woman's arms, "what if I'm just as contagious?"

"Hello?" Tony shrieked at them, fed up with being ignored.

The man slammed the notebooks down and stared out of the grimy window.

"What do you know about what went on here?" The woman asked, "are you part of it? Did he pay you to babysit?"

"I don't know what you're talking about," Tony said. "We broke in, thought the place was empty. Needed somewhere to hide."

"We know who you are," the woman said, and stated their names. "How did your brother get infected?"

Tony was flabbergasted. "Who the hell are you? How do you know about this stuff?"

The man laughed and swiped the moisture from his face, then pointed to the plastic bundle on the carpet. "It turns out I'm her son."

"Whoa, what the actual fuck?" Danny piped up.

The man jumped up from the sofa and dragged Danny's chair around so they could all see one another.

He pointed at the notebooks. "Did you boys not read them?"

"I—" Tony began, but Danny spoke over him.

"Only enough to know they were that old Nazi bastard's."

"Oh he wasn't an actual Nazi," the man said, "but with everything he's done, he might as well have been."

"What's going on?" Tony begged.

"Might as well tell them," the woman muttered.

The man grinned. "I'm Andy, and this is Ginger, and we are werewolf killers."

Neither Scarborough boy said anything.

"Hired initially by Victor Krauss himself," Andy continued, "who in the eighties masqueraded as Doctor Friedrich, a psychiatrist who showed interest in me after I had a series of attacks, where I thought I had turned into a werewolf."

"You're one too?" Danny said in awe.

"No, not as such, but she definitely was," he said, pointing to the body on the floor. "Who killed her?"

"Me," Tony said.

"She was like a fucking zombie, man, all rotting and black and there was this thing in her head," Danny shouted excitedly.

The couple exchanged a look of disgust.

The man pointed at the notebooks and said, "She had been his prisoner since 1955."

He allowed them several moments for that to sink in.

"It's all in the books. His wife, Gwen, attacked her, and he kept her as a guinea pig."

"You're fucking joking?" the woman said, snatching up the notebooks.

"We came here years ago, to this very flat, and saw her, strung up." The tears were back in his eyes. "We should have—"

"He said he'd put her out of her misery," Ginger said, flipping through the pages and gasping at something she saw.

"Well, obviously not," Andy said.

"We came back again," Ginger said defensively. "We found him, saw the headlines about dog attacks, then stuff happened all over the place."

"We tried to get him," said Andy.

"Krauss?" Danny asked.

"Yeah, but there were cops everywhere and these men in black suits, proper Men in Black types." Andy's eyes glazed over. "Bloody werewolves and death everywhere. We couldn't get near any of them, didn't even know how many he had made."

"The park was swarming with the emergency services and the special agents, whoever they were," Ginger said. "We were way out of our depth. After all we did, following him, eavesdropping on his friends, there was so much bloody death, and we still didn't think to check up on this place." Her eyes widened and she looked at Andy in disgust. "We came here first of all, remember? Them kids told us about the café."

Andy nodded. "And he kept her ali ve doing God knows what experiments on her, letting random drunks fuck her, feed her, until she got pregnant, just so he could see what the outcome would be."

"And the outcome was you?" Tony asked, already knowing the answer.

"Yes," Andy spat, "the others, the ones who came out full-lycan, he fed back to her."

"Oh, holy fucking hell," Tony exclaimed, unable to comprehend the allegations.

"This is fucked up on so many scales," Danny said, stating the obvious.

"I don't quite know how you all got involved," Andy said, "or a bunch of OAPs, but I'm glad it's finally over." He paused and looked at them sadly. "Well, it will be."

"You're going to kill me? Do it," Danny said. "Please."

"Was it you who attacked the swimmers?" Ginger threw the notebooks down and wiped her hands on her combats.

Danny nodded. "I didn't want to. Didn't have a choice."

"It's okay," she said, "I know how it is with most of you. Not many of you want this. It's not your fault. It's all that man's fault, he should have never let it leave Germany. To think he wanted to keep this from the Nazis."

"Oh, if they had got hold of it, things would have been much worse, believe me," Andy said. "But the havoc he's wrought is more than enough. Jesus."

"What about my brother?" Danny asked. "He's not infected. Don't hurt him, please."

"We won't," the woman decided.

"This doesn't end with Danny," Tony said, and told them all about a certain vampire and his Renfield.

FÜHRER: PART ONE

Chapter 44

He hadn't been to the lockup for years other than regular drive-bys to check the building remained free from vandalism—although the worst anyone could do was spray-paint the exterior. The building was a three-storey fortress of lockable garages owned by a local housing association, and Cyril had been renting one since the eighties. When he'd had his stall on Felixstowe market, as well as the illegal magazines, certain people would pay good money for weaponry from France. Most of what he bought was to order for local thugs, kids who wanted the bigger, better, louder, more explosive fireworks and bangers, but he did have a liking for certain specialist items himself. He had grown up with James Bond as a hero, and when he'd started travelling on the continent, he had become awestruck by the variety of amazing things that were available. He bought ballpoint pens that had thin stiletto blades hidden in their handles, where if you twisted the barrel, a blade shot out of the lid. Knives were his personal favourite, especially knives that were disguised as or hidden in other things: shoes, watches, even a hip flask.

If you knew where to go and how to get it back undetected, you really could buy anything.

Cyril parked up outside the heavy iron gates and hoped to hell his keys still worked after all this time. The place was deserted, and even though it was secure, he doubted it was maintained very often; most of the lightbulbs inside were dead. The gates shrieked when he opened them. Judging by the amount of litter

FÜHRER: PART ONE

in the entrance, no one had been inside for quite a while. He wondered how many of the lockups were even used. A lot of people in the nearby flats used to use these places for extra storage. Initially when his parents were alive, that was what he used it for. Dusty old family heirlooms his mother refused to sell would sit alongside stacks of illegal pornography, handguns, machetes, knives and fireworks.

As well as working guns and knives, there had been call for replicas of weaponry used in films. Most of what he traded in had been perfectly safe if not indistinguishable from the real-life versions, but were often used in criminal situations: after all, if a crazed maniac is threatening you with what you recognise as a hand grenade, do you really want to fuck around and find out?

He found the key to the lockups' rolling shutter and hoped the lock hadn't rusted over. He jammed the key in the lock and had a mini anxiety attack when the thing wouldn't budge, but finally, with almost enough force to snap the key, the lock gave way. He rolled the shutter up and its high-pitched screech made his teeth ache. Hundreds of red rust flakes speckled his wrists.

Nothing in the garage, aside from his parents' junk, had been labelled, and it had been so long since he had been through the stuff that he had forgotten most of what was in there. The wet stink of mould permeated the air, it was inevitable that damp would get in eventually. Some of the boxes had exploded, spilling photo albums ruined by mildew, and breaking horrendous china ornaments he would have tried to flog at some point. He spotted an orange-hued photograph of a much younger version of himself with shoulder-length hair, brown cords, and a shirt with a wide collar that looked ridiculous in this day and age. The photo had been taken somewhere hot. As ever, he had been trying his best to look cool, to fit in, despite being on holiday with his ageing parents, the two stony-faced individuals standing with him in the photo, both at least a foot shorter than him. He wondered if it had been taken before or after Philippe.

Not wasting any more time, he began to rifle through the nearest boxes.

It wasn't long before he gave up searching. The majority of the firearms he owned had no ammunition, as that used to sell better than the weapons themselves. He doubted they'd have been enough to kill a werewolf in any case. With firsthand knowledge of how Danny had healed when Bartholomew had slit his throat, most of the knives wouldn't suffice, either. He rested against a tower of half-collapsing boxes filled with stacks of water-damaged illegal pornography from the Netherlands, and something right at the back sparked his inspiration. *I don't need to kill him, Bartholomew just wants him captured.* He remembered that the bondage chair in the brothel was enough to restrain the boy, even in wolf-form, and spotted a coil of chain piled in a corner, rusted but solid-looking, and next to that was a rectangular brown package with JAWS scrawled on it in black marker. Cyril's grin almost went from ear to ear as he wheezed laughter into the confines of the garage. "We're going to need a bigger boat."

FÜHRER: PART ONE

Chapter 45

Cyril loaded the box into the matchbox-sized boot of his car and left the lockup.

With a few modifications, his loot from the garage should be more than adequate to help them capture Danny.

Tepes' place wasn't that far away, but Cyril drove much faster than he had ever done in his life, running two red lights and nearly clipping a cyclist when he overtook a bus.

Adrenaline surged through him; what they were about to do was ludicrous and there was no way they would be able to keep a low profile.

Almost an hour had passed since he'd left his little rabbits with the drugged water. If they had drunk it shortly after he'd left to run Tepes' errand, then they should be unconscious still.

If not, then he would have to go through the whole rigmarole again. That would be doubly hard once the boys realised he had tampered with the water, and from their reaction before, they already suspected it.

He slid a palm across his sweaty brow and cursed Tepes for calling on him at the worst time.

Everything is always now, now, now with that bloke. Doesn't he realise that I have responsibilities too? Cyril swore and slapped the steering wheel.

Every vampire needs his Renfield.

Tepes' words replayed over and over again.

"I'm not your bloody servant," Cyril said through gritted teeth. "Not your fucking Igor — "

FÜHRER: PART ONE

"Lurch, more like, haha," Tepes said in his head. It was the sort of reply he would give if Cyril had his little outburst in front of him.

He had always known Tepes was an emotionless freak who only ever surrounded himself with people who were of use to him, but surely all these years of friendship meant something? It did to Cyril, especially seeing as their relationship had become more interesting now they had discovered one another's secret pastimes.

Not your average friendship, but perhaps cathartic for both parties now they had someone other than law enforcement to divulge all their extra activities to. Despite Cyril feeling no remorse or guilt about his own list of crimes, he knew he didn't glorify in it like Tepes did. If he could change the things he had to do to satisfy his cravings, he would.

In another dimension, he was living that ideal life with Philippe, and the afterimages of that fantasy overlapped every single one of his murders.

The fact that he had now tried human meat still sickened him, and he hoped Tepes wouldn't expect him to do it again.

He didn't know what Tepes planned to do once he'd captured Danny, but once he was restrained he wanted nothing else to do with it.

As he turned down Tepes' road he patted a rectangular lump in his shirt pocket. It wouldn't do to be without his little secret weapon.

Chapter 46

He pulled up outside Tepes' house, grabbed the box from the car boot, and stumbled over to the front door, pressing the doorbell with his little finger. After waiting for what felt like two minutes he tutted, put the box on the doorstep, and hammered on the door with a fist. "What the bloody hell are you doing?" Cyril raved, "bloody well tell me to shift my arse and you're not even here, for fuck's sake."

Red with rage, he yanked his mobile phone from his trousers and angrily stabbed Tepes' number.

The old bloodsucker picked up almost immediately and Cyril's voice rose several octaves when he blurted out, "Where the bloody hell are you?"

Tepes' reply was a dark chuckle. In the background, Cyril could hear traffic whizzing by.

"I'll be with you in about thirty seconds."

Tepes hung up and Cyril heard a loud diesel engine nearby before a white Transit van turned onto the road and came towards him. It was covered in the regalia of a national power company: GENSET. Cyril waited for it to pass by but then noticed the driver.

Tepes was almost unrecognisable behind the wheel, his hair scraped back into a ponytail and hidden beneath a baseball cap bearing the power company's logo. The van screeched to a halt mere inches away from the bumper of Cyril's car. Tepes leant from the driver's window and roared with laughter.

FÜHRER: PART ONE

For a few seconds Cyril was lost for words. "I didn't even realise you could drive."

"I've always said I don't drive, not that I can't," Tepes said, and sprung from the van's cabin. "Anything you can do, I can do better."

Cyril studied the van close-up. It was a genuine company vehicle. "I don't believe this. How the hell—"

Tepes put a finger to his lips. "Ask no questions, Cyril, dear. I have my fingers in a lot of pies." He twirled to show off the company uniform. "Don't worry, there's a spare outfit for you." He looked Cyril up and down with a chuckle. "Might be a bit short in the sleeve and leg."

Cyril forced a smile to try and disguise his annoyance. "Where the hell have you been? I've got stuff to do." He pointed at the box on the doorstep. "Stick that somewhere. I'll be back later and we can discuss what we're going to do with the brothers." He fished his keys out and took a lengthy step towards his car but felt Tepes' iron grip on his shoulder.

"Oh no, you don't," Tepes said coldly. "What's more important, right at this very moment, than catching ourselves a werewolf?"

Cyril thought of the two schoolboys. There was no way he was telling Tepes about them. They were his secret. He wasn't prepared to even share their existence until he had done what he needed to do. All his facial twitches erupted in full fury as his anxiety threatened to overwhelm him. "Come on," he said, trying to shrug it off, but the fear was clear in his voice. "It's the middle of the bloody afternoon. We'll be seen."

"What are you hiding, Cyril?"

"I ain't hiding anything. Like I say, it's daylight, man. We can't do what you're thinking during the day." He pointed at the box. "I've not even had a chance to test that stuff."

"I know where they are right now," Tepes stated. "Once we get them, you are free to do what you want with your boy."

"Boy?" Cyril spluttered, choking on his saliva.

"Do you not want the older Scarborough boy for yourself?"

"Yeah, but how are we supposed to snatch both of them?"

"Oh, I'm sure one will follow the other." Tepes slid an arm around Cyril's shoulders and felt him tremble. "When we both have what we want behind closed doors, I promise you'll have as much undisturbed time as you need."

Cyril's mind raced with the prospects of what he would have to do. There was so much bloody work ahead but at least Adam and Taylor were secured. Although, even if he managed to get Tony to the studio without anything going tits-up, he still had to take care of that bloody old man.

He thought about the dog and how foolish he had been to taunt it and let it run off rather than killing it instantly, and wondered whether this was the beginning of the end.

So be it.

If it was the end, then he would make sure Tony had a front-row seat to his performance with Adam and Taylor. It might prove interesting. He'd keep him alive as long as possible and do his best to see them all happily sleeping beneath the bluebells.

FÜHRER: PART ONE

And if he did get found out, he always had his little insurance policy to fall back on.

Cyril picked the cardboard box up from Tepes' doorstep. "Show me this bloody uniform."

Chapter 47

Cyril put the baseball cap on, adjusted to its maximum width.

With the power company's cargo pants at least six inches short in the ankle, and their yellow polo shirt threatening to ride up over his paunch, he resembled an oversized schoolboy, or Stretch Armstrong once his elasticity had perished.

Once Tepes had sated himself and gotten over the hilarity of Cyril's appearance, he ludicrously insisted that the uniform would suffice. After all, it was only the brothers who would recognise them.

Cyril opened the passenger door, but before he could climb in, Tepes shook his head and pointed to the rear of the van.

"What?"

"You and the box go in the back. I'll park up and we'll stake the place out first. When I give you the order, be ready to leap out and do your thing."

This troubled Cyril; once again he was being Tepes' little monkey. "We can't have any witnesses."

"We're in disguise."

Cyril snorted. "You are. There's not much I can do to hide myself. It's alright for you, you looked normal in the first place."

"Which is why we need to be quick," Tepes said. "Their initial reaction will be to the uniform and van. It'll take a few moments for their brains to figure out that you're not just someone who looks like you, and by the time that happens, we'll have them."

He was still doubtful. "So I just grab Danny and expect Tony to follow?"

Tepes nodded. "We've seen how resilient this thing is. I predict you could do anything you want to him aside from lop his head off and he'd get over it. Maim him enough to incapacitate him, and I'll help reel the other one in."

Cyril sat on the step of the van and hugged the box, mentally picturing their plan.

"So what did you find to apprehend our man?" Tepes asked. "I do hope it's nothing showy."

Cyril grimaced. "That's for me to know and you to find out."

Tepes' expression switched from jovial to venomous in the blink of an eye. The stuff inside him was working wonders, ironing out wrinkles that weren't even there and giving him strength and speed where he had never had it before. Rather than snatch the box from Cyril, he thrust his hand upwards and grabbed his throat. "Don't fuck with me, Cyril. I've been lenient up until now." His dark eyes bore into Cyril's soul. "Be a good little Renfield."

That last line was like a live wire. It overrode the fear which threatened to render Cyril a twitching wreck and even though he could barely breathe, he clutched at Tepes' wrist and fought to remove his hand. "I. Am. Not. Your. Servant." He seethed, a weight lightening from him regardless of the potential repercussions. Enough was enough.

It was strange to see a look of surprise on Tepes' face. Very little shocked the man, but Cyril's retaliation had done just that. His wicked grin resurfaced but it had lost some of its potency. He let Cyril go and made a show of patting down his polo shirt collar. "Well, well, well. It seems I may have underestimated you." He stepped back into the road. "I'm extremely sorry." His apology seemed genuine.

"I'm so used to being in charge that I may have mistreated you. Taken you for granted, even. Please, would you show me what you have in the box?"

Cyril's bravado was fleeting. When he opened the flaps of the box, his hands started shaking and he stammered slightly. "I-I f-figured," he said, pulling out a reel of mountain climbing rope, "that this should be a lot stronger than those leather restraints Tony used on him when he had Danny in the cellar."

Tepes frowned and some of his malice returned. "So, what? You're thinking of making a fucking lasso?"

Cyril showed him what else was in the box.

FÜHRER: PART ONE

Chapter 48

Shit.

Tepes wasn't expecting the boys to have company.

His contact said nothing about anyone else.

He scrutinised them from behind a pair of mirrored sunglasses he'd found in the glove compartment.

A man and a woman stood on the entrance ramp to the tower block next to the boys. They wore black militant clothing. They looked like cops. That was the last thing Tepes had expected. "Fuck," he shouted, and slammed his fists against the steering wheel.

"What's the matter?" Cyril asked from behind him.

"I hate to say it, but it looks as though our friends have gone to the police."

Tepes heard the clunk of Cyril banging his head against the van roof.

Seconds later, his bulbous eyes glared over the back of the seats. "What the fuck are we going to do?"

Tepes watched the couple lead the Scarboroughs to a little blue car that seemed a bit on the small side for an undercover cop car.

"They don't look like fuzz," Cyril said.

"What, pray tell, does the fuzz look like? And who else are they going to be?"

"Members of that gang?"

"They're nearly as old as us."

"Surely, if it were cops, they'd be a lot more of them, with what Danny did at the swimming pool?"

FÜHRER: PART ONE

"Bloody hell, Cyril," Tepes said to his reflection in the rearview. "I'm surprised. I thought you would be knee-deep in shit by now at the mention of the police."

Cyril watched the woman, a long ginger braid running down her spine, pull out a bunch of keys hanging from a couple of novelty keyrings, and open the passenger door and push the driver's seat forward to let the boys into the back. It was the keyrings that did it. There was no way cops, undercover or not, were good enough to include a minute detail like that. "I'm telling you," Cyril said, emerging from the back to prove his point, "they are not cops."

Tepes started the van.

"Whoa," Cyril bleated, "what are you doing?"

"You're right," Tepes said slowly, pulling away from the curb. "They can't be cops."

"B-but they might be," Cyril began to protest.

"Fuck it," Tepes said, sounding defeated. "Find something to hold onto, I'm going to ram them."

"What? Don't be so—"

"Get ready!" Tepes turned into the car park. "As soon as you hear a crunch, we get out."

"But what about the other two?"

"Collateral."

The front left corner of the van crumpled the car's bumper and smashed one of the headlights.

"What the fuck?" Danny spat from the back seat.

"Fucking idiot!" Ginger shouted.

Andy stared in disbelief at the front of the power company van towering over their little car. "The bloody prick was probably on his—"

"He's getting out," Tony said as the engineer climbed out of the van, mobile phone in hand.

Andy jumped out of the car and was about to speak when —

"Oh my God!" The engineer gasped and moved around to the front of the vehicles to assess the damage. "I'm so sorry," he said, motioning to his phone, "my mother, she is terribly ill —"

The man spoke with a European accent and fumbled nervously at his uniform, as if he were looking for something. He raised a finger and pointed back at the van. "Come, come, I get my details."

Jesus Christ, Cyril thought, *what the fuck does he expect me to do, sneak around and slit their throats?*

He carefully climbed down from the rear of the van, placed his weapon on the step, and risked a peep around the side in time to see Tepes swing a heavy metal steering wheel lock into the black-clad man's face.

Ginger screamed as Andy hit the floor, instinctively reaching for the handgun she had in a holster beneath her armpit, but the power guy moved so quickly.

His free hand clamped around her face and he threw her into the side of the van.

"No," Tony said when he recognised the wicked grin on the man's face. "It's him."

Danny didn't know what was going on other than they were being attacked. He thrust the driver's seat forward and threw himself out of the vehicle. Andy was flat out on the tarmac bleeding from a gash on his forehead, and Ginger staggered back into him, her hands covering her face. Danny froze, and when he realised who the engineer was, he turned to warn Tony. But it was too late.

"Coo-ee," came a voice from behind him. Danny spun around. There was no mistaking Cyril. He crouched by one of the rear van wheels, a gun aimed at him. Without any hesitation, he pulled the trigger.

Danny felt the shot hit him dead centre of the chest.

Something exploded inside him and he knew his wolf was coming.

Tony shrieked as the bullet went straight through his brother, the car windscreen, and the driver's seat.

A metal spearhead protruded from the back of the upholstery and Tony finally started to comprehend what was happening.

Outside, Danny was staggering backwards and forwards, a thread of wire or rope passing through his chest.

Tepes pushed Ginger aside and got back behind the van's steering wheel.

Tony frantically climbed through the front seats of the car, ducked below the gore-coated rope, and fell out onto the ground. Ginger lay on her side, nose pouring with blood. She opened her eyes and pointed feebly at the Transit.

Tepes turned the van around and Tony finally spotted his partner-in-crime through the swinging rear doors, crouching over what looked like a big fishing reel.

Danny screamed as his body shook with the transformation. He had barely any control over his limbs but managed to hook an appendage—which was somewhere between hand and paw—around the rope coming from his chest.

No sooner had his morphing skin come into contact with the rope than it pulled away from him at an alarming speed, shredding his newly forming skin. Something collided with him and he felt himself being tugged off his feet.

FÜHRER: PART ONE

Chapter 49

A harpoon. A fucking harpoon.

Tony couldn't believe what he was witnessing. The van pulled away, dragging wolf-Danny behind it, leaving a gory trail of flensed skin in the road. He ran after the bucking ferocious thing that was his brother, the harpoon's hook lodged firmly against his spine as Cyril reeled him in. Once safely away from the flats, Tepes stopped the van, jumped out, and aimed a handgun at Tony's head.

Tony watched as the wolf's leash gradually shortened. The beast tore at the van's rear bumper and swinging doors and roared up at Cyril, who was red-faced from exertion in the back of the van and busy loading another harpoon into the gun.

Tepes kept the weapon trained on Tony as he closed the gap between them. "Get out of the van, Cyril!"

Cyril panicked. Danny's monster was firmly attached to the motorised reel but he had no idea how they were going to get the bloody thing into the van. He climbed through to the cabin and soon joined Tepes. "So much for a low profile."

Tepes surveyed the surrounding area.

Pale faces dotted the dark windows of the tower blocks.

He grabbed a fistful of Tony's hair, pressed the gun against his temple and gathered near the captured beast. "Tell him to change back."

Tony laughed. "Do you honestly think he has any control over that thing?"

FÜHRER: PART ONE

Tepes thought for a second and pushed Tony towards Danny. It was a risky manoeuvre, but worth it. Tony yelled as he collided with the wiry furred thing but it made no attempt to attack its brother.

"Just as I thought," Tepes said. "Something of your brother still remains."

Tepes stepped closer to Danny, once more revelling at his magnificence.

Tepes addressed the wolf. "I think you can understand me," he said, and in its big yellow eyes he saw understanding. "My friend here has another harpoon. If you haven't changed back and gotten into the van by the time we hear the first sirens, then it's going to go straight through his fucking head."

It was the second time Tony had come into contact with his brother's wolf. There must have been something in what Tepes said, as yet again, Danny's monster refused to lay a paw on him. If anything, this time it recoiled, shrank away, crushing itself into the van's rear bumper, its torso covered in the blood from its wound.

It made a feeble attempt at reaching for the hooked point of the harpoon dart protruding from its spine. The bleeding had stopped and the flesh around the metal puckered and tried to heal. The remainder of the rope coming from its chest was tightened around a motorised reel;, heavy-duty but not too weighty for a beast of its size. Its claws clacked at the reel and tried slicing through the rope. It roared, head swinging from side to side, jaws snapping at Tepes and Cyril.

Tony looked at the two weapons trained on him. The handgun Tepes held was the one he had found in one of his three cases, along with the drugs, identity cards and money. *I should have just taken everything and run when I had the chance.* Cyril's harpoon gun looked like something Tony had seen people using to shoot rabbits or game on TV, except there was a bloody great spear coming out of the barrel.

"Like it, do you?" Cyril's grin was forced, Tony could hear the fear behind his words. "Exactly the same sort as Quint used in Jaws."

"I don't know what you're talking about," Tony said in disgust. He knew Cyril was a bundle of nerves: his face rippled and twitched and sweat quite literally poured out of him. Although Tony knew what he was capable of, he doubted he would be anything without Tepes. Across the car park, Tony saw Andy had got to his feet and was busy seeing to Ginger.

"Why are you doing this?" Tony asked Tepes, who was still studying Danny's new form.

Danny hunched over against the van, still a lycan.

His breathing was laboured.

Even if the lycanthropy could regenerate, it still had to compensate for the object impaling it.

Tony watched the creature's shoulders rise and fall and saw a gradual change begin.

"I just want to know what I'm dealing with," Tepes said. "Now, get in the van before I shoot your fr-" Bullets thudded through the side of the power company's van. Cyril whimpered and instinctively ducked.

Tepes risked a peep from behind an open van door. Andy stood on the opposite side of the road, pointing a pistol. "I'll kill them both," Tepes roared and popped a shot off.

FÜHRER: PART ONE

Cyril still cowered from more potential shooting.

Tony used Tepes' distraction and tried to slip away.

Tony ran down the road, he had no idea what he was doing other than seizing the opportunity to escape, whether it killed him or not. More gunfire, Cyril's girlish squeal, Tony's long, skinny shadow running ahead of him, stretched out by the late afternoon sun. He saw another behind him giving chase and it leapt, travelled an impossible distance, collided with him and brought him down.

Tony face-planted the tarmac, scraping the skin of his palms, nose and cheeks instantly.

The revitalising powers had worked wonders on Tepes, he wasn't even out of breath. He cradled Tony in his lap, one arm choking him as he pressed the gun into his temple. At the van, Cyril was still acting the cowardly buffoon, but Danny had reverted back to a naked teenage boy and was still firmly attached to the harpoon and rope. The two mysterious additions stood at the roadside, bloody-faced. Not too near, but not far away enough, sirens sang. Tepes congratulated the thing inside him for bestowing these gifts upon him, and for the first time spoke to it in his head as though it really was a sentient personality. *We have so much work to do, my friend. So much we can show each other. Just help me through this.* A surge of energy filled him and he sprang to his feet, Tony squirming beneath one arm. "Now I have your undivided attention," he boomed, taking centre stage like a perverted ringmaster. "Cyril, you're pathetic, really, aren't you?" He couldn't still his tongue from telling the truth. The gangly fucker looked like he was going to burst into tears at any point. "Get that fucking boy in that van now."

Cyril diverted his shame into passive aggression and thrust the butt of the weapon into Danny's spine.

"What the hell are you doing?" Andy said, stepping into the road. "We know about you."

Tepes couldn't fathom this fellow out. Who the hell was he? "This doesn't concern you, and if you step any closer I will shoot him first, and then the pretty redhead."

"Come on." Andy pointed to Danny, struggling to climb up into the van, the harpoon point still sticking out of his back. Every movement reopened the wound. "You know what he is? What's growing inside of you? You can't stop it. You'll have to hide forever."

Tepes chuckled. "That's where you're wrong. Up until now I've hidden, but I have a feeling none of that will matter very soo-"

A red hole braised the side of Tepes' throat; he slapped a hand over it and tightened his hold on Tony. "Well, that was stupid," Tepes said to Ginger, blood seeping through his fingers. He lowered his gun and fired it down at Tony, obliterating one of his knees.

"No," Danny screamed from the back of the van.

Still Ginger aimed her gun.

"Gin, no," Andy said in just as much shock as everyone else. "Let them go."

Ginger looked at the two boys and their captors and spat a mouthful of bloody mucus from her busted nose. "We'll find you."

Tepes took his hand away and showed them the wound had healed already, merely a red welt slashing his neck. He hefted Tony over one shoulder, never once taking his obsidian stare off them. "Get back into your little car and toddle off."

Ginger made to step forward but Andy grabbed her arm and dragged her towards their car with a promise of, "Later."

Tepes waved them off, scowled at Cyril and thrust a finger at the back of the van. Cyril sheepishly climbed up and pushed Danny to the rear of the space.

Tepes threw Tony up onto the van floor. "Tie them up. If either of them get away I will eat your heart."

Cyril flushed red, tears in his eyes, his lower lip, and whatever words were about to leave his mouth were drowned out by the slamming of the van doors.

Tepes couldn't afford to take his eyes off the couple. As he moved around to the driver's seat, he was fully aware that the approaching sirens were getting too close.

"The hunt is on," he called across to them and started the van up.

Andy and Ginger stood defeated by their little blue car and watched the power company's van drive off in the opposite direction of the sirens.

Chapter 50

Cyril felt like his head was going to explode.

Everything was going wrong.

There wasn't supposed to be anyone else who knew about this. The moment Tepes had slammed the van doors, he had set about binding Danny's legs with the mountaineering rope. He ducked Danny's batting hands. "The longer it takes me to secure you, the more your brother will bleed out."

Tony lay on the floor, pressing both hands to the wound on his knee.

Danny let himself be restrained; his attempts at hitting Cyril had been feeble anyway, the harpoon skewering him had sapped him of all fight.

Behind Danny's head, a small hatch slid open and Tepes spoke. "Everything alright back there?"

"Yeah," Cyril said with a grunt. "Danny's secure. I need something to bind his knee with."

"Use his top."

Tony made no protest as Cyril dragged his hoody over his head.

"Who were those people?" Cyril said, taking his eyes off Tony and looking through the hatch at Tepes and the road ahead.

"Tell us who they were, Danny," Tepes ordered, "they looked too old to be part of your crew."

Danny spat a mouthful of blood on Cyril's chest.

"Cyril," Tepes said, "hurt the older one."

"No," Danny cried out. "I don't know who they were. We only met them a few hours ago, I swear."

"Cyril, punch Tony in his injured knee."

FÜHRER: PART ONE

Cyril pulled his fist back ready to carry out Tepes' instruction but once again Danny intervened.

"It's the fucking truth. They're something to do with the Nazi guy, Krauss."

The van slowed and several turns were taken before anyone spoke.

"I can see there's a lot of stuff I'm not aware of," Tepes finally said. "Don't worry, we'll be able to have a good natter when we get back to mine."

Cyril wrapped Tony's hoodie around his knee and used the sleeves to tie it as tight as possible but the blood began to soak through in a couple of seconds. "He's bleeding loads, Bartholomew," Cyril said, panic-stricken.

"Have you not got anything at your little holiday home you can use to deal with it?"

"The studio? I don't know."

"Well, I'm sure you'll figure something out."

Cyril pressed hard against the wound, felt shards of bone grating against one another. Tony shrieked and passed out from the pain.

"We'll be there soon," Tepes said.

"Where are you taking us?" Danny wished the agony of the harpoon would make him lose consciousness, too.

"You're coming back to my place for a little chinwag," Tepes said. "Tony's going with Cyril. We're going to see if your stories corroborate. My friend there has sworn to be the perfect host until he gets my word."

"I have?" Cyril asked.

"Yes, you have," Tepes replied angrily. "However if you've not heard anything from me by," —he checked his wristwatch— "nine o'clock tonight, then feel free to go to town on him."

Cyril thought about the other guests at his *little holiday home* and knew he had his work cut out for him, but as it was one of his most treasured pastimes, his butterfly mind made quick, calculating decisions.

If both the boys are unconscious, smother Taylor and move him. Adam will be nothing on his own; a compliant little zombie, who knows there may be some fun to be had whilst he's still alive. Keep him and Tony alive for a few days until it's the next one's turn.

He smiled at the thought of having his own mini harem; it really was going to be his holiday home.

Through the partition, Cyril saw woodland encompassing the road like a green tunnel.

They were nearly there.

Thirty seconds passed.

They travelled in silence and then the van slowed and Tepes banged on the van wall. "Can't get any closer, as you know."

Cyril pushed his face forwards and took in the surroundings. "Fuck."

Tepes laughed. "Oh, come on, it's not that far."

"Yeah, but every other time it's been dark," Cyril said, thinking of the minute or so he would have to walk with Tony.

"I'll stay here long enough for you to get away from the road."

Cyril felt his excitement dilute into fear. He prodded Tony, who was well and truly out of it still. "Shit," he said, and took a deep breath. "Okay, let me know if the road's clear and I'll make a run for it."

"You're good to go, Cyril," Tepes said. "Remember if I've not contacted you by nine to come and rescue me."

Cyril climbed down from the van and dragged the comatose Tony towards the edge.

"Oh, Cyril," Tepes said, poking his head through the partition. "Good luck."

Cyril lifted Tony up onto his shoulder, surprised at how little the boy weighed, and nodded at his friend. "See you later."

Cyril kicked the van door closed and jogged towards the overgrown path, pleased that Tepes kept his word and didn't drive away until he was deep in the foliage.

The area was deserted as usual, no sounds other than birdsong and the far-off bark of a dog.

Tony's wound leaked down over Cyril's shoulder, he could feel the blood wetting the left breast of his shirt.

He quickened his pace.

The last thing he needed was another body to bury; there was already Samuel Ellington's father to bury when it got dark.

His pulse rate reduced when the studio came into view and he took out the keys.

He managed to get the place open one-handed, laid Tony on the floor beside the headless corpse of the old man and bolted the door.

Behind the reception desk was a tin box containing a load of first-aid stuff; he threw the contents across the desk, selected two patches of gauze, adhesive tape and bandages, then spotted the splintered door frame and froze.

The boys.

He flew towards the soundproofed room knowing full well he would find the schoolkids gone.

The thought of how they had managed to accomplish their escape bubbled up fleetingly in his head as he pushed open the door, and the sight before him made him fall to his knees.

Adam and Taylor were still there, spread in naked cruciforms, chains still attached, fingertips touching on the filthy concrete floor, their throats torn wide. On the wall, across faded band posters, was one word written in what he presumed was their blood. *Renfield.*

Cyril looked at their sweet, dirty little faces and it hurt like finding his own sons butchered.

"No," he screamed, falling forwards and reaching out for their messy hair. "No, not my boys."

Tepes. Tepes had done this.

But why?

Cyril rolled onto his back and put the studio's soundproofing to the test by letting loose all his anguish and sorrow to the ceiling. As his own cries petered out, he heard, through the open reception door, the sound of barking again. Only this time, it wasn't just one dog.

He slowly got to his feet, shuffled towards the studio's entrance, opened the door, and squinted through tear-blurred eyes.

The stinging nettles around the studio were stained with blood from Tony's wound.

The sound of dogs approaching grew louder and he remembered the blood he had wiped around Daisy, Samuel Ellington's father's dog, hours before. Voices crept between the dogs' barks and Cyril slowly turned back into the studio.

It was all over.

FÜHRER: PART ONE

Tepes had betrayed him, and the old bloke's dog had done a Lassie and got help somehow. An unnatural calm came over him as he stuck his thin fingers into his blood-soaked shirt pocket to retrieve the little tobacco tin he had been carrying for the past couple of days.

Outside came the crackle of police radios.

Cyril opened the tin. Inside were two triple-wrapped red bundles the size of marbles.

Ever since he was a kid, he had been into James Bond. He had read books on real-life spies and although he had never managed to procure one, he'd always wanted to get his hands on the fabled cyanide pill and false tooth certain agents were rumoured to have used. That was the idea behind these tiny parcels. He popped the two balls into his mouth, the cellophane sticking to his tongue, thought back to the night he'd drugged Tepes and taken a vial of his blood.

Once he'd realised Tepes was turning into something else entirely he knew he might need a little insurance policy, but he hadn't made the packages until he was sure they were going after the Scarborough boys.

Nodding once at the now semi-conscious Tony, Cyril walked out into the daylight and bit down on the blood capsules.

Matthew Cash

PART FOUR

FÜHRER: PART ONE

Chapter 51

The Dehaneys coach sat beside two others.

The Novotel in La Chapelle-Saint-Ursin was elaborate, an off-white building fitted with all mod-cons.

The passengers inside the hotel feasted their eyes on the restaurant's buffet bars.

These folk were professional eaters.

Buffets were the highlights of some of their meagre existences and were usually the reward for enduring a dull or depressing occasion, such as a funeral or a wedding.

"Pity the drinks aren't unlimited too," Ted half-joked for the third time since joining the shuffling queue, just in case anyone within listening distance hadn't heard him the first two times He had crafted a sturdy wall of hash browns and roast potatoes around the edge of his plate and filled the circular clearing in the middle with everything that could cause spillage: beans, peas, rice, pasta. He roofed this food fortress with bacon strips and sausages. A tower which threatened to avalanche.

Despite the hefty plateful, he still managed to find something to complain about. "Bog-standard fare this is, though, Oliver," he said, carefully topping his triumph with a battered prawn buttress.

"Probably a Lidl nearby. Still," he added before thoughtfully covering the whole lot with gravy and hoping like hell it wouldn't spring a leak, "mustn't grumble."

FÜHRER: PART ONE

Ahead of him, Ollie the Scotsman put just enough food on his own plate to feed an anorexic sparrow.

"Ey, Jock," Ted said with blatant disregard as to whether the term was now classed as racist or derogatory, "you don't want to be traipsing back and forth with them bloody sticks. Get as much on as you can, lad."

Norman, crutches hooked on his elbows, tipped his head towards them. "Och, I only want enough to line my stomach."

Ted rolled his eyes. "Don't tell me you lot watch what you eat and all? Jesus, ain't it enough being teetotal and doing yoga? We're still gonna die, you know."

"My body is a temple," Herbert said profoundly as he came up behind them gazing at his own meagre salad.

Ted studied his mountain of fried carbs and red meat. "Think mine's a bloody Wetherspoons."

It was Ted's first experience of Trevor's sudden explosive laughter and it almost made him drop his plate. "Christ on a bloody bike, lad, you need to give us a ten-minute warning before you let that off!"

Trevor winked at him when he caught Ted's disapproval at his plate of light snacks. "Restaurant's open until ten, man. Once we've stretched ourselves out we'll come back and see if you pair have left us anything."

"You'll be lucky," Ted said, cocking a thumb at Ollie, "this one eats me out of house and home. So, are you lot off upstairs to get into your leotards and go all Jane Fonda on us?"

"You sure you don't want to join us?" Herbert beamed.

Ollie mumbled something which was indecipherable but which ended in the word *fuck* and, as ever, it was left to Ted to translate.

"No, remember, we were going to prop up the bar with your daughter and her mates."

Herbert nodded. "Don't let them lead you astray."

Juliet and Charlotte joined the queue with Gustav and his newly acquired mother-and-son combo.

Ted eyed Gustav, Valerie, and her son Vince and whispered to Herbert, "Ought to make those fat fuckers go with you."

Herbert cringed. "One doesn't do this type of yoga to lose weight, just to retain one's flexibility and mobility."

"Yeah," Ted started and looked at Vince, "but man-mountain there don't look too mobile, does he?"

Valerie, who had been in deep, still openly flirtatious conversation with Gustav stopped mid-word and glared. "Oi, what are you looking at?"

"Nowt, love, nowt." Ted flashed his filthy mouthful at her innocently.

"Besides," Herbert said with seething venom, "I think that someone who resembles an exhumed Jimmy Savile doesn't exactly have the right to comment on people's appearances."

For the first time in a long while, Ted was speechless, even more stunned when Ollie let loose a loud woof of a laugh at his expense.

He scowled at his red-faced boyfriend and took his heavy plate to a nearby table.

"Mind if we join you?" Charlotte said, sidling over to the four-seater table where Ted and Ollie were sitting.

"Free country, ain't it?" Ted said through a mouthful of food.

Charlotte sat opposite him, with Juliet beside her.

Across the restaurant, Norman, Trevor and Herbert took a table for themselves and picked at their plates.

"Ey up, Ponsonby-Toff has stolen the jock's bird!" Ted chuckled and nodded in the direction of Leopold Alcocks, who led Ivy by the elbow to a table for two.

"Ted, isn't it?" Charlotte said, offering one of her nicest smiles.

Ted nodded.

"Am I right in remembering that you two are a couple?" Juliet said, setting down her cutlery.

Ted nodded but Juliet detected an air of wariness about him and offered him a reassuring smile.

"You can take the piss if you want," Ted said, "we're used to it. You should've heard the blokes down the Bus Club when we came out of the proverbial closet."

"Bus Club?" Juliet asked.

"Yep. We used to be bus drivers," Ted said, spearing a sausage.

"Used to be?" Charlotte said. "What do you do now? Neither of you look old enough for retirement!"

"Look after him, don't I?" Ted said somewhat vaguely, "he's got that fibro algae thing."

"Fibromyalgia."

"That's the one. I've never been one to get them long words right. You should bloody hear me when I'm listing the fucking meds he's on, I swear to God I thought I was going to summon Cthulhu or something."

"Lovecraft," Ollie said between mouthfuls.

Charlotte smiled.

"Yeah, some of the names of medication are ridiculous, aren't they? When I first started medical training, I used to think Simvastatin sounded like a place in Wales."

Ted snorted.

"Yep, he's on that one. No grapefruit. Mebeverine sounds like something one of us would say when we're pissed." He coughed awkwardly at Charlotte's polite smile. "So, are you a nurse, then?"

Charlotte felt Juliet's kick under the table. "Yeah."

"Hear that, Oliver?" Ted said, nudging the man beside him. "We'll be in safe hands this trip."

Ollie continued to shovel food in.

"You look like you've got each other's backs," Charlotte said, and waved to Gustav who looked fearful as Valerie dragged him to a table.

"We've always been close," Ted said, with no sign of his usual scorn or sarcasm. "We both pretended we were something we weren't, all through the eighties. Halfway through the nineties, too. I doubt you pair will remember, but it's never been completely okay to be the way we are. You have to learn to give as good as you get, whether it be physically or verbally."

"Paddington Station," Ollie said, scraping baked beans onto his fork.

Ted groaned. "You wanna tell them about that, you tell them."

Ollie stared at them like a frightened, bug-eyed child.

"It's okay," Charlotte began, but Ted sighed and put his knife and fork down.

"Alright, you pair," he said, leaning over the table conspiratorially, "you want to hear about Paddington Station, might I suggest that we finish this and get over to the bar, pronto."

"I'm not sure I want to hear about Paddington Station," Juliet offered politely.

Ted gasped with overdramatic offence. "Trust me, you'll want to hear about Paddington Station."

"I do, I definitely want to hear about Paddington Station!" Charlotte laughed.

"He looks just like his dad," Valerie said, staring lovingly at Vince. "The bastard."

"You sure you don't want me to leave you two to it?" Vince said, feeling like the prickliest of gooseberries.

"No," Gustav said with genuine fear.

"Don't be a twat, Vin." Valerie reached over and swatted his shoulder. "We're just getting to know each other. We're going to be spending a week or so in each other's company, after all."

Gustav gulped.

"So," Valerie said, swooning over him, "tell me about Iceland."

Gustav paled as all knowledge of a country he had never visited left his mind. "Umm, it is nice place."

"I don't really know much about it, to be honest with you, Gustav," Valerie said, "aside from the black sand, and oh, that volcano that went tits-up the other year."

"Eyjafjallajökull," Vince said.

"You what?" Valerie said.

"Eyjafjallajökull," Vince repeated, "that's the name of the volcano that erupted in 2010."

Valerie leaned against Gustav's arm. "Is he right, Gustav? Has he pronounced it proper?"

"Yes," Gustav said nervously, not having the slightest clue. "Very good pronunciation."

Valerie smiled proudly. "My Vincent's dead clever. Always reading, aren't you, Vin?"

Vince nodded and tapped at an e-reading device that rested by his plate.

"Very, very well read, my Vincent," she reiterated. "Tell Gustav what you're reading at the moment."

"Oh, no," Vince declined shyly, "he's not interested in that type of—"

"Of course he is," Valerie snapped. "From the moment I saw him, I could tell he was an intelligent, educated man."

"Yes, yes, I would very much like to hear," Gustav said, and caught Trevor's laughter across the restaurant.

"See," gloated Valerie, "he's interested."

Vince lowered his face and mumbled something into his chest.

"What?" Valerie said. "Speak up."

"*Zombie-Bratwurst in the Daddy-Hole of Death.*"

A aeons-spanning silence befell the table, civilisations rose and fell, humankind, well at least two of the three at the table, de-evolved into goldfish-mouthed Neanderthals.

"You fucking what?" Valerie said with arctic vehemence.

"Please don't make me say it again," Vince whimpered, but one look at his mother told him he had no other choice. "*Zombie-Bratwurst in the Daddy-Hole of Death.*"

Valerie spat each word like clumps of regurgitated poison: "Zombie bloody Bratwurst in the fucking Daddy-Hole of Death?" She sagged and one of her hands went to her face.

Her ring-heavy fingers rubbed at her temples.

"I read Crime and Punishment last week," Vince offered, far too late.

Gustav studied the food on his plate and tried not to look like he wanted the world to swallow him up.

"He has A-levels, Gustav, A-levels," Valerie said, close to tears, shaking her head.

"I believe," Gustav said, raising a finger, "that the same author wrote wonderful stories about the lizards in the jism."

Vince's face lit up as though all his birthdays had come at once.

Valerie wondered what other secrets the Icelandic held and asked herself whether she actually wanted to discover them after all.

Chapter 52

The three old-timers stared across the zipping streams of six lanes of traffic. The Novotel was separated from several hundred acres of maize by a hellish motorway.

Herbert pointed to the dark expanse. "Yoga time, gentlemen."

They meandered along the edges of a flyover which linked the small industrial estate the hotel was on with the endless farmland.

"We're probably going to get picked up by the Gendarmerie," Trevor whined.

"It's alright, we'll tell them Herbert's campervan broke down," Norman said, nudging Trevor. "Yoga?"

Herbert marched on ahead. "Did either of you have a better excuse?"

Neither man answered.

"At least this way, if we appear more agile than normal people our age, we'll be covered."

Trevor sighed. "How are we supposed to do this, Herbie, man?"

Herbert turned and walked backwards. "Trevor, do you remember how you felt when we attacked the soldiers at the barracks?"

"No way, man. All I remember is the shock at finding that my babies were still alive and these people were going to hurt them." Trevor thought back to the bloody-minded rage that had taken hold. His lycanthropic shift just seemed like an addition to his anger.

"Whatever it was you did, you need to do it again," Herbert said, "focus inwards rather than outwards, be more self-aware, feel every aspect of your body and visualise what you want it to do, to become."

"Is it like meditation?" Norman asked. His own experience at the facility was a blur.

"In a way," Herbert said. "It's a matter of concentration and mindfulness."

"Great," Trevor groaned, "because those are some of my strong points."

Herbert tried to explain. "Don't look at your hands and imagine them changing, believe that they will, just like you have faith that if you lift your arm your hand will raise, have faith that they will change. These things inside us are wily bastards but they also want to be let out. As soon as it's established that you can prevent them from doing as they want, they give in."

Norman sighed heavily.

Herbert slipped into a darkened field and they followed suit.

Since their infection, Trevor and Norman's night vision had improved, but as they wove through the knee-high maize, Trevor realised things were even clearer. Perhaps his wolf sensed possible danger and was offering its gift freely.

No! Trevor snapped his eyes shut. *I'm the one in charge, mutt. You want to see in the dark, you'll do it when I say.* He opened his eyes and couldn't see a thing. "Right, now you can help."

"Trevor?" Herbert asked from the darkness.

"Just trying to kick myself into shape," Trevor said, as his night vision reactivated.

"Right," Herbert said, beginning to remove his clothes. "Let's strip off and get started."

"Whoa!" Norman shouted. "What the hell are we doing here?"

Herbert folded his clothes and laid them down. "Well, we can't buy a new wardrobe every time we change, and I for one don't fancy walking back into the Novotel starkers. Do you?"

"Point taken," Norman said, loosening his tie.

"It's bloody cold, man," Trevor said from beneath his pullover.

"Bloody braw," Norman agreed, reluctantly removing the last of his clothes. He gestured to his heavily bandaged body. "What about all this?"

"How do you think you're healing?" Herbert said, now completely naked.

"I'm not as itchy, so that must be a good thing." Norman said pulled a strand of bandage away to see if his skin had finished rebuilding.

Herbert strode ahead of them. "The first thing I'm going to focus on is the cold." He spread his arms. "I noticed, as my wolf seems to be a baldy just like me, that when I change, my skin becomes thicker, almost leathery."

Trevor and Norman gazed in wonder as Herbert closed his eyes and muscles bulged and popped beneath his thickening skin.

"I'm not," Herbert said, as his nose caved in and he sprouted something more canine, "the most hirsute of werewo-lves." The end of the word came out as a half-animal growl.

Under any other circumstances Trevor and Norman would have found his distorted vocals hilarious, but standing naked in a field waiting to change into monsters wasn't conducive to humour.

FÜHRER: PART ONE

"Close your eyes." Somehow, Herbert managed to shape vowels and syllables with his lycanthropic mouth. "Focus on your breathing and your inner thoughts."

Trevor cupped his hands over his genitals. "My inner thoughts are images of you two in the buff. They're seared onto my retina, man."

"Looking at your hairy arse and clackersack isn't exactly our idea of fun, either," Norman said, covering himself.

"You're cold," said Herbert in a voice that would make Barry White sound like a chipmunk.

"No shit, Sherlock."

Herbert ignored Norman's sarcasm. "You have it in you to do something about this. Thicken your skin, let your pelts grow. Find your own way to master this."

Trevor screwed his eyes shut and puffed his cheeks out, trying to push the fur from his facial pores, but only managed a mournful, baritone fart. "This is useless, man."

"Aye," Norman added, "Trevor's right, you're a natural."

A loud roar in front of them made them jolt back and open their eyes.

Herbert was in full werewolf form. He was bigger than they ever remembered seeing him before, a muscular behemoth, completely bald and pink, more like a mutated baby rat than an actual wolf.

His gigantic, clawed hands shot out and grabbed each man around the neck and lifted them off the ground. With one swift motion he manipulated his head into something more human and spoke. "Do you feel it now? That fire inside you knows how easily I could snap your necks..."—he looked at Norman—

"...rip out your tongue, *again*. So harness it. Think of Kiran and Kayleigh. Think of Dolores and Bridget. Think of the people we need to save and what we have to do to achieve this."

Trevor felt it the moment Herbert clamped his hand around his throat. Like acid or poison coursing through him, flooding his veins and setting fire to his nerve-endings. Pain exploded in his stomach and he thought of his grandchildren, his daughter. and willed it to stop, relaxing in Herbert's clutches. *No!* He directed his thoughts to the alien inside. *My way or the highway. I'll let him kill us both, I swear.* He let himself flop, released the tensions and stresses of his body, and focused on what he wanted to change.

His wolf rose to the surface, tore his body apart, and reacted more quickly and fluidly than ever before. Norman felt Herbert's claws dig into his flesh as his neck swelled and he remembered their fight in the park. Claws burst from his fingers and toes and he raked them down Herbert's forearms, muscle and skin hanging in tatters.

Herbert felt Trevor go limp and his pulse slow but Norman's sudden attack made him cry out in agony. He relaxed his grip on Trevor as the visible signs that he was trying to control himself started to show, his vulpine features flickered back and forth from animal to human and came to rest somewhere in between.

Trevor dropped to the ground in a squat, a bulky muscular thing covered in fur from head to toe.

Herbert needed both hands to fend Norman off. He had changed fully, a snapping, lethal whirlwind of tooth and claw.

FÜHRER: PART ONE

"Norman," Herbert shrieked as one of Norman's talons sheared his lips in two, "remember Bridget, your wife. Fight this. Be the stubborn old bastard you've always been."

A pair of giant furry arms appeared from behind Norman and wrapped him in a bearhug.

Now it was two against one.

Norman's wolf-form was still inexplicably quadruped and it was this that gave him an advantage. He squirmed and twisted between the two bipedal half-men, tearing with tooth and claw, and slipped from their clutches.

The moment he was free he fled; his wolf knew it was outnumbered by its two stronger opponents.

There was still a vague awareness, though: Norman felt the crops whip past his slender body as his wolf rocketed through the maize field.

Both Trevor and Herbert gave chase but their current forms weren't built for speed.

Herbert fell to all fours and tried a second transformation, his back snapping, his legs unknitting and reforming into canine hindquarters.

Trevor had never felt so powerful. As he tore through the field, he let the wolf take over to the limit of its physical capability. His skull cracked, a snout burst from his face, and he roared and went after his best friend, galloping towards the six-lane motorway.

Herbert, now in a speedier form, took the lead and was almost on Norman's tail, but Norman leapt into the road — and the path of a small car travelling at a hundred-and-ten miles an hour.

Herbert paused on the hard shoulder and watched the car screech across the two other lanes, smashing into three other cars and the side of a coach.

The mangled tangle of metal shrieked along the central reservation, sparks hissing as they came to a gradual halt and more and more cars ploughed into them.

Just then, Trevor jumped into the melee without a second thought.

He ran across the sea of car roofs, metal crumpling beneath his bulk.

Herbert had no choice but to follow. In the heart of the cacophony, he saw something drag itself between the first car and up on top of the coach. He stuck to the shadows of the hard shoulder and ran as fast as he could to try and get ahead of Norman.

Severed limbs.

Someone was thrown through a windscreen and spread across the tarmac.

Trevor ignored the carnage after learning that concentrating on any aspect of it would haunt him forever. As he neared the end of the pile-up, the outcome became worse, more graphic. The car that had hit Norman was a flattened lump, half-embedded in the rear of the coach. Suitcases spilled from the luggage hold and unidentifiable viscera spilled out from the mashed car.

Norman stood on the roof of the bus and howled out his frustration, his head snapping side to side as he plotted his next move.

Trevor climbed up on the coach roof and made his wolf retreat, leaving him completely exposed. "Norman!" he shrieked, and his friend's wolf, red-furred and battered, dragged itself around, ready to attack.

Although the car crash wasn't enough to kill him, Norman suffered a lot of physical damage. Trevor could see his back legs and hips were crushed, but even as he turned, the regeneration process was underway.

Trevor held his arms up and stepped across the roof.

Norman pulled himself along by his front paws, jaws gnashing the air in front of him.

"It's me, Norman," Trevor yelled above the mayhem, "stop fucking fighting, man. I'm stark-bollock naked in front of hundreds of people. If that's not enough to shock you out of this, then you'll have to just kill me, put me out of my misery."

A loud thunk made them both flinch.

Herbert landed on the roof behind Norman.

Seeing Trevor had changed back into human-form, he chose to do the same; it was too late to worry about what people had or had not seen.

"Norman."

Norman thrashed between the two of them. He knew he was incapacitated, knew what these two could do, and he knew there was nowhere to run.

"Norman," Herbert called again, "we are your friends. I know you can hear me. Fight this bloody thing before anyone else dies."

Inside Norman, the part that wasn't overrun with the alien parasite picked up on certain words and these conjured images in his mind.

He tried to cling to them through the psychological storm.

Bridget.

His wife's face swam before him, the key to opening other memories, vaults where the good stuff was stored for safekeeping: friendship, love, happy times, sex, being a good copper. He grabbed hold of these things and bound them to himself like armour, added the endless drunken escapades with his best friend Trevor, their companionship longer and more honest than either of their marriages.

With the support of a lifetime's worth of good energy, he lowered a heavy metal collar around his snarling wolf's throat and felt it cower and retreat.

Norman rolled onto his side, his legs bloody and disfigured, and looked solemnly at Herbert. "So, how the hell are you going to explain your hand?"

Herbert held his hands in front of his face as if he had never seen them before. He noticed the fully regrown, healed appendage, then took in Norman's massacred limbs.

"What about your legs?"

FÜHRER: PART ONE

Chapter 53

Bellies stuffed, Ted and Ollie led their female companions across the restaurant to the bar area, where a few other members of the coach party were already drinking. Charlotte saw Gustav at the bar and took Juliet and the gents' orders before instructing them to sit down. "You're making friends?" she said, sliding in next to the Ukrainian.

He turned to her, embarrassment reddening his cheeks. "The lady, Valerie, she is becoming emotionally attached, I think."

"And you aren't interested in a wee holiday romance?" Charlotte said with a smirk.

"We are hardly on holiday," he replied.

"No, we're not. But, Jesus, Gustav, with what we're getting into, none of us knows how much longer we even have left. Why not have a bit of fun beforehand?"

Gustav sighed and watched as the bar staff tended to his order.

"Aren't you interested?"

He casually studied the chunky woman with her copious amounts of gold jewellery and bleached blonde hair. "She is a very beautiful woman but I do not wish to be the breaker of hearts."

"She's probably only after a random fling, a drunken fumble."

Gustav's complexion grew even more scarlet.

Charlotte saw that Juliet, Ted and Ollie were sitting at a table big enough to accommodate half a dozen other people. "Come and sit with us. Ted and Ollie are a hoot."

FÜHRER: PART ONE

It seemed to take a few seconds for Gustav to grasp the meaning of her words. He slowly nodded.

Back at the table, Valerie's stare could have melted lead. "What chance have I got if trollops like that have got their claws into him?"

Vince ogled Charlotte's slight but shapely figure. "She's so pretty."

"See? She's even got you drooling."

"Chill out, she's way out of his league."

"Oh," Valerie said, turning to her son, "and I'm not?"

Vince grimaced. "No, what I'm saying is when men see a woman like that, they don't even bother doing anything other than looking. They know there's not a hope in hell that someone like that would ever look at them, or me, in anything other than pity or disgust."

She took one of her son's huge hands. "You could have any woman you desired."

"Yeah, maybe with a heavy dose of Rohypnol."

"Don't say things like that, that's vile."

"True, though."

"It ain't all about looks, you know? You're the dead spit of your dad, and I was a slender size ten when I went for him."

Vince didn't really remember much of his father as he had died of a massive heart attack when he was forty-five and Vince was seven. He remembered his mum being skinny, though, and how as they'd both got over the loss of a husband and father, eating had become the only comfort. "I don't remember him much."

"I don't suppose you do. But he was a real gem, larger than life, clever, funny and lovely. Just like you."

"Yeah, and I'll probably go the same bloody way, but at an even younger age," Vince said scornfully.

She slapped his hand and pushed it away. "Don't be so bloody morbid. What have I told you? Nobody knows how long they have left. I've read stories about bloody marathon runners dropping dead of dicky tickers. Doesn't always have to be about size, you know? And besides, you've more muscle than he did."

Vince smiled sadly. She was always in denial about how serious his obesity really was. He thought about the 'roided-up American wrestlers and how a lot of them had died of heart failure way too young. "It all weighs and adds to the pressure on your body."

"We'll get there, son," she said, and her whole demeanour elevated as Gustav ventured back to their table.

Charlotte placed a tray of drinks in front of Juliet, who was batting Ted's words away like they smelt funny and at the same time trying to stifle laughter.

"It wears the soap," Ted repeated with a gutter-level cackle. "Wears the soap."

"Nuns," Ollie grunted.

"You three look like you are having fun," Charlotte stated.

"These two are worse than my dad and Norman," Juliet said with fond recollection, before her expression changed to one of horror as she remembered their charade of not knowing one another before the trip.

"I've asked them three if they want to join us," Charlotte said, pointing at Gustav's table. "I hope you don't mind."

Ollie shrugged with indifference, but Ted appeared irate. "Thought we had you ladies to ourselves, didn't we, Ollie? Thought there was a chance you'd try and turn us."

Ollie grunted.

"Oh, I'm sure nothing could tear you two apart," Juliet said.

"Ah, he's alright I suppose."

"Uh-oh, here comes trouble," Juliet said, reminding herself of her father and wondering how their yoga session was going.

Gustav brought Valerie and Vince to the table.

Brief introductions were made.

Charlotte tapped Ted on the arm. "You were going to tell us about your Paddington Station incident."

Ted groaned. "Do I have to?"

"Yes," Juliet and Charlotte exclaimed in unison.

"This lot don't want to hear about Paddington Station," he said sheepishly, about the three newcomers.

"Yes we do," Vince said, and the others agreed.

Ted faked reluctance once more, took a large gulp of his drink, let out a burp that sounded like a T-Rex's mating call, and began his story.

"It were some time in the eighties, I think, I know the main topics on the news were AIDS and the bloody IRA—"

"1984," Ollie snapped.

"I said the eighties, didn't I?" Ted rolled his eyes. "Why don't you tell the bloody story if you know the details so well?"

Ollie grumbled something foul into the head of his latest pint.

"No?" Ted said, "Well, shut thy pie hole, Oliver." He turned back to his captive audience. "So, I know I said we didn't come out, as it were, 'til halfway through the nineties, but we knew how each other was inclined and how we felt about one another, too."

"Whoa," Vince interrupted, "you two are a couple?"

"Do you have a problem with that, Sunshine?" Ted said with such malice that the people at nearby tables fell silent.

Vince shrugged. "Nope. Just getting all the deets of the backstory. Nothing new and shocking about homosexuality."

"Fucking was back then, mate," Ted said. "If we were on telly it was always as a bloody comedy element, but we weren't all like Mr Humphries or Julian bloody Clary."

"Still plenty of prejudice about now," Vince said, "I don't know why people give a shit so much about where another person sticks their bits, as long as they ask first."

Ollie barked laughter.

"Good man," Ted added with mild surprise. "Well, anyway, me and him used to nip down to London for the weekend. It's a big place and there were a lot more places that were, let's say, more liberal than up north."

"In the Ukraine, they are still as bad as in the eighties," Gustav chipped in.

FÜHRER: PART ONE

"What's the Ukraine got to do with owt?" Ted asked and wondered what he had said to make Gustav pale so much.

"Umm," Gustav stumbled, desperately trying to find a suitable excuse for bringing up a country he wasn't supposed to be from. "I mean, there are parts of the world, due to their customs or religions, that still frown upon same-sex relationships."

"Fuck 'em," Ted spat.

"Yes, I agree," Gustav said awkwardly, "fuck them all."

"As I was saying, we used to go to London for the weekend, were too scared back then to be ourselves in our own town. Anyway, that day, there were a load of football supporters clogging up Paddington Station; I don't know what team they were for, nor do I care—"

"Tottenham Hotspurs," Ollie growled.

"Whoopee-fucking-doodle-doo," Ted said, seething sarcasm. "Anyway, fuck's sake I'm getting fed up with saying bloody 'anyway'. *Anyhow*, somehow they knew we were a couple, whether it was because we had more freedom to express ourselves in the capital or something else I don't know, it weren't like we were prancing around wearing pink bloody tutus and shitting rainbows like they all do now, but they knew, and it all kicked off."

"Newky Brown ale," Ollie said.

Ted rolled his eyes and dropped his head to the tabletop.

Charlotte and Juliet tried to stifle their laughter but Valerie, less subtle, didn't. "You're a right pair, aren't you?"

Ted faked heavy sobs and forced himself back upright. "I'm getting to that bit," he said, cocking a thumb at Ollie, "photographic memory, this one, but still forgets to put the milk away."

"Bollocks."

"Yours or another pair?" Ted replied and tried to get back to his story. "Anyway, oh, there it is again, this bunch of Tottenham supporters started on us. I reckon it was coz we were pissed as newts and gobbing off about something, but they were, too, and one thing led to another and a bloody great riot started up on the bloody station, fists, feet and fags everywhere. You could smoke at stations, back then. Someone called the rozzers and fucking matey here goes and smashes his half-empty newky brown bottle across someone's head, but it weren't a football supporter, oh no, it were just some random bloke with his suitcase."

"Oh my God!" Juliet exclaimed.

"That's terrible," Charlotte agreed.

Ted quickly held up a hand to silence his audience's reactions. "That's nothing."

Ollie laughed and leant back in his chair, hands across his belly.

Everyone waited in anticipation as Ted taunted them all by taking a slow sip of his beer and yawning wide. "I think I'll call it a night," he said, winking Ollie, "bloody knackered, I am." He made to stand but Charlotte grabbed one wrist and Valerie the other.

"Don't leave us hanging, you daft old bugger," the latter said with a cackle.

Ted grinned mischievously at them. "When they searched this poor unconscious man's suitcase to try and find some identification, they found all the makings for a ruddy bomb, didn't they? Ollie here had inadvertently saved hundreds of people from being blown to smithereens."

"Holy fucking shit," Vince blurted.

"Was it the IRA?" his mother asked.

"Don't know who it were, love, the bloke kept schtum, didn't he?"

"Talk about accidental heroes!" Charlotte said.

"That's us alright," Ted said, "don't give no fucks about anyone but ourselves and inadvertently save hundreds. Typical."

Chapter 54

"I can't believe I can walk on them already," Norman said, as Herbert and Trevor hauled him down from the coach roof and onto his feet.

They began to make their way through the carnage toward the field where they'd left their clothes. Trevor stopped and stared at the devastation they had caused, at the crash victims who were slowly starting to leave their vehicles. Shell-shocked, they barely noticed the trio of naked old men.

The car that was flattened into the rear of the coach, where there could be no possible survivors, had caught fire, and together with the overflowing spilled luggage, caused the back half of the coach to become engulfed with flames.

Frightened, pale faces screamed in the windows.

Trevor saw that one of the other cars had obliterated the door at the front of the coach, leaving the passengers trapped inside.

"We can't leave them," he said to his friends.

Herbert and Norman looked guiltily at the coach inferno and each other.

"Ohm bloody hell," Herbert sighed. "Come on."

He jogged towards the flattened car, and without hesitation thrust himself into the flames and pushed against the crumpled metal.

"Come on, give us a bloody hand," he shrieked as his skin began to blister and char.

"Jesus Christ," Norman said, staring in shock.

Trevor ran into the melee and threw his shoulder against the car.

FÜHRER: PART ONE

"This is insane," Norman said, but knew with how his healing had accelerated, whatever damage the fire did wouldn't last.

He joined his friends, pushing against the red-hot metal, his flesh melting and sticking to everything he touched.

Finally, they moved the burning car away from the coach, clearing the emergency exit and moving the main source of the fire away from harming anyone else.

They staggered, black and seeping, towards the car crushing the other exit, and thrust it out of the way and into the central reservation.

Inside the vehicle, a bloodied woman stared in horror at the three saviours whose blackened, weeping skin regenerated before her eyes.

A wailing cacophony of sirens tore the night apart.

The coach passengers spilled out and were simultaneously awestruck at the three naked figures who made their way hastily into the dark fields on the roadside.

Herbert led his friends towards their stowed clothing bundles and shook his head at the bright, colourful carnage. "God knows how they're going to explain that one."

Chapter 55

"I can't believe I'm sitting here with a real-life hero," Juliet said, with a trace of her father's sarcasm. That sarcasm went undetected by Ollie, who beamed like a lighthouse and blushed with pride.

"Pfft," Ted scoffed. "I've done my fair share of helping old ladies cross the road too, you know?"

"One-four-eight Wake-field City Cen-tre," Ollie managed to get out in monosyllabic grunts.

Ted paled, and all humour drained from his face. "Forget it. You've had too much to bloody drink, you have. You always try to bring that up when you've had too much to bloody drink. Well, you can forget it, or I'll sleep in the foyer."

The atmosphere thickened between the two men; neither would meet each other's eyes. Ted swilled the last quarter of his drink around in the glass, and Ollie stared shamefully at his empty.

"You need to be a bloody hero just to drive a bus these days," Charlotte said, in an attempt to break the stony silence. "You wouldn't believe the amount of people I've treated, who..." — she flinched as she felt Juliet's foot connect with her shin — "... have been attacked on buses."

"Are you a doctor, then?" Vince asked, his cheeks flushed with embarrassment at just talking to her.

Shit. She couldn't remember what she had already told everyone. She rarely drank alcohol, and just a few drinks had addled her brain and loosened her tongue. She knew she was a useless liar, but remembered reading something somewhere about the secret to successful lies was keeping them as close to the truth as possible. Ignoring Juliet's rigid stare, she nodded. "Yeah, I'm afraid so."

Ted and Ollie shook off their sullen moping and Valerie even sat up straighter and took her eyes off Gustav for a moment. *Oh, here we go,* Charlotte thought, *onwards with your lists of medications and ailments.*

"I've got an unsightly lump," Ted began. Charlotte groaned inwardly. "It's about seventeen stone, covered in grey hair and smells like feet and stale cider." He gave Ollie a gentle pat on the shoulder. "You got anything to remove it?"

Charlotte smiled and prayed it wasn't a precursor to a never-ending list of genuine aches and pains. "I'm afraid I can tell from just one look, it's terminal."

"Oh bugger," Ted said with mock sincerity, "looks like I'm stuck with it, then."

Charlotte felt Valerie's eyes on her. "Do you have anything you're worried about? Valerie, isn't it?"

With a jangle of golden jewellery, Valerie shook her head. "No, and I wouldn't be telling you if I did."

"You're not a fan of doctors?"

"Seen that many in my time it's hard to be."

"For yourself," Charlotte started to ask before looking at Vince, "or for your son?"

"See?" Valerie harrumphed and folded her arms across her ample chest. "I know that look," she said to Gustav.

"What look?" Charlotte asked, although she had an idea of where this was going.

"The same expression I've had since he was a baby," Valerie said scornfully, "always bloody well obsessed with his weight. Take him in for a sore throat, they'd make him get on the scales." Before Charlotte could interrupt, she continued. "Do you know what one of your lot said to him when he was six years old?"

"Of course she bleeding don't," Ted butted in, "she's never met you before in her life and she's at least ten years younger than him."

Valerie ignored the retired bus driver and answered her own question. "He said to him, I remember it as clear as day, he said, 'if you don't stop eating and lose weight, you'll be dead from a heart attack by the time you're twelve.'"

Juliet slapped her hands across her mouth.

"That's vile," Charlotte said with such disgust it took Valerie by surprise. "Let me guess, it was an upper-class village GP wearing a bowtie, with a horrendous combover?"

Vince roared with laughter so loud the table shook. He clapped his hands together. "Oh my God. Are you sure you weren't there?"

Charlotte grinned and spread her fingers over her scalp. "I was his combover."

This even softened Valerie's hardened exterior.

"The thing you've got to remember, where health and medical stuff is concerned, is that things are constantly evolving. Back then, I presume the eighties, they didn't know as much as they do now, especially about mental health. I mean, mental institutions were still in force in a lot of towns until the mid- to late-eighties, and they really didn't have much of a clue about things like eating disorders, which obesity is."

"Everyone's got a label these days," Ted ruminated.

"These things are being recognised more," Charlotte continued, "they never saw the psychological side of overeating, or never took it seriously, just put it down to greed. It's less to do with the stomach and more to do with what's up here," she said, tapping her forehead with a finger.

"You're amazing," Vince purred dreamily, and then gasped in horror when he realised he'd put a voice to his thought.

"Aye, aye, big lad's in love," Ted bellowed, heightening Vince's embarrassment.

"Ignore the Blackpool Pier comedian here," Charlotte said, giving Vince her sweetest smile, "I'm just saying that us younger generation of medical professionals have got our fingers on the pulse."

"Aye," Ted crowed, "I bet matey here would like you to put your finger on his pulse."

"Enough," Juliet joined in, "leave the poor man alone."

Now it was Charlotte's turn to blush. "Okay, but to be honest, I've got more in common with you pair where romance is concerned."

"What? You fancy smelly old men, too?" Valerie cut in.

"You're never a dyke?" Ted said, not caring whether the term was the correct vernacular.

"Doctor Dyke," Charlotte stated.

Ted and Ollie revelled in the banter, Gustav started to say something to be included, but Ted cut him off with, "I bet you've ruined all his fantasies now."

Vince, still crimson, fought for the table. "Actually," he said matter-of-fact, "they're now a lot more interesting."

"I thought you said you were a nurse?" Ted said over the laughter.

FÜHRER: PART ONE

Chapter 56

"Could've sworn that blonde 'un said she were a nurse at the beginning of the night," Ted said, as he unlocked the door to his and Ollie's room.

Ollie grunted.

"Can't believe you brought up the one-four-eight," Ted said with disapproval. "I weren't a fucking hero, I just didn't want my arse on the line. Literally."

Ollie gave a guilty pout and turned away, ashamed.

Ted sighed, took his flat cap off, flung it on a nearby chair and sat on the bed to remove his shoes.

Ollie sauntered over to the window and pressed his face against the glass. He'd seen the flashing lights when they'd entered the room, and from where they were situated across a dark field, he could just about see an obstruction on the motorway, jams running in both directions. "Crash."

"Say what?" Ted said, appearing beside him in just his boxer shorts and Whitesnake t-shirt. He squinted into the darkness. "Can't see jack."

Ollie tapped on the glass. "Coach."

"Fucking eagle-eye, you are," Ted said. "Coach, you say? Good job it weren't us. It's these bloody foreign autobahns and their speed limits. Seen some driving like maniacs when we come out of Calais."

"Autoroutes," Ollie corrected.

"Oh, hang on," Ted said with sudden animation. "Haha, looks like bloody matey caught his chakras or something."

The three old yoga enthusiasts were coming across the carpark. The Scot didn't have his sticks but was walking bow-legged and the rotund, bald one was now waving his hands in the air.

"Must be a prosthetic," Ted said, when Ollie pointed his hand out.

Chapter 57

When they re-entered the hotel, the place was practically deserted. Two night staff sat behind the reception desk and Herbert felt the need to explain to them in pidgin-English that the three of them had been for a bit of fresh air. He had been the quickest to heal. In the field, they had stood naked beneath the stars whilst the worst of their injuries healed. His skin tingled under his clothing and he couldn't wait to strip it off and allow this freak of nature take its course.

Norman was right to query their rapid healing; his bones repaired themselves enough for him to walk within minutes.

Their burns from the pile up healed to a sunburnt red, leaving them looking like they had simply overexerted themselves at yoga.

On the journey back to the Novotel, they'd discussed possible reasons for this rapid regeneration, but none of them knew much at all about their condition. Lycanthropy had been bestowed upon them without an instruction manual and every day it offered new surprises.

They retired to their individual rooms ignoring the raging hunger the evening's antics had summoned.

Norman could feel the sinew and flesh knitting together. It was an unholy sensation, something that threatened to overwhelm him, his body alive with incessant crawling. He resisted the urge to scratch at his rapidly healing body, knowing there was no stopping this process.

He stumbled across the hotel room, elbowed open the ensuite door, and began to fill the bathtub with water. It was the first time he had been on his own since the night he'd found Trevor with his grandchildren, and the shock of everything slammed him to the floor. "Oh, fucking hell," he cried, slapping his hands over his face and resting his head between his red knees.

How the hell are we supposed to do this?
How long can we expect to live like fugitives?
If we get the kids, what then?

He mourned his past, the everyday stuff, pointless conversations about the same old bollocks, and he had more ailments than friends.

Norman hoped the cold water would numb his livid skin and hopefully the hurt inside. He closed his eyes and saw scenes from the pile-up.

He saw a man in a business suit explode through the windscreen as his car smashed into him side-on. Faces screaming in the dark as their vehicles joined the destruction he had caused. Throats ripped from soldiers' necks, blood-soaked army fatigues.

How can anyone live with this? Will the visions of what I've done haunt me forever?

Norman let out a low moan and forced his tired eyes open; even the brightness of the ensuite was better than the horrors behind his eyes.

Across the hotel room he spotted the answer to some of his current problems, but most likely the cause of some to come.

The mini bar.

She would never get used to seeing how miraculous this thing was.

Charlotte listened intently as Herbert told her what had happened. But now, sitting on the twin bed opposite her in a shabby tracksuit, he looked better than ever.

She studied his reformed hand, turning it over and back repeatedly. "Why didn't it regrow at the caravan site?"

Herbert shrugged. "Your guess is as good as mine. I really don't know. There's no understanding this thing at all."

"You said you think your regenerative abilities have improved?"

"They have. I don't know why, or what it is that powers this thing," he offered, sounding both amazed and confused.

"At least with vampires we know it's blood," Charlotte said, half-joking, "and there's not been much of a moon tonight."

"You know, I really would like to investigate that side of things more," he said with childlike glee. "I mean, I don't really recall much about the last full moon as we were in the facility and heavily sedated, but Victor seemed to think it affected us somehow."

"How can it provide sustenance? It's not like werewolves experience some kind of nocturnal photosynthesis." Charlotte laughed.

"Maybe they do. Maybe there's something about this thing that can be attracted and changed, not just the Earth's orbit and the tides."

Charlotte pulled the covers up to her chin and laid down. She hardly knew Herbert but felt at ease in his presence. "Do you think they've found out more stuff at this place in Germany?"

Herbert thought about this. "I don't think so. When that doctor snatched me and ran his own experiments, he was just as amazed as anyone else would be. Surely if they understood this thing they would have used it by now? I'm willing to bet they're just as bloody clueless as the rest of us. I think lycanthropy has aspects that won't show up under a microscope."

"Why haven't they sent anyone after us?"

Herbert's face fell and he turned away. "I've been thinking about that too. There's no rational reason why they haven't. Unless they don't care if this gets out, or they know we're coming straight to them."

Charlotte sat up. "How the hell would they know that?"

"Expectation, most likely."

"Or," Charlotte began but shook her head, "no, that would be silly."

"What?"

"What if they've tagged you?"

"How do you mean?"

"Like they do dolphins, rhinos or other animals. There's a million ways they can do that sort of thing now. Sometimes they drill holes in the rhino's horn and insert a GPS tag."

Herbert looked disgusted for a moment but then relief washed his face. "But surely our transformations would ruin that idea? When we change, surely the tag will fall out?"

"That's a good point," Charlotte said, relaxing again. "Although who says your organs change?"

*

Norman held the little bottle up against the light shining in from the bathroom, the amber liquid inside promising to comfort and numb.

Just the one.

The moment the first drop of whisky hit his lips, Norman knew he had fucked up. The miniature bottle was empty before he knew it, and he clawed for the others without even thinking.

FÜHRER: PART ONE

Chapter 58

Gustav rolled over onto his other side and tried to get images of Valerie out of his head. It had been a long time since he'd been romantically involved with anyone, and even then, the closest he'd got to a proper relationship was a drink with a friend of his brother's back home in Antratsyt. Iryna was a good, loving woman but he knew she was more interested in his more handsome brother.

In the corridor, after she and her son had walked him to his room, she had given him a peck on the cheek and whispered her room number, and now it was all he could think about. *What if this is my last chance? Thoughts* of reaching Offenberg and being annihilated straight away were constantly preying on his mind. They really didn't have a hope in Hell. He cursed himself for not just carrying on with the gutless loyalty he had shown Mortimer and Butcher and taken up with them when they left. But he had done what he knew was right. It was easy to see who the good guys were, and at least if he was killed, he would know it was trying to do the right thing.

I released werewolves on a platoon of soldiers and yet I am too nervous to knock on the door of a beautiful woman.

"Enough!" Gustav snapped. He threw back his duvet and marched towards the bedroom door in nothing but a t-shirt, boxer shorts, and Star Wars slippers.

He stared at his reflection defiantly, beat his chest with his fists, and growled. "I am Viking. Albeit from Ukraine."

FÜHRER: PART ONE

He knew it was late, but he tapped on the door anyway. Juliet opened the door a crack and froze.

"Can I—"

"You'd better come in," she said, and let her father into the room.

Trevor wandered in nervously; this was the first time he had been on his own with her since he'd done what he'd done. Just looking at her brought it all back, and no matter how strong his new powers made him, he still collapsed before her. He dropped to his hands and knees on the laminate flooring chastised and weak.

He wanted—but knew he didn't deserve—her forgiveness, but nevertheless, felt her hand against his head as she fell down beside him. "I'm sorry. I'm so sorry."

Juliet let her own rage and sorrow out on her father and rained a few angry fists down across his broad shoulders before wrapping her arms around him and joining him in grief.

Gustav raised his hand to knock on Valerie's door when one of the doors down the corridor exploded and Norman's red quadruped wolf leapt onto the plush carpet. "Shit." Gustav fell back against Valerie's door and tried to keep calm.

The wolf immediately turned in his direction.

"Norman," Gustav whispered. "I know you can hear me. Think about what you are doing. You must control yourself."

It staggered towards him, bumping into the other hotel room doors and walls. Gustav was confused; he had seen these things in action and knew how agile they were. The wolf looked drugged, its eyes glazed over. As it came closer he saw its tongue lolling, dripping drool onto the carpet.

"Have you taken something?" Gustav asked, still backing away, praying no one would open their door.

The wolf shook its head, bashed against another door, and tried to focus on him.

"No!" Gustav shouted as he heard the lock being unfastened. "Stay indoors!"

The door opened, revealing an old man with a pencil moustache. He patted down the lapels of his tartan pyjamas. Gustav recognised him from the coach but they hadn't been introduced.

"Who's let this ruddy dog in here?" the man barked, sounding like a sergeant major at the red-furred beast that came up past his waist.

"Go back in your room," Gustav said calmly.

"You?" The man said in surprise. "You're the Icelandic, aren't you?" He cocked a thumb at the wolf. "Is this your doing?" He scolded and took in its wobbling frame. "Looks bloody ill."

Gustav stared at him in disbelief.

The posh old man went goggle-eyed for a second as if realising he might be in danger and stepped back across the threshold to his room.

"You need to be careful, boy. Bloody things have got all kinds of lurgy here on the continent, don't you know? Probably rabid."

Gustav backed away.

There was something obviously wrong with Norman's wolf, but he had no doubt that any quick movements would cause it to spring.

FÜHRER: PART ONE

Further along the corridor came the sound of more locks being fumbled with. A lump rose in Gustav's throat as Valerie's door began to open and he admitted defeat, knowing the chance of romance had been too good to be true. He was a bit player, a nobody, not even a comedy sidekick. The wolf's snout swivelled towards Valerie's door and Gustav stuck his index and little fingers in his mouth and whistled. "Oi, you big stupid dog," he said—there was no point in getting these people mixed up in the truth. He flicked his left leg and a size-nine slipper in the shape of Darth Vader's head flew from his foot and struck the wolf in the nose. He had just enough time to lose the other slipper before the wolf growled and staggered towards him. As he fled, he heard the toff say something about his actions being stupid and Valerie's blood-curdling cry when she saw the man of her dreams being chased by what looked like a fox on steroids.

It was the shriek that made Herbert fall out of bed whilst he was fumbling for the bedside lamp. Charlotte beat him to it and they stared at one another in horror.

"Stay here," Herbert said, springing up and heading towards the door. Out in the corridor, other guests were loitering outside their rooms, clutching their bedclothes to their chests. "What's going on?" Herbert said to a couple from the coach.

"Just heard some screaming, I'm as clueless as you," the man said.

"Alright, back in your rooms. I'm sure there's nothing to worry about," Barry the coach driver said, elbowing his way through the concerned guests in his vest and trousers. He pulled up the straps of his black braces and headed towards the source of the screaming.

"No chance," Vince said, towering over the portly coach driver, "my mum's up that end."

"If I may." Herbert smiled politely and attempted to get in front of Barry.

Barry gave a patronising grin. "If you don't mind, it's mine and Cheryl's responsibility to see to your welfare and I do have a black belt."

"They look like braces to me," sniggered Ted as he and Ollie came storming up the corridor. He nodded to Herbert as further screams echoed their way. "I don't think yoga's going to sort that out, matey."

Barry didn't know what the hell was going on at the other side of the hotel but the shouting had escalated. "Come on, then, but don't come crying to me if you get your heads blown off."

FÜHRER: PART ONE

Chapter 59

"Oh, Christ, what the bloody hell was that?" Trevor groaned. He pulled out of Juliet's embrace and stood as heavy footsteps raced past the door, followed by something that snarled. "Oh shit," he said, and ran out into the hallway.

Gustav's admirer hurtled down the corridor towards him, shrieking, her blonde hair wild and her thick arms and legs moving a lot quicker than she seemed capable of.

"Wha—" was all Trevor managed before she bounded past him. He caught the furry red tail and butt of Norman's wolf as it rounded a corner chasing whoever it was pursuing.

"Bloody stray has got in somehow," Leopold Alcocks announced as he took great strides in his tartan pyjamas.

"That's no stray," Trevor said. He spun around to Juliet. "Go and find Herbert."

"It's going in his direction."

Gustav had never run so fast in his life. He had never really run at any speed, and although running on the hotel's plush carpets was a pleasure, the physical exertion wasn't. He could hear Norman behind him. If not for repeatedly bouncing off the narrow corridor walls, he would have caught him. His pounding footfall alerted the two night staff, distracting them from whatever they were doing behind the reception desk.

FÜHRER: PART ONE

One man, painfully thin, geeky-looking with glasses and spiky hair, leaned back on his office chair whilst the other, hunched over, all nose and scraggly hair, instinctively reached for a telephone handset on the desk.

"Hide," Gustav managed to grunt as he ran around the back of their desk.

"Sir, please not behi—" the geek started, pointing dramatically at a sign reading 'Staff Only' in French, but then the red wolf staggered into the reception area.

"Oh no, Monsieur!" the older man said, jumping to his feet. "There are to be no pets—"

The red wolf launched itself at the reception desk, an easy feat if it wasn't intoxicated, and skidded across the surface, sending laptops, telephones and office stationery everywhere.

Gustav and the two men jumped backwards.

The wolf clattered over the desk and flopped onto the floor.

"Run," Gustav shouted as the wolf quickly scrabbled about and righted itself.

The three of them ran around the now empty desk, Gustav leading them towards the entrance across the foyer, but whatever substances had addled the wolf's responses were wearing off fast.

Gustav felt the rush of air over his bare arms and the wolf's fur brush him. It hit the geeky receptionist, its front paws striking his upper body, claws digging into his shoulders and mashing him against the thick glass in the foyer entrance. They slid down the locked automatic door, blood already beginning to speckle the glass.

Gustav grabbed the older receptionist's arm and dragged him away from the massacre of his colleague.

"I have to save him," he said, but when he looked back the wolf was already tearing the man's throat out, his screams strangled mid-cry as the creature's teeth yanked free skin, muscle and sinew in thick, messy strands.

Valerie's shriek momentarily stunned Gustav as she bumbled into the foyer and saw the horror.

"Fucking hell," Barry shouted, puffing with exertion. Herbert was right behind him, followed by Ted and Ollie. Vince barged past them all, eyes only on his distressed mother.

Throwing all caution to the wind, Gustav hid behind Herbert. "Herbert, please see to your friend."

"Herbert?" Ted began, "who the bloody hell's Herbert?"

Barry was the only one who didn't just stop and stare. Without any hesitation, he ran at the savage beast and slipped his arms around its neck.

"Oh, for God's sake," Trevor shouted as he elbowed both Ted and Ollie out of the way and darted forward to help the coach driver.

Barry looked like he was wrestling a bear. He straddled the thing's back, legs wrapped around its ribs, and tried to pull the snapping face from the receptionist's throat.

"Don't let it bite you!" Trevor pulled the injured receptionist from underneath the animal but knew the guy was dead straight away. The wolf bucked beneath Barry's weight, twisted, rolled him off onto the floor, and went for his throat, too.

"Norman, no," Herbert cried out and, to the onlookers' amazement, leapt four feet across the foyer and grabbed hold of the animal's tail.

Herbert yanked hard.

FÜHRER: PART ONE

The wolf's hellish growl turned into a high-pitched whimper, almost comical coming from something so ferocious.

He dragged it away from the receptionist and Barry. "Help me, Trevor," Herbert said as the wolf snapped its head back and around, narrowly missing one of Herbert's thighs. Trevor mimicked Barry's hold, pounced on its back, tried to get his arm beneath its throat, and felt the thing's jaws snap at the flesh of his forearm.

"Don't change," Herbert spat, knowing Trevor would be having the same compulsions as him.

Trevor ignored the pain and got the monster in a headlock; its head thrashed about but it couldn't bite. "What now?" Trevor grunted. There was no way they could hold Norman's wolf for long, not in their current state.

"Get it outside," Herbert shouted, directing this mostly at the remaining receptionist, who took keys from his pocket with trembling hands.

"That glass won't stop him, man," Trevor moaned.

Herbert could feel the wolf's tail slipping through his grasp. "Barry," he shouted, "have you got the coach keys on you?"

Barry stared at him as though he were completely demented but then patted a lump in his trouser pocket and nodded.

"We need to get this in the luggage hold," Herbert said, renewing his grip and causing the wolf to whine in Trevor's face.

"You're fucking crazy," Barry said as the receptionist unfastened the lock and the automatic doors swished open, but he got to his feet regardless and stumbled out into the night.

"Fucking yoga my arse," Ted said, side-eyeing Juliet and the now approaching Charlotte.

"Oh, Gustav!" Valerie all but fell into the Ukrainian's arms. He tried to steer her away from the calamity but she pressed onwards, eager to watch Herbert and Trevor struggling with the animal, which began to buck and fight with renewed vigour.

Vince strode past them, an expression of defiance on his face.

"Vince, no!"

Vince turned back to his mum. "They're not strong enough on their own. I can help. Finally my size can be useful."

Herbert saw Barry get to the coach and raise the door of the luggage hold.

"I can't hold this bastard much longer, man," Trevor said, his one arm all but useless where the wolf's teeth had sliced through muscle. They lifted the wolf upright, dragging it across the car park on its hind legs, its forelegs paddling the air as it tried to rake its claws at them.

Vince stormed towards them like a Viking beserker: massive, hairy, and angry. "No," Herbert screamed, not wanting the lad to get infected. This distraction enabled the wolf to pull out of his clutches, leaving him nothing but fistfuls of red fur.

Seizing the opportunity, the wolf thrashed and threw Trevor onto the tarmac and ran straight for Vince.

Vince knew one of the main things with animals was proving to be the bigger, more aggressive opponent. He had read all the myths around bear attacks being thwarted using this methodology and had a split second to decide whether he was going to use it for himself.

The huge dog sprang towards him, a fiery excitement in its eyes, the fur around its mouth and on its chest pink with blood, and for the first time in his life he let his inner anger out. All his life he had been tormented by adults and children alike, but what was worse than their jibes was the endless looks of pity he received from both loved ones and strangers. He channelled all that rage, let it out in a roar much louder than the dog's, and threw himself at it.

The hotel guests rushed out of the foyer. Gustav grabbed Valerie around the waist; her shriek was as loud as Vince's as she tried to stop him, but it was too late.

They all watched as the red wolf leapt at the man in a direct trajectory for its jaws to meet Vince's throat, but he swung a huge fist that connected with the wolf's nose and it dropped to the ground, lifeless.

Everything went quiet whilst everyone came to terms with what had happened.

Vince stood over the fallen animal, ready for another go if necessary.

It was Ted, ever the motor-mouth, who broke the silence with his filthy gurgling-drain-laugh. "Fucking matey's KO'd the fucker."

Herbert was stunned, and thought for a few seconds Vince had killed Norman, despite his still being in wolf form, then he saw his ribs rise and fall and snapped out of it. "Get his back, legs," he told Trevor, and quickly picked up the comatose animal's front end.

"Holy Mary," Trevor said in awe, relief temporarily flowing back to his face. "I can't believe the bastard knocked him out. If only he knew what he'd done." They got to the coach and threw Norman's wolf into the luggage hold and watched as Barry shut the metal door.

"Good show, that man," Leopold Alcocks yelled as he led Ivy out into the night.

Vince turned towards them beaming with victorious pride and held his fist up like a trophy.

Ted and Ollie whooped and applauded.

Valerie slipped free from Gustav and sped past them all in her nightie, wrapped her arms around her heroic son, and smothered his cheeks with kisses. "Oh, my baby. You were so brave," she said, looking up at him with tears in her eyes.

"Three cheers for...err..." Leopold quietened as he realised he didn't know the man's name.

"Three cheers for Vince," Gustav shouted, taking over Leopold's chant, but then saw the ragged, bleeding tooth marks across Vince's knuckles.

FÜHRER: PART ONE

Chapter 60

"Right," Barry said, taking charge once they were back in the hotel. "Better call the authorities, tell them we've got one fatality and a dangerous animal that needs destroying."

"What about Vince's hand?" Valerie complained, "that thing could have been carrying anything."

"Rabies!" Leopold shouted.

A look passed between Gustav and the Boxford crew.

"I'm sure the medics will sort him out, love," Barry offered.

"Yeah," Ted said, uncharacteristically optimistic, patting her on the shoulder. "They've got drugs and vaccines for everything nowadays."

Charlotte saw to Vince's bitten hand and tried not to meet her friends' eyes. She knew what they would be thinking. *What if he's infected?*

Vince didn't even know the thing's teeth had caught him when he'd hit it, the pain was bearable.

The receptionist dithered behind the trashed desk, putting everything back where it should be and searching for the telephone in order to make the appropriate calls.

"Ummm," Herbert said, holding a sleek black telephone and showing the frayed end of the snapped wire.

In unison, Barry, the receptionist and Ted all whipped out mobile phones.

FÜHRER: PART ONE

"Shit!" Herbert grimaced and looked at Trevor, who went bug-eyed and instantly snatched Ted's phone.

Juliet lunged over the desk and knocked the receptionist's mobile phone from his hand.

Barry glared as Gustav reached for his phone but he thrust a palm into his chest and held his phone aloft out of Gustav's reach. "Err, what the fuck is going on?"

Ted was transfixed by the scene frozen around him. Barry had one arm outstretched, hand full of t-shirt, mobile phone raised in the air like a sporting trophy.

Gustav stood on tiptoes, a semi-circle of doughy, hairy white belly spilling out beneath his crumpled t-shirt and over a pair of boxer shorts decorated with cartoon avocados and wearing a solitary Darth Vader slipper.

Herbert, eyes wide, held the reception landline the broken wire like bitten licorice.

Trevor was grasping Ted's four-month-old Google Pixel 5, knuckles lightening as though he was trying to crush the thing.

Juliet was sprawled across the empty reception desk, straightening the oversized t-shirt she was using as a nightie back down over her thighs as the shocked receptionist slowly tore his eyes away from her exposed flesh.

Charlotte's face was a portrait of fear, one hand still on Vince's bandaged wrist.

There was a distinct silence that seemed to last a lifetime, but Ted couldn't keep quiet to save his life.

Or anyone else's, for that matter. "Oh fucking hell, it's like one of those Mexican jerk-offs."

"Stand-offs," Ollie barked.

Barry sighed, let go of Gustav, and lowered his mobile phone. Looking at the group before him, he said, "Please, tell me what the hell is going on?"

The two Boxford pensioners' exchange was lingering but neither said a word. Herbert sheepishly gave the broken landline to the receptionist and stepped forwards, hands raised in a placatory manner.

"Ey," Ted spat, "your hand's grown back."

Herbert grimaced and spoke directly to Barry. "If I may have your attention."

"I'm all ears, me," Barry said.

"I wonder if it would be too much to ask if us few here could go back outside for this conversation."

"This a hostage situation?" Barry said with a hint of disbelief that a pair of old codgers would be capable of such a thing.

"Not as such," Herbert said, "but it would be beneficial to everyone here not to involve anyone else."

No matter what the situation was, Barry thought that sounded like a sensible option. "Okay, everyone outside."

"If I cause a scene, run!" Vince whispered to his mum and Charlotte.

Charlotte smiled with sympathy. "Just do as Herbert says, please."

"You and all?" Ted complained, "how deep does this go?"

"Just get outside, man," Trevor whined, shuffling towards the foyer doors.

FÜHRER: PART ONE

Herbert led the pack towards the coach and stopped beside the luggage hold, which was severely dented but hadn't released its prisoner. He banged on the metal with the fist of his recently reformed hand. "Norman, you alright?" He smiled at the seven members of the coach party and the French receptionist and waited.

From inside the coach, they heard something scrabbling about.

"Was that your dog?" Leopold spoke up but was silenced when a Scottish accent came from behind the buckled metal.

"Aye," said the voice, followed by a throat-clear and a wet spit. "Umm, I take it everything has gone tits-up?"

"That's the jock!" Ted said, clutching hold of Ollie.

"What about the dog?" Ivy asked Leopold.

Trevor sighed heavily and slumped against the coach. "The dog is Norman, Norman is the dog," he looked at their confused faces. "And it wasn't a dog, it was a wolf. Norman is a werewolf." He put his hands on his knees and laughed until he cried.

"I'm afraid it's true," Herbert added before anyone could say anything over Trevor's laughter. "Trevor and Norman and I are, for want of a better word, werewolves."

"I knew it weren't yoga," Ted blurted.

Herbert nodded and waved a hand towards the emergency vehicle lights twinkling on the motorway. "We caused a bit of bother earlier, too."

"I don't believe this," Barry said, and started to walk back to the hotel.

Trevor continued to laugh hysterically, as if something had finally flipped inside him.

"Bloody fools," Leopold tutted, put an arm around Ivy's shoulders, and began to lead her back inside.

Taking heed of Leopold, the receptionist offered his arm to Valerie. She scowled at Gustav and let herself be led. "Bunch of fucking nutters."

"Come on," Ted said to Ollie, "might as well crack open that bottle of Jameson's."

"Mum," Vince called, still standing with Charlotte.

There was a terrific tearing noise then something big flew over their heads and landed on gigantic feet in front of Barry.

Trevor walked through the still-falling tatters of Herbert's exploded tracksuit, through the suddenly immobile people, and stopped next to the muscular bald werewolf in front of them. He slapped a hand on its broad back. "And this is Herbert's wolf."

Herbert lowered his head; his wide tongue slipped across his sharp white teeth and drool dripped on Barry's vest.

Valerie opened her mouth to scream but Juliet clamped a hand over her mouth. "I know it's scary but I promise you he won't hurt you." She turned to all of their frightened faces, "Any of you."

With a ripple of flesh and a clicking of bones, Herbert transformed back into a portly, naked man in his seventies. "Maybe we could go back inside now," he said, blushing as he cupped his genitals.

"No, no, no."

FÜHRER: PART ONE

"Ah, come on," Ted said, pleading with Raoul, the receptionist, who leant against the shuttered bar. "Emergency measures, and all that."

After a little coercion, Herbert and Trevor convinced the bewildered bunch to hear their story now they had been privy to some evidence. They released a bloody Norman, found some clothes and milled into the hotel restaurant, the three OAPs standing before them whilst Gustav, Charlotte and Juliet subtly covered the exits just in case.

"Come on, man," Ted begged, "this is going to need booze."

Raoul ran a hand through his hair and cast a brief look through the wire shutter at the bottles.

"If you want," Herbert offered, you can say we forced you."

There was a demonic little glint in Raoul's eyes for a second and then he yanked out a ring of keys and searched for the one belonging to the bar shutter.

"Fucking come on," Ted cheered, ducking under the rising shutter.

The others looked at Herbert for permission. "Please," he said, "but nothing for me and my two friends here."

Everyone helped themselves to free drinks apart from Barry and those guarding the exits. "This is insane," the coach driver said, looking at the three old men in turn.

"You don't know the half of it," Norman said sadly.

Herbert waited for people to sit down before he began. "Now, this is obviously a shock to you all."

"No shit, Sherlock," Ted muttered into a whisky glass.

"Not that long ago, we discovered a friend of ours was a werewolf. You may have seen or heard some rather tall-sounding tales these past few months. Deaths. Wild dog attacks. Gang wars. Hoodlums disguised as monsters."

Barry nodded. "And this stuff that happened last night at the swimming pool in Suffolk?"

"Boxford," Herbert said. "It's where we all come from."

"We were infected before we found out about our friend," Herbert continued.

"Against our will," Norman said.

"Yes, as my friend says, against our will. Another friend saw only the good things about lycanthropy: extended lifespan, invulnerability, regenerative abilities, heightened senses and increased strength."

Ted laughed. "And on the flip side, you turn into ruddy great hairy bastards at full moon and tear people's throats out. We know, we've all seen the films, Kojak."

Herbert glared at him. "We didn't want this. We didn't ask for this. But it can be controlled. I can control it."

"With your yoga lessons?" Ted asked sarcastically.

"I can control mine too," Trevor joined in, "it's like a psychological part of you, man, that manifests itself into the embodiment of all the rage and animal urges inside of you, but it can be controlled."

All eyes were on Norman. "Aye, I'm getting there."

"So," Barry said, "what's all this got to do with us?"

FÜHRER: PART ONE

Between them, with the occasional quip and confirmation from Juliet, Gustav and Charlotte, the Boxford seniors told them the rest of the story.

Chapter 61

"This is completely insane," Barry said, rubbing his hands over his face as if he could wipe it all away, "and if I hadn't seen it with my own eyes, there's no way I would believe anything you just said." He paused and gave a hollow laugh. "The fact that you're all so bloody nice about it all just adds to the plausibility."

"It's ridiculous, I know," Trevor said, crashing onto a chair next to him and resting a hand on his shoulder. "Like a cross between Cocoon and An American Werewolf in London."

"With Nazis," Ted chipped in.

Trevor nodded slowly. "With Nazis."

"And you think they're planning something big?" Barry aske.

Gustav, still guarding the exit, agreed. "It stands to reason. The only thing I can't understand is what has taken them so long."

Barry focused on the hurt and longing in Juliet's eyes. "Your children?" He pointed a finger at Trevor. "Your grandchildren?"

"All we ask is that you get us to Offenberg as soon as possible," Herbert pleaded. "Make up whatever story you like about what we did to make us take you there. If we survive this, which is highly unlikely, then we'll be on the run for the rest of our lives."

Valerie jumped up, knocking her chair over. "We could've been killed by that bloody thing he turned into."

FÜHRER: PART ONE

Gustav stepped away from the exit. "I am so sorry, Valerie. I led the wolf away from your door. I never thought that Vincent would do something so heroic."

"Humph, well, you don't know him at all." Valerie put her arm around her son, and upon seeing his bandaged hand, the truth dawned on her. She roared hatefully at Norman, "Wait, you bit him!"

Norman lowered his eyes; there was nothing to say.

Herbert winced. "Yes, I'm afraid your son is going to have to come with us, regardless."

"He's gonna turn into a bloody monster, isn't he, my poor Vinnie."

"We can't be certain—" Trevor started but was interrupted by Herbert.

"Yes," he said, locking eyes with Vince, "it's probable. I'm sorry, but it would be for the best if you came with us. Safer for you, for your mother."

Vince scrutinised his wrapped hand. "It doesn't even hurt now," he said in a half-daze.

"No, we'll sort this out on our own. I'll take him to the doctor. They can give him a blood transfusion," Valerie ranted hysterically.

"No, Mum," Vince said, enveloping her in his arms. "We all know what good that will do. Whoever gets hold of this thing will be just as bad as the people they're against."

Herbert nodded sadly.

"I'll go with them, help them if I can. It's about time I did something with my life."

"Wherever you go, I go." Valerie looped her arm around his and held on firmly.

Ted, Ollie and Raoul were halfway drunk, and Leopold and Ivy looked like they had mentally gone to another planet away from the craziness. "Can't you let this lot stay here?"

"Ey, speak for yourself, Bazza," Ted said, "me and Oliver here are willing hostages. This is the most excitement us pair have had in fucking years."

"I'm afraid we can't chance that," Herbert said. "Everyone in this room..." he paused and looked at the mother and son combo— "...aside from those who wish to join us, will be free to go once we get to Offenberg. As I said, you can tell everyone everything once we get there, but we need you to stay with us until then."

Barry thumbed the screen of his mobile. "I'm just seeing how long it'll take to get from here to Offenberg."

They all waited whilst Barry typed in the details to his SatNav. "Says here about five and a half hours, but if we left now we could probably do that in four and a half, five hours tops. We could be there for sun-up. But Offenburg is a big place."

"I think I know where they are," Gustav said, bringing gasps from Juliet and Trevor. "I have been looking at the area, and there is an asphalt mine on the north-west side, which is beside two lakes and miles of forest, the Gottswald Nature Reserve. There are a leftovers of the war around that area, wall bunkers of the old Siegfried Line."

"Hang out your washing on the Siegfried Line," Ivy sang in the singsong voice of someone who had finally lost their last marble.

FÜHRER: PART ONE

"Have you any dirty washing, Mother dear," Leopold joined in.

Gustav eyed them worriedly. "It would be an optimum location."

"You're sure, Gustav?" Herbert asked.

"No, but like I say, it is the prime location in the area."

"Right," Barry said, getting up and grabbing everyone's attention, "take whatever you need for the trip: food, drink, medication, et cetera, talk to no one about this and we'll convene at the coach in thirty minutes." He strolled behind the bar and helped himself to a bottle of Coke. "But you," he said, thrusting the bottle at Norman, "are riding in the luggage hold."

Chapter 62

04:35

Offenburg, Germany.

Bargeld snatched the report from the printer before it fully ejected the paper and ran across the comms area beneath several giant screens to a black door adorned with a golden plaque. The reflection in the brass showed just how nervous and tired he was, how gaunt, with darkness below his eyes.

He had been stationed on comms for six weeks. So far, he had avoided having to report to General Liebermann due to there always being someone of a higher authority above him. Since the targets had begun their journey they were being watched around the clock, every important detail to be given to Liebermann in person.

Liebermann was feared amongst most people at Wolfschanze; he was a psychotic madman at the best of times.

Bargeld braced himself, looked at the symbol engraved in the wood, a modified version of the swastika with a right-facing wolf's head dead-centre, and rapped on the door.

"Enter!" A firm voice came from a speaker embedded in the wolf's head alongside a pinhole camera.

Bargeld opened the door, stepped into Liebermann's office, stamped his right foot down and

FÜHRER: PART ONE

thrust his right palm forward and up. "Heil, mein Führer."

"At ease, Bargeld, at ease."

Liebermann sat behind a huge black desk, tall, slim, Aryan, pristine in uniform. Some said he never took it off, that he never slept.

The office was decked out with Nazi regalia, genuine artefacts that were nearly a century old.

A brief smile graced the general's face. "You have news on our targets, I presume?"

"Yes, sir. The targets are heading south-west on L-ninety-eight. We have drones mapping their course and mobile units around lake Waltersweier and along Gottswaldstraße."

"Good work, Bargeld." He ran a palm over his slick blonde hair and once again showed his shark grin. "Are they still using the same mode of transport?"

"Yes, sir. Scania coach from England with DEHANEYS insignia."

"Very well, continue to map their journey, and once they leave L-ninety-eight, choose somewhere to ambush them."

"Yes, sir. Just to confirm, we are to take no casualties?"

"Affirmative. Kill everyone on board and clean up after yourselves. Usual procedure, bring everything down here and the appropriate teams will trawl for anything useful. You are dismissed."

Bargeld saluted again and left Liebermann's office.

05:03

Forty figures lay belly-first along the verges beside the forest road, their automatic rifles primed and ready to use. Several hundred yards along the deserted road was a strip of explosives camouflaged to blend in with the tarmac.

"Target estimated forty seconds," Hoffman, the soldier in charge, muttered into a radio on his chest just as they saw the headlights of the coach appear in the distance.

"Do we know how many civilians are on there?" asked the man beside him.

"Only half a dozen; doesn't matter, you know that? Get ready."

The coach wound through the forest at a steady pace and when the tyres activated the mines, the front of the bus rose into the air several feet, Hoffman saw the driver scream and raise his arms to cover his head as the windscreen blew in and fire obliterated him. It crashed back down, the front wheels gone, nose crunching into the tarmac.

"First strike was successful," Hoffman said as the coach screeched along the road like a comet. "Take the back wheels out."

A rocket zipped from the forest and struck the rear left wheels and the bus rolled onto its side. After grinding away the asphalt for several metres, it slid down the steep verge and ground to a halt against the crowded trunks. A tree gave a sad creak as it crashed down and flattened the coach's middle section, its canopy blocking the road.

FÜHRER: PART ONE

"Okay," Hoffman shouted to his men. "Get ready to move in. No survivors, remember."

They surrounded the devastated bus and waited for the first movement.

EPILOGUE

1.

"I can't believe they kept you in overnight," Jez said when a male officer led Elizabeth through to the reception of Sudbury Police Station. He glared at the police constable as if it was personally his fault.

The day before, Jez had told them everything he knew about the situation but had also added that he didn't believe the werewolf spin, despite Elizabeth's seemingly coming back from the dead. That was surely some mix-up.

"Oh, I'm a suspect for the swimming pool murders too," she said, sounding quite cheerful about it.

"You said you had no recollection of that," Jez said after the officer left them alone.

"I don't, but with what I am, isn't it safer for everyone if I'm locked up?"

"When are the blood tests back?"

"Oh, they're back now, Jeffrey—"

"Jeffery?"

The police officer returned with a polystyrene cup with tea in it. "Black, two sugars. It's extremely hot."

Elizabeth smiled. "Jeffery, this is Jeremy, the lovely young man I was telling you about."

The officer nodded and gestured towards a door opposite them.

"I have to go and see that pretty police lady now," Elizabeth said, "my, she's a looker. It's a pity you're so anti-establishment, Jeremy, I could have asked if she was single."

"I can't believe you're being so cool about this."

"Oh, Jeremy, there's no point in being anything else at the moment." she let the police officer take her by the arm. "I'll ask if I'm allowed to speak to you later." She darted forwards, pecked his cheek, and went with the constable.

DS Grace Brown was already waiting in the interview room. "Good morning, Elizabeth," she said without raising her head from the wad of papers she was sorting out.

"Good morning, DS Brown," Elizabeth said, sitting opposite her. "May I say what a beautiful suit you have on today? It really highlights your eyes."

"Thank you," the DS said, meeting her gaze. "I got your notes back."

"And?"

Grace leant back in the chair and pressed her palms against her temples. "We can't believe what they're saying."

"And what is that, exactly?"

"That you're exactly who you say you are."

Elizabeth nodded. "Anything else?"

"No. Everything else is normal, no canine DNA, nothing out of the ordinary. In fact, the bigwigs at the hospital made a comment on just how well you are for someone your age."

"And reputedly deceased?" Elizabeth offered.

DS Brown grimaced. "Yes. None of this can be explained!" She laughed and held up a sheet of paper. "I have your post-mortem papers right here, it lists the toxins put into your bloodstream by the Scarborough kid. But these results show none of that, and you definitely didn't have any post-mortem scars when you were examined. I don't understand. No one does."

"But there's nothing alien in them now?"

"No," Grace said, and gave a sarcastic leer, "perhaps we'd only get them if we were to take a sample when you were in wolf form."

"I should imagine you don't believe all that nonsense, do you? OAPs with regenerative abilities who turn into monsters at the full moon."

Grace threw her hands in the air. "I don't know what's going on with all that, but I know it's not monsters, Elizabeth. That's impossible."

"Werewolves are real," Elizabeth snapped, "I could be very dangerous. I could kill people."

Grace sighed. "Look, this is all strange for everyone involved and I understand you're upset about your friends, but—"

Elizabeth slammed her face onto the desk.

"Oh my God," DS Brown shouted and jumped up from her chair. Police Officer Jeffrey rushed across the room as Elizabeth sat back up, nose like a squashed plum.

"Get a first-aider!" Grace said, ripped a handful of tissues from a box, raised them towards Elizabeth's face and stopped at the old woman's red smile.

"You'll see," Elizabeth said, blood covering her lips, "that the bleeding has already stopped."

DS Brown gasped.

"Lean forwards." Elizabeth bowed her head towards her.

Grace could hear a faint crackling coming from Elizabeth's face.

"If you listen carefully, you might be able to hear the cartilage repairing itself."

FÜHRER: PART ONE

DS Grace Brown recoiled as the old lady's broken nose finished healing itself before her eyes.

2.

They had sat outside the house all night, taking it in turns to sleep.

"He's obviously not coming back," Ginger said when Andy woke up.

"Pass me another one of his books and give it another hour," he said groggily.

Ginger took one of Victor Krauss's notebooks from the glove compartment and gave it to Andy.

Tony had told them where Tepes lived but knew next to nothing about Cyril other than his godawful car.

An overwhelming sense of defeat engulfed them both.

"Maybe it's for the best," Ginger said after a while. "There's only so much we can do. Maybe we should just sta—"

"Jesus Christ," Andy exclaimed and pointed at Victor's scrawl. "He was testing viruses and diseases on that woman, seeing which ones the lycanthropy could eradicate."

"He's just as bad as the people he ran from!" Ginger seethed. After all the things he had done all in the name of research and a bid to save his wife.

"The old man was crazy. He could've released anything with what he was testing on her." Andy thought back to the captive the Scarborough boys had killed and how Danny said she'd coughed up a mouthful of black gunk in his face. All colour fell from his face when his eyes met Ginger's, knowing she had thought the same thing. "What if he has?"

FÜHRER: PART ONE

3.

This thing is amazing, Tepes thought as he stared at the rolling road. He had been driving all night without tiring. "Thank you," he said aloud at his own dark eyes in the rearview mirror.

"Wha—?"

Tepes adjusted the mirror so he could look through the partition into the back of the van. During one of his pit stops, he checked on the boy and moved his position so he could keep an eye on him whilst driving. He sat slumped against the rear doors, still bound tightly and still skewered with the harpoon. Although the interior of the van was in almost total darkness, Tepes could see him clearly, a pale, withered thing. It seemed remarkable that Danny was the progenitor to the powers that were running through him so fiercely. "I wasn't talking to you. I was talking to the gift you gave me. I think we're going to be good friends."

Danny spluttered and a black gruel spilled from his lips. The agony from the harpoon was nothing compared to the forest fire of his lungs. Something was wrong with him, something the lycanthropy couldn't alter. He spat a mouthful of the vile blackness towards the partition and saw Tepes' look of disgust. "I think," he said, his breath reeking of decay, "we're all going to die."

FÜHRER: PART ONE

Matthew Cash

Author Biography

Matthew Cash, or Matty-Bob Cash, as he is known to most, was born and raised in Suffolk, which is the setting for his debut novel, Pinprick. He is compiler and editor of Death by Chocolate, a chocoholic horror anthology, and the 12Days Anthology, head of Burdizzo Books and Burdizzo Bards, and has numerous releases on Kindle and several collections in paperback.

He has always written stories since he first learned to write, and most, although not all, tend to slip into the many-layered murky depths of the Horror genre.

His influences —from childhood to present day—include Roald Dahl, James Herbert, Clive Barker, Stephen King, and Stephen Laws, to name but a few.

More recently, he enjoys the work of Adam Nevill, F.R Tallis, Michael Bray, William Meikle and Iain Rob Wright (who featured Matty-Bob in his famous A-Z of Horror title, M is For Matty-Bob, plus Matthew wrote his own version of events, which was included as a bonus).

He is a father of two, a husband of one, and a zookeeper of numerous fur babies.

You can find him here:
www.facebook.com/pinprickbymatthewcash
https://www.amazon.co.uk/-/e/B010MQTWKK

FÜHRER: PART ONE

Matthew Cash

Other Titles by Matthew Cash

FÜHRER: PART ONE

Matthew Cash

PINPRICK

All villages have their secrets, and Brantham is no different.

Twenty-years ago, after foolish risk-taking turned into tragedy, Shane left the rural community under a cloud of suspicion and rumour. Events from that night remain unexplained, memories erased, questions unanswered. Now a notorious politician, he returns to his birthplace when the offer from a property developer is too good to refuse. With big plans to haul Brantham into the 21st century, the developers have already made a devastating impact on the once quaint village. But then the headaches begin, followed by the nightmarish visions.

Soon, Shane wishes he had never returned, as Brantham reveals its ugly secret.

FÜHRER: PART ONE

VIRGIN AND THE HUNTER

Hi, I'm God. And I have a confession to make.

I live with my two best friends and the girl of my dreams, Persephone.

When opportunity knocks, we are usually down the pub having a few drinks, or we'll hang out in Christchurch Park until it gets dark, then go home to do college stuff. Even though I struggle a bit financially, life is good, carefree.

Well, it was.

Things have started going downhill recently, from the moment I started killing people.

FÜHRER: PART ONE

KRACKERJACK

Five people wake up in a warehouse, bound to chairs.

Before each of them, tacked to the wall, are their witness testimonies.

They each played a part in labelling one of Britain's most loved family entertainers a paedophile and sex offender.

Clearly, revenge is the reason they have been brought here, but the man they accused is supposed to be dead.

Opportunity knocks, and Diddy Dave Diamond has one last game show to host — and it's a knockout.

FÜHRER: PART ONE

KRACKERJACK2

Ever wondered what would happen if a celebrity faked their own death and decided they had changed their minds?

Two years ago, publicly shunned comedian Diddy Dave Diamond convinced the nation that he was dead, only to return from beyond the grave to seek retribution on those who ruined his career and tainted his legacy.

Innocent or not, only one person survived Diddy Dave Diamond's last ever game show, but the forfeit prize was imprisonment for similar alleged crimes.

Prison is not kind to inmates with those type of convictions, as the sole survivor finds out, but there's a sudden glimmer of hope.

Someone has surfaced in the public eye claiming to be the dead comedian.

FÜHRER: PART ONE

FUR

The old-aged pensioners of Boxford are set in their ways, loyal to each other and their daily routines. With families and loved ones either moved on to pastures new or maybe even the next life, these folk can become dependent on one another.

But what happens when the natural ailments of old age begin to take their toll?

What if they were given the opportunity to heal, and overcome the things that make everyday life less tolerable?

What if they were given this ability without their consent?

When a group of local thugs attack the village's wealthy Victor Krauss, they unwittingly create a maelstrom of events that not only could destroy their home but everyone in and around it.

Are the old folk the cause or the cure of the horrors?

FÜHRER: PART ONE

Matthew Cash

YOUR FRIGHTFUL SPIRIT STAYED

Something happened deep in Charlie's past to make him the way he is. Something causes the visitations, the disturbances, the ghosts. Is it something in his current life or something from a previous existence? Something haunts Charlie, has followed him for years. Something relentless and unstoppable. Something that only wants to torment, torture and ruin. Something that will chase him to the grave.

FÜHRER: PART ONE

THE GLUT

FREE YOURSELF

What would you do if you found out your compulsions were not your fault?

That something else had been controlling you all along?

What would you do if you discovered there was a dark part of you, a part of humanity, that was put there by an entity older than the stars?

Vince is binge-eating himself into an early grave. He cannot resist the voice inside that encourages him to gorge, an instinctive reaction to every strong emotion. Finding it increasingly more difficult to live with, he vows to do anything to rid himself of it.

Even if it means stooping to new lows and levels of degradation of which he never considered himself capable.

FÜHRER: PART ONE

Matthew Cash

THE DAY BEFORE YOU CAME

When Philippa spots the bungalow it's love at first sight — and she is filled with the sense of safety and warmth whenever she's there. She's not a believer in the supernatural, unlike her best friend, Niamh, but she has to admit there is an energy about the bungalow, a vibrancy that fills her with joy.

Her boyfriend, Ryan, is an angry waste of space, a compulsive liar and petty criminal. He's not frightened of anything - living or dead.

THIS IS NOT YOUR HOUSE

Roger and Vera have been married for years. Everything is a slog, everything is a burden, to Roger, anyway. Having to spend the majority of his life living with his elderly mother-in-law is enough to make anyone bitter.

Vera puts up with her husband even though he doesn't hear the strange noises in the house.

The everyday tedium continues until Roger devises a way to get rid of his mother-in-law.

FÜHRER: PART ONE

Matthew Cash

Other Releases by Matthew Cash

Novels
Virgin and the Hunter
Pinprick
FUR
Your Frightful Spirit Stayed
The Day Before You Came
The Glut
FERAL

Novellas
Ankle Biters
KrackerJack
KrackerJack 2
Clinton Reed's Fat
Illness
Hell and Sebastian
Waiting for Godfrey
Deadbeard
The Cat Came Back
Frosty
The C Word

Short Stories
Why Can't I Be You?
Slugs and Snails and Puppydog Tails
OldTimers
Hunt the C*nt
Werwolf

Non-fiction
From Whale-Boy to Aqua-man

FÜHRER: PART ONE

Anthologies Compiled and Edited by Matthew Cash of Burdizzo Books
Death by Chocolate
12 Days STOCKING FILLERS
12 Days: 2016
12 Days: 2017
The Reverend Burdizzo's Hymnbook*
SPARKS*
Under the Weather [with Em Dehaney & Back Road Books]
Burdizzo Mix Tape Vol.1*
*With Em Dehaney
Corona-Nation Street

Anthologies Featuring Matthew Cash
Rejected for Content 3: Vicious Vengeance
JEApers Creepers
Full Moon Slaughter
Full Moon Slaughter 2
Down the Rabbit Hole: Tales of Insanity
Visions From the Void [edited by Jonathan Butcher & Em Dehaney]

Collections
The Cash Compendium Volume One
The Cash Compendium Continuity
Come and Raise Demons [poetry]
Stromboli and Other Sporadic Eruptions

Website:
www.Facebook.com/pinprickbymatthewcash
Copyright © Matthew Cash 2024

Printed in Great Britain
by Amazon